JANE LOUISE NEWHAGEN

Sand
Dollar

a tale of old Key West

Outskirts Press, Inc.
Denver, Colorado

Sand Dollar
a tale of old Key West
All Rights Reserved
Copyright © 2007 Jane Louise Newhagen
www.janenewhagen.com

Cover painting © Fran Decker
Used with permission.
www.frandecker.com

v 3.0

Outskirts Press
http://www.outskirtspress.com

ISBN-10: 1-4327-0166-5
ISBN-13: 978-1-4327-0166-6

Library of Congress Control Number: 2006939582

Outskirts Press and the "OP" logo are trademarks belonging to
Outskirts Press, Inc.

Printed in the United States of America

SAND DOLLAR

The tropical sand dollar is a flat, firm, chalky-white sea animal. It displays a symmetrical five-petaled flower centered on its gently domed top. A small, smooth, oval hole pierces it through as if it were waiting for a calcified chain to convert it into a pendant necklace. You can't harm the sand dollar by knocking on it with your knuckles, but when you persistently twist it or dig at it with the point of a knife, the shell gives way and hundreds of minute teeth and delicate chambers spill out. The smooth shape is gone and so is the integrity of the shell. All that remains are incomplete fragments and the sand dollar can't be mended.

So it was for Mary.

CHAPTER 1

"**N**o!"

Mary slammed the door to her mother's sitting room and pounded down the narrow stairway. Her long black skirt ballooned around her hips as she took the steps two at a time. She grabbed the brass knob and yanked open the door to her father's office.

"Mother gave me your message," she snapped, disrupting the afternoon tranquility of the shuttered room. "I refuse to marry Richard Randall! It's only been three months since Michael died at sea and already you're trying to pawn me off on someone else. Are you feeling crowded around the house?" Mary combed her straight black hair away from her face with her fingers, crossed her arms across her chest, and glared at her father.

William Thorne looked up from his ledger. His icy blue eyes met her azure ones. His were absent of emotion. Hers overflowed with it. He nestled his pen into its holder, screwed down the cover on the ink bottle, and looked over the top of his wire-rimmed glasses.

Mary wasn't fooled by his calculated composure. She noticed the measured tapping of his leather soles on the wide pine floor-boards under the desk. He was irritated, but so was she. She persisted.

"When my sweet Michael drowned, my heart drowned with him. I loved him and I'll never be the same."

"Michael Wellmet drowned because he didn't have enough sense to go below deck or lash himself to a mast when the storm came up. He may have been book-wise, but he lacked practical sense. You know very well he was the only man lost that day. All the others knew how to take care of themselves."

Mary wanted to bolt from the room and slam the door on her father and his insults, but she knew it would just make matters worse. William Thorne was stubborn under the best of circumstances. When he was angry, he was intractable. She drew a deep breath.

"Father, if Michael had lived, our wedding would have been next week. How could I consider marrying some other man so soon, if ever? Please try to understand. Michael and I shared a passion for botany. We studied Andre Michaux's books about collecting wild flowers and trees and we planned to complete his work. Michael was such a gentle soul; the mockingbirds didn't even scold or peck when he went near their nests.

"Even if I were to consider another man, it wouldn't be a nine-fingered pirate like Richard Randall. He's an adventurer and an opportunist and his only thought is of the profit to be made from other men's ships."

"Richard is no pirate, and you know it," countered William. His feet tapped faster and louder.

"He's a wrecker, a salvor, if you will. He saves sailors and their cargo. He's shown unusual courage over the years, sometimes risking his own life to save others. Yes, someday I think he'll be rich. I hold him in the greatest respect. You should, too. He has his eye on you and you could become his wealthy wife with silver on your table and children dressed in velvet and lace. Consider what a pretty prospect that is. As your father, I wish all of those things for you." William leaned forward in his earnestness, his feet suddenly still.

"This is no time for you to be controlled by sentiment. You know as well as I do that if you continue much longer without a serious prospect, you can look forward to being in this house for the rest of your life. You must be practical. It's past time for you to marry."

"I'm only twenty-two. I can still . . . "

"You think you're still young, but you're not my little girl anymore. Maybe I've spoiled you into believing you are. Sooner than you know, you'll be thirty and still the child of my house. Then all of Green Turtle Cay will remark how the spinster Mary is growing old, still seated at her father's side. A sorry life for such a promising girl as she was!"

Mary dropped her hands to her sides and slapped her thighs through the layers of skirt and petticoat. She sank onto the chair opposite the desk, coming eye to eye with her father.

"I mean no disrespect," she said. "But I have some knowledge in this, too. I have known Richard since my earliest childhood. I have no illusions about his gentle manners or cultured habits. And I have no illusions about my future, either. With Michael I learned what real love is. My dream of a life filled with devotion and passion sank when he drowned, but I dare to hope I can regain it. Now you tell me to choose prosperity and comfort and forget my feelings. I won't do it."

Mary trembled and her eyes brimmed with tears. William Thorne looked away. A warm breeze drifted between the slats of the Bahama shutters and ruffled his neatly-stacked papers. As he reached to keep them from blowing off the desk, he turned to Mary and his features softened.

"Remember how when you were six you slipped off to the beach at sunrise and hid in the mangroves? When we finally found you, you claimed to have spent the morning watching tiny crabs scurrying up and down the roots and wondering what they were thinking. Remember how you lifted your skirt and walked barefoot into the surf to find sand dollars? You dug them up with your toes."

"I still have some of them, you know," Mary smiled wistfully. "I wrapped them in one of Grandma's lace hankies and put them safely at the bottom of a drawer in her cherry bureau."

William rose and stepped around the desk. He lifted her chin with the thumb of his right hand and smiled down at her.

"Mary, once you were full of joy and energy, but since that Wellmet fellow, you do little other than sit in the parlor and stare at the locket he gave you. I admit once I scolded you for being too reckless, but I'd welcome those days back. Now I'm afraid you'll be a victim of your sadness."

He stepped back, pursing his lips.

"You must heed what I say. My only concern is your well-being. I know a thing or two about the world and you should know enough to be obedient."

"Yes, Father," Mary forced a smile. She recognized that the interview was over and the arguing had tired her. She smoothed the folds of her skirt as she stood. "Sarah and I promised Mother to go down to the docks when the fishing boats come in. We should go now or we'll miss the first catch."

"Go then, but remember what I've said. And remember that this father's love only wants the best for his girl, even if she doesn't agree." He placed a gentle kiss on her forehead before she turned to go.

Mary crossed the dusty courtyard to the kitchen house squinting in the hot Bahamian sun. She kicked at the little stones in the sandy, dry dirt, coating her black boots with the fine brown powder. Too bad! She'd just have to wipe them clean before she went into dinner.

It would have been pleasant to sit in the shade of the mahogany tree for a few minutes to rest and organize her thoughts, but Sara was ready to go.

"It's a good thing we have honest slaves," Sara said, patting her pocket. "Mother left the shopping money, all five shiny pennies, sitting in plain view on the kitchen table. Any of them could have taken it. She's lying down with another headache. I gather you two had an unpleasant conversation."

"We spoke briefly," replied Mary. "My conversation was with Father."

"I can't wait to tell you about the plans for the church social!

We had a meeting at Daisy Tyler's this morning and it's going to be the best yet!" exclaimed Sara as they walked down the lane to the fishermen's wharf.

How typical. Sara always seemed busy with parties and gossip. Mary didn't have a very high opinion of her younger sister's intelligence or her judgement either, for that matter. On the other hand, she seldom provoked arguments or strong opinions in others. Mary decided to ask her advice. Maybe her sister's soft ways could give her some insight into her own predicament with her father.

"Sarah, how can I change his mind?" Mary asked. "You always know what to say to him. I just seem to make him more stubborn and angry."

Sarah didn't answer right away.

"I think it would help if you acted more sweetly. Maybe you could start out by asking his advice in small things. He does like to feel respected, doesn't he?"

Sara knows a thing or two about being sweet, Mary thought as she watched the other woman's rounded form move slowly and deliberately ahead of her. Sara was so docile! Sometimes Mary wanted to light a fire under her skirts just to see if she could make her jump and run.

"I don't know if I can do that," replied Mary. " I doubt if he'd believe me if I did. I don't know if he really likes Richard. I think he's impressed by Richard's success as a wrecker and ambitious for my future."

"I think, Dear Sister, that you spend far too much time thinking about romance, wealth, and comfort and little enough energy considering womanly values and humility. Perhaps you should give more thought to your character before you move on to your future."

Mary bristled at her sister's superior attitude. Well, she'd asked, hadn't she? There was the answer whether she liked it or not. Never mind. She'd had enough arguing for the day so she silently scrutinized the dusty toes of her boots for the rest of the walk down the narrow street to the wharf.

CHAPTER 2

T he boats had just arrived and the men were cleaning their catch. Silvery tarpons roiled the water with their splashing as they clamored for the smelly offal the fishermen tossed from the boats.

The odor of sea water and fish flesh rolled over Mary in waves. She held her handkerchief to her nose to filter the smell, but it wasn't much use. Sara raised her eyebrows as Mary pushed her forward to bargain with the fishmonger. Mary always insisted that it was she herself who drove the harder bargain and chose the better fillets.

"Mary, are you well?" asked Sara as they turned toward home. "You're pale and you seem weak."

"I'm fine, Sister," Mary replied. "Just a little tired."

Mary was more than a little tired; the short walk had exhausted her. For days she'd suffered from this malaise and it had developed a disturbing pattern. She slept deeply every night, but by midmorning she wished she could slip away and lie down, if only for a few minutes. Where usually she had a robust appetite and cooperative digestion, now she got queasy at the slightest provocation. Some mornings she vomited weakly even before she ate. She tried to ignore her symptoms, but they persisted in calling themselves to her attention.

"Sara, please take the fish to the kitchen," she asked. "I'd like to check the garden for marauding snails and see if there are enough beans for supper."

"Of course," said Sara. This had long been their habit. Sara stayed close to the hearth, supervising the kitchen and sewing. Mary was more likely to be found outside in the vegetable garden or the fields where she gathered wild herbs and flowers.

Today the climb up the small rise to the garden was laborious. Mary panted as she knelt at the end of two rows of climbing green beans. She closed her eyes and leaned heavily on a rough piece of coral rock that had been dragged to the perimeter when the garden was cleared generations before. She breathed deeply and slowly, willing her heart to stop this unaccustomed pounding.

"Miss Mary?"

Mary didn't respond.

"Miss Mary."

Still grasping the stone, she opened her eyes and turned her head toward the source of the voice.

Phoebe, one of the household slaves, squatted on her heels nearby, apparently untouched by the heat in spite of the black shift that covered her from neck to ankle. Her curly black hair was cropped close to her head and her big hands rested on her kitchen-stained white apron, long fingers neatly interlaced.

Phoebe had been a member of the household for as long as Mary could remember. As children they played together in the dusty courtyard outside the cook house. When Mary's parents hosted dinner parties, Sara and Mary were relegated to the kitchen to eat and Phoebe always sat at the table with them.

Phoebe was younger, or smaller, anyway. It was hard to tell the ages of slaves since nobody paid attention to their birthdays. The slave child's impetuous nature exceeded even Mary's daring and she took risks that frightened the other girls. She jumped down from stone walls and climbed over picket fences that were half again her height. She often tore her clothes and her mother finally gave up trying to keep the little scamp properly dressed.

Mary would never forget how Phoebe screamed when she bumped into the handle of a pot of steaming water that sat on a trivet in the fireplace. It splashed all down the youngster's left leg.

One didn't call a doctor for a slave child, but the girl's grandmother eased the child's pain and treated her wounds with plants and herbs. In a few months Phoebe again played in the courtyard. She limped a little and carried an ugly scar that started up under her skirt somewhere and ran all the way down the outside of her calf and her heel. It was even more horrifying because of the contrast of her suede-smooth dark brown skin with the hard, rough scar. The accident burned the recklessness out of her. She played quietly in the shade and often sat with her grandmother, learning about the mysteries of natural healing. Often Mary would join them.

Phoebe often came to the garden or sat under the nearby sapodilla tree. Mary wasn't sure if the slave had been there before her or if she'd arrived while Mary caught her breath.

"Miss Mary, I can help you," Phoebe murmured. "I know what's wrong. I was that way myself. You can stop it. It doesn't have to go on."

"I don't know what you mean," protested Mary straightening herself to regain some sense of dignity.

"I don't mean harm," said Phoebe. "I just know some things that maybe you want to know too. And I'll be glad to tell you. I know you missed your monthly because your clothes in the wash haven't been bloody for a long time. And anybody who cares to look can see you're feeling sickly and tired. I don't know for sure, but I can guess that you were very close to that Mr. Wellmet before he died."

"Stop!" Mary hissed. "What business is that of yours? Even if it were true?"

"It's no business of mine," replied Phoebe. "I'm a slave, but maybe I've learned some things. I know this. If you don't take certain steps, you're going to have a baby. I can help."

Mary's skin broke into goose flesh. There it was. Phoebe cut through all the dark layers of Mary's denial and spread the situation out in the sun where it couldn't be ignored any longer. Mary had lived for those lazy afternoons lying with Michael on the soft ferns in the shady hammock on the hill overlooking the docks. The sea breezes would cool them after their passion was spent and they'd lie drowsily staring at the leaves waving gently overhead. At first she'd wake up at night and fret about getting pregnant, but it didn't happen, so she didn't worry anymore, at least, until she didn't menstruate the month after Michael died. Then the month after that. She'd been hoping against hope that her regular cycle would return and her fears would be unfounded, but now she had to admit that the girl was right. She was pregnant.

That was about the worst thing that could happen to her right now. Not that lots of girls didn't get married after they found themselves in a family way, but they married the father of the child, not somebody else. This pregnancy could propel her right into the marriage to Richard that she wanted to avoid. As if Richard would marry her now! No one would know better than he that the child was someone else's and it wouldn't take a second to guess whose!

When Phoebe spoke again, her manner was tentative, almost childlike, but her inky eyes mirrored experience beyond her years. She repeated, "I can help you."

"What can I do?" Mary asked.

"You see the aloe there in the sun by the rock?"

"Of course! I know it well. It heals burns and softens the skin."

"It has other uses, too. Break off the leaves and squeeze them until you fill a cup half up with pulp. Crush it with a spoon and drink it down all at once. It's thick and slippery and it tastes bitter, but do it anyway. Soon your blood will come again and you will be as before. You may get cramps and feel sick, but ask for me and I'll sit with you until it passes. Believe me. I know."

Mary stared at her, silently weighing the advice. Finally she nodded. Phoebe rose and walked toward the house without looking back.

Later, as the sun slid low in the sky, Mary returned to the garden with an old cracked tea cup and a filleting knife. Nobody ever paid any attention to her when she went there, but still she felt nervous lest someone should discover her purpose. She pulled succulent aloe leaves and, careful not to cut herself on the saw-toothed edges, cut the thick skin and pushed out the gelatinous pulp. The musky vegetable smell was neither attractive nor repelling and she wondered what it would taste like. She defoliated one plant and moved onto the next. It would never do to leave the leafless stem there to provoke questions. Jerking it out of the ground, she hurled it as far as she could into the nearby scrub, then smoothed the ground where it had been. Two more plants later, she finally filled the cup halfway. She tiptoed upstairs to the bedroom she shared with Sara and hid the cup under her bed. She'd drink the aloe tonight when everyone was asleep.

* * *

"Be a dear and rub my neck while we wait for your father." Ann had dressed and seated herself at the dinning table. She'd brushed her white-blond hair into a tight knot at the nape of her neck. Blue pockets under her eyes and nearly transparent skin testified to her frailty.

"Of course, Mother." Mary rose and went to stand behind Ann's chair, gently stroking her neck and shoulders.

"Over to the right. There. That's the spot. Be gentle, Mary. What on earth are you thinking about? My skin is so thin and your hands are rough. Sara, you take a turn. Your hands are always softer and gentler."

Mary shrugged at the rebuff. It was the same in just about everything. Mother preferred Sara's softness and malleability to Mary's more energetic ways. She sat down and half-watched as Sara soothed their mother's tension. Mother was right. She hadn't been concentrating. She was preoccupied by the cup of aloe hidden behind the bed leg and the green gelatinous mystery it held. She wished she'd taken just a little taste so she'd know what lay ahead. But she hadn't. She'd just have to wait until later.

"Good evening, my dears. I'm sorry I kept you waiting,"

William said as he took his place at the head of the table. "The guild meeting went on and on. We're to advise the governor on salvage regulations. The trouble is, we can't seem to agree among ourselves. Some favor strict regulations and high taxes while others completely oppose any government involvement whatsoever.

"Well, all that can't possibly interest you ladies. Let's enjoy our supper. Unfortunately I have to go back later. We need to reach an agreement as soon as possible."

Some other evening Mary would have relished a discussion of guild business, but not tonight. She picked at the dolphin fillet and boiled beans. Sara monopolized conversation with tales of the plans for the church social.

"Mary, you really must come to this one!" she exclaimed. "Churches from seven towns will be there and we'll all go to Marsh Harbour."

"You know I won't go on a boat since what happened to Michael," Mary replied. "I would no more sail to your social at Marsh Harbour than set out on a transatlantic voyage for London."

"I'm sorry. I forgot for a moment." Sara blushed.

That ended dinner conversation and Mary took the opportunity to excuse herself before dessert.

She went upstairs, glad finally to be alone. She stood by the window to brush the dust from her skirt and jacket and hung her petticoats to air. Sara startled her as she came into the room.

"I must be suffering from a slight miasma," she complained. "The air smells stuffy and sour and I am so tired. Mother offered me some calomel, but I refused. It has such a biting taste and I sometimes think it makes me feel worse than before. I'll just join you in retiring early, if you don't mind."

Mary did mind. She didn't want company for what she was about to do. She wanted to be alone to gather her courage, then to quickly and quietly do what had to be done.

"Is there anything I can do to make you more comfortable?" asked Mary, feigning concern.

"No, no. Don't bother yourself. I just want to rest. I'm sure this will pass by tomorrow."

Mary rinsed her face in cool water from the porcelain bowl on the washstand. She paused to caress the smooth surface of the ornate cherry bureau beside it. It had been a wedding present to her mother's mother and it and glowed with years of dusting and polishing. In general, she didn't care much for furniture, but this piece was like an old friend.

She dried her hands and face on a linen towel, pulled her sleeping chemise over her head, and slid between the sheets, hoping that Sara would soon doze off.

Sara tossed and turned. In the end it was Mary who slept first.

When she awoke, it was still dark. Her throat tightened in panic. She hadn't drunk the aloe.

Sara's regular breathing reassured her that her sister was sleeping soundly. Mary's plan hadn't failed; it had only been delayed. She rolled to her left side and reached under the bed, casting about with her hand for the cup. Finally her thumb brushed against its handle and she froze, wanting to avoid spilling the liquid and awakening her sister. She gingerly slid the cup out from under the bed and sat up, easing her bare feet onto the floor. Already she was starting to feel the queasiness that had plagued her mornings these last weeks.

She took the cup firmly in both hands and drank deeply and quickly. The bitter, viscous liquid caught in her throat, and she swallowed again to force it down. Then she gritted her teeth and held her breath to make it stay there. Her heart pounded against her ribs as she lay down to wait. Phoebe hadn't told her exactly what to expect or when, but now she was committed.

Nothing happened. At least half an hour passed and she didn't feel anything.

Idiot! She thought indignantly. She sat upright and plumped her pillow. *How naive of me to take the word of a slave girl at face value. I've been a victim to the whole story and now look at me, drinking that foul juice! Well, it won't happen again and Phoebe will get a piece of my mind in the morning!*

She seethed with mortification and anger. She was so

consumed by her emotions that at first she didn't notice the wet warmth between her legs. As it spread across her thighs, she realized she was bleeding!

She carefully turned on her side and slid from the bed taking care not to stain the sheets. As she leaned to pull some rags from the bottom drawer of the bureau, she was pierced by violent cramps from her waist to her thighs and the blood began to flow strongly in clots. She doubled over and she jammed rags between her legs. Clutching more in her arms, she ran down the stairs and into the slave quarters next to the kitchen. She slid open the lockless door without knocking and hissed, "Phoebe! Phoebe! Help me. I think I'm dying. I'm bleeding to death."

Phoebe sat up groggily on her sheetless cot. "What is it Miss Mary? It's the middle of the night."

"I drank the aloe. The pain is so bad I can hardly stand and the blood is coming faster than I've ever seen it. Please, help me. You must know what to do!"

"Lie down now. Lie down on my cot," Phoebe instructed. "Pull your knees up and breath deep. And be quiet. Whatever happens, be quiet. You don't want the whole household knowing you're here and what you're doing."

The cramps became so intense that if Mary had tried to speak it would have come out as a scream. She stuffed an unused rag in her mouth and bit it as hard as she could. Sweat ran from her forehead into her hair and she closed her eyes tight.

"Relax now, Miss. It will be over soon. Just relax and you won't hurt so much," Phoebe said. "So, so, so easy, easy, easy, now." She crooned, as if to calm a child. Phoebe wiped her forehead and soothed her with her voice.

Mary lost all sense of time and place. She only knew that eventually the pain began to subside. She allowed her knees to fall open and a last great gush of blood pushed its way out. She whimpered with relief.

"Shhh," Phoebe cautioned. "You just rest real quiet like. I think you're going to feel better now. And when you do, we're going to move you back up to your own bed where you belong. It won't do for your mommy to wake up and find you sleeping in no slave's quarters. That might just be worse than her finding out about that baby that you're not going to have any more."

Mary followed obediently as Phoebe led her up the stairs and helped her into bed, carefully arranging a thick layer of rags around her to absorb the continuing trickle of blood.

"You just lie still, Miss Mary. Sleep now and when you wake up it will be just like your regular bleeding came on you in the night. Nobody will ever know any different except you and me and we won't tell." Phoebe's voice was as quiet and gentle as the rustling of the mosquito netting over the bed. She gently patted Mary's head, then picked up the soiled tea cup as she padded out of the room.

Mary lay quietly, exhausted by pain and fear. Lulled by Sara's breathing, she slipped off into deep, dreamless sleep.

CHAPTER 3

Wﾃﾇhen Mary woke, sun glared between the slats of the
shutters and cast irregular golden stripes on the
bedroom floor. She felt the warm sogginess of the rags between
her thighs. She must have bled steadily throughout the night,
although she hadn't felt the slightest flicker of pain. She replaced
the soaked rags with fresh, wrapped the soiled ones into a bundle,
and pushed it under the bed.

She wished someone would bring her tea. Lying back on her
pillow, she listened for sounds of activity. She heard her mother's
voice and Sara's and the clatter of dishes being put away.
Somebody would check on her eventually. She waited, reviewing
the events of the last twenty-four hours.

She was sure she'd been pregnant. A baby had been pushed out
with all that blood. Michael was dead. His child, once growing in
her, had been flushed out and lay, indistinguishable from clots of
blood, in the disgusting rags that would soon be burned or
bleached in the laundry. Was it a boy or a girl? She'd never know.
She only knew it was gone.

Her grief resurfaced as she contemplated the fact that she had
willingly destroyed the last living trace of Michael and only she
knew about the child to mourn it. She was alone, surrounded by

the tall thick walls of her deceit and secrecy. There was no one to share her burden.

She stared at the ceiling and knew that a part of her had died, too. Her girlish trust and spontaneity had drained from her with the fluids of her pregnancy. From now on, she would deliberately choose her way and protect herself from more pain.

Petticoats rustled outside the door and the knob grated quietly. Ann entered carrying a breakfast tray. "My dear, you're awake. You must eat something. I've brought you tea and toast. Are you indisposed?"

Mother, Mary observed, would never have entertained the idea of a love affair, let alone a premature pregnancy. Since she could remember, Mary had disdained the authority of convention in her mother's life. Yet that was what had protected her from complicated and painful situations. She was touched by her mother's kindness and her throat tightened at the realization of her own duplicity.

"Don't worry, Dear," Ann said. She rested the tray on the bureau arranged the pillows so Mary could sit up and hold the tray on her lap. "Rest until you feel better. I've planned a fish chowder for dinner. Maybe that will help restore you. I'll have it brought upstairs if you prefer. Would you like to wash? I can send Phoebe with a bowl of warm water if that would refresh you.

"By the way, Captain Randall asked after you. He wanted to visit you this evening after dinner. I told him you weren't feeling well and asked him to wait a few days."

"I suppose I'll have to see him, but not before Sunday," said Mary. "Yes, Sunday will be fine."

In the meantime, Mary kept to herself and weighed her options. For the first time, she pondered the idea that maybe the conventional life her father wished for her with its wealth and comfort might be the armor she needed to protect herself from more disappointment and suffering.

* * *

"Why did you make me wait so long to see you, Mary?" Richard's blue eyes crackled with impatience when she met him at the parlor door.

She didn't answer, but smiled in amusement at his efforts to impress her. Evidently he had tried to dress the part of the proper suitor. His sun-bleached red-blond hair still showed furrows from the wet comb he'd used to smooth it before he tied it back with a piece of twine. A little red cut showed where he'd nicked his skin when he trimmed his sideburns. His shirt and trousers looked clean enough, but there was sand in the seams of his boots and a faint salty odor hung about him.

She stepped aside to allow him into the parlor and perched on the upholstered seat of the hunter green arm chair, indicating with a formal sweep of her hand that Richard should take the matching chair on the other side of the lamp table. As he sat, he slid his damaged left hand out of sight between his thigh and the arm of the chair.

Earlier Mary had carefully measured oil into the courting lamp. The duration of its burning would determine the length of his visit and she didn't want him to stay too long. Normally, filling the lamp would be her parents' role, but she'd gotten to it first and evidently they hadn't altered the amount of oil she rationed. She'd lit the wick and replaced the glass shade when she heard Richard's knock at the door.

"I'll come to the point," he said. "I want to marry you. I believe we'll make good partners in life. I love you as much as I can love any woman and I love gain and adventure. I offer you comfort and elegance. I'll give you a fine house for you to raise a family, elegant clothes, as many books as you can read. What more can you want?"

"Evidently our match pleases everyone but me, but maybe I've been too harsh," she replied. "Most women would rejoice at the comfortable life you offer. I wouldn't like to think of myself as a fool if I refused. Let me think on it." She lowered her eyes to hide any hint of insincerity he might see there.

"Tuesday I'm sailing out on another wrecking trip. I can't

guess how long it will take for a ship to pile up on the reef nor for us to take the salvage and the court to grant us the reward. But when I get my money, I'm going to the mainland to buy the best heart pine I can find. I'm going to come back and build a house. When you see that, you'll understand that I mean to give you a good life, better even than what you have."

He looked squarely into her eyes. *This is more like a business deal than a proposal of marriage,* she thought. *Well, that suits me, too.*

"Now look, that damn lamp is flickering out and I should go."

Mary offered no argument and they stood at the same time.

"Good evening," she said.

They parted without touching.

* * *

Richard sailed without fanfare early Tuesday morning.

Mary woke before dawn, but she lay in bed pretending to sleep until Sara dressed and left the room. She'd pulled the wool blanket up under her ears against the January cold and lay in a dark, moist cocoon warmed by her own body. She shivered a little as she forced herself to leave the womb-like bed and slid her feet onto the chilly floor. The knit shawl that she'd worn last night at dinner lay on the chair where she'd dropped it. She wrapped it around her shoulders to quell the chill and hurried to dab her face and rinse her hands, leaving the clammy soap untouched. She stepped into her petticoats and pulled them up, then reluctantly pulled her warm night shirt over her head to put on her camisole. As she buttoned her white blouse and tucked it into her skirt, she reaffirmed yesterday's decision to stay home when Richard sailed. She didn't want her presence at the harbor to signal concern she didn't feel.

She lingered by the bedroom window. It was cloudy and cool with a blustery, brisk breeze to fill the schooner's sails, a much different day than the hot, windy morning when she ran to the dock to say good-bye to Michael. He'd stood on the deck, exuberantly waving both hands over his head as the schooner rolled beneath his feet. Mary leaned out over the end of the pier, the southeast wind whipping her hair and blowing her skirts out behind her. She was like a bowsprit, balanced between the winds and her yearning, until the ship disappeared from view.

Today, Mary silently pledged never to allow herself to be so vulnerable again. She'd had enough of the pain that grows from intimacy and defenselessness! She'd take care of herself from now on. As she turned from the window, she straightened the seams of the jacket's peplum over her hips and straightened her back.

Sara met her at the foot of the stairs.

"Captain Richard sailed this morning, you know. Didn't you want to bid him Godspeed?" she asked.

"It's only been two days since we spoke," replied Mary. "I had nothing more to say to him, nor he to me."

"You don't make very interesting lovers," quipped Sara. "What will they have to talk about at the women's meeting?"

Mary's feathers were ruffled now. "You know perfectly well that Richard and I aren't lovers. I'm not even sure we're friends. And if for once those old ladies have nothing to talk about but their cakes and handiwork, maybe there will be something worth looking at this year. It gets tiresome buying silly dolls and aprons out of good will, doesn't it? I don't think we've ever used anything you bought there."

Sara looked at her ruefully. "I gather you won't be going this afternoon, then."

"Not even to protect my good name."

On the dining room table there was hot tea, the pot warmed in a crocheted cosy, fresh crusty bread, and creamy goat cheese.

"You see, there is something useful we got from a church sale! That tea cosy we use every morning." Sara exclaimed.

"Indeed," replied Mary. "Would you please pass the bread?"

The young women ate in silence. When she finished, Mary slid back her chair and left the room, abandoning Sara to clear the table and carry the dishes to the kitchen house.

* * *

The winter days drifted into tedious monotony. Mornings, Mary weeded and picked flowers and vegetables. In the afternoons, she shopped or helped polish silver and dust. Often before supper and early in the evenings she read and reread the books and magazines that came from the mainland or stitched pretty work on pillow cases and hand towels.

Darkness arrived early. After supper, the family sat in the parlor in the yellow glow of the oil lamps. They discussed the trivialities of their days and whatever plans they'd made for the morrow. Sometimes Mary and her father became involved in more lively discussions about politics and commerce. Mary watched with fascination as her mother and Sara nodded their heads together and chattered, hardly stopping for breath, about the minute details of Mrs. This's new granddaughter or Mrs. That's hat that she wore for the first time last Sunday. She noticed how more and more often the members of the Barlow family would wander into the conversation. She was sure John Barlow had been selected for her sister and soon plans would be unveiled for their wedding.

* * *

Richard's first letter took six weeks to arrive. According to the sketchy notes on the outside, it had zigzagged its way from ship to ship, then to Key West, over to the mainland, and finally to a freighter delivering flour, yard goods, and salt pork to Green Turtle Cay.

Mary had spent the morning in the garden transplanting basil and vervain seedlings that she was cultivating in hope of relieving her mother's persistent headaches. As she headed back to the kitchen to wash her hands, Ann met her in the courtyard, closely followed by Sara.

"Look. It's a letter from the captain! It came on the Emeline this morning," her mother burbled. "The first mate just brought it to the door. It was passed to him when they lay in port in St. Augustine. It must be from Captain Randall. Who else would write you a letter?"

Such excitement! Mary wondered if they had held it up to the sun to try to see into it before she got there. She brushed the dark garden soil from her hands. "Let me see."

The letter was no bigger than a lady's handkerchief and was folded twice and sealed with brown wax. Water stains on the paper and runny spots in the ink testified to its ocean voyage. Mary supposed she was lucky to receive it at all. Letters sometimes were mislaid or thrown away and some just wandered about at sea in the possession of sailors who forgot who sent them or what port they were intended for.

Although in itself the prospect of news from Richard didn't excite her, Mary's eyes brightened and her heart beat a little faster when her mother handed it to her. She'd never gotten a letter before! People seldom went far enough away from home to write letters. Even Michael had never written to her.

"Oh, Mary, open it now!" Sara pleaded.

"I don't see any rush," replied Mary. She slid the letter into her deep apron pocket. "I'll read it later," she said.

Ann regained her composure and some sense of propriety. "Of course Mary would like to read her mail in private. I'm sure she'll tell us any news that concerns us. Come now, let's finish our stitching. Soon we'll have to put everything away to prepare for supper." She wrapped her arm around Sara's shoulders and escorted her into the house.

Mary savored the suspense of the unopened letter. She felt its shape through her apron pocket and glanced down at it often while she washed up and sorted the table linens she'd promised to put away. Then, knowing that her father had gone to meet with his banker for the afternoon, she slipped into his empty office. She picked at the wax trying at once to preserve the seal and open the letter. That wasn't going to work! She took the pen knife from the desk and slit the seal, revealing not one, but three handwritten pages. The lines were slanted with elaborate flourishes on the capital letters and narrow, uneven margins.

"My dear Mary,

I hope this letter finds you and your family well.

As I write it has been two weeks since I left the comforts of Green Turtle Cay. The weather has been fair. I and my little crew are nearly overcome with boredom. Without some bad weather and a few ships cast up on the reef, a wrecker's occupation is neither interesting nor profitable.

Most days we lay at anchor in the deep water off the coast of Florida. From time to time we sail to the north or the south to confirm the well-being of our fellow wreckers and they sometimes call on us, too. You wouldn't recognize these visits to be like the social calls you and your sister pay on your neighbors. Most of the men are not very clean, since we must save our fresh water for drinking, and being exclusively in the company of rough men, they don't much care what they say or how they say it.

There is a large island to the southwest where we discovered a freshwater spring for bathing and to replenish our water supply. We killed two large turtles that provided us with fresh meat and soup. We'll take the shells to the mainland when we go and I promise to have a fine comb made especially for you.

We hear a rumor from the other boats that the United States has passed laws regulating the activities of wreckers off their shores and requiring ship captains to be licensed by their government. I don't know any man who has first hand information or who has changed his practices. I will continue as I have always done until someone proves to me that I should do otherwise.

Although life at sea involves confinement and discomfort, we are privileged to see beautiful sights that are available nowhere else. The sun's rising in the haze fills the sky with pastel shades of pink and blue that can never be captured, even in the delicate threads of your embroidery. On clear nights, the sunsets are so intense that sometimes I must turn my head away. We watch always for the green flash when the sun sinks into the sea because it assures powerful good luck to all who see it. We on the Osprey would much appreciate some luck like that to replace this tedium.

Dear Mary, I have gone to some pains to describe my life here at sea with the hope of helping you to know me better. I hope my stories have at least amused you.

Most sincerely,
Richard Randall"

Amused? Mary couldn't look away from the sheets of paper that had traveled so far and told such exotic tales. She read the letter twice more before refolding it and carefully tucking it back in her pocket. She imagined the island spring and the brilliant sunsets. Such a contrast to the monotony of her day-to-day life! To think the sailors were bored! Briefly, the haze of depression that had hung over her lifted and she smiled at the images Richard's words evoked.

At supper that evening there was no mention of the letter. Sara prattled on about the cunning baby bibs she was sewing for the church fair and wondered if she should limit her color selection to pink and blue or if she might venture into the more daring yellows and greens. William recounted the banker's predictions for a stable island economy. Ann reported the quality and quantity of fresh flour and meat she had procured from the Emeline and suggested that the girls should go with her to the haberdasher's the next day before the new selection of yard goods was depleted.

As they moved to the parlor in the fading winter light, Mary lit the big oil lamp and finally volunteered, "Would you like to hear part of Captain Randall's' letter?"

"Of course," the family responded in unison.

She leaned near the lamp and read clearly, omitting the last paragraph.

"Is that all? Didn't he say anything personal?" asked Sara.

"That's all I'm going to read to you," said Mary, implying by her secrecy more personal comments than in fact were there. She realized she would have to invent a very safe place to store her mail if she didn't want her sister snooping through it.

"Sara, mind your manners," scolded Ann. "You must respect your sister's privacy. It was generous of Mary to read to us at all.

Of course, you are going to reply to the captain, aren't you? News from home can mean so much to men at sea."

"I fully plan to respond," said Mary. "As soon as I can think of something to write about that might interest him."

CHAPTER 4

Mary kept the letter in her pocket until she went upstairs to get ready for bed; then she slipped it under the mattress. In the morning, she stuck it in the space beneath the old bureau's top drawer. She slid the drawer in and out three times to make sure the letter didn't catch and rip. It was safe.

What could she possibly say in reply? She knew little about sailing ships or wrecking. He had mentioned rumors of laws changing for wrecking off the shores of Florida. Her father should know about that, and he might be pleased if she showed interest in his affairs.

What else? There was nothing interesting about the number of napkins she folded in a week or the social calls she was obliged to make to the neighbors. Those things didn't even interest her!

She liked watching the bean seeds peek out of the ground in the kitchen garden and the orchids lavishly proclaim their sensual beauty hidden from all but the patient and inquisitive who wandered off the usual paths in the forest. She enjoyed sitting quietly, waiting for a brightly-colored woodstar to hover on beating wings to draw nectar from a flower with its thin, pointy beak. And she could spend hours watching the colony of silly stilt-legged pink flamingos stupidly scratching out their nests in the mud where their eggs made an easy meal for the iguanas and gulls.

Yes, she would write about these things and see how he responded. Maybe he would be amused. Or maybe he would disdain her natural interests. She'd find out something about him from his reaction. She began to write, and promised herself to finish by the end of the week, but she hadn't finished it when another arrived from Richard. This one was delivered into her own hand as she walked from the cookhouse to the garden. The sailor who brought it had crewed with another wrecker until he allowed himself to be caught in a rigging line and nearly lost a leg, a careless mistake, by his own admission. Dismissed from service, he found passage on merchant boats and eventually bought passage on a shrimper that brought him to Green Turtle Cay.

He waited, apparently he expecting a reward for his efforts. Mary smiled thinly as she fumbled in her pocket for the halfpenny she'd set aside for a horticultural magazine.

"Thank you, Missus."

"Miss," Mary corrected. The sailor's assumption was an unpleasant reminder of her father's comments about her advancing age.

She sat down on the wooden bench in the kitchen yard and broke the letter's seal. There was just a single sheet. Its uneven lines and crooked script testified to the haste in which it had been written.

"Mary,

Our luck arrived Friday with an English schooner headed for Mexico. It was captained by a minor nobleman who meant to prove his manliness by leading a voyage. Because of his inexperience the ship was caught in a squall and tossed on the reef. The ship was battered and several of the crew were injured, but there was no loss of life. I and my sturdy Osprey were the first to the wreck and claimed it. We've spent the week relieving the ship of her salvageable cargo and carrying it to the warehouses in Key West. The insurance monies and freight will certainly be awarded to me and there will be plenty left over after I divide a generous portion among my crew. All that will take time, but when it's done, I'll set out for the mainland to buy the wood to build your house.

The captain was terribly frightened by his experience and exceptionally generous in his gratitude. I have a pretty gift for you, but I'll speak no more of that because I want to surprise you.

Think of me busily shuttling from ship to shore and back, and I'll envision you patiently waiting for my return.

Sincerely yours,

Richard Randall"

"Patiently waiting for his return, indeed! Build *my* house!" Mary exclaimed. "What nerve! I never promised to wait for him at all. His success has gone to his head."

Phoebe looked out the kitchen door to see what the fuss was about, but Mary ignored her as she turned back to the house. She took the stairs two at a time and latched the bedroom door behind her. She fished her unfinished letter out from under the bureau drawer where she'd hidden it with Richard's and sat down to write. She bent the nib of the pen as she scrawled her new comments right below what she had neatly penned about the flamingos.

"I congratulate you on your recent good fortune. However if you think for a minute that I am eagerly waiting your return you should reconsider. I never said anything to give you that idea. While I enjoy your account of your travels, I am quite indifferent to your return.

Mary Thorne"

Folding the letter in three, Mary pushed back the hair that had fallen in her face and took a deep breath. She descended the stairs and knocked on the office door.

"Father, I've finished my letter to Captain Randall. May I have some wax to seal it?"

William's warm smile and the alacrity with which he handed over the sealing wax showed his pleasure at Mary's new interest in the wrecker captain. She didn't bother correcting him.

"Can I help you seal your letter?" he asked.

"I can manage," Mary replied. "How do I go about finding a ship with a trustworthy person who will deliver it?"

"I'll take it with me to the Maritime Board tomorrow morning. Those men are all honest and reliable."

The blood rushed to Mary's cheeks as she thought about what he would probably say about this budding relationship as he winked knowingly at his friends. *Never mind! Their opinion doesn't matter,* she thought, *as long as they take that letter where it's intended to go.*

Mary expected a quick response, but she was disappointed. In fact, there was no response at all. Weeks passed, a month, then two. Mary's indignation had plenty of time to cool and she started to wonder if Richard would ever write. She'd meant to reprimand him, not to alienate him. Was her letter lost? Did he have second thoughts? It was one thing for her to scold him, but she didn't like it at all that now he seemed to be rejecting her. She hated this uncertainty and her inability to do anything about it. She began to write another letter so that when his next one arrived there wouldn't be a delay in her reply.

* * *

April was beautiful that year. Northwesterly winds brought cool, dry days and breezy nights. Mary arose at dawn to enjoy the spring weather and walk the well-worn paths of the wooded coppice. She admired the nodding tips of the. She smiled at the persistence of the wild orchids whose green-tipped roots sought their way through the crevices in the buttonwood bark. It was her favorite time of day and her favorite time of year. For this short time the tranquility of the early hour and the promises of the lushness of the season filled her senses and soothed her thoughts.

On the Wednesday before Easter Mary turned from the cool, moist shadows of the coppice toward the smoking chimneys of the village to find a great fuss at the waterfront. A ship had just docked. Men shouted directions and called out greetings. Dogs barked and waves slapped against the pier. The gulls chattered crazily, adding to the clamor.

Mary's first thought was that maybe Richard's answering letter would be on the newly-arrived ship. When she listened closely to the men's banter, she realized that wouldn't be the case.

"And here's to ya, Captain Randall!" called a dock hand. "Nobody's ever brought a whole house-worth of wood from the mainland like that. It must be you're planning to build a palace right here on Green Turtle Cay."

"It'll be finer than Victoria's castle in London, I promise you," replied the captain. "And better, because here we have the fine Bahama climate." He laughed loudly.

Mary withdrew into the shadows. Her heart smacked in her chest so loudly she was surprised the men at the dock didn't turn and look for the source of the racket.

He'd brought the lumber to build the house, just as he'd said he would. She pressed her back against the shaggy bark of a pigeon plum tree. She felt trapped. She hadn't agreed to anything, but there was no question this house would be built for her. She bristled at the enormity of the assumption.

Still, Richard was a commanding figure standing high on the stacks of wood. His hair was tied back with a garish red and yellow kerchief that gave him a jaunty air. The weeks on the Osprey's deck had tanned his skin darker than the rich pine that was his trophy and, in his excitement, his blue eyes sparkled like the sun's reflection on calm waters on a bright summer day.

She let her mind wander and was carried away by fantasies that had grown bit by bit during his absence. Yes, his wiry frame, toughened by hard work, was just a little taller than her own softer shape, but he was tall enough. And those eyes! That demeanor! His children would be lovely. Their children? A physical pang shot through her abdomen. She covered her womb with both hands as if to protect those future babies. Her lost love and her aborted child must not intrude into her future. She pressed her hands against her skirt so hard the seams pressed into her flesh. Nothing would bring her that kind of suffering again. Nothing!

Mary's first impulse had been to run down to the ship to greet Richard and view the cargo, but she thought better of it. Instead, she skirted the far side of the coppice and made her way home unseen. Richard would call soon enough and she'd receive him graciously, with a modest reserve to conceal her excitement and confusion. How foolish she'd be to allow herself to be carried away at the prospect of a pretty house!

It was still early when she got home and the household was just beginning to stir. Phoebe had laid out bread and tea on the dining room table and Mary helped herself. Sara was the first downstairs.

"Mary, there's a lot of activity down at the docks, did you notice? A ship arrived early this morning. All I can see from our window are its masts. Maybe it's carrying interesting merchandise from the mainland. I can always use fabric to make a new dress."

Mary shrugged her shoulders. Next Ann entered the room with the same questions. Finally William joined them and suggested practically, "When I finish my tea I'll go down and see what's going on. I'll bring you a report at noon."

Mary relaxed. She was glad to postpone questions about Richard's return and all that wood he'd brought with him. And Father would find out more details than she had been able to glean from her remote hiding place in the coppice.

* * *

William was late for lunch and the women sipped their fish chowder while it was still hot. Ann and Sara chatted about Penny Alburton's approaching wedding. Evidently they'd forgotten about the Osprey's arrival. Mary could think of nothing else.

"I heard she is going to have a white wedding dress made just as Victoria did," said Sara. "I'd like that. I'd like to have a white dress to wear just that one time on my wedding day. Then I'd pack it away in a trunk to save for my daughters."

"What if your daughters didn't like it?" asked Mary.

"Of course they'd like it. It would become a tradition. They'd be honored to wear it."

"The Alburtons must have been very successful lately to afford the extravagance of a fancy dress to be worn only once. To my mind there's nothing wrong with a bride who wears her best dress to her wedding and again at Christmas and Easter," said Ann. "A queen will do things as she likes, but the rest of us may find it sensible to continue as we always have."

Weddings! Is there nothing in this world but weddings? thought Mary. As she tipped the bowl to sip the last of her soup, her father took his seat at the table. He was puffing from hurrying up the lane and filled with the importance of the information he'd gathered.

"It was the Osprey that docked this morning, Captain Randall's' vessel," he announced. "It's riding low in the water loaded with fine heart pine he bought on the mainland. He means to build a house."

He paused so they would appreciate the weight of his words. Mary felt as if he were looking straight through her and she could offer no resistance.

"He asked me if he might call this evening. I've invited him for supper. I trust that will suit you ladies."

Ann and Sara exchanged knowing glances. Ann winked almost imperceptibly as she said, "I've planned roast pigeon for supper. I'll be sure there is enough."

Mary studied the bottom of her soup bowl. "Of course, Father," she murmured. "Please excuse me." She dropped her napkin into the empty bowl and left the room without pushing in her chair. Overnight the situation had progressed far beyond flirtation and fantasy. This was loaded with finality just as the Osprey was loaded with lumber. Had she been a ship, she, too, would have ridden low in the water with the weight of the moment.

She set out walking again, this time striding purposefully to the sheltered beach where she'd played as a child. She kicked the sand so hard it flew up into the wind and blew back in her face. She blinked to dislodge the fine grains from her eyes and tears rose to wash them clean. Then she couldn't stop the tears and they coursed down her cheeks as she sobbed with frustration.

I took pride in my independence, she thought. *In everything I've learned and studied. But look, I'm really no more self-reliant than a penned chicken that picks among the scraps that are thrown to it. When it comes to the important things, the decisions are all made beyond the fence. I don't have much more say in my life than that poor hen.*

I don't like Father's insistence on my marrying Richard Randall or anyone else for that matter. I don't like Richard's presumption that his favors are all I've ever hoped for in life. But what does it matter what I like and don't like? The alternative is very bleak indeed. I pretend to be indifferent to the plight of unmarried women, but I see what finally happens. Once they reach a certain age they're not called "unmarried" anymore. They're branded as spinsters, maiden aunts and old biddies who are only tolerated out of duty. She smiled. *How many of those maiden aunts are really maidens? How many, like me, have secrets they don't tell?*

It would have been so easy if Michael had lived. Have the months since he died embellished his memory? Probably, she admitted. *Nevertheless, this possible union with Captain Randall is different. It's motivated by practical concerns not affection. I will have a house, position in the village. Richard will have a wife and family. My parents will be divested of the lingering responsibility for an older daughter. Sara can proceed with her plans to marry John Barlow.*

"It all hinges on me," she muttered. She could gratify her parents' wishes, open the door to Sara's wedded bliss, and satisfy Richard's desire for a wife. And what? What about her?

She bent and gathered up a handful of sand, savoring its moist coolness against her feverish palm. She lofted the sand downwind into a flock of gray and white gulls at the waters' edge. It fell in a fine drizzle on the gulls' backs. They ruffled their wings and flew down the beach where they wouldn't be disturbed. If only she could fly away from her distress like the gulls. She pulled off her shoes and stockings. Wading into the shallows, she dug her toes into the watery sand until they hit a sand dollar. She bent to pick it up and threw it hard, sending it skipping over the water like a stone. So much for dreams and fantasies!

Quiet certainty enveloped her as she stared after the sand dollar. She'd guard the memory of her romance with Michael like her other girlhood treasures and take it out only at special times when she was alone. Like her childhood, it had been a time of butterflies and budding flowers and birdsong. She knew she'd never know anything like it again, but nobody could take away her memories.

She turned to go back to the house and get ready for dinner and the interview with Richard that was sure to follow. She'd wear her good linen blouse with the lace collar and cuffs and her new black shoes. She'd brush her hair until it glowed like crows' feathers. If she was to be part of the dealings to be settled tonight, she would show her value. She would not be lightly given or taken. Maybe she could even have a hand in the bargaining.

CHAPTER 5

Richard arrived early. Mary watched from the kitchen yard as William vigorously shook his hand, ushered him into the office, and shut the door. There could be no doubt about the subject of their conversation. Mary felt like a fecund she-goat at auction. She didn't know what to do with herself and wandered into the dining room.

A leaf extended the normally square table into a broad rectangle decked out with a crisp white table cloth and embroidered napkins. Silver flatware and crystal glasses reflected myriad golden flames from the lighted candelabra, and the Dutch china service added soft tones of ivory and blue. Well, definitely better treatment than for a goat, Mary admitted to herself.

The men finished their business quickly. They walked briskly into the room with Ann and Sara close behind. William took his usual position at the head of the table and Ann sat at the foot. Richard was seated to William's immediate right with Mary next to him. Sara sat alone to her father's left. The plump pigeons lay in a pool of rich drippings. Each was stuffed with bread crumbs redolent of rosemary and parsley and was sliced cleanly down the middle. Richard made short work of half a pigeon and gratefully accepted a second helping. Mary picked at her food.

William inquired about Richard's recent travels and his opinions about regional politics. Ann and Sara adopted attitudes of studied attentiveness. Mary silently studied her plate and wished the meal would end.

At last Phoebe served dessert, a vanilla pudding richly flavored with beans Mary herself had collected from the orchids on the east side of the coppice. When he'd scraped the last sweet drop from his bowl, Richard turned to her and asked, "Mary, with your father's permission, I'd like to speak with you alone."

Mary smiled. *Of course Father would give his permission. Wasn't that what all this was about?* She refolded her napkin, placed it neatly on the table and rose. "Shall we go to the parlor?" she asked.

Before she could even invite him to sit down, Richard began.

"Mary, I'm not good at social pretenses and I don't like them much. I want to speak openly and I'd like you to do the same. I received your letter."

Whether he paused for effect or to compose his thoughts, Mary couldn't tell, but she held her breath until he spoke again.

"I didn't think before I wrote those unfortunate words. I should have said I *hoped* to find you waiting; I had no reason to assume that you would be. Your letter had such lovely descriptions of the life on this island. I knew I'd made you very angry because your closing words were so abrupt. They seemed even harsher from such a distance.

"In the weeks since then I've had plenty of time to think about my plans and my feelings."

"Richard . . ."

"Let me finish," he said firmly. "I'm an adventurer, but I have feelings and I've reached a time in my life when I want to have the comforts of a home and a family. This is not to say that I want to change my profession or stop taking risks. I recognize that any woman who will be my wife must share my adventurous spirit or she will be miserable. Mary, I see in you the independence that I hope will help us form a happy partnership.

"While I appreciate some of your qualities and respect you, I don't love you. And I don't expect you to love me. Nevertheless, I wish to propose marriage. Your father has already given his blessing. But I want you to understand my proposal for what it is.

"If we marry, you will have a fine house. I saw you up in the trees this morning looking at the lumber, so I don't have to tell you about that. You'll have all the pretty things I can provide to furnish your life. In the course of time, I hope we'll have children. Many men can offer as much as I've described." He paused.

"But I offer more. I promise you the freedom to pursue your own interests, whether that means wandering in the coppice at dawn or raising crayfish in your bathtub." He smiled before he went on.

"You must understand that my proposal requires concessions from you, too. I'll continue to sail as a wrecker. The promise of wrecking, as I'm sure you know, is great wealth. The threat is long absences from home and grave physical risks. I'm not blind to the grief you suffered and perhaps still suffer from the loss of that scientist you were engaged to. Understand from the very beginning that if we marry, you risk losing another man at sea."

Mary lowered herself onto the settee. She'd expected a polite exchange of conversation that would lead to Richard's asking for her hand. Then she would have insisted on a decent interval in which to make up her mind. Instead, she'd just received a proposal -- no, a proposition -- with specific terms and conditions. Richard stood before her and looked down at her intensely

"I know you're capable of being decisive, Mary. I ask you to be so now," he said. "There's no value in putting off your decision. You've had months to think. Make your choice, yes or no. I hope you'll choose me. I believe I can make you happy and we can live together satisfactorily."

She inclined her head and closed her eyes. She knew what she wanted. She desperately hoped it was the right thing! Looking up, she met his gaze with determination.

"What I dislike about marriage is the possibility of losing my independence and solitude," Mary said, smiling ruefully. "You seem to understand my need for them. How can I refuse your offer?"

Richard's shoulders visibly softened as he relaxed and smiled again. He sat beside her on the settee. "Well then! I'll do my best for you, Mary.

"I promised you a gift," he said. "Will you accept it? It will be a token of our agreement." He pulled a royal blue velvet bag from his vest pocket and lay it on her lap untying the satin ribbon that held it closed.

"I want you to know that however wonderful this thing is, it is only a token," said Mary. "My affection cannot be paid for. I won't willingly enter an arrangement where my behavior is assumed or my feeling is owed. I won't lose myself. Do you understand?"

"I understand, Mary," Richard whispered, returning her earnest gaze.

Mary tipped the bag's contents onto her lap. Dainty blue enameled flowers and buds linked by delicate silver work formed a necklace bouquet so realistic she hesitated at first to touch the little petals. At each end a silver ring was secured to a single flower.

"It's beautiful!" exclaimed Mary. "What are these little blossoms? I've never seen anything like them."

"I was told they grow wild in the fields in England," said Richard. "The young lord said the necklace reminded him of his lady friend at home and he meant to give it to her on his return. When I allowed that there was a lady in my life, he insisted that I take it as evidence of his gratitude. I bought a ribbon to fasten it. It's the same color as the flowers. May I?"

He took a narrow velvet ribbon from his vest pocket and threaded it through one of the silver rings. Mary held the necklace to her throat and turned so he could pass the ribbon through the other end and tie it in a bow at the nape of her neck.

"I can make it longer or shorter if you like," he said.

She touched her throat and turned. "I think it's perfect." She smiled and looked at her hands lying palms down on her lap. A thin black line around her right index fingernail showed where she hadn't been able to scrub away the dirt from this morning's weeding. A fine contrast to my pretty new jewelry, she thought. The pair sat without speaking until Mary broke the silence.

"I suppose we should share the news with my family. I wouldn't be surprised to find Sara listening outside the door," she said.

Sara wasn't outside the door, but she wasn't far off either. They found her in the dining room industriously trimming lamp wicks, a job Mary knew she would never volunteer to do under ordinary circumstances.

"I am so excited for you!" she exclaimed. She hugged Mary enthusiastically, paused momentarily, then hugged Richard, too. "Have you set a date? Who are you going to invite? I know! We must have a double wedding. Wouldn't that be fun?"

"Sara, I haven't even talked to Mother yet. I'm sure she'll want to have her say in the plans. As for a double wedding, I didn't know you were betrothed. Has something taken place since lunch that I haven't heard about?" Was Sara's excitement prompted only by her enthusiasm for Mary's engagement to Richard or was she really giddy in anticipation of being able to move ahead with her own plans? It didn't matter.

"Mother and Father are in his office," said Sara. "They said they wanted to go over some accounts. Don't make them wait any longer."

There was a very brief pause after Mary's knock. "Come in children," said Ann.

"Richard and I have decided to marry - with your permission, of course, but I understand that has already been granted." Mary nodded deferentially to her father.

William smiled. "I have no objection."

"What a lovely necklace! Richard is that your gift?" asked Ann. "Those are forget-me-nots, aren't they? Forget-me-nots mean constant love. Such a good omen for a new marriage, and flowers never lie!"

"I'm sure you two have much to talk about," said William. "Why don't you go for a walk and enjoy the evening while it's still light?"

Richard led the way through the weeds to the space where he planned to build their house. It sat to the west of Mary's home and overlooked the water. The plot had been passed to him in his father's will and had lain idle for years.

Richard took Mary's arm to guide her around a thorny shrub. Mary winced at the sight of the scar on his left hand where his little finger once had been. Seeing her revulsion, he slid his hand out of sight behind her.

"You'll get used to it. I did," he said laconically and looked away.

"What happened?" Mary asked, trying not to shrink again when he touched her back.

"Carelessness. I was sixteen and thought I knew everything. Another sailor dared me to climb up to the topsail. I scrambled right up without so much as a glance at the sky. My finger got caught under one of the rigging lines when a gust filled the sail and drew the line taught. There was a water spout to starboard. It didn't hit us, but I was trapped up there hugging the mast for dear life with my right arm while my left hand was pinched mercilessly. I knew if I fainted I'd fall to my death, so I clung to consciousness just as I clung to the mast. After the weather subsided, the captain himself climbed up and carried me down, cast over his shoulder like a bag of sand. My finger stayed up there between line and mast. It's still there for all I know. The cook poured rum over the wound and tied it up tight in clean cheesecloth. I guess he did a good job. The bleeding stopped and I didn't get infected.

"I learned my lesson. You can never trust the sea or the weather. I never take anything for granted now. I cheated death once. I don't want to tempt fate again. Sometimes at night when there's a storm I feel the finger being ripped from my hand again. It's a forceful reminder to watch out for myself."

Mary's thoughts wandered briefly to that other man who hadn't cheated death at sea. She stopped. This would never do! She pulled her attention back to the present. Fortunately, Richard was busy planning and didn't notice her distraction. She concentrated on his words.

"We'll need a much better path than this one," he said. "I'll bring some men out here with machetes to clear it before we start to build."

"Let me come with you and look at the plants in the daylight," said Mary, following his lead. "There may be something worth saving that we can't see now. I think I remember daisies growing around here somewhere. Wouldn't it be nice to see them in bloom from our windows?"

"The woman's touch is coming into my life already," quipped Richard. "It would never occur to me to locate a house on account of a patch of daisies." He put his arm around her waist and gave her a little hug. "Let's sit on the hill and watch the sun set," suggested Richard. "Maybe there will be a green flash just for us."

It was a splendid sunset bursting with pink and azure clouds and crowned with golden rays that didn't disappear until the sun was completely below the horizon. There was no green flash, but it didn't matter. As they strolled home, Mary stopped twice to look back for lingering traces of the spectacle. Before Richard left her at her door, he kissed her once on the forehead.

CHAPTER 6

The next morning when Mary came down to breakfast, Ann was already making lists.

"Do you want to invite people from off island or shall we limit the guests to our friends on the Cay?" she asked. "It makes a big difference. A home wedding can be very sweet, but for a large group we'll have to go to the church in Marsh Harbour. I suppose the Methodist church here is big enough, but I won't have you married anywhere other than Church of England. I'm sure Mister Wiley will be amenable to having the service at St. Harmony. You don't go to church, but Sara and I are there often enough."

"I want a small wedding right here in the parlor," said Mary firmly as she lifted the cosy from the teapot and filled her cup. "The only people I want present are you and Father and Sara and my godparents. Richard has no family, but he may have some friends to include. I'll wear my best dress and pick wild flowers for my bouquet. We'll have a hearty meal and end it with a white cake with candied fruit." She dropped a half-spoonful of sugar into her tea and tore herself a generous piece of bread.

"Well!" exclaimed Ann as she put down her pen. "You've thought this through in a short time. I wish you'd consider something a little bit more elaborate. This is the biggest celebration of your life. I definitely want to include a few more guests. We must ask John Barlow and his family. It would be rude to exclude them. Perhaps a fancier cake. It would be so pretty in the middle of the table."

"Mother, I know what I want," Mary said. "You're quite right about the Barlows and I'm sure you'll have many more important things to say, but please understand that 'elaborate' is not an idea that fits with my wedding. Besides, I'm sure Sara will want every fancy thing you can invent. You don't want to wear yourself out before then." She grinned and walked around the table to give Ann a warm hug."Here's a list I want you to make for me. You know the meanings of flowers. Write down every one you can think of so I can choose the very best for my bouquet. Wouldn't it be terrible if I picked something that stands for sadness or infidelity because it was pretty and I didn't know any better? I want only pretty flowers with happy promises!" She buttered her bread as she waited for her tea to cool.

"What a lovely idea," said Ann. "I'd like to do that. I think I may even have an old book in my trunk that tells about those meanings." She sipped her tea and fingered the edge of her writing paper. As she continued, her voice took on a reflective tone.

"I remember the preparations for my wedding as if it were yesterday," she said. "I was only nineteen and I was so frightened and excited. Your father seemed like royalty, being nine years older and so well-known and respected. We had a fine big wedding. My cousins even came all the way from London."

Mary smiled. She'd heard this all before.

"I'm rambling, aren't I?" Ann poured herself another cup of tea and patted Mary's hand. "All right. Let's talk about the present. Have you thought about how you want to furnish your house? You'll take your bed, of course, and your trunk. You'll need some kind of dresser, at least one. It's up to Richard to provide most of the furnishings, and I'm sure he'll have no trouble in his profession. But you'll want things from home that will bring back happy memories and that you'll pass on to your own children when they marry.

"You also should think about servants. Even though there will be only two of you at first, you don't want to do the heavy work yourself and you want someone to cook and do the laundry. Consider whether you want to hire a woman from the village or if you want someone to live in. I can't imagine that you'd want Phoebe with that limp of hers. It's only because of your father's kindness that she's allowed to stay here at all. Her mother is too old to make such a change and I'm afraid I couldn't do without Deborah. My knees aren't what they were and with you girls out of the house, I'll need a young servant to go up and down stairs."

"I could manage this household without worrying much, but setting up a new one is a different matter, isn't it?" asked Mary. "I'll think about it. I wonder how long it will take Richard to build that house. I'd better get started making these other arrangements so I'll be ready when the house is."

* * *

Every morning Mary worked in the house helping her mother and stitching linens. She'd thought she had plenty, but when she stopped to consider the quantity that was used here, she realized her trunk wasn't nearly full enough. Towels and face cloths and bed sheets and pillow cases didn't stay fresh for more than a few days. Then they had to be washed and replaced with another set, especially in the summer. She had just enough personal linen, but when she looked at it critically, she saw that much of it was worn and grey beyond the sun's power to bleach it. Yes, like it or not, there was plenty of sewing to do!

When the day was fair, she took lunch in a basket to share with Richard. At first they sat on the piles of lumber. As the house progressed, the stacks shrank and they were able to sit on the floorboards and steps of the house itself.

Mary's lunchtime forays to the building site began as an excuse to get away from the tedious work of preparing her dowry. Then gradually she began to enjoy Richard's company and conversation. His life at sea was filled with adventure and the ocean environment was a totally different world from the one that she knew on land. He told stories of dolphins that leapt out of the water as they raced beside the Osprey and giant groupers the crew caught that would feed them for days. She was fascinated by his practical skills, the management of his sloop under sail, his planning and building their house. Her impression of him had been dominated by his dangerous profession and nonchalant appearance, but now she began to respect this side of him that was smart and masterful.

"Building a good house isn't much different from building a seaworthy ship," he explained. "You get the best wood you can and then you build it strong, but not rigid. It needs to give and sway a little with the wind. That's why we're using wood pegs to fasten the boards rather than nails. They'll swell and contract with the rest of the house as the seasons change. Everything will stay together and not break."

The construction crew consisted of Richard, Mary's godfather, Uncle Jack, and Seth, a freed slave, who sailed with Richard. Every day they started soon after dawn and worked until mid-afternoon when they sought comfort and companionship in the shady waterfront warehouses.

Mary hadn't seen the drawings for the house. Richard kept them on the Osprey, but as the work progressed she could appreciate the simplicity of its design and the sturdiness of its construction. She came to enjoy the smell of freshly sawn pine and the rhythmic sound of hammers systematically building her home where there had been nothing but a pile of wood.

One day before lunch, she watched the men at work on the second floor and realized something was terribly wrong. She couldn't believe that Richard had made such an enormous mistake. As soon as he jumped to the ground from the tall wooden ladder she exclaimed, "Richard, you've forgotten the stairs! We can't climb a ladder to go to bed. And think of our children; they'll fall to their deaths."

Richard put his hands on his hips and sternly contemplated first Mary, then the house, then Mary again. Oh dear, she thought. I'm right and now he's angry with me for finding the fault. Then he started to laugh so hard he had to sit down.

"Come over here, Mary," he said when he could finally catch his breath. "Look. The stairway goes right here on the outside of the house. That way I don't have to make the rooms smaller to fit stairs on the inside. Think of your mother's house. See how the size of the dining room is reduced by the stairwell? I'm sure the same thing is true upstairs. If I were to put the stairs inside, I'd have to build a much bigger house to get the same size rooms as we have here. It's been done for years on Abaco. Ours is the first house on Green Turtle Cay that will have the design."

"I see your point, but what if it rains?" she asked.

"There will be a roof over the verandas on both floors," Richard explained patiently. "Since it almost never gets cold here, winter won't be a problem. It's a great innovation. You'll see."

I think it's going to look peculiar, Mary thought as she set down the lunch basket, but she didn't say anything because she didn't want him to laugh at her again.

"That Seth is a good worker," Richard observed as he wiped his hands. "He sailed with me on my last wrecking trip and he knew a thing or two about sailing and cooking, too. I want to keep him on. Do you think you can use him around the house when he's not occupied working for me? I'm afraid he'll get grabbed up by somebody else if I can't give him enough work."

"I'll need a man to help with the heavy work," she replied. "I haven't yet gotten other help. I know I must take care of that soon, but I don't know how to tell if a person is capable and trustworthy. Those whom I know to be qualified are either employed or other people's slaves. A few Africans have recently arrived by way of Jamaica, but nobody knows much about them and they're very hard to understand. It's a problem for me."

"Why don't I ask the men at the docks? Maybe someone's wife or daughter is looking for work," Richard suggested.

"That would be a great help." Mary shook the crumbs off the napkins, used one of them to dry the glasses, and slowly put everything back in the basket. Lunch had made her contented and lazy.

"We'll start framing the bedroom this afternoon. Why don't you and I lie down on those boards for a little while, just to make them more familiar when we move in? They're smooth and in the shade over there. We could have a nice time before I have to get back to work." He took her arm and tugged.

She jerked away. "Absolutely not! I can't imagine that you'd say such a thing." She turned quickly and walked home without looking back. She'd spoken like a prude, she knew, but he'd moved so quickly from the role of genial companion to that of amorous suitor. She wasn't ready for that yet.

"You'd best start getting ready," said a quiet little voice inside her. "The wedding gets closer every day."

She tried to regain her composure before she returned the basket to the kitchen where Phoebe was shelling beans. The slave looked up from her work and said hesitantly, "Miss Mary?"

Mary stopped. Slaves didn't start conversations, but she would never forget the one time Phoebe did start one it was important.

"Miss Mary, you will be taking slaves to your new home when you marry, I guess."

"Yes, I will need a servant," Mary replied.

"Then you will take me."

Mary wasn't one to put on airs with anyone, but she was flabbergasted by Phoebe's audacity.

"Since when do you tell me what I will do? You don't make decisions, Phoebe. You follow instructions. Get back to work. Please."

Phoebe stood to face her and Mary could see that she was shaking.

"You will take me or your father will hear about that baby I helped you get rid of last winter." Phoebe paused to be sure the importance of her statement was understood. Then she sighed deeply as if to force out the next words. "And I don't think you want your mother to know how many times I've had to drink that awful aloe to get rid of your younger brothers and sisters."

"What do you mean?" Mary sucked in her breath and steadied herself against the doorway. Her brothers and sisters? Her father?

No! "You're lying!"

"I mean nothing more than I said," replied the slave. "I never wanted to have Mr. William's attentions and I surely never want to have his children, but it's not in my power to refuse him, he being the master and me the slave. So I've done what was necessary. But I can't bear any of it anymore. I just want to have a peaceful life taking care of you and your Captain Richard and all those cute little babies you're going to have. And nobody will be hurt or afraid anymore."

The words spilled from her mouth. "I may limp a bit, Miss, but I can sew and I can clean better than most and I've learned all about cooking and healing from my granny and my mother. I've been faithful to your secret. You know that. I will keep all the secrets I know and take them to my grave. Take *me* into your new home, Miss. No one can be as faithful as I'll be or as hard working."

Phoebe's tearless eyes melted from bold to pleading. The two stared at one another as the seconds throbbed like a pulse uniting them in womanly understanding.

"I didn't know," Mary murmured finally. "I didn't know."

She spun and ran from the kitchen and didn't stop until she came to the coppice. Panting, she embraced a balsam tree to keep from falling. "My own father," she wept taking a perverse pleasure in the scratches the bark made on her cheek. "How could he do that?" She remembered the lamplight that seeped out from under his office door and up the stairs late at night. So many nights. So many years.

Just this morning she'd regretted the prospect of leaving the safety of her childhood home and her father's protection. She'd thought him to be generous, kind and honest. Now she saw that was an illusion.

Nothing was as it seemed. Nothing!

CHAPTER 7

Mary lowered herself to sit on the leafy cushion of the forest floor. She hugged her knees and rocked slowly back and forth staring out at the ocean. She hadn't always agreed with her father, but she believed him to be an honest and decent man. She'd always assumed he would protect her and anyone helpless who came to him. Phoebe shattered that image with just a few words. She stood again and walked deeper into the woods, deaf to the birds' songs from above and blind to the panoply of color painted by the spring flowers at her feet. She wandered aimlessly until the angle of the sun alerted her to the passage of time. She should start home. She didn't want to cause her mother worry, especially now. Still, she dragged her feet as she headed back and tried to make sense of what she'd heard. What if Phoebe was lying? There was no way for Mary to know. One thing was certain - the slave desperately wanted to get out of this house. She risked severe punishment when she spoke out as she did. As Mary climbed the path, each step took her closer to her childhood home and further from her youthful innocence.

Ann was by the stair when Mary came in. "My dear, what's the matter?" she asked. "You don't look well at all."

"I've been in the sun too much this afternoon, Mother. I'm

going to lie down. Please excuse me from dinner." *The bedroom is the only place I can possibly hope to be alone,* she thought. *And I can't face anyone now.*

She lay on her bed in her clothes and closed her eyes. The image of her dignified and virtuous father formally dressed for a guild meeting stared pretentiously out of the darkness. She snapped her eyes open and concentrated on a knot in one of the ceiling planks as she pulled a pillow up around her ears to muffle the echoes of conversation from the dinner table. She must have dozed because Sara surprised her as she bounced into the room and tugged on the pillow. "It's bed time, Mary. Get undressed and hang up your clothes. You can't be as sick as all that." Mary complied lethargically.

She slept on and off, kicking the sheets and pushing the pillow from one place to another. In the morning she refused to get up. She'd slept all she could, but her disillusionment sucked away her energy. Ann brought her breakfast on a tray, but her stomach was clenched in a knot. She could only tolerate broth, and not much of that. On the second day, she forced herself to sit on the edge of the bed. The room spun around in a dizzy haze and she sank helplessly to the stability of the mattress. Her breath was quick and shallow and her body was drenched in cold sweat. She wrapped herself in the sheet for warmth and counted slowly, struggling to match her breath to the cadence of the numbers.

If only she could talk to someone, but who? Certainly not her father! She dreaded to think how he would react to her knowledge of his faithlessness. What might he do to Phoebe as punishment for speaking out? Confiding in her mother or Sara was out of the question. For once she wished she had friends from the village. There was only one possible solution. She must go to Richard. He was used to making hard decisions and he had no emotional involvement. He'd understand.

She lay quietly with her eyes closed and tried to summon the strength to go find him. She sat slowly, then stood, steadying herself on the dresser. This time her sense of purpose kept her calm. She sipped the remaining tepid broth from her lunch tray and dressed hastily, dabbing at her face with a damp cloth and scarcely bothering to run the comb through her hair.

She had no difficulty slipping unnoticed out of the house. She climbed to her familiar lookout on the edge of the woods and paused to compose herself. Doubts crept in again and scurried furtively around the dark corners of her thoughts. What if Richard laughed at her? What if he didn't believe her? What if he thought her father's pleasures were the justifiable right of a slave owner? She didn't know if she could stand more disappointment. *Stop it!* She scolded herself. *You've been through all this before and you've made your decision. Now act on it.*

She didn't have to wait long until she saw Richard and his helpers leave their construction work for the cool breezes of the waterfront. They stripped off their clothes and leapt into the water, shouting and splashing like boys. When they finally crawled back up on the dock, Richard shook his long hair like a big dog and sprayed water in every direction. The men gathered up their discarded clothing, pulled on their trousers, and ambled into one of the storage shacks, presumably to smoke a pipe and maybe drink a little rum.

Although she'd often observed the pier from above, she'd never been beyond the fishmongers' at the landward edge of the docks. The seaward side was a mystery to her. As she walked, she looked furtively toward the house and willed herself to be inconspicuous. She followed the tree line until it ended and, holding her breath, ran across the open grass and onto the dock. She slowed to a walk so her shoes wouldn't drum on the planks and crept to the open door of the shack.

She jumped at the sound of a familiar voice. "Well, it's time for me to go. The wife will be waiting and when I'm late and there's rum on my breath, there's hell to pay. Funny, she doesn't seem to mind the rum if I'm there in time to wash up for supper."

Uncle Jack! He mustn't see her and report to the family. She snuck around the seaside corner of the shack and hid until he came out and was well on his way home. Still afraid that he might look back, she hurried into the darkness of the shack without knocking.

"Richard," she gasped. Usually she took pride in her daring, flaunted it, even. She was unshaken by walking alone in the woods at night or handling scary-looking reptiles, but now she was terrified.

"Mary, what on earth brings you here?!" Richard exclaimed.

Seth looked at her briefly, then stared intently at the floor and left.

"Richard, I have to talk to someone. I have to talk to you! Please take me seriously, for this is so terribly serious." She stumbled and leaned against the wall, feeling lightheaded again.

Richard wrapped an arm around her waist and guided her to sit beside him on a pile of empty burlap flour bags. He tucked a bag behind her to ease her leaning on the wall.

"What is it, Mary? What is it that can be as bad as all this?"

She began slowly and talked faster and faster until she couldn't have stopped if she'd wanted to. She told him about Phoebe's pregnancies and all the nights she had lain safely in bed, unknowing, while her father forced his attentions on the slave. She told him about Michael's child. The tears rolled unheeded down her cheeks and when she finished she sat dumb and still.

Richard took her in his arms and held her against his bare chest. "Oh Mary, look at you! You act so brave and strong, but you've already suffered more than a woman should. You've loved and that one died, and now you've been betrayed. I promise you, no matter what I've done before, I will never betray your trust in me. And I will do everything in my power to see that I'm not lost to you."

He cradled her chin in his right hand and tipped her head up to look at him. "Can you believe me?"

"Yes," she whispered.

He kissed her tear-salted lips once and stroked her hair. As he ran his fingers along her neck to her throat, he slowly undid the first button of her blouse. She started to protest.

"Richard!"

"I'm not joking. I was joking the other afternoon, but this isn't a game. You need me now, not in four weeks after some wedding party. Trust me now," he said. "It won't wait."

She leaned back against the burlap cushion and tentatively wrapped her arms around his naked back.

After Michael died, she'd thought she would never enjoy another man's body. She'd expected only to tolerate someone else's touch and she wondered how she could possibly endure the intimacy of another man inside her. How wrong she'd been! They were different, of course. Where Michael had been soft and smooth, Richard was muscular and hairy. Where the one was thin, the other was burly. Michael had smelled of mint and lemon grass. Richard smelled of sea salt, tobacco and rum. His long hair fell over his face and tangled with hers and his touch radiated manly authority. Her resistance melted away and she closed her eyes and willingly surrendered. Tears and sweat mixed and trickled through the fine dusting of flour that powdered them both, creating little channels like water running through sand.

When they were still again, they lay side by side on their backs without speaking. Richard knelt and covered her with his shirt, brushing the hair away from her face. He looked down at her earnestly.

"I meant what I said. From this day I will never be unfaithful to you. I swear it. But you must make an equally heartfelt promise to me. You will never destroy a child of my body. From now on, you will use your knowledge of herbs and plants for health and growth. And Phoebe, too. You tell her."

"Richard, I was desperate when I did that. You'll know your children, I promise."

He helped her to her feet and traced an index finger along the edge of her lips.

"Look at you! You're completely covered with flour. You didn't look very good when you walked in here, but now you could pass for a ghost. Come outside and get in the water. It's the only way you'll ever get clean."

"I can't swim," she confessed.

"Can't swim?! Then let me splash you clean. Stand over there."

She stood on the pier in the shadow of the shack and he poured jar after jar of cool sea water over her naked body until the flour washed away. Then he turned her to face him. Mary felt herself stripped clean of all the fear and sadness that had troubled her. She took a step toward him and was soon in his arms again kissing and being kissed. This time she had no thought of another time or place. There was only now. They lay on the rough boards of the pier exploring each other with their hands and lips. He brushed her cheek with his left hand and she drew it to her lips and kissed the scar. If it hadn't been for the mosquitoes, they might have lain there for a very long time, but evening was falling. Richard sat up.

"So, how long do we have to wait for this wedding? I can hurry the house along, you know. Once it's finished there's no reason to wait, is there?"

"The sooner we're married and living in our own house, the better it will be for me," replied Mary. "I won't be happy until I cross that threshold with you."

* * *

Mary crept up the stairs. She quickly stripped off her clothes and cleaned the last traces of sand and flour from the creases of her knees and elbows. As she washed between her thighs, she saddened at the thought that she was removing the last trace of their lovemaking. Never mind. There would be many more times. She dressed quickly. A glance in the mirror reassured her that she looked wan enough to be considered sick, but recovering.

She went to the laundry and pushed the wad of soiled clothing into the center of the dirty clothes basket. Phoebe turned from stirring the stew, then returned to her work without comment. Had there been a knowing look in her eye? Was this another secret they shared? Had Seth told her Mary was out at the docks? She had no way of knowing.

"Phoebe, I'm feeling better. Please set a place for me for supper," she said.

"Darling, I am so glad to see you up and about," said Ann as she came in to check the sugar bin. "I was ready to call for Doctor Padget if you hadn't improved by tomorrow. Come, sit with me until supper. There's no need for you to strain yourself." She hooked her elbow in Mary's and ushered her into the dining room.

The meal was soon served and Mary marveled that everything appeared so normal. She wasn't the same person she'd been three days ago, but nobody could see the change and nothing else was different. Ann and Sara prattled about plans for the church bazaar and the approaching wedding of one of Sara's friends. William played the wise and benevolent patriarch. Phoebe served the food and took away the empty plates wearing a serene smile. Mary sat primly erect as if she hadn't spent the afternoon naked in a waterfront shack. *We're all marionettes,* she thought. *Now we behave as we want the world to believe us to be, even in front of the people we're closest to and say we love. But our real lives happen when the lamps are out and our strings are slack and we think nobody's looking. What would happen if all the pretense was stripped away?* She dreaded to think.

"I don't guess you'll want Gram's cherry dresser, will you?" asked Sara. When Mary didn't respond, she repeated the question more loudly.

"Excuse me. My thoughts were elsewhere. You're quite mistaken. I do very much want that dresser. I've used it ever since I can remember. I've been meaning to talk to Mother about it."

"Don't bother trying to get it now," said Sara haughtily. "It's been promised to me."

"I didn't know you cared about it, Mary," said Ann. "I did agree that Sara should keep it."

"She'll do no such thing!" exclaimed Mary. "Sara, you're like a vulture around here laying claim to this and demanding that. Ever since my engagement to Richard you've acted as though you're determined to grab the best things in the house before I can even think of them. Understand me clearly, Sister, there are very few things that I want, but the few I cherish will go with me. I leave all the rest for you."

"Girls, remember yourselves. You're at the table," interjected

William. "Stop your quarreling and act your age."

"Excuse me!" Sara exclaimed. She knocked over her chair as she stood and left the room without righting it.

So that's the sister I so want to protect from hurtful truths, thought Mary. *It is so tempting to hurt her out of spite!*

CHAPTER 8

Mary wouldn't have wanted to live these last days over again, but she had to admit that the outcome was better than anything she could ever have hoped for. Never in her most optimistic fantasies had she conceived of the happiness she felt as Richard smiled when he saw her.

"You're looking much brighter today. How about a little trip to the docks before lunch?" he asked, patting her bottom when she arrived at the house site with the lunch basket.

"Don't be silly. That's not why I came and you know it. Besides, we might never come back and the house would remain unfinished and we could never be married. We would live in sin as dock tramps for the rest of our lives."

"Would you mind that?" he asked.

"Maybe not so much." She smiled impishly and winked.

In spite of her unconventional fantasy, Mary laid out the lunch like a lady. They sat on the bottom step of the newly-completed stairs and used the step above as a table.

"You're a ship's captain and captains have the authority to marry people, don't they?" Mary asked. "Why don't you just declare us married and we can be done with all this foolishness?"

"I don't think it works quite that way," said Richard. "Anyway, at this point I'd hate to deprive your mother of the fun of organizing this party. From what you say she doesn't have much joy in life or much to look forward to. Let's give her this.

"We don't have to wait long. It should only take two more weeks to finish the house if the weather holds. Let's set the wedding for three weeks from Saturday. We'll both feel better if we have a date to look forward to and it will put a limit on the silliness those women can create."

Mary looked up at the house and sighed. In three weeks she would be married and live in the nicest house on the island. She would go to sleep and wake up with Richard at her side. Someday there would be children. The boys would learn the wisdom of the sea from their father and the importance of gentleness and faithfulness from their mother. The girls would master the secrets of plants for healing and food and they would never be obliged to do needlework or embroidery unless they wanted to. They would always be able to take shelter in their father's protection and trust his goodness. She and Richard would live to white-haired old age surrounded by loving children and grandchildren.

"What are you thinking about?" Richard asked.

"I was thinking about the future," she replied. "You get back to work. I don't want to wait a day longer than I have to." She kissed him on the lips, lingering with the touch of his skin and moved by the odor of heart pine and sweat. He responded by pulling her to him, but she stepped away.

"No, no. We have to get on with it," she said as she picked up her basket and glided back along the path with a flirtatious sway to her hips. She heard Richard mutter something that sounded like Dammit! But she didn't look back.

* * *

The date was set, Saturday, June 6 at 4:00. Mister Crocker was pleased to be called upon to officiate. He would sail over from Marsh Harbour in the morning and gratefully accept room and board for the night and a small honorarium. Ann busied herself planning the menu for the bridal supper. Sara conceded possession of the cherry dresser on the condition that she could have the carved oak chair and the mahogany washstand. The former was a problem because Ann hadn't planned to part with that chair at this point in her life, but Sara's persistence prevailed. William attended an unusual number of meetings that kept him out of the house most days.

Construction of the new house was finished a week before the wedding. As a finishing touch, Richard hung a heavy brass knocker on the front door. It was cast in the shape of a dolphin and had been part of the rewards of a French wreck he had saved the year before.

The house was almost twice as long as it was wide. The two main floors were extended by wide verandahs on both sides. The doors and windows were precisely measured to match side to side and front to back so that every breeze passed freely through the house. The peaked roof enclosed a spacious attic and came all the way out over the verandahs, making the structure look larger than it really was.

Mary would cheerfully have moved in immediately, or at least met with Richard in the afternoons, but there was no privacy. Everybody seemed to have business there that couldn't be delayed and they left the doors unlocked so they could come and go. Ann breezed in and out with extra table linen she wanted to bestow, seemingly one piece at a time. Sara came on the pretext of measuring for furniture, although what little they needed was already planned for. Uncle Jack never seemed to be able to remember where he left his tools. Mary soon realized that their comings and goings were as much to keep her and Richard from succumbing to temptation as to accomplish anything of real value.

However, there was plenty to keep her busy. She and Phoebe swept up the sawdust and washed the windows. She had Seth turn over the dirt for a garden and they transplanted herbs and vegetables to the new beds.

"My dear, I don't think it's suitable that you work alongside your servant like that," said Ann. "It will give her ideas of importance beyond her place in life."

"I'll only feel that the house is truly mine after I sweep and polish it myself. Besides, there's too much work here for just Phoebe. The men say they tidy up after they've finished a job, but you know they leave a mess," replied Mary. She knew her mother had been surprised by her announcement that she wanted to take Phoebe to her new home. Seeing them working side by side clearly disturbed her more. What would her poor mother say if she knew all the secrets they shared? Fortunately, she'd never know.

The men lugged the heavy dresser up to the second floor and on the first floor they arranged the dining table, desk, and sofa Richard bought. Fortunately, the new cast iron stove could be taken apart and reassembled in the cookhouse or they might never have gotten it off the boat, let alone past the dock. Mary's four poster bed would be the last piece of furniture to make the move. They would carry it from her childhood bedroom to her new home as soon as she got up on her wedding day.

"Sara, will you miss me after I'm married, or will you simply enjoy the privacy and space my absence affords you?" Mary asked one morning as she brushed her hair. She was awash in childhood memories of sitting on the floor playing pick-up-sticks together and huddling under the covers in one bed during a storm. She was vividly aware that soon she would walk away from a part of her life to which she could never return except in memory.

"I'll miss you. I'll be the only young person left in this house. And who will I quarrel with? I'll just have to come visit when I feel contentious." Sara grinned mischievously.

* * *

Ann was excited to find the book that described the traditional meanings of flowers. "See how old it is. My mother gave it to me when I was a young woman. Look. Here's her signature and the date inside the cover. I leafed through the pages and I think I appreciate it now more than when it was given to me. Notice the drawings as well as the words. Their detail is remarkable! I'm just sorry roses don't grow here. The pink rose stands for perfect happiness. It's ideal for a bride, don't you think?"

"Roses would be lovely," said Mary, "but I'm sure I'll find others that are equally appropriate."

She took the book with her the next time she met Richard for lunch. They sat on the veranda in full view of anyone who would care to look. They'd figured out that when their whereabouts were known, they seemed to be left to themselves. By accommodating everyone's inquisitive and protective impulses, they gained privacy to talk, if not to touch.

"There are lots of plants in the Bahamas that will bring us luck," Mary said. "Can you imagine that the common fern stands for magic, fascination, confidence and shelter? I must have some fern. Palm leaves mean victory and success. It doesn't say what kind of palm, so I guess I'll take tender young tips from the coconut palms that grow by the path to the waterfront. This is best of all. Orchids symbolize love, beauty, and refinement. Richard, do you think they can make me refined?" She laughed. "The Chinese hold that the orchid is the symbol of many children. Yes, I'll have lots of orchids!"

* * *

June 6 arrived with showers that delayed until afternoon both Mary's foray into the coppice for her flowers and the minister's arrival. When finally the sun peeked out, she loped down the stairs and into the woods where she wandered happily looking for unblemished blossoms and greens. She picked an armful. The soft, moist leaves of the plants she knew so well and loved felt like a living benediction on her life with Richard. She picked more. Why should she stint on a blessing?

She carried the cuttings to the kitchen and tied them together into a lavish arrangement, tucking leaves around the string to hide it. She slid it into a shady corner of the table where it would stay cool and fresh until she needed it. When she came into the house through the dining room, she was confronted by mayhem.

"Where have you been, Mary?" her mother shrieked. "You're dressed for a picnic, not a wedding, and you've just tracked in mud. Get someone to sweep that up and get yourself dressed." She held her handkerchief to her apple-red cheek and sighed deeply. Mary helped her to a chair and briskly fanned her.

"There's plenty of time, Mother. You must have forgotten I was going out to gather flowers. Remember, we talked about it. I'm going to get dressed now and you must calm down. Let Sara oversee the table while you rest in your room for a while."

"I'm just a little agitated, my dear. It's not every day my eldest daughter is married, now is it?"

Mary took her arm and helped her to stand. "Of course it's not. Come on now. We'll go upstairs together and soon it will be time."

* * *

Mary had never worn the ivory silk blouse her mother had given her for Christmas. With its leg-of-mutton sleeves and lace jabot and cuffs, it was far too elegant for daily wear. Ann never said so, but Mary understood the gift was meant for her wedding. It was her mother's effort to dress her up. At the time she didn't appreciate the expensive and elegant gift. Now she was glad to have it. She pulled her newest long black skirt from the wardrobe and checked it for dust and stains. Phoebe must have anticipated her choice. It was immaculate and freshly ironed.

Ann tapped quietly at the door before she entered.

"I'm feeling much better. A few minutes alone was all I needed. Let me help you dress."

She held Mary's skirt for her to step into and tied the sash, smoothing the folds and gathers. She slid the blouse over Mary's upraised arms and fastened its tiny pearl buttons. She piled her hair high on her head and held it with what seemed like dozens of scratchy wire hairpins.

"Now, look in the mirror. You're beautiful!"

Mary could hear the latent tears in her mother's voice and she hastened to calm her own feelings. If Mary started crying, she knew her mother would, too, and she'd never get control of herself.

She turned to the mirror and was astonished by the woman who stared back at her. The sophisticated hairdo revealed her long, smooth neck and her angular chin looked more classic than assertive, which was how she usually thought of it. Wisps of hair fell delicately at her nape and lay daintily on the fine lace collar. Her eyes sparkled with excitement and her cheeks blushed in the velvety pink of the roses that Ann had coveted for the bridal bouquet. As she watched, Ann tied the forget-me-not necklace so that it fell just below the lace jabot and lay against the curve at the top of her breasts.

The doorknob squeaked and broke the spell as Sara breathlessly announced, "Everyone is here. You must come down. It's time to start!"

Mary wrapped her mother in a gentle embrace. "Let's go down together," she murmured.

* * *

Phoebe was waiting at the foot of the stairs with Mary's bouquet. "Don't you think that's a little much?" asked Sara, surprised by its size.

"Not at all. It's perfect," replied Mary as she cradled it against her left arm.

William stood impatiently by the parlor door. He offered his arm and Mary took it stiffly and forced a smile. She looked to the end of the room where stout, good-natured Mr. Crocker waited with Richard. Well, she wasn't the only one to have taken care with her appearance! Richard sported a freshly boiled and starched shirt and collar and an immaculate pair of black breeches with rich brown stockings and shiny leather boots. He'd brushed his hair into submission and tied it back with a black velvet ribbon.

As William withdrew to one side, Mary whispered, "Where did you get those clothes? You are so handsome!"

"I've always been handsome," Richard replied. "But your

Uncle Jack lent me the finery."

Mr. Crocker looked at them sternly to stop their banter. "Dearly beloved, we are gathered here . . ." he intoned.

Mary drifted away, caught in the rhythm of the ritual and the magic of the moment. "I, Mary, take thee Richard . . ." As she repeated her vows she hardly recognized her own voice. Richard's seemed to thunder, "in sickness and in health until death do us part."

"I now pronounce you man and wife. You may kiss the bride."

She had expected a perfunctory kiss. Instead, he crushed her in his arms and pressed his lips long and hard against her mouth. Mary heard her mother gasp. As he stepped back, he whispered, "Finally!" and winked. Holding her right hand in his left, he turned and formally shook Mr. Crocker's hand.

"Your dinner is laid out in the dining room. I'm sure there will be something for everyone's taste," declared Ann proudly.

"And for the gentlemen, there are several bottles of premium Jamaican rum and glasses on the desk in my office," announced William. "Please help yourselves."

Mary was glad she had refused a big wedding. As it was, there were more people here than she would usually see in a month and they all wanted to talk to her. She felt guilty that she didn't really care much about their stories of friends and children and relatives, but she pretended a polite interest in the news and gossip. She was hungry, but every time she took a piece of fish or a bowl of beans someone would come to offer their congratulations and she would put aside the food, which became decidedly uninteresting once it was cold. Richard stayed at her side and she could see that the social pleasantries were wearing on him at least as much as on her. At least now and then he could slip away to her father's office and enjoy a tumbler of rum.

"Richard, take my glass of punch and pour a little rum in it the next time you go in there. It's not fair that you should have that moral support and it should be denied me."

He raised his eyebrows, but the next time he left the room he returned with a glass of punch that he had clandestinely improved.

"This isn't very ladylike, you know."

"If you cared about my being ladylike, you would have found a different wife long ago."

Jack Kemp took out his fiddle and began to play a waltz. Richard took Mary's hand in his and guided her to the open space by the door. Soon everybody was dancing. Richard clearly had not spent much time waltzing. "That's the third time I've stepped on your foot and I've bumped into your parents twice. I think this is a very bad time for me to learn to dance. Do you mind if I ask Jack to play a polka? I know how to do that."

The tempo increased and the older generation dropped out, but the others spilled out the door into the courtyard where there was more room and only paused when the fiddler himself needed to rest.

"Richard, slip a little more rum into this, won't you? It washes away the dust and gives me the energy I need," asked Mary handing him a tumbler of punch. They danced and drank gaily until the sun began to drop toward the horizon and the guests started to leave.

At first Mary thought she was dizzy from the dancing, but the dizziness didn't go away when she sat down and her head throbbed relentlessly. "Richard, I'm not shuure . . ." She paused to look at him, but his features were all blurry. She squinted to clear her vision.

"Oh Mary, I'm quite sure. You're drunk. It's time for us to leave this party. Now."

He put an arm around her waist and propelled her toward the path to their house, smiling and nodding all the way. "Thank you for your good wishes. I know you have assured our happiness," he cried with unusual loquaciousness. They got as far as the daisy patch before she began to wretch.

"I feel terrible," she moaned. "Please get me more punch to wash this taste out of my mouth."

"Punch is the last thing in the world you need. Come on."

She held tightly to the railing and Richard supported her from behind as they climbed the narrow stair to their bedroom. Mary sighed when she saw her bed draped in new white mosquito netting with satin bows at the corners. Lovely, but she didn't know if she could keep her eyes open much longer what with the pounding in her head and the ringing in her ears.

She leaned against the bed post as Richard undressed her. Then he helped her climb between the sheets. "This wasn't exactly what I had planned, you know. Move over now. At least maybe I can get some sleep."

Mary held the side of the bed with one hand and his shoulder with the other as the world spun faster and faster around her. She closed her eyes.

CHAPTER 9

When Mary woke she was alone. Bright light filtered through the shutters. It must have been midmorning, maybe later. She rolled onto her side and her head throbbed so hard the pulsation was almost audible. She held still until it subsided.

Feet hammered the stairs and the outside door slammed. Mary winced and squinted through burning eyes as Sara threw open the bedroom door so hard the knob banged on the wall behind it. She planted herself in the doorway, feet spread and arms akimbo.

"I have never been so embarrassed in my life! Your wedding day and you got drunk. You got drunk in front of our friends and my fiancé and his family. Do you remember that you threw up on your way home? I hope you're ashamed of yourself."

"Where's Richard?" asked Mary weakly, trying not to move.

"I don't know where Richard is. For all I know, you'll never see him again and it would serve you right. You've humiliated me and everyone in the family. I hope he never comes back."

Mary gritted her teeth as she rolled over to face the wall. "Get out, Sara. This is my house and I don't want you here." She pulled a pillow over her head.

Sara left as she had arrived, slamming everything that moved.

After some time, Mary felt a gentle hand on her shoulder. "Who's there?" She shifted the pillow just far enough to allow her to hear.

"I brought you some food and herb tea, Miss Mary. This should help you feel better."

Phoebe pushed aside the mosquito net and helped her sit. "Here, take some bread and honey. It'll give you strength and the tea will calm your stomach and ease the pain in your head."

Mary grimaced and coughed after the first sip. "It's bitter! What is this?"

"It's black haw. It tastes terrible, but it will help you feel better."

Mary drank the infusion with childlike obedience and sank back on the pillows. Gradually her head stopped pounding and she could think beyond her discomfort. As the darkness advanced, she wished Richard would come to bed. She was lonely and she wanted reassurance that he still loved her. He would never be angry with her drunkenness like Sara, would he? Of course not. But a tiny speck of doubt, no bigger than a grain of sand and just as rough and irritating, lay in the back of her mind. As she drifted off, she wondered if, in her drunken reveling, she had destroyed something very precious.

She awoke to his hand as it traced a gentle line across her cheek, down her chin and neck, and under the sheet where he pressed the warm skin between her breasts.

"Your heart is still beating," he said.

"I wasn't sure there for a while," she replied. "Where have you been? I was afraid you wouldn't come back."

"I was down at the boat. I've been drunk a few times myself, you know. I figured there wasn't anything I could do for you so I just stayed out of the way and let time heal you. Somehow it always does. Phoebe says she has some kind of potion that really helped you. I'd like to know about that one. Not that I'll be getting drunk, of course." He winked. "Move over. Let me in that bed."

Draped in its white netting the bed was like a cocoon insulating them from the rest of the world. His touch was purposeful; his kiss, long and deep. She quivered with anticipation, remembering when they'd made love at the waterfront. Richard drew her to him gently, but with undeniable passion. Mary wouldn't have considered denying him anything. They moved together, then apart; hurried, then slowed; panted and sighed and moaned. Finally they lay side by side on their backs with the sheet thrown back to cool their sweaty skin in the air.

"Do you think you can leave your bed today?" he asked, rubbing her thigh.

"I can, but I don't think I want to. I'd like to stay like this forever."

"It's time, my dear. Phoebe promised us chowder and fresh bread for lunch and I'm ready for it. You've made me hungry."

It was odd having him there as she washed. Modesty hadn't been a consideration when they made love on the dock, but now she stood naked next to her grandmother's dresser and her childhood bed. She didn't know where to look or what to do. She clutched a towel in front of herself and lowered her eyes.

"Do you find me ugly, Mary?"

"Not at all, but I've never lived with a man before. This is very new to me and very strange."

"You'll get used to it." He took the towel from her and wrapped it around her waist to pull her against him. He placed a long and gentle kiss on her lips before he turned her to face the wardrobe. "Now get dressed so we can go down and eat." He was right. She was hungry, too. The assurance that they could lie together again tonight and tomorrow and whenever they wanted was a headier brew than anything she could drink from a glass and she drifted dreamily around the room dressing and straightening, feeling a wifely responsibility for the room, the house, the world. Life was wonderful.

After lunch they strolled down to the dock and sat for a while. "I suppose I should visit my mother. I wonder if she's as mad as Sara. Do I look all right? I want to seem healthy, not suffering for my sins."

"You look fine. I'll go with you."

Ann met them at the door. "Mary, you look radiant. How are you Richard? Come in and sit down. We'll have tea."

The young maid brought tea and sweet biscuits to the parlor and Ann poured. Richard's big rough hands looked incongruous holding the delicate cup and saucer. He clearly felt out of place and he drank quickly and gingerly deposited the porcelain on the nearby table. Ann chattered about household affairs and Mary soon realized that if her mother once was angry about her behavior, she had now forgiven her. They made plans for Ann to return the visit in three days and Mary and Richard set out for home.

"I don't have to be there when she comes, do I?" asked Richard. "Fine china makes me nervous."

"You've done your duty," Mary laughed. "You won't be expected at tea again. You didn't see my father around, did you? I'm glad he wasn't there. I know I have to see him from time to time, but I'm not ready. I'm so happy to be with you and out of his house and mistress of my own. I don't want to spoil it."

They went to the garden where Mary checked to see which plants were becoming established and if any needed stakes or clipping. Richard leaned against a nearby buttonwood tree and watched. "We need a strong bench out here. I'd rather sit than stand when I watch you in the garden."

"If you're going shopping, we can use a few things for the house," teased Mary. "We're three chairs short of having my family for dinner, and that's before Sara marries. I'd love to have a pair of armchairs and a small table in the bedroom so we could have our morning tea before we come downstairs. And each of us needs a desk, you for business and I, for household accounts and garden records."

"I'm sailing at the end of next week," interrupted Richard.

Mary sat back on her heels and looked up at him. "What did you say?"

"I said I'm sailing next Friday."

"You can't!" Mary stood and ran to him, stepping on a row of basil seedlings. She threw herself against his chest and held him to her with all the strength in her arms. "You can't go. Not yet. Not ever, if I have my way about it."

He pushed her back just far enough to look into her eyes. "By the time I sail it will be eight weeks since I've earned any money. I've been building the house and I wanted to be with you. But you know as well as I do that we need an income and wrecking is what I do. It will be as it was when I sailed before we were married. I'll come home as soon as I can, and when I do, our lives will be the better for my trip."

She pressed her forehead against his chest. She'd known this would happen sooner or later, but she'd pushed the idea out of her mind. The present was so sweet, why dwell on the future? In retrospect, those weeks of building and anticipation seemed like days. Next Friday cast a shadow with the immediacy of tomorrow.

When Mary was seven, Sara was just learning to walk. She stumbled and fell, smashing a big white sand dollar Mary had found on the beach just that morning. It was only the second one Mary had ever uncovered and it was as big as her palm - a treasure. When Sara smashed it, it disintegrated into lacy particles of calcified chambers and could never be put back together. Mary shrieked until her throat vibrated and burned, barely catching her breath between screams. She pounded irrationally on her little sister's back until Ann pulled her away.

Now she was overcome with that same sense of loss and futility. She wanted desperately to wail and pound on Richard's chest until he changed his mind. However, the tantrum hadn't changed things all those years ago, and there was no question of its being of any use today. She was mistress of her own house and she'd better be mistress of herself, too. When she looked up, she'd arranged a smile on her face and her eyes were perfectly dry. "Of course," she said. "I didn't realize it would be so soon."

Richard immediately began to prepare the Osprey for the voyage. Seth worked with him and some men she didn't know and her Uncle Jack, who would be second in command. They worked steadily scrubbing decks and polishing fittings, testing lines and mending sails, securing water barrels, tarps, and fishing poles. Mary brought lunch to the pier every day and after they'd eaten, she'd linger to watch their progress.

"It's much like our house," explained Richard. "Only the Osprey has to stay afloat. What we're doing now is the basis for our success or failure later on. The ship must be perfectly seaworthy if we are to help save a ship that has blown aground in a storm. That ship might be lost if even one of our lines breaks. Then we would have failed to save human lives and cargo and we'd have nothing to show for it ourselves."

Watching the preparations, Mary gradually came to realize that, as attentive and loving as Richard was to her, he loved this seagoing life, too, and he was looking forward to his excursion. She could see that wrecking would be her rival for his affection for a long, long time.

CHAPTER 10

The night before Richard was to sail, Ann invited them to dinner, but Mary invented an upset stomach so she could have her husband to herself.

"What time will you go?" she asked.

"Soon after dawn if there's a good wind. Shall I write?"

"I don't think so, not after what happened last time. It's too easy to misunderstand and be misunderstood. Just send me a page saying you are well and safe and when you expect to come home."

"Will you send me news? I want to know about your days and your thoughts," he said.

"My letters will be boring."

"Let me be the judge of that."

They had an early supper of fried grouper and boiled pigeon peas. Richard wanted to check the Osprey one last time and Mary went to the wharf with him. He walked so briskly that sometimes she had to run to catch up. As he looked into the darkness where the night sky met the ocean, she realized his thoughts were running ahead to the voyage and knew without a doubt that the uncertainty that frightened her, invigorated him.

When they made love that night, he stroked her slowly and gently, lingering over every kiss and looking deep into her eyes.

Then he lifted her from the bed and carried her outside. They stood naked in the shadows on the veranda, barely illuminated by the fading moon. He hugged her against his chest.

"I'll miss you more than I can say." His breath tickled her ear as he spoke. "I have more than any man deserves, two lovers, a beautiful woman and her majesty, the sea."

For the first time since he'd announced his departure, Mary wept. Her tears ran unheeded down her cheeks and slid along the creases where their bodies met. She breathed deeply and felt such lightness that she imagined she was rising to glide among the stars in Richard's embrace.

"We should go inside. It will be dawn soon and we won't have slept at all." Mary winced as Richard's practical words broke the spell and she returned to reality as she felt her bare feet on the damp boards of the verandah.

Soon gray light filtered through the shutters, announcing the approaching dawn. Richard slid out of bed and dressed. Trying to delay the inevitable, Mary waited until he went downstairs before she got up. She dawdled unnecessarily over simple details like drawing her socks up smoothly and tying her boots with even bows, but finally she was dressed and there was nothing to do but to join him at the table and face the goodbyes.

"Will you come to see me off?" Richard asked.

"Of course. This isn't at all like before." She smiled and affectionately traced the veins on his right hand with the little finger of her left.

"Come in a half an hour or so. We still need to load some flour and stow the men's gear. I won't sail until you're there."

When he left, Mary carried their dishes to the kitchen house. "Phoebe, you know they're leaving this morning, don't you? Will you come with me to wish them well?"

"To be sure, Miss Mary." Soon the two women walked to the wharf where The Osprey bustled with activity. The morning stillness was shattered by men's shouted orders and raucous joking.

"Not a moment too soon," observed Richard as he strode down

the plank to Mary's side. He kissed her lightly, a public kiss, she thought.

"Godspeed," she said. She tucked her lace handkerchief into his shirt pocket. "This will bring you home safely."

"I love you," he replied and turned and mounted the ramp.

Mary looked around for Phoebe. She stood far back from all the bustle staring solemnly at Seth as he stood by the mizzen mast. He raised his hand to his heart as if making a pledge, then turned to man one of the lines.

They cast off and raised the sails, which filled gradually, then puffed with wind and carried The Osprey to the west. Away, away, away, thought Mary and she waved in rhythm with the word until her arm ached and the ship was no more than a blur in the morning haze. She turned to leave and discovered Phoebe at her side. The two women walked home in silence.

* * *

With Richard gone, the days were bland and uniform. Mary seldom knew or cared if it was Tuesday or Sunday. She spent most of her time alone in the house or walking along the seashore and into the woods. She slept poorly and often got up in the middle of the night to stand on the veranda to watch the moon and try to recapture the bliss she'd known there with Richard. The moon inched through its phases, passing through new moon darkness to a growing hint of light. When it approached fullness, Mary realized she'd already been married a month. How ironic that she should feel so alone! Several times as she turned to step inside, she was sure she saw Phoebe in the shadowed doorway of the kitchen house staring at the moon just as Mary had done. Did she share Mary's loneliness?

Mary began her letter the day after Richard sailed. She wrote a little every day describing the weather, which was abnormally hot for the time of year; the robust growth of the daisies, nearly a foot tall; and what she perceived as the silliness of the turmoil that was building around Sara's betrothal to John Barlow and their approaching marriage. One day as she wrote, Phoebe stood in the doorway.

"Miss Mary, in your letter to Captain Richard, will you be so kind as to include a word from me to Seth? I can only write my name and he doesn't read, anyway. But if you could write a little for me and the captain would read it to him, it would make us both very happy."

"I wish I'd thought of it myself. What do you want to say?"

"I'm not quite sure yet. I'll think about it tonight and you might make that a part of tomorrow's writing."

"Here's my message," said Phoebe the next day. "I miss you. Love. Phoebe."

Mary realized how hard it must have been to compose words that would be known by both her mistress and her master. "Is that all you want to say?" she asked. "I could put in more if you want me to."

"No, Miss. That says it all." *I suppose it does*, thought Mary. *The only important thing in all the pages I've written here is just what she said.*

Two weeks passed. It seemed as if there soon should be a ship to carry her letter to Richard, so she went to the docks every day. While she didn't succeed in sending the letter, she heard sailors' legends and maritime gossip, some of which had a ring of truth to it.

"Is it true that the new lighthouses along our coast are warning the sailors too well and ruining the wreckers' incomes?" she asked one evening over supper at her parents' house.

"Very true," replied William. "Where did you hear that?"

"I heard it from the dock workers. They also said that the United States is demanding that ships wrecked on the Florida reef be brought into American ports for salvage. Don't you think the policy will affect our business here in the Bahamas?"

"There's no question about it. President Polk just asked his Congress to pass a law to that effect. But don't you worry. I'm sure the guilds will resolve the problem. We had another meeting on the subject only last week. You shouldn't frequent the waterfront, my dear. Those men can be rough and ill-mannered." He frowned his disapproval.

Mary did worry. If there were fewer wrecks and the proceeds of them diminished, Richard would have to work harder, be at sea more often, and make less profit. Even after her letter went on its way, she persisted in visiting the waterfront and kept abreast of rumors and news.

* * *

Three weeks passed and Mary began to despair of hearing news from the Osprey. Then late one Friday afternoon, Mary saw an unfamiliar sailor making his way up the path to the house. She met him at the front door.

"I have a letter for a Missus Captain Randall," he said. "Have I come to the right place?"

"Yes, you have!" Mary exclaimed as she exchanged a penny for the long-awaited letter. The penny was generous beyond the value of the service rendered, she knew, but the extravagance was in proportion to her excitement. The sailor paused as if waiting for her to realize her mistake, but Mary nodded and went into the house, so he shrugged and went on his way.

There was a single sheet folded in thirds and addressed on the outside in Richard's hand. She went into the sparely-furnished parlor and sank to the sofa. She pried open the wax seal and read.

"Dearest Mary,

I miss you terribly. I think I work harder during the day so I'll fall asleep quickly at night and not be tormented by loneliness.

I have no inkling of when we'll turn toward home. In fifteen days there has been no sign of a wreck here and no news of one anywhere else, either. I propose to sail southwest along the Florida Keys in hope of better luck. I hope my next note will bring better news.

Seth sends his regards to Phoebe. I love you. Richard"

Mary read it again, then she went upstairs where Phoebe was sweeping. "I have news from the Osprey," she said as she held out the letter. "They haven't been lucky finding wrecks, but they're safe. Seth sent his regards."

Phoebe looked up and smiled warmly. "Thank you Miss. Thank you for telling me."

Mary left the letter open on the dining table and every time she passed she smiled as she pictured him working hard so he could sleep peacefully. "I have no inkling . . ." he wrote. She'd never heard of "an inkling" until he said it one day when he was building their house. "I haven't the slightest inkling of how we're going to get that heavy dresser of yours up those narrow stairs and into the bedroom." She'd asked him what "inkling" meant and laughed when he explained how it was an old word he'd learned from his grandmother when he was little and she'd wondered out loud what would ever become of him if he didn't learn to behave. "I don't have an inkling how we're going to stop you from spending your whole life in the jail," she'd worried. It was Richard's word and she laughed quietly as she reread it. I made him seem closer.

She was glad to have left the letter in plain view. Several times she noticed Phoebe lingering by the table to look at it. She can't read the words, thought Mary, but its presence seems to give her comfort.

The next day she sealed her second thick letter and took it to the wharf to dispatch it on the ship that had brought Richard's. She was pleased to discover that, along with household supplies and personal messages, the ship carried magazines and books from England and the United States. She bought a copy of Emerson's *Nature* because she remembered Michael had talked about it and she couldn't resist a copy of the "Saturday Evening Post" with articles that ranged from politics and business to history and stories. It would certainly relieve the sameness of her days. "Ladies' Book," filled with fashion plates and etiquette pointers, would delight her mother and Sara, so she bought that, too. After her extravagant tip for the sailor and these expenses, she would have less to spend on groceries, but eating conch and beans for a while seemed a small price to pay for such luxuries.

The magazine opened Mary's eyes to situations that she didn't know existed. Reading the Post, she learned that England and the United States had prohibited transporting, buying, or selling slaves. There was a passionate essay asserting the rights of the descendants of black Africans, like Phoebe, who were widely owned throughout the Bahamas and the southern United States. Another article, equally intense, defended the prerogatives of the slave owners who had, after all, paid good money for their property and deserved full benefit of their investments. Those who supported slavery averred that black slaves were fundamentally inferior to whites - things, like pieces of furniture or goats. Evidently, she thought ruefully, her father was well versed in his rights as a slave owner.

Having grown up with what she had thought to be a benign form of slavery, she hadn't questioned it. True, all the white women she knew were in charge of black women, but they often shared many household tasks. Evidently it wasn't that way everywhere.

There were so many contradictions! For example, Phoebe hadn't learned to read and write as Mary had, but she was far from stupid. She had a vast understanding of medicinal herbs that Mary could only hope to master some day. Mary would never forget that her own ability to read hadn't helped her one bit when she was pregnant and didn't know what to do. She was increasingly aware that she and Phoebe provided one another with companionship and support that transcended social mores. Both lonely and anxious for their men at sea, they were united in their yearning for the safe return of the ones they loved.

CHAPTER 11

It was the morning of August 5, a Wednesday, when they sighted the Osprey. A dock hand spied her through a glass while she was still a half-day's sail from port. There was loud shouting and somebody shot his pistol into the air. Mary set out for the waterfront as soon as she heard the ruckus and almost literally ran into Dan, a young man she'd seen hanging around the docks hoping for odd jobs.

"I came to tell you, Missus. It's the Osprey. Captain Randall will be in port by nightfall!"

"Wonderful news!" After so much waiting, Mary could hardly trust her ears. "Are you sure?"

"Quite sure, Missus. All the men know the Osprey and every one of them recognizes her out there. They say the crew will be eating supper on dry land tonight."

"Thank you! Oh, thank you for this wonderful news!" She laughed as she turned and hurried back to the house.

"Phoebe, they're coming home," she panted as she sat down hard on a kitchen chair. Phoebe's eyes brightened and she took a quick breath when she heard the news. Then she smoothed her apron and resumed dicing peppers for vegetable soup.

"Slow down and take a glass of water, Miss Mary. It's too hot for a person to be running around like you're doing. That would be a fine how-do-you-do for the captain to come back after all these weeks and find his bride in a muddle because she had too much sun."

Mary gratefully accepted the glass, drained it, and held it out to be refilled. "Of course, and there's no rush because they aren't expected to make land until the afternoon." She dipped her handkerchief in the water and patted her temples.

"We'll plan a good supper to make the captain glad to be home. What foods do you suppose he's missed? I'm sure he's eaten so much fish he never wants to see one again. Maybe young Dan will go out and shoot a couple of pigeons for us to roast. There are mangoes ripe and ready to fall. They'll clean the salt out of his mouth and refresh him. And bread and lots of butter. I'm sure they ran out of bread and have been living on dry crackers, and the butter must have gone rancid so long ago it's only a memory. We'll prepare a feast to delight this returning seaman, a feast he'll not soon forget! Oh, if the captain only knew what pleasures await him."

Pleasures that await us both, she thought, because her anticipation extended well beyond the dinner table.

So many things needed to be done. Mary wanted everything to be perfect for Richard's homecoming. She pulled on a simple shift and tied an old kerchief around her head like a pirate, then she changed the bed and polished the wooden furniture. As she worked, she looked out the bedroom window and saw Dan at the kitchen door with two plump pigeons. He shook his head vigorously when Phoebe put her hand in her pocket for money to pay him. Evidently he, too, was taken up in the spirit of gaiety that surrounded the Osprey's homecoming. Mary made a mental note to make it up to him. Dan's family was large and not very prosperous. Foregoing payment for the pigeons was a sacrifice.

The aroma of baking bread filled the kitchen when Mary paused there to rest and watch Phoebe pluck the pigeons. "They're funny birds, aren't they?" mused Mary. "They often seem almost too heavy to fly when they flap their wings so hard to stay in the air. They're not graceful at all. But aren't those blue-black feathers beautiful? We should clean them and put them to some decorative use."

She'd just begun to peel the shaggy skin from a mango when Sara burst in.

"Is this how you prepare yourself for the arrival of your husband, Mary? Have you become the kitchen help around here? Look at you. You're sweaty and you smell. At this time of day you should be resting with a cloth over your eyes. Today, of all days! I can't imagine what you're thinking."

Mary hadn't seen much of her sister during the last few weeks. Sara was preoccupied with her own wedding plans. In fact, she'd been doubly absorbed since Mary had given her that women's magazine.

Sara didn't pause for Mary's reply. "I came to tell you that Mother wants you and Richard to come for dinner tomorrow night. She and Father want to welcome Richard home. I think they're going to invite some influential guild members and their wives. The contacts should be socially and commercially beneficial. Hopefully you can make yourself presentable by then. She said she'd like to see you at five. It suits her because she likes to go to bed early these days and she sleeps better if she has time to digest her supper."

"Richard and I won't be available for a few days," Mary said firmly. "Please tell Mother that we will be delighted to come on Sunday. If Father wants to invite his important friends, that will be fine. Five o'clock will be fine, too."

"Mary, you don't seem very grateful for the invitation," Sara said.

"If you truly love your John Barlow and not just the idea of him and a big wedding, you'll come to understand why I insist on being alone with Richard for a few days. I hope some day you will appreciate what I'm saying," Mary paused. "For right now, dear Sister, I think it would be best if you go on home and leave me to my preparations. I'll plan to see you Sunday."

"I understand. Well, goodby until then." Sara's manner lost its imperiousness as she turned to go.

No, I don't think you understand at all, thought Mary. "Yes, goodby," she said.

Mary waited until Sara was out of earshot. "She's right," she admitted to Phoebe. "I'm sweaty and dirty. I'll finish peeling the mangoes and cut up the star fruit and then I think I'll clean up."

"I'll finish with the fruit, Miss Mary," Phoebe said. "And I'll put a wet rag over the bowl so they'll stay moist and cool. You freshen up and make yourself pretty. Your captain has missed you even more than a roasted pigeon or a bowl of fruit, I'd guess."

"I certainly hope so," Mary replied.

* * *

Mary washed her face and scrubbed her hands free of the garden dirt that had collected around her nails. She brushed her long hair until it crackled with electricity. She put on a crisply-ironed green summer dress that flattered her slender waist and complemented her rich brown eyes. Pinning a sprig of fragrant jasmine to the bodice of her dress, she was as pleased by the sultry scent as she hoped Richard would be. Then she sat quietly on the veranda on the shady east side of the house near the front door. There she would be comfortable and she could see the lane that led up from the docks.

And now I will wait. Waiting seems to be what I do best, she thought as she cooled herself with a palm leaf fan. *At least I spend more time waiting than doing almost anything else.* She gazed listlessly at the hazy sky. From here she wouldn't see the Osprey's approach, but it didn't matter. It would arrive whether she was watching or not. She would have liked to have gone down to the waterfront to see the schooner come in, but she knew she would have been in the way, especially after the ship docked and had to be secured and unloaded. It was better to stretch her patience this little bit further. Her reward would be finally having Richard to herself.

The still heat lay on the day untouched by any breeze. Lucky

Richard, she thought. At least there is some wind out there if they are under sail. She dozed, tired from the morning's heat and exertion.

"A fine welcome this is."

Mary's eyes popped open. There he was leaning against the veranda railing and smiling down at her.

"Oh Richard. I didn't mean to fall asleep. I've waited for you so long and now look. How could I be so unfeeling? I only . . . " She started to cry. Big hiccoughing sobs burst from her throat as tears streamed down her cheeks and her chest heaved as if she were choking. Richard lifted her from the chair and held her snugly in his sun-cured arms. She tried again to explain and was again defeated by the intensity of her emotions.

"Oh, Mary, Mary, Mary," he repeated, rocking her gently from side to side and kissing her forehead. Finally she was still. He put his hands around her waist, lifted her up, and deposited her firmly on her feet.

"I watched you for a while before I spoke. You're such a soft and gentle vision for these sea-weary eyes. I've missed you. This trip was different from any other I've made. I left a part of myself here with you when I sailed this time. I'm glad to be home."

Mary slid back onto the chair and fumbled through her pockets for a handkerchief. She wiped her nose and dabbed at her eyes as she observed her husband. He was thinner than when he left and his skin was as brown as boot leather. His hair had grown at least an inch and, even tied back, it hung below his shoulders. But his eyes hadn't changed - those bright blue eyes that could look right into her soul. She smiled. "Yes, I'm glad you're home, too."

Richard consumed a pigeon and a half and slathered butter on slice after slice of warm bread. Even before the summer sun dipped below the horizon, they went upstairs and closed the doors.

* * *

Now the household assumed a new rhythm. Richard went to the waterfront early, before the heat set in. Mary did the shopping and household tasks. Early in the afternoon they stopped for a plain lunch of chowder or bread and cheese. Then they'd linger at the table for hours and talk.

"It's not that our trip was a failure," Richard explained. "We did come upon two ships in trouble. The first one was a big barque. There were three wrecking ships at that one and since Henry Alston got there first, he was the wreck master and we were only consorts.

"We managed to pull the barque away from the rocks where it threatened to smash into pieces and we thought we'd saved ship, crew and cargo, but the wind changed and she swung around again. The rocks bashed a great hole in her side and she began to take on water. We had to move quickly to transfer the cargo, because it was almost all bales of cotton and the water would quickly ruin it. We couldn't pull our schooners alongside the wreck because the seas were too rough and we risked getting stove in ourselves, so we ran rowboats back and forth as fast as we could to carry the cotton to safety.

"I guess we finally saved about half of it. The rest went down with the ship. The captain was grateful, of course, but the salvage award didn't amount to much once it was divided between the owners and the three wrecking vessels. We did a whole lot of work there for not much pay."

"How could that ship have been more profitable?" asked Mary.

"I've wondered that myself, but there's no good answer. The obvious thing is if there had been only two ships or even if I had been the only one, then the shares would have been bigger. But the loss would have been greater, too, and the award, smaller. I don't think the court was unfair with the salvage award. After all, it was raw cotton, not gold ingots, that we saved. No, I'd have to say that nobody's going to get rich from that kind of situation."

"And the other wreck?"

"Happily, the other one was both simpler and more profitable. She was carrying barrels of molasses, tobacco, and some wooden furniture, things that aren't as absorbent as cotton. We were the only ship to come to her aid. We tied her off with two anchors and were able to slide right up alongside so we could unload the cargo directly.

"We took off the tobacco first because it was most vulnerable to saltwater damage. Next we removed the molasses because it was heavy and would weigh the ship down if she started to sink. The furniture came off last. We worked quickly and there was no damage to any of the cargo. I think you'll like the chairs I claimed. I didn't forget your shopping list." Richard smiled as he spread butter on his third piece of bread. "There weren't any desks, though."

"It was all very routine and we thought we were finished. I had just shaken hands with the captain - Andrews, his name was - when the boom of his jib swung around and knocked one of his crew into the water. The man was completely stunned and sank like a stone. Seth saw him go overboard and jumped right in after him. Otherwise, he surely would have drowned. As it was, he threw up sea water for most of the afternoon."

Mary shivered at the idea of the sailor's close call. Every time she heard of a drowning, it reopened the wound of her grief over the loss of Michael.

"I suppose the salvage award was much greater because you saved a life."

"Not at all." Richard shook his head. "There's no reward for saving lives, although some years ago one was given because slaves were saved and they were considered as merchandise. This second wreck was a more profitable venture because we managed it alone and saved the boat and the entire cargo. Oddly enough, we made more money on the easier job. It often happens that way, but no wrecker with any integrity will turn his back on hard, dangerous work. To my knowledge, no one has ever been killed at it. There must be an angel who protects us, although I don't have an inkling what his name might be."

"I surely hope there is such an angel," Mary whispered.

* * *

Mary luxuriated in the three days she'd set aside to be with Richard. On Sunday as they dressed to visit her parents, she realized she no longer viewed the dinner party as an intrusion. Rather, she welcomed the occasion as an opportunity to bask publicly in her happiness.

Ann outdid herself as a hostess. The meal began with a spicy conch chowder, followed by roast manatee, fresh fruit, baked yams, and pudding for desert. Sara's intended, John Barlow, was there as well as two members of the Maritime Guild and their wives.

"I've done some wrecking," John said. "But I find I'm best suited to building the ships for you more daring men to sail. I love the smell and feel of the wood and the challenge of shaping it into a seaworthy vessel. I like the solidity of the work and of the land under my feet. I confess, the rocking of a ship makes me queasy and I'd just as soon avoid that."

"I think I can understand your love of wood from my experience building our house," said Richard. "I became fascinated by the timber and what I could do with it. For myself, though, I think I got that out of my system. I'll sail your ships any day, John. A life spent only on land would seem dry and still to me. I love to see the wind in the sails and feel the salt spray as I stand on the rolling deck."

The men's conversation drifted to news and rumors about commerce and law. The older women were absorbed in the plans for Sara's September wedding. Mary was seated between Richard and John, so she was able to enjoy their conversation.

"I fail to understand the new energy they're putting into enforcing old laws," commented Richard as he helped himself to another slice of manatee. "Take the law requiring salvage acquired in American waters to be taken through a U.S. port of entry. That's sat dusty on the shelf for over twenty years and nobody cared. All of a sudden it's important. Today I wouldn't venture to bring my salvage straight home. I'd lose my license and probably be sent to prison. I'll take the goods to Key West. It takes longer and costs me more, but I think the magistrates are fair and I'd like to stay in business!"

"There's little hope of the Bahamas ever exerting enough influence to change the law," observed one of the guildsmen. "We don't agree with one another often enough to present a united front. Even if we did, we don't represent much population. I wonder that more of our wreckers don't pick up and move to Key West or St. Augustine."

"There are still Loyalists alive who fled here because they were persecuted on the mainland during the American Revolution. It's their children who are doing the wrecking now. I doubt they would feel welcome in America, or be made welcome, for that matter. Richard, weren't your parents Loyalists?" asked William.

"My grandparents came to Green Turtle Cay from Massachusetts before the war," replied Richard. "My parents described them as whalers who turned to wandering. They went first to Nova Scotia, then to the Carolinas, then they came here and stayed. I have nothing against the Americans, but I don't know enough to say much in their favor, either."

"Have they also begun to enforce the law against trading in slaves?" asked Mary. "Unless I'm mistaken, Britain outlawed slave trade at about the same time as the wrecking legislation was passed. I think maybe the United States did, too."

"Mary! Where did you get that information?" asked her father. His fork clattered against his dinner plate and the women abandoned their conversation to see what was happening.

"I read it in The Saturday Evening Post. I'm sure you've heard of it, too."

"I'm aware of the statute. What surprises me is that your interest extends to maritime law, my dear."

"Anything that affects my family interests me," Mary replied sweetly. Under the table she slid her hand from her own lap to Richard's thigh and gave him a little squeeze. While they didn't dwell on William's attitude toward slaves and his behavior with Phoebe, neither one had forgotten the secrets Mary had revealed that day on the dock nor the pain they had caused her.

"That Seth who crews for me says he's a freed slave," observed Richard, giving no sign of what was going on behind the drape of the tablecloth. "I've accepted his statement at face value, but now that you mention it, I haven't seen his papers. It would be a terrible thing to see a freed man go back into slavery because of lack of documentation. Even worse, if he were mistaken for bonded, I could be accused of trafficking and transporting. I think I'll check into that more closely."

Both Ann and Sara were feeling left out of this serious conversation and they spoke simultaneously.

"Father, what do you plan to wear when you give me away in marriage?"

"William, have you seen those gold cuff links I gave you as a wedding present? It would be so lovely if you could wear them for Sara's wedding."

Conversation turned to jewelry, waistcoats, and what other fathers had been seen to wear at fancy weddings. When the last speck of bread pudding had been licked from Ann's silver spoons, the party broke up.

"John seems like a pleasant man," said Mary as they walked home in the gathering dusk. "Do you think Sara will drive him mad?"

"He's nobody's fool, Mary. There must be aspects of her that he likes very much or he'd never have asked for her hand. Maybe your perspective as a big sister is different from his as a suitor." Richard patted her on the bottom and gave her a playful pinch.

"Ouch!" Mary exclaimed, feigning distress. "You'll pay for that."

Richard wrapped his arm around her waist and drew her close in step with him. "You may have saved me a lot of trouble by mentioning the slave trade legislation at dinner. I hadn't thought of it for years."

* * *

At lunch the next day, Richard reported his conversation with Seth. "He doesn't have any idea what became of his manumission papers," he said. "Everything he owns is in his duffel and he went through it right in front of me. I absolutely believe that he once had a letter guaranteeing his freedom, but it's nowhere to be found today. The fact that I've been paying him like any other sailor wouldn't be much use as evidence in court. Without that letter, they could make a case for my being stupid enough to pay wages to a slave. I figure the best thing to do is to free him again. Ironic, isn't it?"

"What has to be done?" asked Mary.

"I talked to Benjamin Fine, the lawyer. He says all I need is a new letter with Seth's physical description and a statement of my intention to free him and pay him from now on. It's really nothing but a repetition of what is already the case. He strongly suggested that there be two signed copies of the letter and that I should keep one in a safe dry place. I can't disagree with that."

Mary glanced toward the kitchen. "I think we should free Phoebe at the same time," she said. "I don't think we'd be obliged to provide much more than the housing and food we give her now and a standard wage is about a pound a year. I hope she'll stay with us. I think she would."

"Has she said anything to indicate she wants her freedom?"

"No. She's very aware of her status as a slave, but she's never complained about it to me. This is my idea."

"If it's what you want, I have no objections. Of course, if she decides to run off, you'll be left without a servant. I can't imagine that she would refuse her freedom, but why don't you talk to her before I make any arrangements with Benjamin?"

* * *

Phoebe's reaction wasn't what Mary expected. She'd anticipated elation or gratitude or, at least surprise. She was met with postponement.

"I'd like to think about that, Miss Mary, if it's all right with you."

Finally on Friday Phoebe approached Mary and Richard. "Miss Mary. Captain Richard. I've thought about your idea of giving me my freedom and I've talked to Seth about what you're doing for him, too. We think it's a good thing you're offering us and we thank you. We want to stay with you folks. This island is the only life I've ever known and it's the best that Seth has seen. There's just one other thing."

"One other thing?" asked Mary. She glanced at Richard and couldn't tell if the spark in his eyes was humor or irritation.

"What would that be, Phoebe?" he asked.

"You know that slaves aren't allowed to marry. Well, me and Seth, once we're free, we'd want to be married and we'd like your blessing."

Mary jumped up and threw her arms around Phoebe.

"Of course you have our blessing! We'll be very happy for you."

* * *

The lawyer duly executed the manumission papers and a wedding certificate.

"Seth asked us to come to some kind of party back in the coppice on Sunday," reported Richard. "He was a little vague about the time. I guess we should go. I never expected so much activity to stem from a legality."

Mary laughed. "Nor did I. I'd like to go. I'm sure there will be more surprises."

Mid-Sunday afternoon Richard and Mary walked in the general direction Seth had indicated. Emerging from the trees, they looked down the slope to see that the celebration was well underway. At least a dozen servants from other households had come and several had brought their children. Bright ribbons bedecked the women's and girls' hair and the men wore broad sashes woven from rainbow-hued scraps of fabric. They stood in a circle and clapped in a slow, muted rhythm. Seth and Phoebe stood in the middle with their hands alternating along the handle of a palm broom.

"Let's stop here," said Mary. "We shouldn't interrupt." They sat in the shadow of a buttonwood.

A white-haired man lifted his hands and raised his voice. "Today Phoebe and Seth sweep away their old lives and welcome a new one together," he said. The clapping became louder and faster and the pair moved around the circle raising puffs of dust as they brushed the ground. When they completed the circle, the old man spoke louder and louder, "This is a new beginning. Our brother and sister have chosen to move from their separateness to form a household."

Then they lay the broom in the dirt and Phoebe and Seth jumped over it in unison, Seth giving support to Phoebe's game left leg. With that, the well-wishers rushed to the middle of the circle to congratulate the bride and groom. The men slapped Seth on the back so often and so heartily that Mary wondered that he could still stand. Phoebe disappeared among the women and little girls.

Mary and Richard stood silently and turned toward home. When they were a distance away, Richard said, "I've heard about that custom of jumping the broom, but I never expected to see it. Slaves brought it from Africa. It's sacred and, as I understand it, secret. It was a great privilege that we were asked to be there."

The next day the household went along normally as if nothing special had happened. Midmorning, Mary went to the kitchen. "You were a beautiful bride, Phoebe," she said.

Phoebe lowered her eyes and smiled. "Thank you, Miss Mary. I didn't know you were there."

"We watched from a distance. We hope you'll be very happy together."

"We aim to be, Miss, just like you and the captain."

CHAPTER 12

"I mean to stay in port for a month this time," said Richard one morning at breakfast. "We Bahamian wreckers are losing our commercial advantage. I want to talk with the guildsmen and any captains that may pass through to see if there are more profitable ways for us to do business. For example, maybe we can devise new kinds of contracts besides the traditional consort partnership at the wreck sites. In any case, I plan to sail the last day of August and I'll return in plenty of time for Sara's wedding at the end of September. I wouldn't want to miss that," he grinned wryly.

The tropical August drifted by in a humid haze. Early mornings found the newlyweds walking barefoot in the lukewarm surf or tracing circles in the moist sand with driftwood. In the evenings they refreshed themselves walking in the leafy shade of the coppice. Sometimes Mary wished their lazy lovemaking would never end, but there were times when lying in bed talking seemed like an even greater pleasure. They would fall asleep wrapped in each other's arms or, when there was no breeze, leaning their naked backs together, their arms and legs stretched out searching for a bit of coolness.

When the day came for Richard to sail, Mary went to say good bye. She smiled and chattered confidently. There was continuity to their life. She knew when he planned to come home. She felt safe.

"I feel sorry for Seth and Phoebe," said Mary. "The last time you sailed it was our first separation. Now it's theirs."

"Will you miss me, even though it's not the first time?" He put an arm around her waist and pulled her against him.

"I'll miss you, all right. You know it." She melted against his chest until he gently pushed her away. He gave her that public peck on the cheek that signaled his transformation from lover to captain and turned to the task at hand.

* * *

True to his word, Richard returned four days before Sara's wedding.

"I'd started to wonder if you were going to avoid the whole affair," said Mary.

"If it were up to me, I might have, but I promised, didn't I?"

William had rented the guild hall to accommodate the fifty wedding guests. Sara proudly displayed the long white dress that she'd stitched herself after a pattern that was said to be copied from Queen Victoria's wedding gown. William wore his gold cuff links. Ann fussed and wept prettily. It all went according to plan, but it seemed to Mary that it was less grand than expected. Maybe it couldn't measure up to such an enormous prologue. Apparently Richard was right about John's affection for his bride. The respect and tenderness he showed toward Sara amazed Mary. Well, she hoped they'd be happy.

The intensity of the weather didn't diminish, rather, the heat mounted in an unrelieved crescendo and the beginning of October was hotter than August. The narrow streets were powdered with fine sandy dust and the drainage ditches beside them lay parched with nothing to drain. This was usually the rainy season, but there had been few clouds and fewer showers. Nobody remembered for sure when there had been a decent rain storm. September? Maybe the end of August? The cisterns were nearly empty. Fresh water was precious. Slaves and servants carried buckets of sea water for household chores. They were ordered to thoroughly wipe the plates and flatware before they washed them and the dishwater was saved for days. Then it was poured into the privies to try to dilute the pungent odor of human excrement. Clothes weren't washed until they became unbearable. A few of the wealthier citizens, including William Thorne, paid for barrels of fresh water to be shipped from mainland Florida and shared it with everyone. People looked forward to the refreshing tin dipper of water and no one commented on the fact that the water was tepid and stale-tasting, if indeed they noticed.

On her morning walks, Mary noticed the birds acting peculiarly, especially the pigeons and the mockingbirds. They flew out to sea facing into the balmy southeast breeze, then raced back to shore where they perched low in the trees as close to the trunks as they could get. The poor things were quite likely going mad without enough water in the relentless autumn heat, she thought. Or else they were dying.

Early on the ninth of October the winds started to pick up and the barometers fell. Everyone predicted high tides and squally weather. Fishing and transport came to a halt. All the boats were firmly anchored, checked, and then checked again. The men spent the day carrying equipment below decks and into the warehouses where it couldn't blow, and tying down what couldn't be moved. The birds stopped flying out to sea.

"I've tied up the Osprey as well as I can," said Richard. "You and Phoebe bring all the loose things inside from the porches and the garden. Seth and I will check the roof and secure the shutters."

"A good rain would settle the dust and replenish the cisterns," said Mary, grunting with the effort of dragging a wicker chair in the house from the veranda. "But there's no good in a violent storm. I remember one when I was a little girl. It went on for two days and stripped every leaf from the trees." She wiped dusty sweat from her forehead, not noticing the brown stain on the sleeve of her blouse.

"I'll be right back," said Richard. "I want to be sure your parents are ready, too. Your father's too old to climb on the roof on a sunny day, let alone in a building wind."

By nightfall, every building on the island was shuttered or boarded. Slivers of light escaped through cracks in the few houses where lanterns burned, but most were completely dark. The rain began as gentle drizzle, but soon the burgeoning wind drove it hard against the houses.

Mary had piled blankets and sheets on the floor of Richard's first floor office for a makeshift bed. It might not be comfortable, but it was better than risking exposure in their upstairs bedroom if the winds and rain breached the roof.

"Is this what it's like to sleep when you're at sea?" Mary asked.

"Not really," replied Richard. "At sea there's always the movement of the boat. Here on land we don't sway. But this floor is as hard as any ship's cot I've ever felt. At sea is no place to be tonight. As safe as we are here on the lee side of our little island, we'll be lucky to close our eyes for long, "

As the night wore on the wind roared and rain drops drove against the shutters like thousands of unguided nails. Mary lay on the thin cushion of bedding as stiff as the boards underneath, waiting for the storm to end. Even Richard's embrace couldn't soften her tightly strung muscles.

Once the winds calmed and it seemed like it might be over, but soon they roared again with their previous fury. No one slept on the island that night. Mary held her breath as the wind abated, hoping that this time the calm would last. The sun emerged as the storm clouds blew out to sea.

Mary cracked open a door and peeked out. Where there had been only dust, now slippery mud filled every depression and angry streams ran across the ground where it was too dry to absorb the sudden onslaught of water. Cisterns overflowed. Leaves had been ripped from the trees and shredded before they fell to the ground, creating green islands outlined by muddy rivulets. Most of the houses weathered the storm well, with only lifted shingles and shutters sprung from their hinges.

"It's a matter of building and maintaining," said Richard. "If you build a thing right the first time and keep it strong, it will serve for generations. That's as true of ships as it is of houses. Still, I think the hurricane went south of us. We have fine strong houses, but I'd say we also had some very good luck. I wonder how they're faring on the mainland and in the Keys."

That news came three days later. A small ketch with tattered sails arrived from the west. It was manned by two teenage boys whose eyes bulged with the enormity of what they had seen.

Key West was devastated. The lighthouse lay shattered on the ground. Fourteen people were crushed when it fell. The graveyard, located on a sandy ridge near the ocean, had washed away. Bodies had blown up on the streets and hung from trees. Homes, warehouses, and churches were destroyed indiscriminately. All but eight homes were uninhabitable because they were blown down, washed into the sea, or without roofs. Ships broke their moorings. A few that drifted out to sea were saved, but the ones that stayed too close to shore were scuttled. Everything was flooded and there was a constant black cloud of mosquitos, little food, and an appalling amount of reconstruction to be done if the town were to survive. Construction materials were in short supply and the ships needed to fetch them were damaged, many beyond repair.

The boys gladly accepted Mary's offer of food and lodging. They gobbled down chunks of bread and cheese and drank tea as if they never expected to enjoy such a luxury again. She guided them to the parlor where she spread out blankets for them to rest. Phoebe brought a basin of water and Mary went for towels and soap, but the boys were asleep before she came back.

Sara and John came to see how the others had fared and the men retired to the office. After two hours they came out, walked down to the pier, and talked some more before they returned to their secluded conference.

"What do you suppose those two are planning now?" Sara asked as she and Mary surveyed the ruins of the vegetable garden.

"I strongly suspect they smell adventure and profit in the havoc the hurricane wreaked on Key West. I'd bet they'll be sailing within a few days," said Mary with a touch of bitterness.

"Sara! Mary! Come here. We have a plan." John's normally ruddy face was redder than ever and tiny beads of perspiration sparkled over his bushy eyebrows.

The women hurried back to the house.

"We're going to Key West!" announced Richard.

Mary gave Sara a knowing look and turned toward Richard, tight-lipped and dour.

"When I say we, I mean we," he said returning her gaze. "All of us. Our servants, our houses and our furniture. Everything. We'll take our houses apart and float them over. I bought some land a while ago as an investment. We'll rebuild our homes there. There's money to be made in the transport and sale of building and shipping materials as well as in wrecking."

Mary stared. They'd lived in their house less than a year. Their whole life was on Green Turtle Cay - their history, their plans, Mary's family. Until this moment, she had never doubted that her entire future lay on the island.

"Richard, what are you thinking of?" asked Mary as soon as they were alone. "You worked hard to build this house. You can't decide overnight to take it apart and put it somewhere else."

"Why not?" asked Richard, sitting in one of the oak chairs by the dining table. "It's a good house and I don't want to leave it behind. I suppose we could, if you'd rather, but I think we should take it."

"You're missing my point entirely, and you know it. It's not about the house; it's about our lives. I've always lived on Green Turtle Cay. I can't imagine living anywhere else. My family exasperates me sometimes, but in Key West I'd probably never see them. We'd be foreigners there and I think I would be lonely."

"You'll only be two days' journey from your family, three at most. When you stop being so emotional, I think you'll see that may be an advantage. The truth is, Mary, if we don't go I may have to find another living. The Americans have got a stranglehold on us wreckers. It's just plain unprofitable to be anywhere but St. Augustine or Key West. I'd rather go to Key West because I'm an islander just as you are and, after the hurricane, the opportunity is there."

"Do you think you have some of your grandparents' wandering blood?" Mary asked, shaking her head in exasperation.

"It may be that their blood frees me to take advantage of opportunities when they present themselves," he replied thrusting his chin forward.

They'd disagreed about trivial matters before - the orientation of the house, the expense for furnishings. They'd seriously disputed the importance of the great cast-iron stove that dominated the kitchen. But this was fundamentally different, a choice between the familiar and the alien; comfort and difficulties; security and anxiety.

Mary's hair had come loose from its pins and fallen over her face in the heat of their discussion. She pushed it back impatiently. "I want to think," she said. "I'm going walking. You needn't come."

The familiar paths welcomed her. In some ways the plants and animals were part of her family as much as her parents and sister. Nodding, she acknowledged the new growth on the orchids and ferns. She stopped to watch a tiny migratory bird with a yellow face and ebony cowl as it feasted on the early-evening mosquitoes. It ignored her when she imitated its song to coax it nearer.

She sat on a fallen log next to a sturdy lignum vitae and her thoughts drifted to the afternoon just a little more than a year ago when she came here to mourn the death of Michael Wellmet. How was it that the men in her life always seemed to lead her away from home? With Michael she had been eager for the adventure. Had she changed so much in such a short time? Science and biology guided that odyssey; this was a mercantile undertaking, but no less worthwhile and exciting for that. Had she become a stodgy old housewife after just four months of marriage? Maybe she should have married a guildsman, she thought wryly.

A ladybug scurried along the hem of her skirt, brightly scarlet against the black cotton. It turned and climbed over the folds of fabric toward her lap, slowing with the effort of scaling each woven height and racing down the other side. What on earth is she doing? Mary asked herself. She's left her familiar world of dirt and grass and trees to climb mountains of cotton twill. It must seem very strange. And maybe it did, because the little beetle paused as if to consider her situation. Then she stretched its wings a few times and flew, first to the trunk of the buttonwood and then out of sight. Mary watched the space where she disappeared.

She brushed her skirt smooth and rose. While she'd been thinking of other things, her decision had formed. She'd asked Richard what he'd been thinking of when he devised this plan. Now she wondered how she could have considered rejecting it.

When she got back to the house, Richard was sitting in the dark by the table. He didn't seem to have moved since she left. Phoebe had put out food, but it was untouched.

"Well?' he asked.

"I think I understand how you'll take the house apart," Mary said. "But I haven't an inkling of how you think you're going to get it to Key West."

Richard stood and embraced her. His kiss was long and hard. Mary sat down to catch her breath.

* * *

The first stage of the project is hardly novel, thought Mary. *It involves another trip.* The Osprey and a small crew were to go to Key West in early November. Richard would make the applications and pay the necessary bribes to get approval for building on his land. Next he would pour the concrete pilings on which the house would sit and put them in place. Before he sailed, he spent an entire afternoon measuring the base of the house. The next day, he measured it again.

"It won't do if we get the house over there and there's nothing to put it on," said Richard. "And if the pilings are in the wrong place, they might as well not be there at all."

Three weeks flew by as Mary made lists of furniture and kitchenware to take to Key West, then changed her mind and rewrote the lists. She sat with her mother nearly every afternoon, explaining and re-explaining why it made sense to leave and promising to come home as often as possible.

Richard was back in plenty of time for Christmas and, after the successful trip, his good humor was contagious. The day before Christmas, he cut a pretty buttonwood, tender and soft with newly grown leaves, and pushed it into a bucket of moist sand. Mary gathered sea shells, strung them with black sewing thread, and hung them from the tip of every branch. Phoebe wedged thick candles into conch shells and arranged them in a circle on the floor around the tree. At ten o'clock the Randalls and the Thornes and the Barlows gathered in Mary's festive parlor. They sang "Oh, Come All Ye Faithful" and "Silent Night," and toasted the Christ child with rum punch. They lit thin white candles from the thick ones at the base of the tree and carried them at arms' length through the night, symbolizing the star that shown over the manger in Bethlehem.

Christmas Day there were plenty of packages to open. Sara's generosity stunned Mary when she gave her a box of vellum writing paper. Mary's gift to her mother was a packet of calming herbal tea, made of plants that she had collected herself. Richard chose an enormous piece of gnarled driftwood for John who promised to carve and polish it as a decoration for the house when it was rebuilt in Key West. They stuffed themselves with wild turkey and pigeon peas and fresh bread and white pudding spiced with cinnamon and ginger and plump raisins. Everyone strolled to the western beach and watched the sun set. Then the couples separated, walking home arm in arm.

"It was a wonderful holiday," said Mary as she turned toward Richard under the fresh sheets. "I'll treasure these memories for the rest of my life."

"I've never known a celebration so filled with tradition," said Richard. "I hope all our Christmases will be like this."

* * *

Moving plans had been put aside for the holiday, but 1847 was less than three days old when Richard and his men began dismantling the house.

First they removed the porches. They numbered the boards and carried them down to the dock. After the porches came the windows.

Soon Mary and Richard moved in with Sara and John, because their own house no longer offered privacy, shelter, nor comfort. Most of their furniture was hauled to the dock and tarped with old sails. Mary's bedroom furniture crowded Sara's parlor and her hooked rugs were rolled and stacked against the wall.

The men climbed thirty-foot ladders to the roof to pry up the shingles and lower them in big wooden buckets tied to thick rigging lines. They loosened the roof beams and rafters and lowered them to the ground, too.

Then came the exterior pine planking, the inside walls, and the posts and beams that formed the skeleton of the house. The pegs pounded out easily at first, but the winter weather became unusually springlike and as the humidity rose, the pegs swelled, requiring more effort to free them from their holes.

"I swear, if those pegs get any fatter, that house won't come apart at all!" exclaimed Richard one hot afternoon as he straddled a floor joist on the second floor and slammed his hammer against the thick wood in frustration.

Mary tried not to contemplate what might happen if the house wouldn't come apart, yet couldn't be reassembled either.

The men swung hammers like battle axes and cursed, at first under their breath, then in full hearing of anyone in the vicinity. Still, they steadily gained ground. Every day more boards were freed and carried to the dock. When the pegs became so moist they lost their solidity and couldn't be driven, they tapered long dowels to drive them out.

"We're going to have to put this thing back together with nails, that's for sure," said Richard. "Whoever invented the idea of pegging a house lived some place other than the tropics!"

Mary chewed her lower lip and tugged at her hair as the outside staircase was reduced to a series of puzzle-like pieces with treads and risers tied together in bundles and newel posts, balusters and handrails stacked in uneven lengths like kindling. Her beautiful home was rapidly being reduced to piles of lumber and buckets of parts.

Finally all the boards lay parallel and clearly marked on the dock with a line of buckets holding pegs, shingles, and tools beside them. The house, which had taken six weeks to build, came down in only three.

Mary felt as if her nerves were shredded from living in close quarters with her sister and brother-in-law and watching her house dismantled and all of her possessions readied for shipment. At night she lay on her back in her four poster bed in Sara's dining room and stared at the ceiling, imagining the next obstacle to the move. Richard slept fitfully, barking orders into his pillow, then wrapping his arms around his chest and sighing. By day she could hardly concentrate to go to the market or work in the garden. Dark circles pooled beneath her eyes and her hair hung lifelessly in a braid.

"We'll load her up on Monday," Richard announced one Friday morning. "That will give us two days to rest and get organized. The long and heavy lumber will go on John's Cynthia May; she's the wider one. Tools and parts and furniture will travel on the Osprey."

Mary still visited her mother every day. She cut herbs and roots from the garden to take to her new home. One morning she rose early and walked to the east side of the island to watch the sun rise. It was curious, she thought, how predictably her family reacted to her approaching departure. Her father appeared untouched, talking of practical things as always. Her mother retired to her bedroom where she could cry privately and pray for Mary's deliverance from the sea and the strangers with whom she would now make her life. Sara seemed so absorbed in her own affairs that, even with Mary and Richard living in the house, their future seemed of little concern to her.

Monday came soon and the Cynthia May was loaded deliberately if not quickly. Mary lost track of which boards were parlor and which, roof. It wasn't until after three o'clock that they began to load the Osprey and the work went slowly because of the irregular shapes and sizes of the load. Finally they brought Mary's furniture and rugs to the dock and began to push them into vacant corners and lash them on top of flat surfaces. It had been dark for an hour when John and Richard came to Mary.

"We've tried everything," said Richard. "There's nothing we can do to make more space. There's room for you and your luggage. But you've got to choose between taking Phoebe and taking the cherry dresser you're so fond of. There's not room for both and the boat's already sitting low in the water."

Mary stared at him in disbelief. "Unpack the settee to make room," she said.

"It's Phoebe or the dresser," said Richard. "We can't start unpacking and rearranging at this point."

Mary paused just long enough to draw a long breath and blow it out slowly. The dresser had been made in England and passed through the family for generations. She'd fought to wrest it from Sara's clutches. But she could never leave Phoebe behind.

"Leave the dresser here," she whispered and she turned and walked toward Sara's house to pack her valise.

CHAPTER 13

Mary fingered the lace collar of the silk blouse she'd worn at her wedding. She folded it carefully and put it in her valise. The lamp flickered as she stared at the night-blackened window. So much had changed in such a short time. It was hard to believe she was packing up the last details of her life in preparation for . . . In preparation for what? she wondered. She could foresee absolutely nothing about her future. Life on Green Turtle Cay had a predictable rhythm based on the tides and the weather and the seasons. Her sister and mother were often irritating and she had come to despise her father, but she didn't know what to expect of Key West. Would she survive the journey over so much frightening ocean? Could Richard rebuild the house as it was before? Was Key West a civilized place or a pirate outpost as some said?

Never mind! This was no time for desperate thinking. There was no limit to the difficulties she could imagine if she didn't discipline her thoughts. She would deal with the realities as they came along and not waste energy on every frightening fantasy that crossed her mind. She buckled the valise and hoisted it from the bed to the floor.

"The weather glass has risen all day without stopping," said

Richard. "It looks like a storm is coming from the northeast. We'd best be off right at dawn if we want to beat it."

Mary grimaced. She'd had enough of storms. Richard took her by the hands and drew her to him, but for once his touch didn't awaken any thrill in her. She just wanted to go to sleep, the sooner to have the journey over with. She pulled away and climbed into bed.

"Good night, then," said Richard and slid between the sheets, rolling his back to her.

She slept lightly, so it wasn't hard to be awake early. She washed and dressed in the dark.

"Richard, it's morning. Get up! We have to go."

"Come back to bed," he moaned lazily, only half awake.

"Richard, you're the one who said we must leave at dawn. If you don't get up, I'll captain the boat myself."

"No such thing!" Richard fought the snarl of bed clothes and stood, still partly entangled in a sheet.

"Get the rest of our things packed while I dress. We'll need bread and cheese for breakfast. And hot tea. Don't forget the tea!"

Mary smiled at Richard's unusual disorganization. When hadn't there been food and strong hot tea in the morning? How silly.

Phoebe had laid thick slices of bread and a wedge of cheddar on Sara's fancy plate painted with peacocks. Sara's black tea kettle steamed on Sara's cast iron stove. Everything was Sara's! Mary's things were all loaded on the ships. She looked out into the darkness. The breeze from the north sent a chill down her back that penetrated her spine.

"Are you ready?" she asked Phoebe.

"I'm ready, Miss Mary. Seth carried my sack to the dock before sunrise and he's down there at work. Soon as I clean after your breakfast, I'll be there, too."

"Have you seen my mother? It will be terrible if I can't say goodbye to her. Maybe I should run to her house now, before it's too late."

"I have no doubt she's drinking her tea right now. And you'd do well to do the same, Miss. There's not much time and those men aren't going to wait patiently for us."

"Where's my tea?" blustered Richard as he sat heavily on the wooden kitchen bench. He picked up his cup even as he spoke and dropped a teaspoon of sugar into it. He gulped tea and bit off mouthfuls of bread.

"You women come directly to the pier. I don't want to leave without you, but I will if I must. It's critical that we sail ahead of this storm!" Richard stuffed a last chunk of bread into his jacket pocket. "I'm talking about minutes, not hours." He gave Mary a perfunctory kiss on the cheek and strode out the door.

Mary and Phoebe shared the washing up. Phoebe had just hung the dish towel from the rod of the oven door when Sara stepped into the kitchen, sleepy-eyed and still buttoning the cuffs of her blouse.

"I was afraid you'd already gone." Sara hugged Mary and kissed her cheek. "I'll miss you. You've always been there for me to imitate when I was uncertain what to do and to torment when I was out of sorts. I've taken you for granted. It won't be the same."

"I'll miss you, too, but soon you'll follow and we'll build a new life in Key West." Mary longed for the courage of her words. She gently pushed Sara away. "I must go. Look after Mother and write soon."

Mary and Phoebe set out silently on the sandy path that threaded through the darkness to the dock. They didn't pause as they passed the denuded pilings that had once supported the house. There was no sign of Ann. Finally, when they came to the wooden steps that led up to the pier, a trembling voice broke the silence.

"Mary my child, stop for a moment and bid me goodby. Only the Lord knows when I shall lay eyes on you again."

"Go ahead, Phoebe. Tell them I'll be right there," Mary said.

Ann leaned heavily on William's arm and tears poured down her cheeks.

"Oh my child, you are going so far away! Promise to write. I shall pray for you night and day."

"Of course I'll write and I'll come home," Mary reached to

embrace her but the older woman fainted, collapsing into William's arms.

"Mother!" Mary exclaimed. "We must take you inside where you can lie down and rest. I'll get a cool cloth for your head. I can . . ."

"You can do nothing, my dear," said William firmly. "I'll take care of her. I've done so for many years. You go to the dock. Go and don't look back. Your future is on that ship and where it will carry you. Hurry."

Mary knew how her father had "taken care" of her. Nevermind. She couldn't help that now. "Of course. Yes, I will. Goodby, Father," she said and she turned and walked quickly back to the dock. As she climbed the steps, she saw Phoebe gingerly make her way across the gangplank between the pier and the Osprey.

"Where have you been?" Richard asked as Mary approached. " What was more important to you than this?":

"Mother fainted."

"Get on the ship if you're going to," roared Richard. "Or do you feel faint, too? I've set out the gangplank to make it easy for you."

How could he be so unfeeling about her mother's anxiety? thought Mary. *How could he insult her in public? Well, she'd show him! She wasn't going to show any weakness!*

Mary deliberately walked to the gangplank and started across. It rocked gently from side to side with the movement of the water. She was unsure of her footing, but she continued, stiff-necked and straight-legged. She was sure all the men were watching her, waiting for some sign of womanly weakness.

She was wrong about that. Knowing the last passenger was boarding, the men returned to their work. Richard went to check the forward moorings as he chewed on the remainder of his breakfast bread. He tossed the last crust into the water. Two enormous tarpons raced for the prize and nearly collided. Mary started at the sound of the splash as the water splattered her face and hands. She recoiled to the left, away from the fish, lost her balance, and reached out for the gangplank, the rail, anything that might keep her from falling. All she grasped was air. She struck the water flat on her back and knew she was about to die. She gave a little scream, then gasped as the cold wetness enveloped her. The water stung her eyes and revolted her as it filled her mouth and her throat.

Phoebe was the only one to see her fall. "Captain Richard, Miss Mary has fallen in the sea!" she screamed over and over again until the words became garbled and came out as an eerie wordless chant. She pointed at the spot where Mary had disappeared, jabbing her finger toward the center of the widening circle of ripples that marked Mary's entry.

Richard took in what had happened. He ripped off his heavy boots and jumped into the water shouting for lines to drag her out. Seth quickly complied and Richard caught the first one he threw and dove toward the spot where Phoebe pointed. The water wasn't deep, only about three fathoms, but it was murky and at first Richard couldn't see. He swam in ever-widening circles until he finally found her, her arm draped around a rock. He was nearly out of breath and he couldn't carry her to the surface. He pushed the end of the line under the rock so it would lead him back on his next try and shot to the surface, gasping.

"I've found her! When I jerk the line, you pull! Her life depends on it," he shouted.

He dove again, following the line to Mary's inert body. He wrapped it around her waist and her shoulders, tying it tightly, then jerked hard three times. It grew taut and Mary began to rise toward the surface. Richard followed, pushing from below to hasten her ascent.

They lifted her onto the boat as Richard raised himself to the dock. Streaming water, he ran across the boarding plank. He hung her over the rail with her upper body hanging seaward and briskly smacked her on the back again and again.

When Phoebe saw him beating her mistress, she wailed louder and louder, sobbing out hysterical shrieks.

"For God's sake, shut up, Phoebe," Richard yelled in frustration as he struck Mary's back again. "Somebody take that woman below!" That blow was the one that counted. Mary began to vomit sea water. She heaved, then panted for air and heaved again.

"She's saved. Thank God, she's saved," murmured Richard, calling again on the deity he seldom acknowledged except in profanity.

Soon Mary couldn't vomit any more. She hiccoughed pathetically but she was breathing again and from time to time her eyes flickered open, then shut. Richard lowered her gently to the deck, pillowing her head on his shirt and stroking her back.

"You'll live to see Key West, Mary," he whispered in her ear. "Cast off," he shouted. "We should have left an hour ago. If we don't get underway, we'll be caught in the storm and we'll all go to the bottom with no one to drag us back up."

Sails billowed in the mounting wind as the Osprey and the Cynthia Mae moved swiftly to the southeast, racing around the south end of Great Abaco to Providence Channel where the island would buffer them from the approaching storm.

Mary lay exhausted on the deck. The wet and the wind chilled her through, but she didn't have the energy to move. Phoebe looked warily through the hatch and climbed onto the deck. She wrapped a tattered wool blanket around Mary's shoulders and lifted her to her knees.

"Lean on me and I'll help you."

Mary stumbled into the cabin and curled up in a corner of the cabin boy's cot. The rough wool blanket chafed her already-abraded skin, but it was a small price to pay for the warmth. She couldn't push the horror of her helplessness out of her mind. Time and time again she saw the murky water close around her and felt its stinging briny clutch. Every time she relived her fall, the water was colder and she sank deeper before she struck the bottom. She clung to the blanket as if it were a lifeline and her hands cramped from the effort.

Phoebe placed a small tray on the floor and brushed a hand across Mary's brow. "Seth's heated some thick bean soup to give you strength and I've boiled camomile leaves to help you sleep. Here, drink the soup first." She held the bowl to Mary's lips and supported her head.

The Osprey led the Cynthia Mae through the moonless night. Only the glow of oil lanterns identified their locations. They had just reached the channel when the storm overtook them. The wind raged and tore at the sails. Gusts drove the Osprey ahead, then abandoned it to roll without direction. Water poured over the decks. The schooner rode up on the waves, bow high in the air, then slammed down as she passed over the crests. Men tied themselves to the masts and rails to keep from being lost overboard.

Mary and Phoebe clung to each other as their cot slid from one side of the cabin to the other. Water forced its way under the door and rose to a depth of three inches before it drained through the cracks between the boards. Mary trembled with the fear that, for the second time in a day, she was facing a watery grave. She heard the crew shouting, Richard's voice above the rest. "Furl those sails, now! Furl them or the masts'll be tipped and the ship will go right over. Steady now. Steady. We'll ride'er out if we're careful. We've got to get the bow turned into the wind. There!"

Mary listened all night as he coaxed the crew to keep going. Sometimes it seemed as if he even commanded the ship and the sea to behave. And maybe he did, because as hazy light brightened the cracks around the cabin door, she could feel the wind abate and the water begin to calm. With each passing hour, the storm receded. Mary and Phoebe relaxed their grasp of each other and tentatively stood on the puddled floor. At first they expected to be thrown down, but eventually they slogged from one end of the cabin to the other without mishap.

"Phoebe, where's the galley?" asked Mary, gathering confidence. "They've worked all night and they have a long day ahead of them. They'll be glad if we can get them bread and tea. We could use some, too."

She stepped onto the deck. Water and sky stretched as far as she could see. The deck rolled under her feet and the sails, again unfurled, snapped in the wind. The ocean rose and fell and lapped at the sides of the ship. It was like riding on a cloud, but she didn't need to be reminded that the ocean wasn't clean and fluffy. She steadied herself on anything she could reach; soon she was pleased to find that she could walk on the swaying deck without falling.

The women tried ten matches before they found one dry enough to light and it seemed like forever before the charcoal glowed with enough heat to boil water. Finally they were able to pass mugs of unsweetened tea and day old bread among the crew.

Under other circumstances, the men might have expressed their thanks, but there was a new and grave problem. John Barlow's ship had disappeared in the storm. All eyes squinted as they looked astern, straining for sight of the ship. Richard didn't lower the scope from his eye, searching. At midday he announced, "She's back there somewhere. We're going back to find her."

Mary stood at the rail and stared into the distance. What if John and his ship and her house had gone down in the storm together? The house and the schooner could be replaced, but what if John was gone, too? She knew well the grief of a woman whose beloved was lost at sea. She wouldn't wish that on anyone, even Sara at her worst.

Winter's early twilight again began to settle in when Richard shouted, "I see her! Look to starboard. The main mast is broken off. It's lying on the deck and dragging in the water, but she's still afloat." There was no telling from such a distance how the crew had fared. As the Osprey approached, the Cynthia Mae bobbed about randomly and it was difficult to come alongside.

There was a welcome cry. "We're all here. No one's been lost. Richard, can you hear? It's John. We need help, but it could be worse."

Richard beamed and his crew gave a victorious shout. "We're coming. Hold on. We're on our way!" he yelled.

The Cynthia Mae was in sorry shape. She was unable to sail, but there were no leaks and no danger of bilging. Richard and several crewmen went across to her in a long boat. They decided, rather than try to lift the broken mast, they would cut it free and take the Cynthia Mae in tow like a barge.

Boats from the Osprey carried lines from the starboard and port beams of one ship to the other and securely fastened them. This wasn't standard wrecking procedure, but logically it should work. When all the lines were secure, Richard ordered the Osprey to move out under sail. Mary held her breath and pressed her palms against the rail as hard as she could as if it would help the boat move forward. The lines drew taut against the damaged ship and the schooners moved ahead together. Progress would be slow, but if nothing more went wrong, they should make it to port.

* * *

It should have been a two-day trip, three days at most. As it was, the Atlantic coast of Key West came into view late in the afternoon of the fifth day. Richard knew the hazards of the reef that lined the island's shore and stayed well away from the tricky rocks and coral that could lead to further disaster. They sailed around the southern edge of the island and into the Gulf of Mexico as the sun dipped toward the horizon. Mary was standing on the deck to admire the setting sun when Richard came to stand beside her.

"Have you ever seen anything so beautiful?" she asked. "The sun rises sweetly and delicately to the east of our home on Green Turtle Cay, but this western view is dazzling. It's vivid and fiery and filled with energy. What a different world!"

"You're describing your home on Key West now," Richard squeezed her shoulder with his blistered hand.

"How can I call a place my home where I have yet to set foot?"

"I've been here many times and I assure you that it's most welcoming."

Lashed together as they were, the two schooners weren't nimble enough to dock at the pier. Richard pulled the boats up parallel to the shore as close as he could and cast the anchors.

"We'll unload the women here and cut the tow lines and use them to haul John's boat to the north pier. Then we can dock the Osprey and call it a day," Richard instructed.

"Mary, you and Phoebe climb into the dinghy," he ordered.

"Take your luggage."

The dinghy was suspended from a winch. As Mary leaned on it, it swung away from her and she looked down into the water. Oh! Not again!

Seth scrambled to the opposite side and steadied the boat.

"Here, you can get in now. Phoebe, you go next. I'll take care of your things, too."

Mary climbed over the side, expecting at any minute to be dumped on the deck or into the sea. She sank onto the plank seat in the bow and grasped the sides with white knuckles. Phoebe joined her. Seth hoisted the luggage into the center of the boat and slid over the side without rocking it. Two crewmen swung the boat out over the railing where it paused, suspended in air.

Rub-a-dub-dub,

Three men in a tub!

They all set out to sea.

Mary giggled hysterically.

The butcher, the baker, the candlestick maker.

Those were the sailors three.

Fatigue and fright had taken their toll. She wished she were a little girl at her father's knee listening to rhymes about imaginary adventures instead of living a real one.

The dinghy splashed gently as it struck the water. Seth released the lines that tied it to the schooner, took up the oars, and rhythmically rowed toward shore. Mary heard Richard shouting orders, but when she tried to turn, the boat tipped a little and she quickly straightened, staring rigidly ahead. When they reached the shore, Seth jumped out and pulled the dinghy up on the shore.

"I'll carry you the rest of the way, Miss Mary. You're tired and the way is uneven."

He cradled her in his arms like a child and carried her across the rocky shore. Phoebe climbed over the side of the boat, following with Mary's valise and her own cotton sack.

"We're going to that white house there with the red doors," Seth instructed. "That's where the captain says you'll live until your house is built again. We're to ask for Miss Caroline Wells and give her this paper. Says she's expecting us. It's not far, Miss. Can you walk with a little help? I think you need to get your land legs back."

He was right! After five days on the ship, it felt funny to be on land, but she would have walked any distance to a clean bed firmly situated in a house on dry land.

"I'll be fine. Thank you, Seth."

The big white house sat just on the other side of a wide path that paralleled the shore. The many doors and windows of the first floor were bright with lamplight. The second floor was dark except for one window where lace curtains gently fluttered revealing only glimpses of a room lit by a single candle.

Mary, Phoebe, and Seth climbed the steep steps to the porch and hadn't time to decide which door to knock at before a short woman with curly blond hair and pale blue eyes opened the center one and stepped out on the porch. Seth wordlessly offered her Richard's note. She tore it open, read it, and stuffed in her skirt pocket in one motion.

"So you're Mary Randall. Come in. Put down the bag and I'll have it taken upstairs. Your woman servant can sleep with mine behind the kitchen house.

"Martha! Put water on to boil for the bath tub. A female guest has arrived. Now where will the man servant sleep? I have no men's quarters here."

"With your favor, Ma'am, I'll get back to the ships. Captain Randall says we're to sleep there and guard them until the house and all the things are safely unloaded. If there's nothing more for me to do here, I'll go."

Seth smiled briefly at Phoebe and half bowed to Caroline and Mary.

"Of course. Be on your way."

Mary climbed the steep stairway to the second floor and was shown to her room at the back of the house. Tears of nostalgia flooded her eyes. She thought of home as she felt the thick braided rug under her feet and stroked the cotton bedclothes and the embroidered counterpane. Civilization!

Caroline called up, "You'll find a dressing gown hung behind the door. It's large, but it will do after your bath. Come down when you're ready. The water is hot."

Mary folded the robe over her arm and smiled in anticipation. The only other time she'd been a guest in another person's house she'd had to put up with her sister's dining room while her own house was dismantled and loaded. Then there had been no oversized robes for after her bath. Tinkling laughter rang from behind a closed door near the stair. Another woman in the house! How pleasant this place was going to be!

CHAPTER 14

Mary slid into the steaming tub and luxuriated in the caress of the water and the aroma of herbs. Rosemary! There was something else familiar that she couldn't name. Maybe lavender. She allowed herself to sink until the water lapped at her ear lobes and wet the nape of her neck. She closed her eyes and languorously swayed her hips from side to side, creating a gentle current. Every inch of her body was pleasurably massaged. After the weeks at Sara's and the days on the Osprey, she reveled in the luxury.

"Take your time and when you're ready I have chicken soup and fresh bread for your supper," called Caroline.

"Please don't worry about me," Mary replied, hoping to discourage further conversation.

She relaxed into reverie and imagined herself in a place where clothing was always clean and smelled of sunshine and starch. There the corners of the furniture were rounded and smooth and the surfaces shone with lacquer and polish. Rugs softened her step and upholstered cushions eased her sitting. It was nothing like the hard, rough surfaces and dirty quarters she had endured these last days making the crossing from Green Turtle Cay to Key West. Filled with renewed hope, she believed Richard was right. This was a welcoming place. She had assumed that it was a rough outpost, but that clearly wasn't true. Caroline's home was gracious and Caroline herself seemed to be considerate and perhaps even smart.

Tomorrow she'd wear clean clothes. How funny that just having clean clothes had become an occasion! She'd never again take fresh clothing for granted after living on that ship for five days! She'd wear the pale blue blouse that set off her pretty forget-me-not necklace. She knew just where the necklace was, wrapped in tissue paper and tucked against the back edge of her valise. If Richard didn't have time to leave the ship, she'd go to the waterfront herself. It would be a good reminder for him that she was waiting and she wasn't the sodden mess he had dragged from the sea bottom. Yes, tomorrow! Tomorrow she would see the spot where her house was soon to be rebuilt and the city surrounding it. She could begin her new life.

When the water cooled, she climbed out of the tub, dried, and shrugged on the big cotton robe. Following the sound of voices, she found the kitchen.

"I've set a place for you in the dining room," said Caroline. "I'll sit with you while you eat. We make a tasty and fortifying chicken soup here. The chickens are brought over from Cuba for fighting. That's a big sport among the men, to see whose rooster is the strongest and meanest. Needless to say, there are plenty of losers, and once a cock has been defeated, he's worthless even if he's still alive. Those losers are turned loose in the streets and if you can catch them, they're yours, although most of them are mean and dangerous. They're tough, but very flavorful. If you simmer them for long enough, the soup is irresistible! You'll see."

Mary's appetite wasn't spoiled by Caroline's earthy description of the soup's ingredients. The aroma was marvelous. She dipped her spoon in the steaming broth and sipped. Exquisite!

"What is the spice? I've never tasted anything quite like it," she asked.

"That's from Cuba, too. They call it annatto. It gives the yellow color and the distinctive taste. You can buy it at the market.

We have quite a few groceries you might not have seen before."

"I hope it won't be long before I have a kitchen of my own," said Mary. She finished her supper and went straight to bed.

When she awoke, bright sunshine peeked around the edges of the brocade curtains that rustled in the sea breeze. She could tell from the clanging of dishes and whispering of a straw broom that the household had been awake for some time. She lay still, savoring the opportunity to be idle.

She was surprised to hear Richard talking to Caroline and went to the window to investigate.

"Nothing has changed for me," said Caroline.

"Everything has changed, and you know it," Richard replied. "It changed last June when I married."

"Nothing had changed this summer when you were here, nor in November. We enjoyed each other as we always have. Do you mean your visits then were only for sport? You reduce me to the status of the other women in this house! Toys of the moment, discarded after use! I could happily have rented you one of my young fillies who would have understood the business arrangement. How is it you neglected to mention that your feelings had changed as well as your station in life? Well, enjoy being a respectable married man. But don't look back, because I'll never be there waiting for you."

Caroline's eyes narrowed and she thrust her neck forward like a snake preparing to strike. Yesterday's pastel prettiness was gone. Now she was frightening in her animal-like fury. She fumbled with her ears and threw something at Richard's feet.

"Tokens of your affection, you said! These are worthless baubles, only slightly more valuable than your meaningless words of love. Take them and get out of my life!

"I'll keep Mary for three weeks. She's a sweet thing, although I wonder if she's very smart if she accepted you. You'll pay for her keep. Yes, you'll pay handsomely. I don't want to see you again. You can deal with my girls if you must come here to pay or give a message. If you want to visit your wife, I expect you to go no further than the parlor and make an appointment before you come so I can be elsewhere."

Caroline turned on her heel and walked across the courtyard, arms akimbo. She slammed the heavy red door behind her and went inside. Richard ground the heel of his boot in the dirt where Caroline had thrown the rejected tokens. Shoving his hands deep into his pockets, he strode out of the courtyard.

Mary stared at the stage where the drama had played out. Caroline had been Richard's lover! He had visited her on his wrecking trips. He'd come to her even after he'd married. Impossible! She couldn't believe he'd be unfaithful to her! The words must have been garbled in the wind.

She dressed hastily and crept down the stairs. Once in the courtyard, she scuffed her booted toe in the dirt where Richard had stood. An enameled earring lay in the dust. Its delicate forget-me-nots matched the necklace Richard had given her as an engagement present. It took just a moment to unearth the second of the pair. He had given half of the set to Caroline, sharing the jewelry just as he shared his affection!

Mary screamed. She started to run from the courtyard, then realized she didn't have anywhere to go. She took the stairs two at a time, slammed the bedroom door, and locked it before she threw herself on the bed. This space that so recently had seemed a haven now was a prison. She was trapped on a foreign island in a house of prostitution run by the woman who had shared her husband's bed and affection. She rolled onto her back and stared at the cracks between the ceiling boards.

What could she do? Women sometimes returned to their parents' homes. Almost always they were widows whose husbands were lost at sea. Presumably she could find transport back to Green Turtle Cay, but what would her life be once she was there? She remembered her father's words when he tried to persuade her to accept Richard's advances. "Soon all of Green Turtle Cay will remark how the spinster Mary is growing old, still seated at her father's side," he'd said. "A sorry life for such a promising girl." The best they would say of her now was that she was a wronged woman. After the story circulated for a while, she would be known as soiled goods unworthy of another suitor, a wife who walked off on her husband, probably unfaithful herself.

There was a tap at the door. "Miss Mary, I've brought you some tea. It's getting mighty late to be having breakfast."

"I'm not well. Please leave me alone."

"Yes, ma'am, if you're sure."

Mary could hear the skepticism in Phoebe's voice. When had Mary been ill and not wanted her help? She would gladly have accepted it now, but this was beyond Phoebe's ability with herbs and plants and Mary had no intention of sharing her marital problems with anybody. She listened to her servant's obedient footfall as she retreated along the hall and down the stairs.

If she chose to stay in Key West, what would she do? She'd be surprised if it was a place where a young woman could live on her own unless she was a nun or a prostitute and neither of those callings appealed to her. She smiled bitterly. The former was too little, the latter, too much, of a good thing.

What if she took shelter in her marriage and made the best of it? She would hide the pain of Richard's infidelity. She didn't have to discuss it or even acknowledge it, for that matter. She could pretend not to know. No! That was silly. She wasn't stupid and it wouldn't help her situation if she seemed so.

Mary sat on the edge of the bed and held her head in her hands. Then what? I've been honest and trusting and what good was that? I'd better be more careful with my feelings and protect myself if I don't want to be hurt more.

What will make my life here pleasant, or at least bearable? she wondered. Comfort. I must have a pleasant household with pretty things. I want my independence to come and go as I did on Green Turtle Cay. And now I want children. I will take solace in them. Surely my innocent children will love me purely as this wretched husband never did and I will love them without fear of betrayal or deceit. These are my goals. I'll face the situation head on and make them happen.

The necklace was in her luggage exactly where she remembered putting it. She took the earrings out of her pocket and rinsed the dust from them in the wash basin. Arranging her hair high on her head to best show off her earlobes and throat, she put on the earrings and tied the familiar necklace high on her chest where it wouldn't be overlooked.

Gritting her teeth and pressing her lips together in a determined line, she unlocked the door and raised her chin as she moved down the hall and descended the stairs, her stately manner belying the trepidation she felt.

"I'd like some tea now," said Mary as she entered the dining room. "And bread and butter if you still have some."

Caroline sat at the table bent over half a dozen ledgers spread out in front of her. Her back was to Mary and she didn't turn to greet her.

"Your maid is still in the kitchen," she said. "I think you can find your way."

Mary walked around the table and sat down facing Caroline. "I want to thank you for your generous hospitality," she said, beaming with what she hoped looked like a confident smile. "It is such a pleasure to be in civilization again after so many long days at sea. Have you ever been to sea, Caroline?"

"No, I can't say as I have. Nor do I care to go," said Caroline looking up with obvious impatience.

Her eyes were cold and her manner, brusque. Mary looked her straight in the eye, holding her gaze. Finally she had the satisfaction of seeing Caroline take in the earrings which until minutes ago had been her own. Then Caroline focused on the matching necklace. She couldn't seem to take her eyes off of it.

She didn't know either, thought Mary. *She didn't know we shared the jewelry as well as the man. And I don't think she knew that I was anything more than a silly girl bride. Well, now she knows.*

"I'll see to your tea," said Caroline, suddenly rising and heading to the kitchen house.

Mary's composed smile spread into a genuine grin. She'd made her point! It was a very small victory, but it felt good.

Soon Phoebe appeared with tea, bread, butter, and mango jam.

"I'm glad you're feeling better, Miss," she said. "You look well and rested." She raised her eyebrows.

She noticed the earrings, Mary said to herself. *If anyone knows my things, it's Phoebe. I wonder what she thinks.*

"I feel much better. Thank you," Mary said.

Phoebe recognized the dismissal and left quietly.

Mary lingered over breakfast, eating more than usual to compensate for the late hour and the fact that she didn't plan to be present for lunch. Although Caroline had left the account books spread over most of the table, she didn't reappear.

* * *

Mary went straight to the waterfront. When she came to the Osprey, nobody was on deck, but she could hear men's voices in the cabin. The distance between the dock and the ship was spanned by that same narrow gangplank. As much as she wanted to confront Richard, nothing in the world could make her walk across that board.

She recognized parts of the house at the landward end of the pier. The stairs and railing were all stacked together with several windows leaning against them. The long, rough boards were part of the siding and the narrower, smoother ones were from a floor. She couldn't tell if they were from the bedroom or the parlor or Richard's office. Richard would know. She remembered him marking every board as he stacked it back on Green Turtle Cay.

Her household furniture was all around on the dock. Evidently it had been unloaded and hadn't gotten any farther. She wondered where it would be stored until there was a house to put it in. It certainly couldn't stay where it was. Spotting a straight back dining chair, she sat down to wait. She felt absurd dressed in good clothes and jewelry and sitting on a nice chair in the middle of the rough-hewn planks of this dock that smelled of fish and rotting seaweed. She didn't see any alternative, so she sat up straight, folded her hands in her lap, tried to look unperturbed, and waited.

The effects of the hurricane were still evident after four

months. A big schooner with a jagged stump for a foremast, floated at anchor. Boards and canvass, presumably from ships that didn't survive the storm, lay on the rocky shore where they had washed up. Caroline's house seemed not to have suffered serious damage, but further down the shoreline was a structure without a roof and another that had been crazily pushed over to one side like a stack of dominoes.

As the sun climbed overhead, Mary wished she'd worn a hat. Never mind. She wasn't going back to that house. Not until she talked to her husband.

When Richard finally appeared, he didn't come from the Osprey. Rather, he came strolling along a wide dirt trail that seemed to connect the waterfront with the interior of the island. He led a pair of enormous gray draft horses that drew a flat bed wagon with high side stakes and no back. Three men sat on the wagon joking and laughing as they dangled their legs over the back.

Richard led the horses near the siding and urged them backward, trying to bring the wagon close to the boards. He couldn't stop them before the wagon ran into the stack and knocked it over.

"Damn!" he shouted. "I can't drive this thing. If one of you can, then do it. Otherwise, you men get off your asses and unhook the wagon and push it alongside the wood so we can load it. Then we'll hook the horses up again to haul it up the street."

Mary didn't move. She didn't want to call attention to herself and stop the drama. She'd never seen Richard unable to do anything he set his mind to. Well! He must be pushed to some limits himself.

"I'm going to get Seth and Jack," he said as one of the crewmen stood at the heads of the horses and the other two unhitched the wagon. "There's no need to stand guard on the ship. We'll get this done a lot sooner with two more strong backs."

He was almost to the gang plank before he noticed Mary seated amid the furniture.

"What are you doing here?" he asked.

"I'm waiting for you," Mary replied. "I can't imagine any other reason to sit out here like this."

"Wait just a minute more. I'll take you to see your new home!" He was on the Osprey in two strides and disappeared below deck. He emerged with Seth and Jack. He pointed them toward the wagon and wrapped his arm around Mary's waist. "Come on! If you see it now, you'll know every step of its construction, just as you did the first time I built it."

Mary had looked forward to this moment for weeks - the day when she could see the lot where their house would stand, when she could sift the dirt between her fingers and search out flowers to replace the daisies she'd left behind. She burst into tears.

"Come on! What are you crying about?" Richard took her hands and pulled her to stand in front of him. He opened his mouth as if to speak, then shut it and stared at the earrings. Mary wiped her teary cheeks with the back of her hand and raised her chin.

"Before you move one stick of wood there are some things I want to say."

"Sit down, Mary. You're tired and upset."

She stood her ground.

"When did you give that woman these earrings? How could you deceive me as you did? I pined for you when you were away. I looked out to sea and wept from loneliness. And you weren't even thinking of me. You were giving that woman gifts and finding companionship in her bed. How many other lovers do you have scattered along the Florida coast? A girl in every port, isn't that what they say? I thought that was only for deck hands, not captains. But I guess that's how you are. You enjoy whomever and whatever is at hand. You must be looking forward to a fine time here in Key West with two of your women within a short walk."

Richard's face was redder than any sunburn and he looked self-consciously at his crewmen to see if they heard. The men looked as if they might be working, but they were abnormally silent.

"Come over here." He took Mary's arm and pulled her aside. A hen and five chicks scampered from behind a stack of floor boards, squawking at the human invasion. Richard kicked the hen and she screeched and flapped her wings. The chicks scattered in every direction.

"What kind of man are you to kick a poor dumb animal?" Mary screamed. "What kind of man are you to lie and cheat with women? You're not the man I love. I believed in a virtuous man who would stand by me and protect me and be faithful. That man was all in my imagination. It was never you."

Richard put his hands on her shoulders and forced her to sit back down.

"Who are you to accuse me?" he hissed through clenched teeth. "Do you think I don't know about what you did in the coppice with that biologist of yours? Maybe you never stood on the dock and looked into the woods as I did. It's a very clear view, right to the top of the hill. Don't accuse me from the pinnacle of your virtue. I saw for myself what you were up to. And I know the signs of a virgin and I know you never showed any evidence of being one. At least not with me.

"You're right. We have things to discuss. I don't care to air my private life in front of my crew or argue with a mad woman and you, my dear, are far from rational. I'll take you back to Caroline's house where you can gather your wits. We'll talk after dinner."

"I don't need you to take me. I can walk perfectly well by myself. Don't neglect to warn Caroline that you're coming. You know she doesn't want to see you."

Good. That would show him she'd heard the whole conversation and he might as well be truthful.

CHAPTER 15

Mary reentered the house through the back door and regained her room without being seen. She took off her clothes and stood naked in front of the window, raising her arms to benefit from the weak breeze that filtered through the louvered shutter. There was fresh water in the pitcher and she moistened a cloth and held it to her temples and the back of her neck. She was panting from exertion and anger and she tried to concentrate on breathing slowly and evenly. Her body cooled and her temper subsided from roaring flames to hot embers.

Phoebe tapped at the door. "Miss Mary, will you be at dinner?"

"Please bring me a tray," Mary replied. "Soup and vegetables, nothing heavy." She lay back on the bed and tried to compose her thoughts, but it was useless. Eventually, another knock at the door signaled Phoebe's return. Mary opened the door and quickly took the tray without meeting Phoebe's eyes. So what if she was naked? She chose to have dinner in her room without clothes on tonight. She giggled giddily, but her defiance gave her energy and she considered her dinner tray.

There was chicken soup, golden with that exotic Cuban spice, and a bowl of cold green beans and onions dotted with shimmering drops of tart vinegar. Five sprigs of rosemary tied together with a long, wide leaf of grass lay on the tray beside the spoon. Mary understood and was silently grateful to Phoebe. She was to place the rosemary under her pillow to ward off bad dreams. She pulled the chair near the window and balanced the tray on her knees.

Her attention wandered back to the problem at hand. *I loathe the fact that Caroline shared Richard's bed,* she thought. *To think he continued the affair after our marriage!* Mary shuddered. Her throat tightened and she spat a mouthful of partially-chewed beans into the napkin.

She lowered the tray from her lap to the floor and stood, looking down at her bare body. Her breasts were small and firm, her stomach flat. Soft curly brown hair at her groin softened the angularity of her long legs and contrasted with her milky skin. How did her body compare to Caroline's freckled buxomness? Had Caroline discovered the softness of the channel between Richard's lean buttocks that Mary loved to stroke? Had she trembled at the touch of his lips on her breasts and recoiled from his damaged hand, then learned to kiss it and rub it softly against her cheek as Mary had?

Mary stooped and flung the empty soup bowl against the wall. The thick pottery crashed heavily to the floor without breaking. She got more satisfaction when she threw the porcelain plate that held the vegetables against the back of the door and it shattered, spraying sharp fragments and pickled vegetables over the walls and floor. She stood and kicked the tray against the baseboard under the window.

Phoebe thundered up the stairs. "Miss Mary, what's happening? Are you all right?"

"I'm fine," Mary snapped. "Leave me alone."

"Captain Randall is here now. He says you're expecting him."

"Damn," she muttered. "Damn, damn, damn. Well, I'd just as well face this now."

"I'll be down presently," she said.

Mary took her time as she dressed and brushed her hair with long, unhurried strokes. She rearranged the necklace and consulted the hand mirror to be sure the earrings were hanging straight. Dusk sifted through the shutters and the room was half-dark before she descended to the parlor.

Richard faced the window, his back to the door. As she entered the room, Mary paused at the threshold and cleared her throat. "Hello," she said.

"Hello."

Richard turned to face her. He seemed to be trying to make a good impression. His hair was combed and his shirt was clean, but there was dirt under his finger nails and traces of mud on the knees of his trousers. Mary was reminded of the evening when he called at her father's house to ask her hand in marriage. She pinched the soft skin on the inside of her forearm. This was no time for sentimentality! Head high, she deliberately crossed the room and stopped three steps from him.

"You were cruel this afternoon. Did you mean what you said?" he asked.

Mary was determined not to lose her composure as she had earlier. She hid her clenched fists in the folds of her skirt and calmly met his gaze as she spoke in measured tones.

"I meant I can't stand your dalliance with Caroline or anybody else, for that matter. I meant I thought our marriage was of some importance to you." She paced to the window and back. When she resumed, she spoke more loudly. "I thought you loved me. If I was cruel, it was because I was injured and angry and disappointed. I still am. I can't believe I traveled here and endured so much fear and danger only for this disappointment. Why did I bother? Why did you? We can call each other names forever, but what is the point, Richard? Evidently we have some very old complaints. I can't see how to resolve them."

Richard clasped his hands in front of him, then dropped them to his sides.

"I visited Caroline because I was lonely and far from home. I never expected you'd know. As for the earrings, that was before you consented to marry me. I'd been successful on a wreck and you'd just scolded me in that letter. I saved the necklace for you and gave the earrings to Caroline. It seemed right at the time."

He had begun levelly as she had done, but as he continued he put his hands on his hips and raised his voice, too.

"What about your lying in the ferns with Michael Wellmet? You enjoyed that willingly enough. I'd call that dalliance, too, wouldn't you? I've known about it all along, you know. It seemed unnecessary to talk about it. I thought it was best lost in the past." He stopped abruptly and lowered his eyes and his voice. "Until today, anyway. I'm sorry. I shouldn't have yelled those things at you. I lost my temper and I'm not proud of it. But I hope you're sorry, too, for what you said and how you said it."

He reached out to her, but she stepped back. Sighing, he looked into her eyes and reached again, this time firmly grasping her hand.

"We're not saints, are we? If we pretended to be, it was a mistake. We know each other better today than we did before, but we're the same people we were when we left Green Turtle Cay. I still love you and I'm pretty sure you love me."

He pulled her against him and raised her chin. At first Mary thought to resist again, but she didn't really want to reject his familiar touch. She softened against him and he kissed her lightly on her closed lips. This is how we should be, she thought. If we could just go on like this, I think I could forgive anything. She felt a little dizzy and leaned against him to steady herself. He guided her to a chair and knelt in front of her.

"We've been through a hard passage. I've never seen one like it. My body aches from the effort of fighting the wind and the sea and my eyes are tired of searching the horizon. I'm exhausted by the seemingly endless problems I've had to solve. You've suffered hardships, too. We need to finish this task we've set for ourselves and rest."

"What about Caroline?"

"Whatever there was between me and Caroline is over. I never meant it should go on. I could have married her. I'm sure she would have had me. I married you."

Mary smiled. She'd been so absorbed with his betrayal that she hadn't thought of that. He'd chosen her when it counted and he was reaffirming his choice now. She leaned over, took his hands in hers and held them against the forget-me-not necklace where it lay against the curve of her breasts.

CHAPTER 16

There was no practical alternative to Mary and Richard's present living arrangements until the house was in place. He wasn't welcome in Caroline's house and Mary refused to cross onto the Osprey to return to the cramped and uncomfortable cabin. Just months ago, there had been two public lodging houses picturesquely situated on the island's Atlantic coast, but they were leveled by the hurricane. The proprietors were lucky to escape with their lives and were living with friends and family until the guest houses could be rebuilt.

Richard found space in Asa Tift's warehouse to store the furniture and household goods. It hadn't rained, but between the salt spray and the morning dew, the finish on the wood pieces wouldn't last long. "I think everything will be safe there," he said. "I'm paying him a nice sum to keep it and I think the stories of his dishonesty are born of envy, not fact. He's a very wealthy man and doesn't need to trifle in used furniture. Still, I'll go check from time to time. You never know who else may have the run of the place."

Every morning, Mary rose before daylight and was out the door before the rest of the household began to stir. She went straight to the dock where she and Richard sat on discarded wood boxes and shared a strong, brisk pot of tea. Seth had his own way with tea. She guessed it was his masculine approach to brewing that made the difference. Or did he just forget it and let it steep too long?

The men hauled pieces of the house to William Street like dedicated ants following a well-worn trail. When the hauling was done, they began to rebuild. Mary would have liked to help, but there wasn't much she could do except fetch a bucket of nails or pick up a dropped hammer. Late in the morning she would walk to the shops on Duval Street. The bakery and grocery had been rebuilt and shared a storefront across from the remains of the Episcopal church. She bought provisions for the crew and a simple lunch to share with Richard. It reminded her of the days before they married when she watched him build the house the first time and they shared lunch from a basket. She felt as if years had passed since then, although it had been less than ten months.

As the house began to take shape, she and Richard lingered after the day's work was done and the crew went back to the Osprey. Now there were no eyes to censor their intimacy as there had been before their marriage. Only insistent mosquitos interrupted their lovemaking on the wide floor boards.

Mary took her supper at Caroline's. Although she often returned late, her place was always set in the dining room. She was, after all, a paying boarder and she was the only one, so she ate alone. She wasn't surprised that Caroline didn't join her or that the menu was plainer since their confrontation. Chicken stew was the meal four days out of seven. At other times there was conch chowder, turtle soup, or fried mullet.

There also seemed to be some problem getting her laundry done. Phoebe reported that often she was denied the use of the wash tub, although no one else seemed to be using it. And Mary's clean clothes sometimes mysteriously fell from the line into the dust before they were dry and had to be washed again. The bed sheets weren't as soft as previously and often there were holes or roughly sewn patches.

Mary recognized the lack of hospitality as Caroline's revenge, although the hardships were more annoying for Phoebe than for herself. She could have searched out Caroline and confronted her with the omissions of service, but her intuition told her that she would only make matters worse.

"Miss Mary, I'll just go back and ask for some better sheets. Those patched ones just aren't suitable. I don't like the way they've started to treat us in this house!" Phoebe burst out one day.

"These will do just fine. It won't be long before we're back in our own home with our own things and we won't have to deal with these problems," Mary replied.

Phoebe looked dubious, but she stripped the bed and remade it, doing her best to bury the patched spots under the mattress.

Mary longed to be settled, too. Every little delay in the construction loomed large for her. One day a window wouldn't go in. Later in the week, half the risers for the stairs were missing. Whenever there was a setback, she despaired of ever seeing the house completed, but then the crisis would be resolved and progress would resume.

"I was worried about finishing before Caroline's deadline," Richard confessed one afternoon. "She's sent me three notes threatening to take me to court if you aren't out in time and the bill paid in full. Not that any magistrate would pay attention to that kind of petty business, but it would be annoying and expensive. Embarrassing, too, to have private business aired in public like that. As it turns out, we'll be done well before then." He smiled proudly. "It helps that all the wood is numbered, cut and drilled. We've been working hard the whole time, but even so, I'm surprised at how quickly the place has gone up compared to the first time. We'll finish hanging the doors and windows by Tuesday at the latest and then we'll move in. I've hired a wagon to cart the furniture from the warehouse.

"I'm afraid Phoebe's going to have to cook outside for a while. The stove will be in place, but I want to complete the main house before I start building the kitchen. She and Seth can use the back room or sleep on the Osprey, as they see fit."

"I can't wait to be in my own home," Mary said. "It's not so much Caroline. Her meanness hasn't been as bad as I'd expected. I'm looking forward to having real privacy again. I always feel as if I'm being watched, even though I don't see anyone. It's probably my imagination, but I don't like it."

"What about me? Don't you also long to live with your husband again or shall I move on?" Richard's eyes twinkled teasingly.

Mary stiffened and looked up quickly, then seeing he meant it as a joke, replied, "Don't go just yet. There's still a place for you here with me."

The rest of the windows and doors went in without a hitch and the stairway again connected the two floors. It was a whole day's work to get the furniture from the warehouse and the sun was starting to set before they could see the end of the job.

"That's it!" Richard announced, raising little puffs of dust as he smacked his hands on his pants. "We sleep here tonight. I'll go get your things and I'll leave the rent on the dining room table. I'm paying the whole three weeks, although you'll have stayed three days less than that. Phoebe will come back here with me and our household will be together again."

Mary kissed him for good luck and went upstairs to find bedding and towels. She carefully tucked the corners of the bed sheets and smoothed the blanket before carrying linens downstairs for the servants' cots. Earlier she'd swept her bedroom free of construction debris, but the downstairs floors were still littered and she set out to clean them before the others came.

The kitchen cupboard was temporarily in the back room along with the boxes of cooking utensils and tableware. We're going to have a fine time of it trying to cook a supper tonight, she thought. Then it struck her that in the hurry to move, she hadn't thought to provision the house. The shops closed over an hour before. She hurried down to the Osprey, hoping to find Seth.

"Bring biscuits and cheese and tea," she said. "What else is there to make a meal? I guess we won't starve, but it's not going to be much of a supper."

"I still have some jarred pork and some white beans," Seth

reassured her. "Phoebe can heat those on the stove and we'll have enough."

The wood was a little green and it seemed like forever before the coals in the stove burned hot enough to heat anything. When they finally sat down to eat, the food, although plain, was satisfying. Mary was so tired. It was an effort to stay awake to eat. When she finished, she excused herself and went upstairs.

"I'll join you soon," Richard promised. "I just want to take one more look around."

Mary heard the crunching of his boots in the stony dirt as he patrolled the property. She imagined him looking up at the house and smiling with the satisfaction of having done a good job and finishing it ahead of time. She slipped into bed imagining his pleasure and was asleep before he laid a foot on the stairs.

* * *

In the days that followed, the hard work fell to Mary and Phoebe. They swept and washed floors and porches, unpacked dishes and linens, and arranged the furniture. Soon it was hard to tell the place had been taken apart and moved. It was home again.

"I want to get started on our garden," said Mary one morning when Phoebe finished clearing the breakfast table. "It's too late in the winter to plant the tender vegetables. We'll have to buy them until next season, but we can prepare the ground and plant some herbs and shrubs."

"I'll be glad to get my hands back in the dirt," replied Phoebe. "It's going to take about a year to make this soil grow much of anything. It's nothing but sand and coral rock as far as I can see. I've been saving food scraps since we moved in. I put them in a hole and let them set and I gather fallen leaves and throw them in, too. That'll be real good for the sand once they rot, but rotting takes time. I guess it won't hurt to plant some herb seeds, but we better not use them up. We'll need more if our first try fails."

They went into the yard to find a likely spot. A big egg fruit tree hung over the street and spread back over much of the yard.

That would provide welcome shade in the summer and the fleshy orange fruit would make pies in the fall. But the garden needed light and should be well away from the tree. They settled on the brushy area beyond the cistern. Mary would ask Richard to have it cleared.

"It's odd," said Mary as they discussed the garden at dinner. "I thought William Street ran east to west, but today as I looked carefully at the sun and shadows, I saw it's not so. The corner of the house points east. The end facing the street faces to the northeast."

"They laid the streets out that way so the corners of the houses, like the prows of ships, would cut into the easterly winds. That's where the big storms come from. Otherwise, the sides of the houses would be broad against the wind in a storm, like sails, and much more likely to be blown down. I've heard it said that if it had been done the other way, there'd be nothing left of the town today."

Once the house was finished, Richard spent more and more time at the waterfront. Mary knew he was thinking of sailing so she was glad when he agreed to cut down the scrub and turn the earth for the garden. When they marked the boundaries, she was tempted to make it twice as big as she really needed, just to keep him home for a little longer.

As she watched the clearing, she was glad not to have made the job any harder than it already was. Her mother's garden on Green Turtle Cay had been cultivated for decades. The stones had been removed and dragged to the edges. The soil there was light and friable and she could easily sink her trowel in up to the handle. This so-called garden was a small jungle that had never known a shovel or machete. The surface would blunt a trowel's point if anyone were so foolish as to try to dig it with such a dainty tool. Mary was astonished when she saw the effort required to tame the patch. Richard and Seth were bathed in sweat, although it was still winter and not hot at all. Their forearms were covered with red scratches and leaves and twigs caught in their hair.

"This garden had better grow the best food and plenty of it!"

exclaimed Richard. "We've bled on this ground and it owes us something in return!"

Mary's reassurances seemed to satisfy him, although she thought it would take a miracle to turn the barren patch into productive land.

It was early March and the days were noticeably longer, but the weather was still fresh and dry. Mary sat on the edge of the cistern, watched the play of the afternoon shadows in the breeze, and considered her new home. The household was falling into a satisfying routine and her life had a relaxed rhythm. Life was good.

Unaccountably, Mary began to feel unsettled. One moment she was placidly happy, then for no apparent reason, she was overcome by ill-defined sadness. She tired more quickly than usual and often slept well into the morning if no one roused her. It seemed to her that she should have recovered by now from the move, but her condition didn't seem to improve, rather, it worsened. She found the fatigue annoying. She'd never felt so run down except for when she was pregnant after Michael died.

Of course! How could she be so stupid? This was exactly like the other time! She'd been too busy to pay much attention. How long had it been since she'd menstruated?

She was pregnant! This time the knowledge brought tears of pleasure to her eyes. She hugged herself in anticipation. The child would have Richard's clear blue eyes and curly reddish blond hair. It would share her love of reading and nature. It would be a girl. No, a boy. Richard would want a boy, she was sure. They would name him Richard, just like his father.

She stood and waltzed in lazy circles between the cistern and the vegetable garden tracing big swooping patterns through the air with her hands and leaning her head back to absorb the warmth of the afternoon sun. She hummed a lullaby her mother sang to her when she was a child.

"You're very happy today."

She had no idea how long Richard had been on the porch watching her. She couldn't contain her delight at seeing him and ran up the steps with her arms flung wide open.

"We're going to have a baby!"

Richard's eyes opened wide and he jerked to attention. Mary couldn't tell if he was pleased or shocked or both.

"We're going to have a baby? Are you sure?"

"I'm very sure. I didn't tell you before because . . . Well, because I didn't realize it myself!" Mary blushed self-consciously. "You can take my word for it. I'm pregnant."

"Should you be dancing around like that? Come inside. Sit down and rest." He lifted her in his arms and carried her to the parlor where he deposited her on the sofa.

"Do you know what to do?" he asked. "Aren't there special things for pregnant women? I never thought I'd long for your mother, but she'd be a great help in this situation, wouldn't she? I don't have an inkling how you should take care of yourself or how to prepare for a child. I'm not sure what I should do as a father either, although I swear I'll do my best."

Mary laughed. She found his confusion charming. "Women have been having babies for centuries," she said. "I trust my instincts and I'm sure Phoebe has more practical knowledge than my mother and all her friends put together. I seem to remember women relying heavily on the servants' knowledge when it was time for the first baby."

She thought of Phoebe's collaboration in ending her first pregnancy and a chill ran down her back. *That* secret must never be revealed! What she did then was necessary, but guilt clung like a dark shadow in a corner of her mind. *All that is past*, she thought. *I won't allow those awful memories to ruin this for me. I'll put them aside as if it never happened.* Still, she couldn't help comparing today's joy with the desperation that accompanied the discovery of her first, brief pregnancy. A terrible idea occurred to her. Would this child be harmed by what she did before?

"Are you all right?" Richard asked. "Suddenly you look sad."

"I'm fine. This is as unexpected for me as it is for you. I think I need a little time to get used to the idea."

She rubbed the sofa's horsehair upholstery against the grain, forcing her attention to the present. She was determined to make this a happy time. Hoping her effort at gaiety wasn't transparently forced, she clasped her hands and exclaimed, "Already I can see a great deal to do! I'll write my mother and Sara right away. A good long talk with Phoebe is definitely in order."

It worked. Richard smiled again and looked relaxed and Mary felt better, too.

* * *

After she cleared the table and washed the dishes, Phoebe usually sat outside the kitchen door to rest her feet and enjoy the evening breezes. Tonight, rather than going to the parlor, Mary waited for her and approached quietly in the dark.

"Phoebe, I'm going to have a child," she practically whispered.

"You're going to keep this one, aren't you?" Phoebe asked matter-of-factly.

Mary took a little step backward, surprised by her tone. She pressed on anyway. "Yes, I want this baby very much. I need your advice about what to do while I'm pregnant."

"Growing babies is the easiest thing there is!" Phoebe's laugh rolled melodically from deep in her throat. "It's getting rid of them that we have to learn how to do. Just take good care of yourself, Miss Mary. Eat fresh food when you're hungry and take a long walk every day and rest when you're tired. You don't need to do anything special. Before you know it, you'll be pushing that little child into the daylight. Maybe you'll want some help then, but I'll be here. Count on me."

Mary watched a gauzy cloud drift past the sliver of a new moon. She wasn't sure she wanted to continue. If she asked the next question and the answer was what she feared, what would she do?

"Is there something more, Miss Mary?"

"When I drank the aloe, did it do anything to change me permanently? Is this baby going to stay inside me, or is it going to come out like that other one? I want it so much, and I'm afraid."

"I can't see the future, Miss, but lots of women have done what you did and gone on to have big families of healthy children. Sometimes babies do get born before their times, but I believe it's always for the best. There's surely something very wrong when that happens and the little ones that die would have lived in misery if they'd been born. Once you feel the child quicken, you can be pretty sure everything is fine. And if it's not, don't blame yourself. Those things just happen sometimes."

Tears of relief welled up in Mary's eyes and streamed down her cheeks.

"There is one thing that every baby needs more than anything," said Phoebe. "That's a cheerful mother. I'm going to make you some chamomile tea with a little peppermint in it. That'll take away the sadness. And another thing you might be afraid to ask. Don't you worry if you and the captain want to do a little lovemaking. I don't believe it hurts a thing and pretty soon you'll stick out so far in front you won't be able to manage a good hug."

Mary giggled through her tears. "Tea sounds good. I'll take it upstairs with me." She paused. "Thank you."

Mary slept deeply, cradled in Richard's arms. The next morning, she wrote letters to her mother and sister, telling them of her news. Richard carried the sealed letters to the waterfront and was lucky to encounter a packet that would stop at Marsh Harbour. From there it was just a short distance to Green Turtle Cay.

Sara's reply arrived in just a little more than a week.

"Dearest Mary,

What a surprise to receive the news that you're expecting a baby. I'm even more delighted because I'm also "in a family way." I love that expression! They say it's quite current in Queen Victoria's England. My child will be born about the same time as yours. How fitting for sisters!

My other news is less pleasant. Mother seems to be afflicted with a sort of wasting disease. She was never hearty, but now she is losing weight from her already delicate frame. She seems to be mentally depressed and has become more pious than ever. I spend at least half of every day there and I'm managing the household for her. I'm not sure if Father understands the gravity of her illness. She's complained for so long, I don't think he pays much attention any more.

It was a strange kind of luck that brought John back to Green Turtle Cay with a broken ship. If it hadn't been for that, we'd be ready to leave here by now. Between my pregnancy and Mother's condition, there is no possibility that John and I will come to Key West in the foreseeable future. How I would have loved to spend these months of expectation with you! I'm sending for magazines to help me choose a stylish layette. I'll be glad to share what I learn. I think I'll use the dresser you left behind for the baby's things. I'm sure you won't mind.

Please write soon.

Your loving sister, Sara"

A stylish layette. The dresser. Sara hadn't changed a bit!

Ann's letter came several days later. Mary was glad to have been forewarned.

"Dear child,

The news of your condition brings me such joy! To have two daughters about to give me grandchildren is more than I could have hoped for. I should be very glad to see you here, but of course that's not possible. My health is poor, although no one can explain it. I fear I draw nigh to the grave. Pray it is the Lord's will we see each other again. If we don't meet in this world, we will be together again in heaven. Be well, my child, and pray for your loving mother. Your father sends his love."

Mary lay the letter in her lap and stared. Her grief was nearly as great as if Ann had already died. She might never see her mother again. Ann might never see her grandchild. "Never" stretched out before her and she felt alone and helpless in the face of that bleak and unknowable infinity.

CHAPTER 17

Mary suspected it was just a matter of time before Richard would sail again and she was right. "I figure I'll leave at the end of next week if the weather's good," he announced. "I've talked to several captains down at the pier and they're willing to include me in the chain of wreckers between here and Indian Key."

"Will you go to Green Turtle Cay?"

"I can't imagine why I should," Richard squinted and scratched his head. "We just came from there."

"I want you to visit Mother and carry my letters. I think the sight of you will be the next best thing for her to having me visit. It's all I can think of to do." Mary's voice was taut with anxiety and she pulled at her fingers in her frustration at not being able to go herself. "And I want you to get my cherry dresser before Sara believes she owns it entirely."

"I guess I can do that. I'll even brave the wrath of Sara to retrieve your furniture." He smiled and hugged her.

Mary wrote a brief response to Sara, then embarked on a lengthier letter to her mother. She added to it at least twice a day and soon it became more of a journal than a letter. Mary described details of the household such as the spacious kitchen house and the capacious cistern that sat near to it. She recounted her experiences establishing trade with the shops - the greengrocer who gave her double the change she was owed and his surprise when she pointed out his error; the fishmonger who always had the freshest catch at the best price and even offered pompano sometimes. She wrote about trying to improve the soil in the garden and the curlews that perched in the scrub right next to it, practically asking to be shot and served for dinner. She shared her happiness about her condition and reassured her mother that she felt well and confident. The letter was ten pages long by the time she folded and sealed it. "Have you thought of writing a book?" quipped Richard when she showed him the fat packet of paper.

"Walk with me down to the pier to watch the sunset," he suggested the evening before he was to leave.

It was a clear, brisk evening with a gentle breeze from the northwest that ruffled Mary's skirt. The western pier was a popular gathering place at the end of the day and a small crowd of sailors and shopkeepers and mothers with children had gathered. Mary recognized Emeline Watlington, a prominent wrecker's wife, with three of her daughters. She started when she saw Caroline.

Mary didn't think much about Caroline these days. She'd glimpsed her from behind several times when she shopped on Duval Street. That was inevitable in such a small town. On those occasions, as if by mutual agreement the two women would turn and go in opposite directions. Mary would have liked to avoid her now.

"Let's go down there to the left. It looks less crowded," suggested Mary.

"It's less crowded because you can't see as well from there," replied Richard, slipping his arm around her waist and guiding her to the center of the group. *He doesn't see what's about to happen*, thought Mary. *Either that or he doesn't care*. Richard steered her to stand in the space just to the left of Caroline.

"See how the view is better from here? This may be the most beautiful sunset of the winter!" Caroline snapped her head toward them, evidently startled by Richard's voice. She and Mary were face to face. Caroline's wide eyes and gaping mouth testified to her complete surprise. Summoning all her composure and confidence, Mary tried to be casual, "Why hello. Isn't it a lovely evening?"

"Indeed," replied Caroline. "Good evening, Richard. I hear you are to be congratulated. You're having a baby, aren't you Mary? How sweet. I hope you're feeling well."

You wouldn't know what sweet is, thought Mary bitterly. "I'm feeling very well, thank you." She was relieved of the necessity of further conversation as the sun dipped into the Gulf of Mexico in a radiant explosion of pinks and oranges and purples. Everyone's attention was focused on the natural extravaganza. When Mary thought to look, Caroline had disappeared.

"I think I saw a green flash," said a sailor.

"You've never seen a green flash," replied Richard authoritatively. "If you had, you'd know one when you saw it. There wasn't a flash tonight."

"I remember how you described that in a letter," said Mary. "It's rare, isn't it? I'd love to see it some day."

"You have to watch a lot of sunsets, and even then it's not guaranteed. My grandfather said anyone who sees it will be granted peace of mind. That sounds like a myth to me. I can't say. I've seen several, but I've never been one to worry much anyway. We'll test it on you. You're the worrier in this family." He held her close and pecked her on the forehead. Mary smiled up at him, hoping Caroline looked back and saw.

* * *

The Osprey sailed at dawn and Mary took her usual position waving goodbye from the dock. These partings had become less emotional for her and this morning she felt like a seasoned seaman's wife. She knew what to expect from his absence and what to anticipate upon his return.

She had more time on her hands when she was alone. Some mornings she'd leisurely sort through the fabrics at the dry goods store in search of the softest cotton. In the afternoon she'd stitch some little garments for the baby. When she felt ambitious, she walked inland to investigate the island. The woodland began just minutes from where William Street tapered into a footpath and it was less than an hour's walk to the Atlantic coast. She liked to sit on a rock and eat her lunch as she gazed at the horizon and wondered if a distant speck might be the Osprey or another wrecker's ship. Often she'd take the longer route home, walking around the southern tip of the island and stopping to watch the construction of the new lighthouse.

The path narrowed as it passed next to the mangrove-choked shallows. Nearby was a dilapidated shanty camp that housed about two dozen men. Richard said they were sailors who'd lost their jobs or impoverished themselves through gambling and drink. Mary was more inclined to believe they were decent men down on their luck. None of them had ever threatened her or even spoken to her, for that matter. Nonetheless, she relaxed a little once she passed the encampment and was glad to forsake the remote path for the wider streets of the city.

* * *

When the Osprey returned at the end of April, it was a fine sight. The Touchstone, a big three-masted barque, had foundered on the reef and was refloated after the cargo was removed. Empty, she rode high in the water as she followed the Osprey and the other two wrecking ships into port.

The captain, Miles Francis, couldn't say enough in praise of the salvage operation and offered to go before the magistrate to speak on behalf of Richard and the other wrecker captains who had saved his ship and cargo.

"Of course, it's the insurer's money he'll recommend they give us," said Richard. "But still, it's generous of him to stand up on our behalf. I feel certain we'll receive a favorable judgement.

"I wish you could have seen Francis' face when he noticed your dresser. 'That didn't come off my ship, Sir!' he exclaimed. 'Where did it come from?' I guess he thought I'd been pillaging on the side. I set him straight." Richard chuckled. "There still are plenty of people who think there are pirates hidden in some cove and that maybe we wreckers are some of them disguised under a different flag."

Mary was glad of Richard's success and amused by his stories, but the news from Green Turtle Cay was most important to her.

"Your mother didn't look as sick as I expected," Richard reported. "She must have improved quite a bit from the time she last wrote. Your sister wasn't very happy to see me take the dresser. In the end, your mother took your side and reminded Sara it was your wedding present.

"Seth and I will haul the thing upstairs this afternoon and that's it! We're not moving again because that dresser is too heavy to cart around any more!" He gave her a hug that softened the harshness of his words. "Go now, I know you're dying to read your letters. I'll join you when I've seen to the cargo and the ship."

Mary hid the letters in her skirt pocket as if sunlight might render the ink invisible. She only removed them once she was settled on the wicker rocker at the shady end of the veranda. She unsealed her sister's letter first. It must have been written before Richard claimed the dresser.

"Dearest Mary,

What a pleasure to see your dear Richard again! You can imagine how he and John enjoyed rekindling their friendship and recalling their eventful crossing to Key West in January.

"Mother's condition appears to have improved. I can't say whether the cause is the anticipation of two grandchildren or the nostrum Dr. Padget prescribed. I tasted it one day and thought there was more than a little alcohol in it, but she only takes a little and it seems to help so surely there's no harm.

"I'm feeling well, although my waistline has already begun to disappear. The midwife guesses that my child will be born in early October if not before. She warns me to watch my diet because fat accumulated during pregnancy usually lasts a lifetime. I do want to get back onto my pretty clothes, but I'm awfully fond of pudding, too. It's a difficult choice to make."

Look at that Sara! Jumping ahead to have her baby first! Mary knew it was silly to resent it. After all, Sara wasn't in control of the child's conception. Still, being second in line made Mary feel even more remote. She opened Ann's thin note.

"My dear child,

"Your long letter is such a treasure for me! I shall read it again and again until the pages become frayed and crumble to dust. Then I'll sweep it into an envelope and cherish it as a memento. Only another long letter will save it from becoming a precious relic, so I hope you will write again soon and at length.

"I am following doctor's orders and find that I am calmer and sleep better than before. My appetite comes and goes and I'm no longer losing weight.

"Richard's visit diverted me greatly. Your father was very interested in his reports of Key West. He even suggested that we should move there, too. I don't encourage that. I doubt I could survive such a change."

Yes, I think she has improved, thought Mary. What could her father possibly be thinking of to suggest moving to Key West? Improvement or not, her mother would never be able to support such a strain.

* * *

Richard sailed again in May and life resumed what Mary had come to think of as its "on my own" pace. She didn't mind being alone as much as before because she was preoccupied with herself and the child growing inside her. Every morning she stood naked in front of the mirror to see if her shape had begun to change. In the end, it wasn't the mirror that provided that information - it was the waistband of her skirt. It seemed as if one day it buttoned normally and the next day the ends of the waistband didn't meet, let alone overlap. She looped a short length of yarn through the buttonhole and around the button to hold it closed and chose a blouse with a peplum to cover the arrangement. The length from button to buttonhole grew steadily. She saw the change from one week to the next.

Mary had always been slim in a boyish kind of way and she'd never been vain about her figure. Now she began to feel perturbed by her growing waistline and swelling breasts. Phoebe sewed some ample shifts from bright-colored floral cottons, but Mary put them aside thinking they were ungainly. However, she began to see the wisdom of a temporary wardrobe - at least she'd be comfortable. But she knew once she switched to the maternity clothes, she'd be expected to stay home. Women in advanced pregnancy didn't shop or stroll on the beach. She was jealous of her freedom, so she tied another length of yarn to the first and left the bottom button of the over-blouse undone.

One day as she strolled along the mangrove path, she felt a thumping against the inside of her abdomen. Alarmed, she sat down on a pile of wood. There was another thumping, slightly to the right of the first. She put both hands on her belly and waited. Nothing. She felt silly sitting there holding herself and decided to resume her walk. As she stood, there it was again! She walked a few steps more and nothing happened, so she set out at her normal pace. Wham! This time it was much more vigorous than before and the pounding repeated itself in a slow, steady pattern. Then she realized what was going on. The baby had quickened and was drumming its arms and legs against her insides! Mary laughed aloud. "You've got my attention now. Stop!"

Obediently, the baby stopped kicking.

"That's more like it," Mary said as she set out for home. "You've gone to sleep now, have you? Well, you rest and grow because I want a big strong child. Are you a boy? I think you are. I'm going to call you Richard, just like your father."

The baby was either asleep or resting. Mary couldn't feel it move at all. Or was it just being attentive? She was quite sure it could hear and she continued her monologue in a quiet, intimate tone.

"You have a wonderful life to look forward to, Richard. Your father is handsome and he's richer every time he sails back into port because he's a bold wrecking captain. You'll have good clothes and a fine clean house to grow up in and I'll buy you lots of toys and books. I know you'll share my love of reading and nature. When you're old enough, your father will teach you the ways of the ocean and one day you'll be a great captain like he is. You'll marry a pretty wife who loves you as much as I love your father and your children will be as handsome and smart as you are yourself. Then when we get old, you'll take care of us, and we'll spend our last days playing with our grandchildren and watching them grow."

The baby kicked her again strongly. "Ooof! Am I keeping you awake, little Richard? Or is it too much all at once, this happy life you're going to lead? I don't mean to make you a father quite so fast! You'll have years to get used to that idea. I'm certainly not ready to be a grandmother. After all, you're my first child and you're not even born yet." There were three more taps, much gentler than what had come before, then nothing.

"I'm glad you have a sense of propriety, my child. It wouldn't do for me to be seen chatting into thin air and we're coming back into town now. She patted her stomach and walked on as if nothing unusual had happened. Phoebe had said that once she felt the child's movement, she could feel confident it was healthy and well. She felt a giggly gaiety almost like when she first knew she was pregnant. When she reached home, she went straight to the kitchen house where Phoebe had just hung the laundry tub to drain on the outside wall.

"Phoebe, the baby's moving. I can feel it!"

Phoebe turned, her big smile shining in her dark face like a quarter moon in the summer night's sky. "That's just wonderful, Miss Mary. Just wonderful!"

Whatever the future held for mother and child, the present became a field of conflict. The issue was sleep. Until now, her condition hadn't prevented Mary from enjoying most of her normal activities. Unfortunately, the child was predisposed to nocturnal exercise. The thumping began as soon as she went to bed. She could visualize the baby as it kicked and waved its arms inside of her, keeping her wide-awake. When she rolled from side to side or got up and walked around the room, the baby seemed to rest, but Mary would no sooner lie down and fall asleep than the activity would start again. In contrast, the child scarcely moved during the day. Mary was so tired she didn't move around much, either.

"You'd best see if you can take a little nap in the afternoons," advised Phoebe. "It's not good for you to be so worn down and it's not good for the baby, either."

"I hate to go to bed like a sick person," protested Mary.

"You're not sick, honey, but you will be if you don't take care of yourself. Look at those big dark circles under your eyes. That's not normal. Not for you."

So Mary changed her ways and spent more time resting and napping. The baby accommodated her by being still in the afternoon and she gratefully enjoyed the uninterrupted rest. At the same time, she realized her method of adjusting her wardrobe to her growing waist wasn't working any more.

"That's a good idea, Miss Mary," said Phoebe the first time Mary came to breakfast in one of the new shifts. "It's not for me to tell you what to wear, but it's high time you did something to cover up that middle of yours. You're too big for your regular things in spite of all the good ideas you've had to make them fit."

* * *

Richard returned to port one afternoon soon after the summer solstice. Mary was napping. She didn't hear his foot on the stair or the quiet squeak of the knob.

"Mary, I'm home," he said softly, so as not to startle her. At the sound of his voice she rolled to face him and sat up drowsily.

"Well look at you!" he exclaimed. "I've just been gone a few weeks, but it looks like I've got twice the wife I had when I left."

Twice the wife! The words confirmed Mary's worst imaginings. She looked fat and stodgy, even to Richard. She looked at him. "I feel ugly enough," she muttered between tight lips. "Please don't make it worse."

"I didn't mean you look ugly. It's just that you've changed a lot in such a short time!" He sat next to her on of the bed and stroked her hair. Finally, Mary looked up at him and smiled.

"We have a surprise for you." She took his hand and put it on her belly on the right side where she'd just felt the baby squirming.

"My God, it's alive in there! Mary, it's not hurting you is it? That fellow's strong. It's sure to be a boy with that kind of strength. A son! I'm going to have a son!"

"We won't know that for sure until it's born, but if it is a boy, I want to name him Richard."

Richard buried his head on her lap and reached all the way around her in a gentle hug. He caught his breath in a poorly disguised sob and Mary felt the wetness of his tears penetrate the thin material of her shift and moisten her legs.

* * *

Mary was happy to discover this tenderness and consideration in Richard. He was as assertive as ever in business and with his crew, but at home it was almost embarrassing how he spoiled her, serving her plate with the best morsels and smoothing the sheets before she lay down. But she knew not to let herself become too spoiled because soon enough he would sail again. Sure enough, July wasn't half over when he announced his next foray.

Writing to Richard, Sara, and her mother helped pass the long days when Mary no longer traversed the island or walked into town. There wasn't much to say because one day was very much like the next, but she talked about the weather and Phoebe's progress with the garden and her own continuing good health. There didn't seem to be any reason to dwell on the persistent late night antics of the little devil inside her. She wondered if Sara's letters glossed over her discomfort, too. Her sister certainly didn't mention any negative aspects of her pregnancy except her constant temptation to indulge in desserts. *She'll never get back into her clothes,* thought Mary. *No doubt she'll enjoy having a new wardrobe.*

Richard came home in four weeks, then sailed again in August. When he returned at the end of September, he hadn't been successful at wrecking, but he brought a letter from Sara that was given him by the captain of a schooner headed from the Bahamas to New England. Richard gave Mary the letter unopened as they sat together in the parlor.

"I was lucky to anchor near Indian Key when he did," he said. "Otherwise Sara's letter might have gone all the way up the coast and back before it reached you. Come on, open it. I want to hear what she has to say."

Mary read aloud,

"Dearest Sister,

Our little family now numbers three. Cynthia Ann was born on Sunday, September 12. She's healthy, nurses strongly, and sleeps quietly much of the time."

"How could Sara's child be other than perfect?" Mary interjected, laughing.

"Mother spends most of every day at my house doting on me and little Cynthia. Sometimes her presence wears on John. He spends quite a bit of time at his shipbuilding lately. Father stops by in the afternoon. He holds the baby until she starts to fidget or cry, then that's the end of his visit. I wonder if he was impatient with us when we were little.

"I won't go into detail about the actual experience of child bearing, but I'd be less than honest if I pretended there was any pleasure in it. Right now I'd be quite content to limit my family to this one beautiful girl."

She went on with a detailed description of the smoothness of the baby's skin and the clarity of her blue eyes and how her toes seemed to be in constant motion.

"I was shocked to see that she was born without a hair on her head, but Mother assures me I was the same and you know how much hair I have now."

Richard listened attentively as Mary read. "I guess my next voyage had better be the last until after our boy is born," he observed. "There's no mother or sister to be with you, so you'll have to make do with me and Phoebe."

Mary was glad he'd thought of that himself, but it worried her that he had his heart set on a son. He'd be very disappointed if the baby was a girl.

CHAPTER 18

Mary's labor started a little after midnight with gentle cramps. She rolled over on her side and gently rubbed her belly and whispered to the baby to be still. When the pains continued, she woke Richard and together they stroked her stomach. Without warning, a rush of warm fluid poured between her legs and soaked the bedclothes.

"I think I'd better get Phoebe," Richard said. He hastily rolled out of bed and pulled on his breeches and boots.

Mary stood to remove the wet bedding, but a strong contraction bent her over and she sat down again involuntarily. She wrapped a dry corner of the sheet tightly around her shoulders and rocked from side to side dreading the next contraction. It seemed like an hour before she heard Phoebe's step on the stair.

"Don't you worry, Miss Mary. I'm here to help you and everything's going to be all right. Let me spread a fresh sheet for you to lie on. Now, you just lie back down and rest." Mary obediently leaned back on the pillows. "Here's a nice cloth I just soaked in water. You suck on that and I'll make it fresh whenever you want. If you start to hurt, you just bite down on it and it'll help." Phoebe pulled the chair next to the bed and held Mary's hand in her lap stroking it gently with her calloused fingers.

"Where's Richard? I want him with me," Mary pled as the contractions strengthened. "I want him with me now!"

"I told the captain to go down to the waterfront. There's nothin' he can do to help here and we don't want to make him worry. I'll go get him when it's time for him to meet his child."

As the pains got stronger and closer, Mary forgot about him for a while, then she blamed him for her suffering.

"That bastard! This is all his fault! I can't stand any more pain and he's out there walking around as if nothing was happening. I'll never let him touch me again. I've learned my lesson." Mary rolled her head from side to side and arched her back as another contraction burned around her abdomen and down her spine. Phoebe slid a fresh wet cloth between her lips.

The labor quieted for a while and Mary rested, eyes closed. Her breath came softly and shallowly. Phoebe slipped out of the room and quickly came back with fresh cloths and towels, her shiny sewing scissors, a bottle of brandy, and another bowl of water. As the sun mounted in the sky, Mary squinted at the brightness of the light that squeezed through the louvered shutters.

"Phoebe, will it be much longer?" she whispered. Her tears ran down the sides of her face and pooled in her ears. Sweat glistened on her forehead and darkened the roots of her hair.

"The baby'll come in its own good time. We're gettin' there. Just try to be patient. Breathe deep and slow. Think about doing that."

With that, the contractions started again, harder than before. Phoebe soaked the cloth in brandy and Mary bit down on it as she sucked. Phoebe went to the foot of the bed and pulled Mary toward her by her feet. "You put your knees up in the air now and spread them." She raised her voice. "Breathe slow and strong like I said. Every time it hurts you push with all your strength to help it come out."

Mary gasped in pain. "Get it out! Get it out of me!" she shrieked.

"Push hard now, honey. Push!"

Finally the little head burst into the air, followed by shoulders, chest, stomach, legs and feet. Phoebe accepted the infant onto a clean towel. It screamed just as vigorously as Mary had done during her labor. Mary sank against the mattress as Phoebe held the baby up in the air by its feet. Well, there was no question about it's being a boy! Mary giggled at the sight of its bright red testicles sticking out from between its thighs. Then she recoiled with horror as Phoebe took the sharp-pointed scissors, dipped them in the brandy, and leaned between Mary's raised knees.

"What are you doing?" Mary wailed. "Don't hurt him!"

"I'm not hurting anybody. I'm just cutting him separate from you. He's ready to live on his own now." She paused and before Mary knew what was happening, Phoebe lay the baby across Mary's deflated stomach and he stopped crying.

"Oh, look at him!" exclaimed Mary. "He's the tiniest little man in the world. Phoebe, he's beautiful!" She held up his hands and then his feet. "Ten fingers and ten toes. His eyes look blue, like Richard's, don't they? I wonder if his hair will stay dark like it is. He'll be a very handsome man with that combination."

"Only a mother could call that bloody mess beautiful," laughed Phoebe. "And you don't look like much yourself, if you'll pardon my saying so. Come on, pull yourself back up on the pillows. I'm going to try to clean you two up so maybe Captain Richard will recognize you as his own."

Phoebe took the infant onto her lap, rubbed him vigorously with soap suds and rinsed him with clean water. When he started to howl, she laughed. "You're a strong one, aren't you young fellow? Those lungs are mighty powerful for such a little thing." She put the baby on his stomach on a fresh sheet she had arranged on the floor and progressed to the mother. Mary lay back passively, and let Phoebe wash her as she enjoyed the sensation of the warm water on her skin and the absence of pain.

"Hold on to me and stand up. I need to wash your back and you can't lie on those bloody sheets anymore."

Phoebe wrapped a strong arm around Mary's waist and helped her over to lean against the dresser. She quickly finished washing her back and changed the bed. Then she helped Mary lie down, drawing up the fresh sheet and laying the now-sleeping baby diagonally across her chest. The child hardly stirred. Exhausted from her exertion, Mary drifted between consciousness and sleep. Phoebe slipped out of the room with another load of soiled laundry.

* * *

When Mary woke Richard sat stiffly beside the bed with his hands, folded in his lap. He stared at her as if waiting for the answer to some unasked question.

"Are you all right?" he asked. "I heard you screaming." He moved to stand by the bed and stroked her hair.

"I'm all right now." She saw no reason to elaborate. The pain was over and she didn't want to relive it in the telling.

"I still want to name him Richard," she said. "You never told me if you agree."

"By all means! He'll be Richard just like his father. I want to hold him!" He leaned down and scooped up the baby in his big hands. Young Richard bawled heartily. Richard held him against his shoulder. When that didn't work, he sat down again and laid his son on his stomach across his knees. The change only produced more howling and a flurry of kicking. Richard's enthusiasm seemed somewhat dampened by the baby's crying and his own inadequacy. "I've never been around babies and I haven't an inkling how to make it stop. What should I do?"

"Turn him over and put your finger in his mouth. Maybe he'll suck on it. Don't forget this is my first one, too. I'm not sure I have all the answers."

But she could feel her confidence growing. *So this is what they call a maternal instinct*, she thought. *The nanny goats and the hound bitches seem always to know what to do and I'm learning, too.*

The finger didn't work, either. Mary pushed herself up against the pillows and Richard handed the child back to her. She dropped the sheet away from her right breast and cradled his head in the crook of her elbow. The baby nuzzled her with his nose, then tipped his head and started to suck forcefully. "Oh," Mary gasped involuntarily. Then she relaxed and smiled.

* * *

Mary wholeheartedly embraced motherhood. She woke cheerfully to the early morning cries that heralded young Richard's hunger and lifted him from his wicker cradle to sit by the window to nurse. She enjoyed his pulling at her breast as his sucking relieved her early-morning fullness. She managed every part of his life except the laundry, which she left to Phoebe.

Only once in a while did she allow herself to think of her other baby that was never born. She'd wonder briefly if it had been a boy or a girl and whether it would have brought her as much pleasure as young Richard. She vaguely realized that part of her maternal devotion was driven by guilt over the dead baby. But she didn't allow herself to dwell on that and when her thoughts became too disturbing, she buried them under the minutia of practical concerns for the household and her living son.

"I never thought to enjoy such menial tasks," she wrote to Sara. "Here I am nursing like a sow and changing dirty nappies and bathing this little creature who smells like sour milk half the time. I seldom leave the house without him. Our streets are so rough that a pram wouldn't make it a block without tipping. At first I carried him in my arms, but he's already gained weight and that was becoming tiring. Phoebe and I concocted a sling that goes around my neck and behind one shoulder. It's like a little hammock and he seems to be comfortable. I think the fresh air does us both good.

"'Richard has moved back into my bed. Although I'm still bleeding and too sore for passion, his warm presence completes my world. I have never been happier."

"Dear Sister," Sara replied. "I'm amused by your fascination with maternal drudgery. Personally, I'm eternally grateful to have two servants now to keep the house and do much of the work involved with little Cynthia. I've engaged a wet nurse for the nights; I put the baby to bed in a second cradle in the nurse's room and retrieve her in the morning after John and I enjoy a good night's sleep. We've always been different, haven't we? You wanted to walk in the woods and root in the garden while I preferred needlework and ladies' meetings."

Yes, thought Mary. *We're very different. I wonder how two women sharing the same parents and the same childhood home could have such contrasting views!*

Mary kept her son with her almost constantly. She bought a cradle for the first floor so she could have him nearby as she sat in the parlor or ate in the dining room. She became a familiar sight on Duval Street and along the wooded paths where she walked every morning with him slung across her torso. At night she was lulled to sleep by his quiet breathing punctuated by a few squeaky hiccoughs and an occasional gurgle as he slept next to the bed.

"Mary, may I have your attention for a minute?" Richard's words were clipped and formal. Mary joined him in the parlor wondering at his annoyance. As she transferred young Richard from his sling to the cradle, her husband sat heavily on the sofa. "Mary, please! May I talk to my wife for once without the presence of that child? Take him to Phoebe. He needs changing anyway." He wrinkled his nose in disgust. "I want to talk to you alone!"

What was this about? He'd never spoken to her like that. Mary grabbed up her son and hurried from the room. She hastily deposited him in Phoebe's arms. "Just for a minute. I'll be right back." The baby started to cry, but Mary didn't pause. She was barely back into the parlor when Richard started.

"Mary, it's been more than six weeks since Richard was born. Do you think he's thriving?"

"You know how well he's doing," Mary replied. "He's eating well and gaining weight. I'm very proud of his growth because I care for him almost exclusively," she added.

"I know you do. You care for him to the exclusion of your husband." Richard folded his arms across his chest and tapped his booted foot on the pine floor. His voice rose with every sentence.

"You never go anywhere without that baby hanging off of you and you seldom speak of anything else. I arranged to stay home until after Christmas so I could be with you and the child, but at this point I question my wisdom. As far as I can tell, I could have sailed the day he was born for all the difference it would make to you. I swear, I feel like I've served my purpose by siring the little brat and now I've been discarded."

Mary's eyes widened and she spread her hands over her heart as if she had been wounded and needed to staunch the bleeding. "How can you possibly call a poor innocent child a brat? Have you become so heartless?" Now she was shouting, too. "The baby depends on me for his life. I feed him and keep him safe and love him as no one else can. Are you jealous of my motherly affection for your own son? Is there no space in your heart for this new little life? I'm not sure I know you anymore!"

Richard stood and opened his mouth as if to go on; then he closed it again and pursed his lips. He strode out the door, nudging Mary out of his way. She flinched at the sharp crack of wood striking wood as he slammed the front door and banged down the front stairs.

Mary stared at the door and shook her head to clear it. He couldn't have meant what he said! Equally astonishing was the anger she felt for Richard. She was consumed by righteous resentment in defense of her child and her motherhood. She extended her long arms and clenched her fists in the folds of her skirt, gritting her teeth as her mind teemed with accusations. How dare he?!

Her rigidity disintegrated into trembling. She collapsed onto the sofa and breathed deeply to try to control her shaking. A cool determination replaced her anger. He had callously criticized her, but she wouldn't allow him to intrude on her baby's well-being. She would wrap that precious little life in a protective cocoon of maternal love and devotion that would defend him from every possible threat.

Mary went back to the kitchen and, without comment, gathered up her son. She carried him to her favorite spot on the east veranda by the front door and gently rocked him in the old cane-seated chair, humming tunelessly as the early winter darkness began to fall. She tried to nurse, but tension held back the milk and he sucked futilely at her hard breast. She'd have to try again later. Finally, she rebuttoned her blouse and went to the dining room where Phoebe had set the table. Richard hadn't come home yet. He'd probably run into friends in town. He'd done that a couple of times and it didn't surprise her anymore. She didn't bother with the cradle and held young Richard on her lap. The richness of the spicy chowder and the crustiness of the warm loaf escaped her as she picked at her meal. When she finished, she nursed little Richard, tucked him in his cradle, and went straight to bed.

Richard wasn't home the next morning, nor the morning after that. Mary didn't know whether to be worried or angry. As much as she hated having to go looking for him, she couldn't think of anything else to do.

"I'm going out," she said as she loaded the baby into his sling. Phoebe acknowledged the announcement with a silent nod. *I wonder what she's thinking*, Mary asked herself as she walked down William Street to the waterfront. *I wonder if she knows what's become of Richard. I don't want to ask her. I don't want to explain that miserable scene.*

Soon Mary saw there was no need to ask anyone. The Osprey was gone from its mooring. Richard had gone to sea without so much as a fare-thee-well. Was he so angry that he'd left her for good? She sat heavily on a flour crate, careless of the white powder that puffed up and coated her black skirt. She hugged her baby against her chest and hunched over him protectively as she stared to the west. Where had he gone? When would he come home? The calm waters of the Gulf lapped gently against the shore. If they knew the answers, they weren't telling.

"I want you to know he didn't come to me. Things are bad enough without your wondering about that."

Mary jerked upright. She hadn't seen Caroline for months, but she recognized her voice. She jerked upright and turned to face her. "What?" she asked. Caroline rested her shopping bag on a barrel before she spoke again.

"Probably everybody in Key West knows more about your husband's whereabouts than you do. He got roaring drunk down on Duval Street a couple of nights ago and then he went around shouting how he'd lost his wife to his baby boy. I'm told he finally collapsed right about where you're sitting and spent the night there, sleeping it off. The next morning he took that black man and some other fellow I've never seen before and set sail.

"Like I said, he didn't come to me. You're going to wonder when you start thinking again, and you've got enough troubles as it is."

"Where did he go, then?" Mary asked feebly.

"He didn't tell anybody where he was going. He left early in the morning and didn't take time to load provisions. He won't be at sea long without food or water. He'll probably be back within the week. It's none of my business, but what was all that yelling about?"

Mary stiffened and the baby started to cry. "It's exactly none of your business. Please leave me alone." She stood and held her son to her shoulder as she paced slowly along the edge of the dock to sooth him. Ignoring the rebuff, Caroline walked along beside her.

"If you were more neighborly, you'd have heard by now that I make things my business when they interest me. I'm going to tell you a couple of things whether you want to hear them or not.

"The first is this: Yes, I was in love with your captain. In love. It wasn't a business arrangement for me and I believe there was a time when he cared about me, too. That's over. Period. Stop. Forget about it. It's only a fading memory for me. Pleasant, but fading." She smiled.

"The second thing I want to say is this: You thought you could live your life alone in your nice house with your precious baby and your handsome husband. Well, that's falling apart already, isn't it? You'd better get out and make a friend or two. Granted, there aren't many women on this little island, but the ones who are here are mostly good. I include myself in that group, by the way. You've got no family here, so you're going to have to substitute some friends. No woman can be happy without other women to talk to and give her advice. What do you have to say?" Caroline pivoted herself in front of Mary so they were face to face.

Mary didn't know what to say. She didn't question Richard's fidelity. She knew he was happy at home, at least until now. It was Caroline's analysis of her solitude that disturbed her. She was right. During her pregnancy Mary had sometimes wished for another woman to talk with, but she had made only a few acquaintances here, not friends. She knew better than to talk with them about personal things. That required the intimacy of friendship, which didn't happen overnight.

"Come on. Let's get out of the sun." Caroline's voice softened as she lifted her shopping bag and slung it over her shoulder. She led the way to the red-shuttered house, ushered Mary into the parlor, and sat down on the sofa. Mary sat on the edge of a chair, unsure how this visit was going to work out.

"May I hold him?" Caroline asked. Mary raised her eyebrows in surprise.

"I never had a child," Caroline spread her hands open on her lap, palms up. She studied them as if she was trying to read her own fortune in their creases. "As it turns out, I never will, now. But there was a time when I was an innocent bride and I was filled with dreams of a family. I got pregnant right away and I thought I was on the verge of a perfect life. I didn't know that George - that was my husband's name - got mean when he drank. And he drank often. When I told him about the baby, he pushed me hard and I fell down on some stones near the water. One hit me full in the stomach. It hurt something terrible. I started to bleed the next day and it got worse and worse. And then there was no more baby."

Caroline looked up and Mary saw in her eyes how much she had suffered. "I didn't have anyplace to go, no family or anything. So I stayed with George until he died. He was killed in a brawl one night. He was drinking peaceably with an English captain, but then he insulted him by making fun of the queen, of all things. The captain defended Her Majesty's honor by pulling a stiletto out of his boot and stabbing George right through the heart until the point came out his back.

"I had to make a living and this business presented itself," Caroline indicated the house with her eyes. "It wasn't so bad, not after what I'd been through with George."

Mary lifted Richard out of his sling and laid him on Caroline's lap. The child looked up at her and wrinkled up his face, but then he smiled and cooed. He reached out for her hand. Caroline hesitated briefly, then she extended her index finger for him to hold. She inclined her head as if to study the child, but when she looked up, Mary saw the sheen of unshed tears over her eyes.

"I guess you're not the only one who needs someone to talk to," observed Caroline. "Thank you for listening." She circled a finger in Richard's hair twisting it into little moist curls.

"We may have more in common than you know," said Mary. "And you're right. I don't have a single friend and maybe it's time I did." A relaxed intimacy had grown between them as Caroline talked. She said, "Maybe Richard was right. Maybe I've neglected him and spoiled the baby."

"What's important is that he thinks you neglected him," Caroline replied. "That's what you need to deal with when he comes home."

"If he comes home," Mary murmured, lowering her eyes.

"He'll come back. You just be ready for him when he does."

CHAPTER 19

Constantly straining for the sound of Richard's step on the stair, Mary barely slept. She had to force herself to eat for the sake of the baby she was nursing. When the afternoon gusts whistled in the leaves of the egg fruit tree, she imagined the Osprey being tossed about in the wind. In the morning when the air and water were still, she feared the ship was becalmed and Richard would starve before regaining shore. "You hear a lot about the danger from high winds," she'd once overheard him warn Seth. "But in the horse latitudes there's equal danger from unfilled sails and still water. Key West is even further into the horse latitudes than the Bahamas and we'll do well to be aware." She shivered at the thought that his words might have been prophetic.

On Tuesday morning, when Richard had been gone for three full days, Mary left the baby with Phoebe and, for the first time since her confinement, walked alone to the Atlantic shore. She was surprised to notice that the gentle slope of the wooded path that had once been an easy stroll now had her panting. By the time she reached the watershed that led to the ocean, sweat dampened her blouse and her heart was pounding. Mary frowned. She hadn't realized her new domestic routine had compromised her ability to roam confidently in the rough areas of the island.

She leaned against a big limestone rock that overlooked the low tide shore line. The beach was strewn with rocks and fragments of coral. So different from the beaches on Green Turtle Cay! There she would slip out of her shoes and walk barefoot for miles swerving in and out of the gentle surf, her feet caressed by the fine white sand. Here she could feel the sharp rocks through the shoe leather and wondered if they'd cut right through the soles to her feet. Everything was more difficult and complicated on this new island.

Mary sat in the shade of the sentinel rock arranging her skirt beneath her as a cushion against the stones. Unperturbed by her presence, the fat gray and white gulls whined and chattered. They strutted on silly twig-like legs with knobby knees and three-toed webbed feet. They'd briefly swoop off alone, but soon returned to the flock. Further off, brown pelicans floated, then rose, broad wings laboring to lift heavy bodies. Finally airborne, they cruised over the water watching, watching. Then they dove headfirst straight into the surf and emerged with bulging pouches, content to float again as they digested their catch. Lulled by the waves' rhythm and the avian routines, Mary's thoughts began to drift away. She came back to her senses with a start as her lolling head bumped against the rock. She held her head in her hands, remembering the awful argument.

"I could have sailed the day young Richard was born for all the difference it would make to you. I've served my purpose by siring your little brat and now I'm being discarded," he'd said. He was jealous and his pride was injured, that was for sure. She saw now that the baby had become an obsession. In some ghostly way, Michael's child was present in Richard's as if the first one had left particles inside of her that were incorporated into this baby. The one helpless infant embodied her love for both men and her sense of loss of the first child. Baby Richard had lost his identity and had become an amalgam of people and feelings that had nothing to do with him. Mary understood now how Richard might think she'd treated him as though he'd served his purpose, just like he'd said. She didn't want to cast him off like a worn garment; she loved him. Most of all, she didn't want to be alone! Her head throbbed and she squinted far out to sea as if the watery reaches of the east would show her how to clean up the murky mess she had unwittingly created.

The sun was high in the sky before fullness in her breasts and a gnawing in her stomach reminded her it was time for her own and baby Richard's lunch. She brushed the chalky coral dust from her skirt as she stood and turned toward home, this time taking the path through the mangroves past Whitehead Point. She didn't see much change in the homeless. What surprised her was the sight of a woman passing among the lean-to's. Her back was turned, but Mary recognized the curly red-blond hair.

"Caroline, is that you?" she shouted.

Caroline turned and beckoned enthusiastically.

"What are you doing here?" Mary asked as they met halfway between the path and the camp.

"I could ask the same of you," replied Caroline, pushing her unruly hair out of her eyes. "I come out here as often as I have time. I bring leftover food and sometimes I buy a little extra, especially fresh vegetables and fruit. These folks are in terrible shape. People say they're just degenerates, but I don't know. Every one of them has a story of how bad luck put him here. Boats ran aground or sank. Sickness and injury kept them from work. Families died tragically. The hurricane just made things worse. It would be foolish to swallow every tale I'm told, but there's truth in there along with imagination and lies and I'm gratified when I help them out a little. They eat only what they pull out of the sea or scavenge from the garbage cans at night and they're almost all sick in one way or another, so my fresh food and little ministrations seem huge to them and I feel like a goddess of mercy. I guess it's selfish of me in a way, but I don't think there's anything wrong with that." She smiled and took Mary by the arm. "Come, meet your neighbors."

"I don't know," said Mary. "I'm surprised you feel safe here. I've heard that these men are rapists and thieves."

"A lot of people would rather pretend these folks don't exist because they're not attractive and they need so much. And they can be ungrateful and resentful. They're not all men, you know. There's a woman here, too. She's a brave one! I wouldn't come here at night, but I've never felt threatened during the day. Come on."

Mary let herself be drawn down the path. She was speechless at the sight of the crude structures. Boards that seemed to be from houses and boats were propped and tied together with sails and tarps laid over for roofs. Even worse than the look of the place was its smell. Mary had never known such a stench of human excrement and garbage. She covered her nose and mouth with her hand and gasped.

"Sanitation is a terrible problem. It should be better soon, though, I've just talked the mayor into having some men come out to dig privies. I convinced him it's in the town's best interest. If diseases take hold here, they could easily spread to the rest of the population." Caroline winked conspiratorially. "It's amazing what can get done when people in power recognize it as their own self interest."

Mary didn't speak again until they emerged on the other side of the shanty village. She dropped her hand from her face and asked, "I didn't see any people. Where are they?"

"They stay in their huts in the heat of the day. You don't see much of them except in the morning and late afternoon. Many of them are so depressed they just sit and rock back and forth and stare at the ground. Sometimes it depresses me too, when I think of what their lives are like. I have to remind myself that I'm doing what I can and that it makes a difference."

The mention of food triggered an involuntary rush to Mary's breasts and she felt warm milk run down her skin inside her chemise. She was long overdue at home and if she didn't get on her way the floodgates would open uncontrollably. "I must go!" she exclaimed.

Caroline scrutinized her. "Are you repelled by what you've seen here?" she asked.

"I need time to think about it," replied Mary. "My immediate problem is that if I don't get home and feed my baby, I think I'll burst!" She cradled her heavy breasts in her hands and rolled her eyes.

"I see what you mean," said Caroline grinning. "Has Richard come back yet?"

"He wasn't there when I left." The admission stung like vinegar on an open cut, bringing her attention back to her fears.

* * *

As soon as she got home, Mary went straight to the kitchen house. Phoebe was pacifying the hungry baby by giving him a cloth soaked in chicken broth to suck on.

"He's been wishing you'd get home, Miss Mary." Phoebe's tone held more humor than reproach.

"I didn't intend to stay out so long," replied Mary as she unbuttoned her blouse and took the child in her arms. She sat down on the bench and put the child straight to her breast. Gentle slurping punctuated the otherwise silent scene as the baby satisfied his hunger and Mary enjoyed relief.

"The captain came home while you were gone."

Mary started. She'd missed his arrival when she was on the other side of the island! The baby lost her nipple and began to fret.

"When was that?"

"I'd say it was about midmorning. I'd finished sweeping the yard and started peeling potatoes for stew. He didn't say much except he wanted bread and cheese and tea taken up to the bedroom. I haven't seen him since. He looked as dirty as when he comes back from a long voyage and his eyes were red. I figure I'll drag out the bath tub this afternoon. He needs it!"

Mary's mantle of anxiety for his safety fell away and was replaced by concern for mending the fabric of their marriage. She rearranged herself and baby Richard reapplied himself to the business of lunch. She would have liked to hurry his feeding, but there was nothing she could do to rush him. *It's probably just as well,* she thought. *I'd better organize my thoughts. I want to be calm and reasonable. I'll accept some blame for our quarrel. At the same time, he must honor my responsibilities as a mother. The most important thing is to make him feel appreciated again.*

Young Richard finally finished and started to doze off. Mary kissed his forehead and passed him to Phoebe. "Will you burp him and lay him in his cradle? I want to see the captain."

She closed her blouse and straightened the gathers of her skirt, brushing off the last of the coral dust. She loosened her hair and smoothed it.

The thirteen steps to the second floor seemed like hundreds. She held her breath in apprehension as she stepped onto the veranda and paused to compose herself before opening the outside door. The bedroom door was ajar.

Richard was asleep. He lay on his stomach diagonally across the bed and his back rose and fell with each heavy breath. He hadn't taken off his boots, let alone his clothes. His unshaven face lay against the smooth white pillow and his scarred left hand hung down as if he had fallen asleep as he reached for the last piece of bread from the tray on the floor.

She tiptoed to the bed and lifted the tray to the dresser. Careful not to disturb him, she moved the straight-backed chair next to the bed and sat. Richard breathed rhythmically and he dug his head a little deeper into the down pillow.

Mary folded her hands in her lap and watched him sleep. She'd never observed him like this. His slack muscles weren't those of the captain who commanded the seas. Shut off from the worries of his trade, he was almost infantile in his repose. How odd that she hadn't noticed before! Their baby had the same pointed ears as his father. They were much the same, weren't they, not only in their physical characteristics, but in their dependence on her? Maternal protectiveness was a side of herself she hadn't known before the birth of their son, and now she realized those feelings weren't limited to her child, but extended to his father. She lifted his hand to her lap, enclosing its roughness in her softness and warming his cool fingertips. She didn't know how long she sat there before Richard opened his eyes and withdrew his hand abruptly, startled to see her.

"What!" he exclaimed in confusion.

Mary's planned speech slipped out of her head. "I love you," she said simply.

Richard rolled to his side and stared at her. She felt as if those blue eyes looked right into her heart, although she couldn't guess what he saw. She squirmed inside. What was he thinking? He reached out and took her hands in his. Without hesitation, he pulled her to lie beside him. He wrapped his arms around her so firmly that she could hardly move, but then, she didn't want to. The familiar contours of his body and the warm odor of his sweat comforted her like nothing else could.

"I love you, too," he whispered.

They lay motionless until the sky began to darken and the aroma of simmering stew and baking bread drifted through the cracked door.

Richard kissed Mary's forehead and swung his legs over the edge of the bed. "Will you think I love you less if I confess that I'm famished? I haven't had a decent meal in days," he said as he stood.

"Will you feel rejected if I insist that you bathe before you eat? Phoebe said she'd drag out the tub and I'll bet the water is hot. I'll sit with you, if you like." She extended her arms and he pulled her to stand in front of him.

"We'll strike a bargain then. Where's my son? I didn't mean to never see him again!"

"He's with Phoebe. I'm sure he's fine," Mary said.

They excused Phoebe from the kitchen and Richard dropped his dirty clothes in the corner. Mary retrieved the baby from his cradle and nursed him while his father soaked away the dirt of his trip and gazed at them. "You look like a madonna with the child at your breast and your hair tumbling down over him." Mary smiled. *How close I came to losing this,* she thought.

Richard dried and put on clean clothes and Mary returned the child to Phoebe. From now on, they would eat alone. Richard wolfed down his food. Mary tried to be more decorous, but she'd missed lunch and was ravenous, too. The night was mild and after supper they reclaimed their son and sat on the veranda.

"Let me hold that mouse." Richard picked up his son. "That's what he looks like, you know. Those pointy ears make him look like a big bald pink mouse."

Mary laughed for the first time in days. "His ears are just like yours, you know."

"Hmmphh!" Richard grimaced. "And what did he learn while I was gone? Does he walk yet or talk? Maybe he learned the names of the stars so he can navigate a ship one day."

"He mostly ate and slept. You'll have to wait for those other achievements."

When they went upstairs, Mary pushed the cradle away from the bed and set it in the corner by the dresser out of the way of drafts. The baby didn't disturb his parents until the rooster announced the sunrise.

CHAPTER 20

The next morning, Mary savored the details of her domestic routine even more than before. She fed and bathed her son, hugging him close and kissing the soft skin on top of his head before laying him down for his nap. Then she trimmed Richard's hair and sideburns. When he went to the waterfront, she tidied the bedroom. After a solitary lunch she decided to visit Caroline. She was curious about Caroline's work at Whitehead Point and warmed by the prospect of female friendship. It was a good chance to practice some independence, so she left baby Richard in Phoebe's care, wrapped a woolen shawl around her shoulders against the early winter chill, and set off down William Street.

Caroline opened the heavy red door to welcome her. " I saw the Osprey returned," said Caroline. "How did it go?"

"We are reconciled," said Mary. She saw no need to go into detail.

A few embers glowed in the fireplace and the women pulled their chairs close to the warmth. "I wonder if Richard had built our house in December if he would have included a fireplace," Mary speculated. "We had breakfast in the kitchen next to the stove this morning."

"So did I. It's so cozy there," said Caroline. "This is mostly for the guests and for show. The candlesticks on the mantle and the gilt-framed mirror remind sailors of home, or at least the home they wish they had. For most of them this place offers comforts they don't see elsewhere."

Mary saw the conversation veering uncomfortably toward Richard's earlier visits and quickly guided it elsewhere. "I'd like to know more about your work at Whitehead Point," she said.

Caroline's eyes brightened and she shook a finger as if to scold. "Talk about comfort, those folks don't have any," she said. "And nobody in town seems to care. The ladies from the churches do nothing but donate worn out clothing from time to time and they feel they've made their contribution. So much could be done with a little money and the courage to show real kindness - the sort of kindness that sits down across the table and listens before it talks. As far as I know, I'm the only one who's doing that. I want your help. You have the time and I'll bet you can spare some money, too. Walk over there with me tomorrow morning. I know you'll want to join me when you get to know the people and the situation."

"Yes, tomorrow will be fine," Mary said. "I'll be glad to go with you. But don't rush into plans for the future. You're right. I'm not comfortable there. I've never seen or smelled anything like it. As for money, I'd want to talk to Richard. I take what I need from the cash box to pay for the household, but I always discuss other expenses with him. Tomorrow, yes. After that, we'll see."

* * *

Soon after sunrise, Mary and Caroline strolled down Eaton Street, turned left on Thomas, and followed it to its end. As they left the village, the street became a rough path and they walked in a single file until they came to the open area near the water.

"Did you talk to Richard about our plans?" blurted Caroline.

"Please don't pressure me! I didn't even broach the subject," Mary raised her voice and wheeled around in front of Caroline. "I didn't talk to him about this morning's walk and I didn't mention money, because I don't even know if I want to get involved in your project. It strikes me that it just might be foolhardy to leave cleanliness for filth and security for uncertainty. That's what you're doing, you know, when you come down here. You may be filled with happiness by doing good for those in need, but surely you realize that there's a dark side to this place. You're leaping in amid misery and disease and death. I can see that after just the one visit. Maybe you're not endangered by thieves and rapists, but you're willingly putting yourself in the way of other hazards. Don't be surprised if I choose not to join you, Caroline! I have a husband and child to think about beside myself."

"And it would be a shame to interrupt your comfortable life, wouldn't it?" Caroline jostled Mary's arm as she brushed past. She strode toward the encampment, looking stiffly ahead and swinging her arms as if they helped propel her forward.

Mary looked back toward the village. She had half a mind to go home, but she didn't. Pride and curiosity pushed her along behind Caroline. She pushed her moist hair back from her forehead and hurried down the gentle slope to catch up. As they approached, Mary saw men sitting on the east side of their hovels, drawing warmth from the morning sun.

"Morning' Miz Caroline." Several baritone voices greeted her familiarly.

"Who's that you've got with you?" A woman's soprano startled Mary and she turned to locate its source. Much to her surprise, she recognized the speaker. It was Julia Miller. Mary remembered last seeing her on Green Turtle Cay when she was just a teenager. Visibly pregnant, she had married a crewman from a wrecking ship and disappeared. A little girl clung to her apron and wiped her nose on it with a thick, mucussy sniffle. She cradled an infant in one arm.

"Julia Miller! Is that you?" Mary asked.

The younger woman smiled in recognition, then frowned and pulled her tattered bonnet down over her face. She took the little girl's shoulder and pushed her into the shadows of the nearest lean-to.

"Julia, it's me, Mary Randall - Mary Thorne. Do you remember me?" Mary took several steps in the direction of the shack and waited. There was no movement and no sound; the place might have been empty. Mary turned to Caroline. "What was that about? I'm sure she recognized me. Why is she hiding?"

"Embarrassment and shame. Julia came to Key West as a newlywed. Her husband was a deck hand on the Merribel. The first baby came early as they often do. That's the little girl. He took to drinking, lost his job, and started beating her. She has an ugly scar from her left eye to her chin where he cut her. He broke into Dr. Hawthorne's house and took money and drugs. When the sheriff came after him, he disappeared. The little boy's father was some sailor who forced himself on her. Fortunately Ephraim Reed has taken her in. He's too old to stand up for her physically, but he's respected, so nobody will go after her again."

"What a terrible story!" exclaimed Mary. She shivered as she recalled her recent thoughts of leaving Richard. Clearly Key West wasn't a place for a young woman alone! "The little girl doesn't seem well. Does the doctor ever come here?"

"They can't afford a doctor and he won't come for free. You've only seen a fraction of the misery here, Mary. You see why I want your help."

Mary didn't reply. She watched as Caroline delivered bread and soup to some men, lingering to talk as they ate. As the sun mounted toward its midday peak, the two women made their way home.

"You haven't said anything since we saw Julia. What are you thinking?" asked Caroline.

"I'm trying to sort out what I think," said Mary.

Scenes of sickness and want troubled her all afternoon. As she fed young Richard and put him to rest on crisp sheets in his cradle in the clean, dry house, she was haunted by images of Julia's infant and his dirty living conditions. That night she told to Richard about her concerns.

"Are you sure this is what you want to do?" he asked, scratching his head. "I'm afraid your good heart is going to lead you into trouble. How will you protect yourself from the disease and depression there?"

"I'll protect myself from disease by being scrupulously clean. And my beautiful home and loving family will be my defense against depression," she replied. "I want to do this. Thank you for not preventing me. I'll make it my New Year's resolution to improve at least one life at the Point!" She glowed with the fervor of her determination and purpose.

* * *

This year the holidays flew by. Having a child in the house heightened the excitement, but even Mary couldn't pretend that baby Richard, less than two months old, could appreciate the celebration. Her sadness at being so far from her parents and sister was buffered by Richard's affectionate attention. On Christmas Day, she gave him a scrimshaw shaving brush she'd bought from a Massachusetts sailor who'd passed through town during the summer. He gave her a brooch with gold stems and leaves surrounding garnet flowers. "That deep red reflects only the surface of my love," he said as he put his hand at the small of her back and pulled her against him.

Soon after the decorations were taken down, Richard went to sea again.

Mary visited the Point several times a week. She routinely brought fresh vegetables and herbs she knew to be cleansing and tonic like the simple nettle and horseweed she picked by the path. Nonetheless, the residents remained wary of her. They welcomed Caroline inside, but if Mary was along, the welcome cooled. If she ventured there alone, people who sat outside would disappear, dissipating silently like the dew vanished as the sun rose in the sky.

Mary persisted. She collected bags of used clothing from the church auxiliaries. She sorted it and mended what she could. She had Phoebe wash and iron everything, then divided it all by size and sex, making a special box of children's garments and labeling it with Julia's name. That was probably unnecessary since Julia had the only children at the Point, but Mary thought it might please her to be singled out.

* * *

With the approach of summer came the possibility of tropical storms and high seas. Richard stayed in Key West only days at a time before he sailed again. Mary understood the necessity of profiting from the calm weather, but finding herself almost constantly alone, she was glad to have a useful outlet for her energy.

"It was difficult to convince me to help you at Whitehead Point, but now I think I'd be bored and lonely without it," said Mary as she and Caroline sorted a new batch of discarded clothing.

"We do it for ourselves as well as for them, don't we?" observed Caroline. "Would you look at this?" She held up a pair of men's trousers. "Do those rich women have no shame? They're worn through at the knees and there's a tear in the crotch that could never be mended. This is barely a rag. Don't they understand that the clothes they give are meant to be worn again? Look. This shirt is in worse shape than the trousers! We're going to have to think of a new use for rags."

* * *

Finally Mary began to gain acceptance into life at the Point. She and Julia were even forging a friendship based on their domestic interests.

"What's in this bag, Mary?" Julia asked one day as she helped unload the donkey cart.

"I'm embarrassed to say I've brought more rags. How many bags of those do you have tucked away? We're so often given clothes that are just used up."

"I remembered an old craft my gram used to do," said Julia. "We'd make fun of her saying the rags were only fit to be thrown away, but she didn't listen. Come inside and I'll show you."

On the rough wood floor lay small, shaggy, multicolored rugs. They were pushed together edge to edge so Mary could scarcely see where one ended and the next began.

"I decided to try it because the floors are so hard on Maggie's bare feet and Jonny's knees," Julia explained. "They don't take long to make. I just tear the rags, draw the strips in and out through the burlap from old potato bags, and knot them. I could make two or three in a day if I tried." She smiled proudly. "I give them to everybody who wants them. You can use them as rugs and you can lie on them, too. It makes the boards more comfortable. Not like a real mattress, but better than nothing. And you can put them on top of you if it gets cold. They shake clean pretty good and, if they get really dirty, you can throw them away. They're rags, after all. Just trash to start with."

"Good for you!" exclaimed Mary, beaming with pleasure at Julia's ingenuity and the fact that the apparently useless rags could be put to good use.

* * *

Mary had something to think about beside her involvement at the Point. Recently food had stopped tasting good and she often felt queasy in the morning. She was pretty sure she was pregnant again. How unfair that pregnancy always seemed to announce itself by upsetting her digestive system! When Phoebe's herbal remedies didn't help, she was positive. It was a good thing little Richard had begun to eat porridge and strained vegetables. He'd be hard pressed to get enough nourishment from the amount of milk she produced these days.

Summer weather enveloped the island more completely with each passing week. Mary did her shopping and went to the Point in the mornings. In the afternoons she sat with young Richard in the shade of the east veranda.

That child wanted to crawl everywhere! She especially had to watch him closely upstairs because he didn't know how to navigate the steps and could easily tumble headfirst to the bottom. Mary hoped he would walk soon. As he crawled, he ground the dirt and splinters into his knees and clothes just like little Jonny down at the Point and it seemed as if he was always filthy. On the other hand, all the exercise wore him out and he quickly fell asleep in his downstairs cradle after lunch. Mary fanned herself and gazed at the street as she absently rocked the cradle with her foot.

A mosquito buzzed near her face and she waved it away with the fan. Another landed on the back of her hand and she squashed it before it had a chance to bite. She took her cotton handkerchief from her skirt pocket, licked it, and wiped off the bloody mess. Disgusting! You'd think the heat and humidity would be enough to bear, but no, these awful insects always came with them. She'd have to move inside if they got much worse, but she didn't want to lose what little breeze drifted in from the southeast. She alternately waved the fan over the baby and around herself to keep the mosquitoes away. Even so, one bit her on the neck. She stopped fanning to swat at that one and when she looked down there was another flying away from Richard's fat little cheek. He awoke with surprise at the sting and Mary swept him up in her arms before he could be attacked again and hurried to the kitchen house.

"Phoebe, please take the duster and brush me off before I go inside. I'm being attacked and I don't want to have any of these creatures as house guests! Why don't they bother you?"

"Garlic, Miss Mary. I learned from my mother that if you eat enough garlic, those mosquitoes won't bother you hardly at all."

"I'll remember that," said Mary. It wouldn't do her a lot of good right now. She'd had Phoebe eliminate garlic and onions from the food because they passed into Mary's milk and upset young Richard's stomach. And she didn't want to take any chances with her own digestion they way things were. She'd just have to wait to benefit from that remedy!

* * *

Mary rose earlier and earlier to take advantage of the

mornings' cool. On days when she planned to go to the Point, she left Richard with Phoebe who fed him porridge with raisins and sugar.

"Are you ill?" Caroline asked one day as they walked together. "You don't seem yourself."

"It's the heat," replied Mary. She thought to leave it at that, but reconsidered. After a pause she continued, "It doesn't make it any easier that I'm expecting another child. I tire easily and my food doesn't sit very well."

"Another baby! Are you glad?"

"To tell you the truth, I hadn't thought about being glad or sorry. It's just the way things are." She might have explained that she knew how to alter the situation, that she'd thought about it and chose to go on with the pregnancy. But she didn't want to reawaken those painful memories and felt confident that Caroline was well-versed on the chemistry of abortion. They walked on in silence.

At the encampment they found the weather taking its toll on morale there, too.

"Will one of you hold this baby while I go in and dress Maggie?" snapped Julia. "He fussed all night and all morning and he has a burning rash on his stomach. Ephraim's come down sick if you can imagine that. He was healthy through all the chills and winds of winter and now the warm weather's come and he has a nasty, dry cough."

"You take the baby," suggested Caroline. "I'll look in on Ephraim. You don't need to get sick from him." Mary sat, laying the baby lengthwise on her knees. She pulled up his shirt to examine his stomach. It was red and blotchy and bled in patches where he'd scratched himself. Too bad she didn't have any aloe with her to soothe it. She'd bring some tomorrow. Come to think of it, she'd bring plants. They'd grow well in the sunny spot on the east side of Julia's shack. It might even be the beginning of a garden.

* * *

The Osprey returned on the last Tuesday of May. Richard was in a darker mood than Mary had ever seen him.

"The politics of wrecking is becoming bizarre," he pushed his beans around on the plate without eating them. "Just months ago men accepted each other's word and acted with honor. Now look. Less than a week ago I watched two captains come to blows over who was to be the master of a wreck. I couldn't believe my eyes."

"I thought the first one to the wreck was automatically the master," said Mary.

"Exactly. That's why I'm so astonished. They argued about what constitutes being first. Owens said he'd seen it first and so he had claim. Howe put three crewmen on the deck, but didn't board the wreck himself until the next day when both captains went together to assess the situation. That's when I arrived. Just after I boarded, they saw the quantity of goods in the hold and the argument erupted. Half of that load is a small fortune and the wreck master will be able to retire if he wants. They pushed each other down on the slippery deck and Howe was kneeling over Owens beating in his face when I broke it up."

"What happened to the captain of the wreck? I should think he would have seen who was first."

Richard scratched his head. "That's even stranger. The guy, I think his name is Perez, just speaks Spanish and he didn't appear to understand what was going on. He ducked into his cabin when the fighting started and bolted the door. He seemed mighty afraid. I wonder if all that cargo was legally his. We'll find out, maybe. The affair is supposed to be settled in court in the next few weeks. I'm a witness, although I don't have an inkling of how I can help straighten things out. I didn't see anything but the fight."

"I'll be glad to have you here for a while," said Mary. "I've missed you and I believe young Richard is starting to know if you're home or not. Wait until you see how he scoots around on the floor! You called him a mouse once. You may have been right!" She paused to emphasize her news. "Richard, the last time you were home, you seem to have left me with an unexpected gift."

"Oh?" said Richard squinting. "I don't recall giving you anything."

"I'm pregnant again," Mary said as she patted her belly. "I'm sure of it, although the baby hasn't started to move yet."

"Think of that! Two boys in as many years! I don't know any man who's done that! What shall we name this one?" Richard jumped up and wrapped his arms around Mary's shoulders.

She pushed him back. "There's a lot more involved than your achievement, dear husband. Remember who carries these children around and feeds them before and after they're born. Besides, there's no assurance that this one will be a boy. I've heard that girls are equally likely."

"I'm just happy to have something to look forward to. As life at sea becomes more uncertain, your news gives me heart."

* * *

The wreckers' trial lasted into the second week of June. Richard was required to be on hand daily at the Court House in Jackson Square to give eye witness testimony. He was called on only twice in three weeks.

"The judge seems irritated that I can't resolve the case for him," he reported one evening at supper. "All I've done is report what I saw. There are those who would have me do otherwise, though. Daniel Howe pulled me aside today and offered $100 if I would alter my memory in his favor. Maybe he feels his case is the weaker. I refused."

Richard pushed back his chair and rose from the table, leaving his napkin in a crumpled ball beside his empty plate. "I'm not sure what I would have done if he'd offered double the amount."

"You're not serious!" Mary didn't try to hide her astonishment.

"I'm very serious. I'd be very happy to have a new source of income."

"Did we make a mistake in coming here?" Mary's throat tightened with anxiety and her words verged on shrillness. They had invested so much of their lives in the move! What if they'd been wrong?

"Things are no better in the Bahamas," Richard replied. "If anything, they're worse. No, our reasons for coming to Key West are still valid, but the world keeps changing. Don't forget we came here because wrecking was a dying profession where we were. We may have to change again, but don't worry. I can take care of matters."

"Of course," Mary replied. She meant her words to give him confidence, but she wasn't reassured herself. She loathed insecurity and Richard's blunt assessment of their situation raised gooseflesh on her arms.

In the end the wreckers' trial was solved with the Solomonic judgement that the captains would divide the wreck master's share equally. The matter might still have been quite profitable for both if the judgement had been delivered timely. But in the three weeks the affair had dragged on, the insurance company took a closer look and determined that the goods on the ship were not the cargo they had underwritten. To make matters worse, the shipment, which had been unloaded and stored in a Front Street warehouse, had mysteriously diminished by half and Captain Perez was nowhere to be found.

"It could have been worse," Richard observed. "At one point the judge considered revoking both men's licenses. That would have been catastrophic for them both; it would have deprived them of their livelihoods. I think the lesson in this is to make the most of the profits that are still available in wrecking. At the same time, I mean to actively investigate some other ways to make money. It's a shame, because I love the sea, but I've become rather fond of the comforts of home, too. I may have to sacrifice one or the other. I hope not."

Mary hoped not, too. On this subject, she knew her mind precisely. She had absolutely no interest in giving up her comfortable life on William Street so Richard could continue to sail around on the Osprey. The only reason his seagoing life was tolerable for her was because it supported them. Without profits, what was the point?

Again Richard stocked the schooner with food. He brought home arms-full of charts and unrolled them on his desk, weighting the ends with books to keep them from curling back. Every night he bent over the water-stained pages and traced the lines that depicted contours of the reef and the depths of open water, muttering softly. Often he only quit his study when the lamps burned out.

Those lamps reminded Mary of the courting lamp that had timed Richard's visits to her father's house back on Green Turtle Cay. Jealous of the time he spent planning his trip, she was tempted to fill them only halfway as she had done when he came to court her, but that was silly. He'd only have Phoebe refill them or do it himself. After all, it was respect for the convention, not the lack of light, that had prompted Richard to leave when the lamp went out. It all seemed so long ago!

"I think I'll head out with the tide on the sixteenth." Richard rubbed his eyes with his knuckles as he joined Mary on the parlor sofa one Tuesday night in June. "There will be a full moon and if a storm doesn't come up, the night will be bright and good for sailing. I can reach open water quickly. Then I'll be well-positioned for spotting the less fortunate who heave up on the sand or stave in their hulls on the reef."

"You sound bloodthirsty and uncaring when you talk that way," Mary said.

"I don't cause the wrecks. You know that. I just make it my business to be at hand when they happen."

"The sixteenth is Friday. It's bad luck to sail then. Why don't you leave earlier or delay for a day or two?" asked Mary.

"Do you believe that? 'A Friday's sail will always fail.' Isn't that what they say?" He looked down his nose in disdain. "There's nothing in my experience to support that idea. I won't base my plans on superstition. Friday is the earliest we can prepare the ship and I want to sail before the solstice when the days will start to shorten. I'll sail on the 16th and make my own luck."

Friday morning as Mary watched the Osprey sail away, she hugged young Richard tightly and turned to Phoebe. "How often have we bade them Godspeed like this? Soon we'll wear a rut in the planks from walking out here to the same spot time after time." *That's probably the picture he keeps in his mind,* she thought. *If I stand here when he sails and again when he docks, it's as if I hadn't moved. How comforting it would be to think that nothing changes unless you're there to witness it.*

"Let's go home," she said. "Please take Richard. He's getting heavy for me."

Phoebe accepted the child into her arms and led the way as young Richard stared wide-eyed over her shoulder as if he were trying to hold the Osprey in his gaze. Lost in her thoughts, Mary watched the swinging of the other woman's broad hips ahead of her and matched her steps. Their movements became so synchronized that Mary might have been alone, walking up the street preceded by her own shadow.

CHAPTER 21

Clouds gathered for two days. The hot and humid air was as still as if Nature were holding her breath. On Wednesday, the season's first tropical storm darkened the sky. The rain began as a series of small squalls, then it poured as if the clouds were determined to squeeze out the very last drop, and that as quickly as possible.

Water streamed from the eaves as Mary and Phoebe fastened the shutters hard against the windows and latched the doors. Phoebe brought water, soup, and bread into the dining room and fastened the door behind her. They sat on straight back chairs, idle but alert. It was too dark to read or do needlework and they wanted to save the lamp oil for night. The wind's angry roar and the staccato beat of the torrential rain against the house almost drowned out their voices.

"Are you afraid?" Mary shouted over the din.

"No, Miss. I believe the house can withstand the storm. I just don't like sitting in the dark not knowing when it will end."

"I feel the same way," said Mary. She covered Phoebe's hand with her own. Her intention was to give reassurance, but she received at least as much comfort from the contact as she gave.

Little Richard sat quietly on the floor between them. He

laughed when lightening brightened the narrow spaces in the shutters and ducked under Mary's long skirt when thunder shook the island.

"Let's make sure he has a full stomach. Maybe he'll nap. This is unpleasant now, but it will be unbearable if he starts to wail," Mary observed. They took turns offering him bread moistened with the tepid chicken soup and he happily gobbled it down. Soon his head nodded and when Mary lay him in the crib he curled up and slept, oblivious to the storm's roar. Phoebe rocked from side to side in her chair humming tunelessly. Despite the violence outside, in the darkened parlor suspended activity and the quiet patience of the two women produced a kind of domestic serenity. Sitting in the dark, Mary lost all sense of time. Finally, she slumped in her chair and dropped off to sleep. When the racket of the storm subsided, the abruptness of the calm startled her and she sat upright. Richard squealed as if he shared her surprise. He rubbed his eyes with his little fists and yawned.

"Do you think it's over?" Mary asked.

"Let's wait a little and see," Phoebe replied, rubbing her eyes, too. "It may have blown itself out, but let's be sure."

It *was* over. The sun peeked in and out of the clouds as they raced off to the northwest, then it shone unencumbered with blinding brightness and surprising heat. They ventured outside and found the cistern filled to overflowing and the garden ridged with muddy streams. An enormous puddle blocked the intersection of Eaton and William Streets and steam rose from the hard pan of the intersection as the intense sun heated it. The shutters had held and the storm hadn't breached the house, but branches and leaves were strewn everywhere.

"This is a fine mess," said Mary. "We may as well start cleaning it up." Energized by the fresh air and the enormity of the task ahead, they collected straw brooms from the cookhouse. Mary attacked the debris on the veranda while Phoebe cleared the breezeway between the house and the kitchen. Young Richard crawled and splashed in the puddle at the foot of the steps by the front door. He laughed as he slapped the fig leaves that floated next to him. "At least that will keep him busy while we work," said Mary. "We can clean him up later!"

"We're going to need to clean us all up," observed Phoebe. "We're getting as dirty as he is."

Muddy water splattered up Phoebe's bare brown legs and drenched Mary's long black skirt. Mary took off her petticoats and her shoes and stockings, laying them inside the door. She pulled her skirt between her legs and tucked it into her waistband to form a voluminous pant. She enjoyed the childlike freedom of bare legs and feet, but soon the exertion of sweeping and the rising humidity made the sweat run down her forehead and sting her eyes. She wiped her forehead with her sleeve and leaned on the broom as she paused to catch her breath.

"You'd best sit down and rest for a while, Miss Mary. Don't forget that baby you're carrying."

Mary down sat heavily on the top step and watched Phoebe work and Richard play. Leaves rustled and twigs broke in the scrub behind the garden. Out came a sodden rooster. He'd traded his accustomed strut for a peculiar shuffle. His proud red comb hung to one side and his feathers, usually gaudily luminescent blues and blacks, drooped dully, coated with the same brown mud that covered everything else. A hen and five chicks followed, dully pecking at the mud as if they entertained little hope of finding seeds or insects. *If birds can experience melancholy, these are overcome by it*, Mary thought. She shared their dismay. Her world seemed overturned, too.

Then she felt a familiar thump against her rib cage. The new baby had quickened. It was almost as if he were reminding her he was there and demanded some consideration. *Oh, there I go calling it a boy,* she thought. *I'm as bad as Richard! Never mind. He'll be a boy for now. The important thing is I can feel him. He's as real to me now as Richard over there splashing in the mud.* The realization helped her accept her relative inactivity. In a few days order would be restored. What was her rush?

It was a time for patience. Dried silt dusted the porches even after they were swept and Phoebe had to sweep them again . . . and again. Leaves broomed from the walk blew back over night, so Mary and Phoebe pushed them back into the scrub once again. The humidity became suffocating. Phoebe washed the dirty clothes, but the clean ones hung wet on the clothesline with little hope of a dry breeze to make them wearable. The heavy muddy odor of mold and mildew pervaded everything. Mosquitoes bred uncontrolled and no longer waited for dusk to fly and bite. By late afternoon they forced everybody inside stuffy, tightly closed rooms and even then, the persistent insects managed to creep in to buzz and prick and generally make life miserable. Sleep was only possible when exhaustion demanded it. Most nights Mary lay naked in the stifling, still bedroom and stared at the motionless web of mosquito netting that draped her bed. She knew from the unaccustomed droop of Phoebe's shoulders that she suffered the same uncomfortable insomnia.

By Saturday morning, Mary had to escape the demands and closeness of the house.

"Phoebe, I'm going for a walk," she announced. "I'll take Richard with me. He'll benefit from some fresh air, too."

"Do you want me to come and help carry him if you get tired?" Phoebe asked.

"I don't plan to go far," Mary reassured her. "And I'd like to be alone for a time. We'll be fine."

As Mary walked, Richard wiggled in her arms and the unborn baby bounced around in her belly. She had to laugh at their antics. She felt invigorated and interested in the world around her for the first time since the storm. She slung Richard up to look over her left shoulder and strode along purposefully. The arrangement seemed to suit the infant because he laughed as he bounced along.

Mary had set out without a specific destination, but she was drawn to the path that led to Whitehead Point. How had Julia weathered the storm? Mary stopped to rest twice before she got there, but the path was mostly downhill and her curiosity propelled her on. When she finally reached the clearing, she gasped. Shanties lay on the ground. Privies were flooded and overflowing. The place stank of sewage and stagnation. All that remained of the garden Julia planted just weeks before was a silty puddle striped by little chasms where the dirt had washed away. The herbs and shrubs hadn't grown enough roots to stop the erosion and the soil they had worked so hard to sift and rake was nowhere to be seen. Neither were the residents.

"Julia! Maggie! Ephraim!" Mary shouted. Surely they could hear her. She waited for an answer, but all she heard were the waves as they brushed against the roots of the mangroves.

"They've got to be here somewhere," she insisted, talking to herself in her frustration.

Hauling Richard over her shoulder like a sack of flour, she dodged the rubble and puddles skirting the impenetrable mangroves until she reached the edge of the rocky beach. Squinting into the sun, she threaded her way among the stones to the shoreline and looked back. Not a soul in sight! She sank to a rock to rest. She'd been borne along by the search, but now she realized she was tired.

The noontime sun scorched her back. She pulled off her jacket and folded it as a cushion for Richard in the shade of a big chunk of marl.

"Mary?"

A hand touched her shoulder with featherlike gentleness. It was Julia.

"Where have you been? I didn't see a sign of you! I didn't know what to think. Why didn't you call to me?" asked Mary.

"I saw you come and sneaked away so as not to wake my children. They sleep fitfully since the storm and last night they only fell asleep just before dawn. So this is your little boy! He's so big. Tell me his name again." Julia's face brightened with pleasure as she looked at Richard.

Another time Mary might have enjoyed a relaxed discussion of motherhood and babies, but she was brimming with more pressing questions. "Where are your children? What happened to Ephraim and the others?"

"We've taken shelter down by the mangroves on the other side. Ephraim is with us. I don't know where the others have gone. I think they spread out along the shore. Ephraim has a fever and he's still coughing. We're all being eaten alive by the mosquitoes. I don't know what to do."

Julia's smile faded. She dropped her hands to her sides in a gesture of hopelessness and tears made little muddy gullies along her dirty cheeks like the grooves in the silt of the garden. Speechless, Mary hugged her and they stood motionless except for Julia's tiny sobs until Richard tugged at Mary's skirt insisting, "Up! Up!"

"Please come with me," Julia said. "I know a baby's rash is different from an old man's disease, but you helped the rash with your herbs. Maybe you can help Ephraim."

Mary doubted it. She knew some mixtures that would calm a cough temporarily, but none that would cure it. Diseases deep in the body would heal themselves with rest and wholesome food. Or else, sometimes they wouldn't. She didn't want to think of that. Julia had experienced enough pain and uncertainty in her life without suspicions that Ephraim's sickness might be fatal.

"By all means, let's go," said Mary. She grunted as she lifted Richard to her shoulder.

"Are you all right?" asked Julia.

"I'm expecting another child and I don't have my usual energy," confessed Mary.

"Let me carry him. You still haven't told me his name, you know."

"It's Richard."

"Come on then, Richard." Julia hooked her hands under his arms and bounced him several times clucking her tongue against her teeth. Richard smiled and leaned against her as they made their way into the mangroves.

The new shelter was even more rudimentary than the first. They had tied three corners of an old square sail to branches to form a roof. The fourth corner hung down and was staked to the ground, forming a crude windbreak and giving the illusion of privacy. The tattered canvas sagged and Mary thought it might collapse soon, but it provided much-needed shade, at least for now.

Boards rested on rocks to span the mucky soil. Julia's two children sprawled on their backs, their arms and legs spread wide and their chests rising and falling in gentle unison. Ephraim, on the other hand, curled on his side at the edge of the platform. Mary could see he was more delirious than dozing. His rasping breath was punctuated by a dry cough. When she touched his forehead, he blinked and tried to push himself up with his arms, but the effort was too much.

"He has a fever. I might be able to brew a tea with bark that will help that. I don't know about the cough. I'll have to ask Phoebe. It's important for him to drink lots of water. Do you have fresh water? Is there enough to eat? I didn't bring anything." Even as she asked the questions, Mary knew the answers. There wasn't enough of anything before; since the storm, there could only be less. She didn't wait for Julia's reply. "Let me go home and bring back the things you need. It would be best if we could take Ephraim to town, but I don't see how we can move him."

"He wouldn't go, anyway," said Julia. "You know how he feels about what he calls 'society.' He'd rather die than live in town."

I hope he's not already dying here. Mary shivered. "I'll be on my way," she said with a confidence she didn't feel.

"Won't you eat before you go?" Julia asked. "I have some bread left and I caught a fish this morning. I'm not sure what it is, but it's big and there's plenty. Please, share our lunch."

"The sooner I leave, the sooner I'll be back," Mary said as she picked up Richard.

She set out briskly, but her energy didn't carry her past the beach. The baby started kicking and nausea rose in her throat. She reeled with waves of dizziness and she leaned on a rock, then sat down hard on the ground guiding Richard's fall to the cushion of her lap. He began to cry. Mary hugged him and started to cry, too. Addled by fatigue and weakness and stung by the bile that kept rising at the back of her throat, she panicked.

"Help me! Someone please help me!" She screamed. Richard wailed louder than before and wet through the diaper he'd worn since early morning. In her frenzy, Mary couldn't be sure if it was she or her child who had soaked her legs with pungent urine.

"Stop it now!"

Mary looked around and Julia slapped her hard on the right cheek, then on the left one. Mary fell silent as she stared wide-eyed at this woman she had so often helped and thought to be a friend. Why was she being so cruel?

"What are you doing?" she moaned. "Don't hurt me." She started to cry again, but this time she could only manage little hiccup-like sobs.

"You're hysterical," said Julia. "Do what I tell you or I'll hit you again. Let go of the child. I'll take care of him. Now, stand behind me and put your hands on my shoulders. Lean on me and only take a step when I do."

The world still spun and wobbled as Mary tried to comply. The three worked their way back to the camp. When they finally reached the shade of the tarp, Ephraim hadn't moved and Maggie was feeding chunks of bread to Jonathan. Julia deposited Richard in front of her.

"Share with this one, too, Maggie," she said, pointing at Richard. "He thinks he's starving, even if he's not."

"Yes, Mum."

"Mary, come over here and lie down!" Mary obeyed. Julia leaned over the edge of the wood platform, wet a rag, and lay it on Mary's forehead, arranging it to cover her eyes and temples. Mary relaxed a little and stopped sobbing.

"Lean up on your elbows so I can give you a drink," Julia instructed.

Gradually Mary gained some control of herself. "What can I do? Phoebe will be frantic if we don't come back soon, but I'm too weak to walk home, let alone carry Richard. It was foolish of me to come so far. But how could I know I would tire so quickly? It's terrifying to think what could have happened. I might have split my head on a rock or dropped Richard in the water. And now I'll have to stay here until I'm stronger . . ."

Julia let her prattle on until she talked herself out and rested quietly. She folded one of her rag rugs under Mary's head and turned to check on the children. The toddlers were asleep and Maggie was breaking up the last of the loaf of bread. "You're quite the little mother, aren't you dear?" Julia asked.

"Mmmm," replied the child through a mouthful of bread. She smiled in acknowledgment of the praise.

Peace ruled the camp for at least an hour and Julia and her daughter sat quietly. The silence was interrupted by women's voices.

"Mary, where are you? I know you're here somewhere!"

"Miss Mary, we want to take you home."

Mary recognized Caroline's and Phoebe's voices immediately. Julia stepped out where she could be seen and waved a torn, grayed bed sheet back and forth like a flag of surrender.

"Mary, what were you thinking of coming all this distance carrying young Richard? Are you mad?" asked Caroline.

"Of course I'm not mad. It was a beautiful day and I wanted to go outside after being cooped up during the storm. I knew Richard would like it, too, and before I knew it we were here. It was only when I set out for home that I became ill. And Julia has taken perfect care of both of us. Phoebe, since you're here, please look at Ephraim. What can we do for him? He's very ill and I hope you can cure his ailments." Mary knew she was talking a lot, but there was so much to account for.

Phoebe sat with Ephraim for a minute while Caroline took Julia aside. *They're talking about me,* thought Mary as she sat alone. *Never mind. They're good friends and only want the best for me. They're planning our return to town. Oh, I can't wait to lie in my own bed and sit at my own table!*

Before sunset they were on their way. Phoebe carried Richard piggyback with his legs thrust ahead under her arms. He gripped her neck in a half-excited, half-frightened hug. Caroline wrapped an arm around Mary's waist and supported her as she steered her along the path.

"Thank you, Caroline. Thank you for coming for us."

"It was little enough to do," said Caroline. "Now if we can just get home before the mosquitoes finish us off! Damn, there's another one!"

CHAPTER 22

Mary devoured her chowder while Phoebe fed Richard morsels of grouper and tipped a cup so he could drink some fish broth. She washed the day's grime from the child and Mary bathed and put on a clean nightgown. Wrapped in fresh sheets and secure in familiar surroundings, they both slept well into the morning.

Caroline visited the next afternoon and found Mary in the garden stripping the leaves and small white flowers from a shrub.

"Good as new, are you?" she asked. She perched on the edge of the cistern and smiled as she watched Mary work. "What on earth are you doing with that pretty weed?"

"I haven't felt new in a long time." Mary looked up and smiled wryly. "The plant's for a tea for Ephraim. It isn't a weed, you know. Its botanical name is *Marrubium*, although people usually call it horehound. I don't know why. It doesn't have anything to do with dogs. We brought this plant from Green Turtle Cay because it's one of the best medicines for disturbed breathing and diseases of the lungs. It's even said to help consumption."

"Do you think Ephraim is suffering from consumption?" asked Caroline.

"I've never seen it, so I can't be sure, but from what I've read,

I wouldn't be surprised. If he does have consumption, I hope it's not too far advanced. I read it can't be cured. Even doctors can only assuage the symptoms. People recover, if they do, through their own strength. Ephraim is old. He hasn't eaten well for years and judging from the smell of his breath, he drinks a lot of rum. I think he's had that cough since the day I first saw him.

"That's not very cheerful," observed Caroline as her smile faded.

"No, it's not cheerful at all, and I hope it's not true. I dread to think of Julia on her own again. But let's not entertain dark thoughts. If Phoebe and I show you how to prepare the tea from it will you teach Julia? I don't think Phoebe's going to willingly let me out of her sight any time soon."

"Of course I'll deliver it. From what you say, the sooner, the better! By the way, I agree with Phoebe. You've had enough excitement for a while. It's not so long ago I prodded you to get out of the house. Now even I think you should stay home. When do you expect Captain Richard's return?"

"He was vague about that before he left and I haven't received any letters. I never know when to expect him."

* * *

Mary played with young Richard and did simple household chores like polishing the silver and dusting the detailed scroll work on the mahogany diningroom sideboard. In the afternoons she sat and embroidered or worked needlepoint while Richard napped or played nearby. He seemed to have reached a new stage in his development; he wasn't as active as before and he slept longer and more deeply. Maybe he was still recovering from their experience at the Point. Mary didn't regain her strength as quickly as she'd expected, either. By Wednesday, she knew she was ill. Her muscles ached as if she had worked all day in the garden and her head felt as if it would burst. She fluctuated between chills and sweats and just the thought of food turned her stomach. Richard developed a fever, too. He begged to be picked up, but when Mary lifted him, he cried out in obvious pain.

"You two breathed miasma down there in that mangrove camp and now you're sick," said Phoebe. "You get to bed and I'll take care of things." Mary readily accepted her authority.

"Poor little Richard looks even worse than I feel." Mary said, "See how he stares at me without reacting? What awful thing did I do when I took him with me that day?"

"Talking like that isn't going to do any good," Phoebe replied. "You take care of yourself and do what I tell you to. Remember that other baby you're working on. Get to bed now. I'll carry Richard up in a minute. You're both going to need rest and some strong teas to help you recover."

Mary was happy to oblige. Her back ached so that she could barely drag herself up the steps holding on to the rail. Her temples throbbed constantly. She fumbled with the buttons as she undressed and left her clothing in a pile on the floor by the dresser. She crawled between the sheets and plumped up the pillows beside her head to cushion any sound that might make her headache worse. She was barely aware when Phoebe lay Richard in his cradle.

The teas were ghastly. The borage infusion was so bitter Mary could hardly finish a cup of it. The safflower was worse. Both made her sweat. Phoebe insisted she drink three cups of each one every day and it seemed as if she spent as much time on the chamber pot as in bed. Then there was the echinacea root, the final ingredient in the trio of distasteful herbs. Its first effect on her tongue was a seductively sweet relief from the previous nostrums, but as she swallowed the infusion, the aftereffect was as bitter as anything that had come before. Phoebe dosed Richard with the same infusions tablespoon by tablespoon, wiped his brow and changed his almost-constantly wet and soiled diapers.

"That echinacea will make you strong to fight off the infection," said Phoebe when Mary wrinkled her face into an unusually graphic protest. "You watch. My grandmother said she once cured a big swelling on her own belly by drinking five cups of it every day for six months. Don't you complain. You're only drinking three. Look at that little child next to you. He doesn't grumble about his medicine. You be like him!" she scolded.

The only pleasant ingredients in the treatment were the little bouquets of clary sage that Phoebe put on the table next to the bed. She freshened them every day and the pretty little blue flowers released a spicy, earthy fragrance that raised Mary's spirits, however briefly.

"That sage would make a good tea for you, too," Phoebe observed as she placed a fresh bouquet on the table. "But it might make you lose the baby and we don't want that!"

"No, we certainly don't!" exclaimed Mary. "And I'm very grateful to be spared from drinking still another concoction. It couldn't taste as good as that bouquet smells."

Phoebe chuckled as she gathered empty cups from the dresser. "I think you're feeling better already," she said. "You're certainly getting more talkative."

After three days, Mary felt her strength began to return. On the morning of the fourth day, she got out of bed and dressed. Richard seemed to have better color and his fever seemed to have abated. She thought he was recovering, too. She carried him downstairs for the first time since she fell ill and gobbled down bread and cheese. It was the first food that had appealed to her in days! Mary held her son as he drank a cup of chicken soup and chewed on a bread crust.

Phoebe insisted they continue to drink the herbal infusions. Mary complied although she made faces whenever she had to finish the safflower. She hoped she'd never have to endure that awful potion again. Maybe if she did as Phoebe said and was thorough in this treatment, she'd be cured for good. It seemed to be working. By Monday evening she felt herself again and enjoyed a plate of fried grouper and boiled beans. She pulverized the fish with her fork and picked through it for bones before feeding it to Richard. He didn't seem to share her enthusiasm for supper, but then, he hadn't eaten solid food in three days. Maybe he needed to get used to it again.

The next morning, he was as sick as before. His forehead

almost steamed with fever and he vomited until there was nothing left to come out. They tried to feed him spoonfuls of tea, but even that wouldn't stay down. When Mary saw the red specks on the cloth she used to wipe his mouth, she paled.

"He needs the doctor, Phoebe. Go get Dr. Hawthorne. 433 Duval Street. Around the corner to the left. Go quickly!" Phoebe shed her apron and dropped it on the table. Duval Street was only four blocks away. She'd be back with the doctor in no time. Mary clutched Richard to her chest and rocked back and forth. "Everything will be all right, honey. I promise you'll feel better soon," she whispered.

* * *

Dr. Hawthorne was only called in cases of extreme illness and Mary had never met him. His gaunt frame supported his black suit like a hanger, but didn't fill it out. He stared through cavernous dark brown eyes that looked like lumps of coal in his chalky skin. When he removed his hat, he revealed a smooth crown unrelieved by even a single hair. What struck Mary most was his enormous hands. She couldn't take her eyes off them. The long soft fingers ended in perfectly groomed nails that would put any woman to shame. He set his black satchel on the bed table and washed his hands in the basin Phoebe provided.

"It's the yellow fever. I'm sure of it," he said as he examined the little boy. "Everything indicates it." He pulled back Richard's left eyelid with his thumb. "Look how his eyes are becoming jaundiced. I think the skin of his stomach is a little yellow, too." His pronouncements about the gravity of the child's illness made his angular face seem more severe, almost threatening. Gooseflesh broke out on Mary's arms and she rubbed her hands together unconsciously.

"We must act quickly and decisively," the doctor continued. "I've read all the opinions of Dr. Benjamin Rush of Philadelphia. He is very respected and influential. We must follow his instructions to the letter. First, we will bleed the boy. For a youngster this size, four ounces should be right for today. Possibly the same amount tomorrow. We also need to administer an emetic to stimulate his bowels. Bring me a small bowl to catch the blood."

Mary gasped. "Doctor, he's already weak from fever and lack of food. Won't bleeding only weaken him further?"

The doctor scowled. "Madam, I know what I'm doing. Herbal potions won't do any good here. The only solution is to remove the poisons from his system. We can't waste time in discussion. He's very ill."

Tears ran down Mary's cheeks as she silently watched the doctor open his bag and remove a shiny scalpel. Phoebe stood just inside the door and Mary looked to her for encouragement. The other woman's face was woodenly inexpressive as she stared at a spot near her toes.

Richard shrieked when the scalpel lanced his skin. He tried to squirm free, but the doctor forced him against the bed with one hand and held his bleeding wrist over the bowl with the other. Dark red blood throbbed into the bowl. When a little puddle gathered, Dr. Hawthorne wrapped gauze bandaging around the wound. Holding Richard's arm aloft, he addressed Mary over the din of Richard's cries.

"Elevate his arm until the bleeding stops. I'll leave you another length of gauze in case he soaks that one through. Have your slave dissolve the jalap powder in a cup of water. It's mild in this dosage. I like to use it with children. Make him drink it as soon as you can. Force it down his throat if necessary. You can expect to sit with him through the night as his bowels open and that system is cleansed, too. I'll be back tomorrow after lunch. If he's not greatly improved, I'll bleed him again. There's nothing more to do until then except to follow my instructions precisely."

Mary picked up her howling son and sat on the bed clutching him against her breasts, his arm still raised, as she rocked from side to side, crooning. The doctor buckled his bag, stood, and replaced his hat. He turned to leave. "I'll let myself out."

"You," he said as he pointed at Phoebe. "Mix the jalap. Good day," he said to Mary and he left.

When Phoebe lifted her head, Mary read the indignation and anger in her pursed lips and jutting chin.

"We'll do as he said. Please prepare the jalap. I'm sorry he treated you badly," Mary didn't know what more to say.

When it was ready, Mary dipped a finger in the jalap preparation and slipped it into Richard's mouth. He spat it out and clammed his jaws shut. Overwrought from the bleeding, he was still crying and when he opened his mouth to gulp air Mary managed to drip a little of the liquid onto his tongue. It took almost an hour, but finally he swallowed most of it. Exhausted, he finally stopped crying and Mary lay him in the middle of the bed, hoping he would rest. In just a few minutes he curled up and began to wail again.

"He's cramping," said Mary. "I thought the doctor said it would be mild. I don't know what to do now."

"We'd best just follow the good doctor's instructions and keep him clean," said Phoebe. Mary could tell from the clipped, monotonic words that she wasn't convinced.

They sat with him through the night taking turns changing diapers and sheets and cooling his forehead with a damp cloth. One woman would doze and then the other but, constantly alert, neither really slept. Richard moaned softly as he tossed from side to side. His eyes closed and every once in a while he whimpered as if he were remembering the torture he'd endured earlier.

When the sun rose, Mary cracked open the shutters and raised a window to admit a little light and fresh air. Her heart stopped as she unpinned yet another diaper. She left him naked and sat heavily on the bed beside him. He was bleeding from his intestine.

"It's not working," she whispered. "He's worse and I don't know what to do."

If only Richard were here! She yearned to lean on her husband's arm and to share her fears and doubts. But Richard was far away. It was up to her. As hard as she tried, she couldn't trust this strange doctor. Maybe he'd read about cures that famous man dictated, but his methods weren't working. Her child was getting sicker and sicker in spite of the bleeding and purgative. Maybe because of them! She wiped his brow with the moist cloth, then held it to her own.

Neither she nor Phoebe thought to eat lunch, but it must have been afternoon, because Phoebe had just carried a load of dirty laundry down the stairs when Mary heard Dr. Hawthorne's step on the downstairs veranda. He mounted the stairs and opened the bedroom door without knocking.

"How is he?"

"He hasn't improved. He's worse. He's bleeding from the intestine," Mary replied levelly. She knew what she must do - what any mother would do - and she needed to gather her courage to stand up to the doctor's authority.

"I will bleed him again immediately," said the doctor.

"You'll do no such thing! You will not bleed him again. Your services are no longer required here." It took such an effort to say the words that they came out as a shout.

"Are you refusing my treatments?" asked Dr. Hawthorne, raising his eyebrows and sniffing.

"Your treatments are violent and painful and they're not helping. I refuse to allow you to hurt my son again. Please go."

"Madam, home remedies can't cure this. The responsibility will be yours if he doesn't recover."

"I will take that responsibility. Good afternoon, Doctor." Mary walked to the bedroom door and formally showed him out. When he was gone she crumpled to her knees beside the bed and began to sob. She covered Richard's cold little feet with one hand and miserably cradled her head on the other.

CHAPTER 23

Phoebe tapped at the door. She carried a basin of cool water to wash the sick child.

"Come in," whispered Mary. Her hair fell over her face and her eyes burned as she looked into the bright doorway. "I sent the doctor away. I couldn't bear to see him slice at little Richard's flesh again and the jalap root is irritating his intestine. The poor thing is only getting weaker with those treatments. I don't know if we can save him, but if he must die, I want him to die peacefully."

"I'll make camomile tea to calm his stomach. And some for you. It will help you compose yourself."

After a dozen or so teaspoons of tea, Richard rested, although his fever continued uncontrolled. They dripped a steady stream of restorative infusions into his mouth and kept cool cloths on his forehead.

"At least he's not any worse," observed Mary. "Let's see if a little chicken broth will give him strength." She didn't have words for her disappointment when he threw up the soup. She gritted her teeth and slumped in dejection. Then she renewed her efforts with the teas. He seemed to tolerate them. *If love and determination can save a life, then I will save his,* she thought.

As the sun set, Phoebe coaxed Mary to eat. She dipped bread in soup, just as they had done for Richard during the storm. How long ago that seemed!

Mary gently rocked her son as Phoebe changed the sheets. She lay him on the fresh bed, washed her face, and lay next to him. She didn't waste time brushing her hair and left her clothes on the chair back. She wanted to be close to her little boy and lend him her strength. *I will give him my breath and the beating of my heart,* she vowed. *I will give him my soul, if necessary.*

She drew the hot little body to her, stroking his back. "I think he'll sleep now. Leave the infusions on the dresser in case he wakes in the night." Phoebe nodded and tiptoed out the door and down the stairs. Richard breathed regularly, if shallowly, and Mary lay perfectly still so as not to disturb him. Soon she was asleep.

Mary woke as the sky began to brighten. At first she had to struggle to reconstruct the previous day's events. When memory did return, she regretted it. She shuddered when she remembered Richard's suffering and shivered as she acknowledged her audacity in dismissing Dr. Hawthorne. Never mind! She must move ahead. She had rolled away from Richard during the night. She sat on the edge of the bed and turned to observe him. He'd turned onto his side and faced her with his eyes wide open. He must have just awakened, too. He was so quiet. Had his condition improved? Mary brushed her fingers over his forehead to check his temperature. He was cool! The fever had broken!

She lifted him to her shoulder and hugged him. His head lolled to one side and his arms and legs dangled limply. She quickly put him down. He lay perfectly still and stared.

This can't be! She thought. *He couldn't have died right there in the bed next to me without my knowing it.* She put her index finger across his palm. When his hand didn't grasp it, she enclosed his hand with hers and formed it into a fist. When she let go, his hand fell open. Unwilling to believe what she saw, she put her ear to his chest. Nothing. Pressing harder and harder, she held her breath and strained to hear just one soft beat of her son's heart or to feel a muscle quiver with life. It was no use.

She sprang to her feet. "Richard! Richard! Richard!" she

shrieked. She beat the marble top of the dresser with clenched fists and pushed the pitcher and basin to the floor where they shattered, scattering water and broken pieces all over. A sharp-cornered shard cut her foot, but she was insensitive to the hurt and blind to the blood. She cried out for her dead child and her absent husband and every loss she had ever experienced. Her determination and knowledge and love had amounted to nothing when it counted most and she was utterly alone in defeat and emptiness.

Phoebe burst into the room. "Miss Mary, what's wrong?" Then she saw the little body on the bed.

"Ohou, ohou, ohou." The deep minor tones of her wailing merged with Mary's shrill cries. They clung together, keening in lamentation for the loss of this beloved child. When finally they tired, they sat cross-legged on the floor facing each other with their knees touching and their hands clasped together between them. Mary searched Phoebe's face for hope or encouragement, but all she found was raw grief. Mary dropped her chin to her chest, unable to control her tearless sobs and powerless to call her son back to life or her husband to her side.

Finally Phoebe gently pulled away and pushed herself to her feet. "We must prepare the body for burial," she said softly.

Mary looked up. Her eyes widened in horror and surprise. "We can't bury him!" she exclaimed. "We will keep him until his father comes home. Richard must see his son before he goes into the ground."

"Miss Mary, we don't know when Captain Richard will return. You know we can't keep a body for very long, no matter how much we love him or how good our reasons. That child is dead and we have to let him go. We have to bury him soon."

Mary pulled herself up against the bed's footboard. Her legs trembled as she stood, but she crossed her arms across her chest and her voice was firm. "My son will not go to the cemetery until his father is here to walk behind him. I will not allow it."

"It's August, Miss Mary," said Phoebe gently, sweeping the broken pottery to one side with her foot. "You know the heat and humidity will soon start to rot that poor child's body. You don't want the captain to come home to witness the boy's spoilt flesh. You don't want to see it yourself."

Mary understood Phoebe's arguments, but she refused to cede to reason.

"There has to be a way! Go get Caroline. She knows everything about this town. She'll find a way. Maybe somewhere there's a great store of ice where we can keep him cool."

Phoebe muttered something unintelligible as she left the room, closing the door firmly behind her.

At nine months Richard had grown heavy for Mary to carry. His dead weight was even harder to lift as she struggled to cradle him in her arms. She sank onto the rocking chair and held his stiffening body on her lap. His vacant eyes stared up at her. She pulled the lacy hem of her nightgown over his face to interrupt the awful, empty gaze. As she rocked, she closed her eyes and imagined his curious crawling and exploration of just a few days ago.

Caroline and Phoebe spoke quietly as they climbed the stairs. Mary pretended not to hear them when they opened the bedroom door.

"Mary." Mary could hear Caroline's grief in the simple speaking of her name. She was so glad her friend was here, but she couldn't open her eyes. If she did, she would see a world she didn't want to inhabit.

"Mary," Caroline repeated. "I have a plan. You know of Thomas Burger, I'm sure. He painted Mrs. Geiger and her children last spring. He also paints oil-o-grams, portraits of people who have died, so their families can remember them as if they were alive. I've sent my servant, Phyllis, to ask him to come. Now, open your eyes and let me help you dress. We'll have him paint you rocking Richard as you've done so many times. The picture will be a comfort to you and Captain Randall."

Mary opened her eyes and allowed Phoebe to take the infant body from her limp grasp. As Phoebe cleaned the boy for the last time, Caroline washed and dressed Mary as if she too were a child. She brushed her long straight hair and twisted it into a simple chignon at the nape of her neck.

"If I'm to be painted, I suppose I should wear my best," said Mary with resignation. "Get my enamel necklace and earrings from the top drawer of the dresser."

Mary intercepted Caroline's hands before she could fasten the necklace. She examined the dainty blue flowers as if for the first time.

"It all seems so long ago, doesn't it?" she asked.

"Yes, very long ago," replied Caroline as she tied the velvet ribbon and centered the point of the necklace on Mary's breastbone.

Mary sat in the rocking chair and they arranged young Richard's body as naturally as possible on her right knee facing the light that filtered through the open door. Soon the artist thumped noisily up the thirteen stairs dragging his easel. His curly blond hair shot off in every direction and his trousers were dotted with a panoply of color, evidence of where he wiped his brushes. The sharp odor of turpentine accompanied him.

"Good day, ladies. Please accept my sincere condolences at your loss. Ah! You've done very well to arrange the subject and his dear mother. Time is of the essence, as you know. We want a realistic likeness and that is a fleeting quality after death."

Mary's first instinct was to despise him for his inane patter but as he worked and chattered she began to realize his ruddy complexion was the blush of combined embarrassment and exertion and his jabbering was intended to help her relax.

"Please smile for me, mother. You can hardly feel gay on a day such as this one, but you will look often at this portrait and a loving smile will bring you more comfort than the scowl of grief. There now. That's better. I'll soon be done. I work quickly to record the important details of my subjects and finish the work in my studio."

True to his word, the artist soon packed up the brushes and paints and hoisted the easel over his shoulder. "I'll return in two days with the finished painting. I'm sure you will want to be alone tomorrow for the funeral. I promise you, the portrait will gladden your heart and bring back happy memories. Until then." He departed as noisily as he had arrived.

Phoebe took the dead child from Mary and placed him on his back in the cradle. She coaxed the little eyelids closed and put a penny on each one.

"He can lay there until the casket is ready this afternoon," said Caroline. "I sent one of my girls to the carpenter's to have him make the box. They'll see that the grave is dug."

Mary choked and doubled over as if stabbed by the brutally factual description of the funeral preparations.

"I can't do this!" she wheezed.

"You have no choice," replied Caroline. "Lie down. I'm sure Phoebe has something to help you sleep. Sleep will help. You'll see."

Sleep did help. At least she didn't have to watch when they carried him down to the parlor and laid him in the casket. She didn't see Phoebe strip away the little sheets that she had embroidered before he was born or smell the smoke when she burned them. She was deaf to the ring of the pickax that carried all the way from the cemetery when it struck hard marl as they scraped out the hole for the grave. Mary slept until morning and when she woke, she found her black serge suit folded over the back of the chair. She dressed carelessly, not even noticing that she'd buttoned her blouse wrong until it came out uneven at the bottom and she had to do it again. She pulled on her shoes without wiping off the dust and missed an eyelet on the left one as she laced it. She went down stairs to the dining room and quickly looked away when she saw the casket on the parlor table. Caroline was already there.

"We'll go to the cemetery at ten. I've hired a donkey cart and Mister Adams will come from St. Paul's to read the service. Everything is taken care of."

Mary picked at a slice of bread and tried to moisten her throat with tea. She wished the time would pass more quickly. Maybe if the funeral was over the pain would stop.

At last she heard the donkey's hooves approach, then stop in front of the house. The sexton climbed the steps to the veranda, tipped his hat to the women as he mumbled something that might have been "Good day," and single-handedly carried the little box to the unpainted two-wheeled cart. They had to wait for Mister Adams. When he arrived, he took Mary's elbow and guided her from the house to her position behind the casket. Caroline and Phoebe stepped into line behind them.

It hadn't rained since the storm and the ground was dry. The cart's wheels threw up fine sandy dust that grayed the dark clothing of the four figures in the little funeral procession. They walked the three blocks to the cemetery in silence. *Angela Street. How fitting,* thought Mary. *I'd never noticed before. All the angels are right here and there is a street named for them.* The summer sky was unrelieved by even a wisp of cloud and the mourners squinted as they walked into the unshaded graveyard. They easily found the grave in the bare field and stood with their backs to the glare. The casket had slid to the front of the cart and it grated across the rough boards when the sexton pulled it back where he could lift it off.

The grave wasn't deep. The day before, the diggers had hit a hard, wide strip of rock and it was late in the afternoon, so they'd quit. Tomorrow or the next day they'd build forms and pour a cement slab over it. The family could add a marble stone later, if they could afford it.

Caroline and Phoebe stood on either side of Mary supporting her by her elbows. Mr. Adams read from the prayer book in his left hand and gestured with his right.

"We entrust this child, Richard, to Thy never-failing care and love," he intoned.

Nothing was real. Mary tried to concentrate on the words, but instead her attention shifted to a mockingbird as it landed on the end of a branch of a lone ficus tree. The branch bobbed up and down with the bird's weight and she wondered if it would fall off and if it did, would it die? Die. The word brought her back as Mister Adams leaned over and gathered a handful of rocky dust. It clattered hollowly on the casket.

"In sure and certain hope of the resurrection to eternal life . . . earth to earth, ashes to ashes, dust to dust."

Mary didn't hear any more. The minister hastily finished reading the service as Caroline and Phoebe struggled to hold her up. They lowered her onto the cart and walked beside it to keep her from falling off. As the cart bumped onto Angela Street, Mary opened her eyes.

"Be still," said Caroline, gently stroking her brow. "You'll be home soon."

CHAPTER 24

The day after the funeral Mary slept until midmorning. Before all the sickness and grief, it had been her habit to rise early on Saturdays and go to Whitehead Point. Today it didn't cross her mind. She drank tea in her room and sat on the veranda, staring to the northeast toward the cemetery and, beyond it, the Atlantic Ocean. She couldn't see either one, but that was the direction of everything she cared about in this world - and the next if there were such a thing. *My Richards both are there somewhere,* she mused. *And both are out of sight and out of my life. I wish my husband would come home. I don't know how I can endure this grief by myself for much longer.*

Restless, she went back inside. At the sight of the little cradle beside the bed, she felt as if the flesh of her heart was being physically ripped.

"Get this thing out of here before the memories tear me apart!" she wailed.

She walked backwards dragging the heavy mahogany cradle. It gave a sharp bang as she pulled it over the threshold and onto the veranda. She tipped it onto its end, bent her knees, and hugged it against her chest as she stood, raising it until one of the rockers hung over the rail. Then she pushed from the other end. It seesawed briefly. Mary put her back to it and shoved with all her strength and the cradle tipped away from the veranda. It paused, almost as if it were gauging the long fall that lay before it. Then it dropped. The polished mahogany splintered as it crashed to the ground. Mary hung over the rail and stared.

Phoebe ran into the yard. "What on earth have you done?" she asked.

"I couldn't stand to look at it," Mary replied. "Put the other one in the attic out of sight."

Phoebe stood for a moment, looking from the shattered cradle to the veranda and back again. Then she slowly and deliberately mounted the stairs. "Come down for some lunch," she coaxed. She took Mary's hand and led her down the stairs. "I've peeled a fresh mango and sliced it for you. It's bright and sweet and juicy. I know you'll like it. After you eat, you'll sit by the garden and watch me weed. You can tell me what vegetables you want for dinner."

Phoebe was treating her like a child. It rankled and it didn't make her feel any better but she didn't know what else to do, so she complied. She picked at her food, moving it around on her plate. Maybe Phoebe would leave her alone if it looked like she'd eaten. She sat at the table long after she stopped pretending. After a while, Phoebe urged her into the garden to sit in the sun. While they were there, Thomas Burger returned. Instead of his easel, he carried the large canvas, covered by a white paint-stained sheet.

"I finished the portrait this morning," he said. "I want you to have it because I know how much it means to a grieving mother to be able to see the image of her little child. The oil paint takes a long time to dry, but we can prop the canvas on a chair and in a few weeks, I'll return to frame it if you like."

Phoebe brushed her hands on her skirt and stood to take the beans to the kitchen house. Mary led the artist to the parlor.

"I'd like you to put it here, Mr. Burger." Mary pushed a straight-backed chair from the dining room to face the sofa.

The artist stood between her and the chair, blocking her view. He positioned the sheet so it hung freely in front and braced the canvas between the caned seat and the ladder back. He adjusted it a little here and there, checking to be sure it was secure. When he lifted the sheet from the front and stepped away, Mary caught her breath and sat down.

"It's a perfect likeness of us both!" she exclaimed. "It's as if he were still alive. Look at his little hands! And you've captured the color of his hair perfectly. It's exactly the color of his father's, you know."

"Phoebe, come look!" she called.

Phoebe stamped her feet free of courtyard dust before she came in the house. She carried clean silverware in one hand and she laid it on the table as she passed through the dining room. When she saw the portrait, she smiled tenderly.

"I've never seen a picture of the dead," she said. "It does seem to bring him back to us, doesn't it?" She stepped behind the couch and patted Mary's shoulder. "This will be a great comfort to you, Miss, just like the gentleman said."

"There's only one problem," said Mary. "The longer I look at the eyes, the less they seem to be real. They're empty of expression."

"That's very perceptive of you," said the artist. "The eyes of the dead in an oil-o-gram always have a vacant look because all feeling has passed from the body. It's good in a way, because so often the eyes expressed pain and fear immediately before death and we certainly wouldn't want to preserve that. But, at the same time, it's impossible to recreate the expression of the happy, living subject without having known him."

"I see," said Mary. She was glad to have the portrait, but she knew she would never look at it without experiencing the deep melancholy she felt now looking into those empty pools of blue that she had known to be so bright and curious.

* * *

Mary wallowed in listlessness and dejection. She firmly rejected more sedation, but now she slept poorly and sometimes woke in the middle of the night in a cold sweat. Once awake, it took her a long time to find a comfortable position, as the fetus in her belly kicked unrelentingly. In the mornings, she barely had the energy to get out of bed. She ate little and spent her days gazing at the portrait of her dead son. She had Phoebe lower the shutters and the room was dark and stuffy. The gloom and discomfort suited her. She rehearsed in her mind the scenes that had led to her child's death. His hair drenched with the sweat of his fever. His screams as the doctor cut his soft skin to bleed him. His unresponsiveness the morning he died. She searched for words to explain to Richard what had happened - what it had been like - but even when she managed a description in her mind, she didn't think she could say the words out loud.

Phoebe encouraged her, practically begged her, to eat and step out in the sun, but even her earnest reminders of the welfare of the unborn child went unheeded.

Caroline came to visit three days after the burial. She admired the portrait, but Mary's only response was a wan smile.

"Walk over to the Point with me. We'll go down and see how Julia and her children are faring in the new tent city they're building," she suggested.

"I don't care if I ever go there again! See what I got for my previous generosity of spirit. A dead son!"

"Mary, you didn't cause Richard's death. No one even knows the source of the fever. There's no possible way you can hold yourself responsible."

"It doesn't matter. Even if that's true, he's no less dead," Mary replied. "You can keep your ideas to yourself from now on."

"I'll be going," said Caroline as she raised her eyebrows and pursed her lips. "Please, Friend, try to regain some enthusiasm for life. You have a new baby coming and Captain Richard will be home soon. There's so much for you to look forward to."

"Indeed," Mary replied flatly and she turned back to the portrait.

Caroline shrugged her shoulders. "I'll call again in a few days," she said and she turned to the door. "Send Phoebe if there's anything I can do for you."

JANE LOUISE NEWHAGEN

* * *

Six sultry August days had dragged by since they buried baby Richard, each one indistinguishable from the other. Mary was sitting in the gloomy parlor when she heard Richard's familiar heavy steps on the front stair. She jumped up, shedding her despair like waves running off the sand in the receding tide. She collided with her husband in the doorway. Steadying herself against the wall, she beamed at him joyfully.

"You're home! I'm so glad you're home. I don't know how much longer I could have waited for you to come!"

"Well, that's the most enthusiastic welcome I've ever enjoyed!" Richard exclaimed, laughing. He slipped his hands under her arms and lifted her like a child. "It's been a long trip and I'm glad to be home. Where's my little son? Did he grow while I was away? Wake him from his nap. I want to say 'hello' to him!"

Mary looked away and her body went rigid.

"What's the matter?" he asked as he put her down on her feet. "Come on now, bring me my son." He gave her an affectionate slap on the buttock to encourage her.

Mary clenched her fists at the end of rod-like arms and tilted her head back to look him in the eyes.

"He's dead. The baby's dead," she said flatly. "He got sick and the doctor came and bled him and he got worse. He died and we buried him on Saturday. I wanted to keep his body for you, but it's too hot. So we buried him without you and you'll never see him again. There's just that picture over there that I had painted for a memory, but the eyes are wrong. The hair is just perfect, but the eyes are wrong because they're dead, too." This was not what she'd planned, not what she wanted to say, but she couldn't stop herself. The dreadful words became an inarticulate scream. Richard stared at her. He took her by the arms and shook her. Finally her screaming turned to tears. Her knees weakened and her head rocked back and forth as he shook her. Richard guided her to the sofa. They fell, more than sat. Mary sobbed as she buried her head in his lap.

"You're hysterical," he said. "Calm yourself and tell me what happened."

She tried to catch her breath between sobs. She wiped at her cheeks and nose and pushed herself to sitting.

"It's all true. Our child is dead. Look." She gestured toward the portrait.

Richard stared mutely. He stood and walked over and tentatively touched the cheek of the child in the portrait. Wet flesh-colored paint came off on his index finger and he rubbed it against his thumb, staring at it incredulously. He wiped his hand on his pant leg and walked out the door without speaking. Mary listened to the sound of his footsteps as he went down the steps and turned in the direction of the cemetery.

She hoped he'd come back. They could go to the cemetery together. But the steps grew fainter. When she accepted that he'd gone without her, she assumed her accustomed position in front of the portrait. *So, I wait once more,* she thought. *Richard is gone. Who knows when he'll be back? This waiting has become my life. I wait for my husband to come home, wait for babies to be born, wait for their healing, wait for their deaths.*

"Was that the captain's voice I heard? Has he come home?" Phoebe's matter-of-fact question called Mary back to reality.

"Yes, it was the captain. He's gone to the baby's grave. I don't know when to expect him back"

"I think I'll make a chicken stew," said Phoebe. "I have some yeast dough left from this morning's bread that will make fine dumplings. The captain always likes dumplings. I'll boil them when I know he's back in the house. There's nothing worse than a soggy dumpling that's had to sit."

"You're so worried about Richard. What about me?" wailed Mary as she tugged at her hair. "I'm in need of comfort, too!"

"I've been trying to ease your pain, Miss, me and Miss Caroline, both. But you haven't let us help. Maybe now with the captain home to share your grief things will be better for you."

Mary nodded without speaking and returned her attention to the image of her dead son. She didn't care if she had to wait until midnight for dinner. She couldn't eat anyway. Her unborn child kicked. She pushed back at the place she'd felt him. "Don't be in a hurry to get out of there," she whispered. "You see what can happen? Stay where it's safe."

Richard came home just before sunset. He was covered with dirt and tears had carved muddy channels along his cheeks. Soil was ground into the knees of his trousers and blackened his fingernails. He must have thrown himself on the grave and clawed at it in the irrational hope of regaining the young life that once occupied the body that lay there. He stood silently in the doorway and the tortured expression in his eyes said everything.

"I'll go wash for dinner," he muttered.

They barely spoke as they sat across from one another. Mary made no pretense of eating. Richard squashed his dumplings with his fork and mixed them with the stew, taking a bite only when the food was reduced to a paste that didn't require chewing. She didn't want to break the silence for fear of losing control of herself and driving him out the door again. She fiddled with the napkin on her lap and stared at her plate willing him to speak first. Finally, he pushed his plate away. He reached across the table and lifted her chin.

"I want to know everything that happened," he said. "Come to my office where we can be alone. I don't think I can stand to sit in the parlor and look at that painting right now."

Mary seldom had reason to go into Richard's office and she felt out of place. Here he did his business accounts and met with insurers and city officials. The dark, narrow room at the front of the house held only an ornately carved oak desk and matching armchair, four Spartan chairs for visitors, and a wall of bookcases filled with legal briefs and sailing charts. It made her think of her father's office in her childhood home on Green Turtle Cay.

Richard sat behind the desk and looked expectantly at Mary. She sat on the edge of a chair and recounted every detail of the last few weeks. She told him what a fine day it had been; how she took young Richard with her to the homeless camp; and how Phoebe and Caroline had come to find them and bring them home. She recounted the details of her illness and the baby's soon after; how she had recovered and he had seemed better, too, before he took a terrible turn for the worse. She described the measures the doctor had used to try to cure him.

"What did Doctor Hawthorne say when there was no improvement?"

"He wanted to bleed him again and continue the purgative. I dismissed him. The treatment wasn't helping and it was tormenting the poor child."

"You what?" Richard's elbows banged on the desk as he leaned across it. "Doctor Hawthorne is very well respected. He is a student of Benjamin Rush from the mainland. What made you think you knew better than he did?"

"The fever was worse. The bleeding and purging made him weaker."

"So you sent the doctor away." Richard's words grew louder while Mary's became quieter.

"Yes."

"And my son is dead." Now he was shouting.

"He was my son, too. I tried to save him. He was too sick and it was too late. I was here alone and I did the best I could. If you had been here, I believe you would have done the same as I did."

Richard was suddenly quiet. Mary stood and approached him, making her way through the narrow space between the desk and the bookcases. She held her arms open wide, offering comfort and hoping for understanding.

"Leave me alone," he said stonily. "I need to think."

"You're blaming me for something that wasn't my doing," cried Mary. "No power on earth could have saved that child. He was so sick! If you'd seen him, you'd understand."

"But I didn't see him."

Mary dropped her arms to her sides. Her shoulders slumped as she turned and left the room. There was nothing more to do. Surely Richard would understand when he'd had more time to think. After all, he'd just received a terrible shock! How could he be expected to act rationally? Mary climbed the stairway to the second floor.

She'd questioned the wisdom of having those thirteen steps when Richard built the house on Green Turtle Cay. She'd been afraid they would bring bad luck. He'd laughed at her superstition, saying that the number was necessary to maintain the proportion of the risers to the treads. She'd accepted his explanation and put the thought out of her mind. Now, as she slowly retraced the familiar stairway, she wasn't so sure.

She left the doors open and sat by the bedroom window. When the lamp started to flicker out, she lay on the bed without undressing. Weak rays of waning moonlight flickered through the shutters. Once in a while she heard the clump of heavy boots on the hardwood floors below, but Richard didn't come to bed. Mary finally dozed as the sun lightened the sky and she only woke when a construction wagon clattered along William Street. She rose, smoothed the counterpane, and washed her face. Downstairs, Richard was nowhere to be found.

Mary shoved her bonnet down on her head without bothering to arrange her hair and tied the ribbon in an uneven bow. She walked out of the house with determination, but stopped at the street. Which way did he go? To the right to visit the cemetery again or to the left down Eaton Street and into town? Her intuition prodded her to the left and she walked toward Duval Street.

She'd only gone about a block when she saw her husband approaching on the other side of the street. She waved as she crossed over, then stopped and watched him approach. *It's so good to have him home! I've even missed the sight of him,* Mary thought. *I love the way he swings his arms when he takes those long strides of his. He's not a tall man, but he covers a lot of ground in a short time.*

"Hello," she said, blushing from the unaccustomed exertion and her pleasure in watching him.

"I'm glad you came to meet me," said Richard. He slid his arm around her waist and she turned to walk with him. "I've just been to visit Dr. Hawthorne at his surgery. He described young Richard's sickness in detail. He said it was a classic case of yellow fever. That's probably what you suffered from, too, only you were strong and recovered. Unfortunately, infants and the aged have more difficulty resisting virulent diseases. That's why Richard seemed well, then relapsed and fell into the critical stage."

His words comforted her. His anger had dissipated, he was seeking rational explanations. She leaned comfortably against his shoulder as they strolled.

"Dr. Hawthorne was pursuing the classic treatment for the disease," he continued. "He feels confident that if his treatment hadn't been interrupted, the child would be alive today."

Mary stopped and Richard swung around to face her.

"He blames himself in part. He says you were probably slightly delirious from your own fever days before and your judgement was impaired. He didn't think of that at the time, but now he wishes he'd been firmer with you. He feels strongly about the role Phoebe played in the tragedy. He says you are obviously very much under her influence and that her folk remedies are dangerous to you and potentially to our other children."

"That's absurd!" exclaimed Mary. "I think Dr. Hawthorne's memory has altered the facts. The infusions we gave Richard weren't harming him. It was the bloodletting and cathartics that weakened him. The good doctor is trying to defend his reputation." Mary's words tumbled out and her eyes flashed with indignation.

"No one is accusing anyone. I want nothing more than your well-being. Dr. Hawthorne agrees." Richard's tone was calm and reasonable. "He suggests that in light of your illness and the experience of losing this first child that you so doted on, you're probably suffering from hysteria. He gave me a bottle of Godfrey's Cordial to settle your nerves. And he strongly suggests that we dismiss Phoebe. He thinks you're very impressionable in your present condition and her influence is not to be desired. You should have an older woman from town, someone more stable and trained to follow instructions and limit her activity to cooking and cleaning." He removed a small amber glass bottle from his pocket. The glass stopper was sealed in place with white parafin. Mary cringed at the sight of the medicine.

"Nonsense! Don't you know that Godfrey's Cordial can

poison? It's mostly laudanum, a mixture of opium and alcohol. I won't risk poisoning just so I can sleep soundly or avoid sorrow. As for Phoebe, she may be a servant, but I rely on her wisdom as well as her abilities. I won't consider dismissing her."

"I can't force you to take the medication, even if it's for your own good. But I am the head of this household and I pay Phoebe's wages. If you won't fire her, I will. I say this at no small personal sacrifice. Her husband, Seth, will certainly leave my employ when she goes. He's a good sailor, but I'll find another. And we'll find another maid."

Mary cringed at the harshness of his words. *Who was this tyrant? Did he really believe he was acting in her best interest? Two days ago she couldn't wait for his return. Now he seemed set on destroying what was left of her life.*

"No!" she shouted. "I won't allow it."

"This isn't yours to allow or prevent, Mary," said Richard in a controlled tone that again reminded Mary of her father. "Phoebe is an employee. I'll give her some money in consideration of her years of service, but she must go immediately. I'll talk to her as soon as we get home. Now quiet down. We don't want the whole town to hear us disagree."

He turned to walk beside her and, firmly taking her elbow, propelled her back up Eaton Street. Mary wanted to lash out to defend herself. But what was the use? There was nothing she could do.

CHAPTER 25

"I'll be going now." Phoebe drew her lips tightly together. She stood with military stiffness, only bending to hoist the canvas bag that held her belongings. "You go look through the house before I leave so you'll know I didn't take anything," she said in an uncharacteristic monotone. She blinked twice and turned her head away.

Mary wanted to embrace her, kiss her, and beg her not to go. She wanted to cry, but Richard was right there and his firm proprietary grip on her arm served as a warning that she'd better control herself. "Here are your last wages and a little bit more," he said as he handed Phoebe the envelope. "There's no need for us to check up on you. You've always been honest and if we have questions, we'll come to your new employer's and ask."

Dismissing Phoebe was the cruelest thing he could do, Mary thought. *And yet as he took away with one hand he was in his own way generous, giving her more money than she had any reason to expect. And he hadn't required her to leave until she found another position. Granted, it had taken only a day and a word from Mary before Caroline hired her. Still, many servants were sent packing the moment they were fired. At least Phoebe was spared that.*

Mary smiled sadly. "Be well, Phoebe." She pulled her arm free from Richard's grasp and walked outside and up the stairs where she shut the bedroom door with audible firmness.

Maude Simms arrived that afternoon. Richard had hired her sight-unseen on Doctor Hawthorne's recommendation. He immediately ushered her into his office and closed the door. Mary sat in the adjoining parlor, straining to hear, but their subdued tones were unintelligible through the closed door. She absently fingered some old letters from Green Turtle Cay that she had retrieved from the sideboard as she gazed at the portrait of her dead son. When Richard and Maude finally emerged, Richard spoke with great formality. "Mrs. Simms, I want you to meet my wife. I'm sure there's much she wants to tell you about the management of the house."

"I'm pleased to meet you, Mrs. Randall." Maude bobbed in a little curtsey that made Mary think of the plovers she often saw on the beach. The woman's drab brown skirt and jacket were relieved only by a starched white blouse that matched her pale white face. A few wisps of yellowed white hair trailed over her temples from beneath her close-fitting brown cap. She did look like a plover! And like the bird, the servant had no visible neck. Mary stifled a giggle. This wasn't funny. Maude was to take Phoebe's place in the household if not in her heart and Mary ought to demonstrate her own authority from the outset.

"Good afternoon, Mrs. Simms," she said cooly. "Come to the kitchen house and I'll show you your quarters and the equipment we have here. I'll expect you to be responsible for the garden as well as cooking and cleaning. I'll show you that, too."

"Please call me Maude, Mrs. Randall."

Mary winced at the sound of the respectful "Mrs. Randall," after all these years hearing "Miss Mary." Not that she wanted this stranger to be more familiar! She simply ached for the way things used to be.

Maude was very cooperative and cheerfully accepted all her duties. The single difficulty was the garden. She was willing enough, but she didn't seem to be able to distinguish a tomato plant from a thistle. Mary could only hope that with patience, she could teach her to discriminate weeds from vegetables.

While Maude did what she was told, she totally lacked initiative and sometimes was forgetful. It seemed, though, that Richard had given her one instruction she wouldn't forget.

Twice when she found Mary weeping as she sat before the oil-o-gram, she said, "Mrs. Randall, nobody wants you to suffer from grief this way. Captain Randall gave me the laudanum to keep in the kitchen for you. Let me get you some. Just a teaspoon or two will make you feel so much better."

"I'll have none of it!" exclaimed Mary. "And you stay away from it, too. Put it at the back of the cabinet behind the flour and forget about it. It's not to be dabbled with."

* * *

Wanting to avoid further maternal suffering, Mary tried to ignore her second pregnancy. Sometimes she even was able to forget about it. In contrast, Richard was very aware of the approaching birth and often talked about it when they were together over dinner.

"I want to name this child Richard, too," he said.

"And what if it's a girl?" Mary asked.

"Then we'll name it something else."

She figured the pregnancy must be about five months along, but her body hadn't changed much and she seemed far from needing those awful shifts she had to wear the first time when she got too big for normal clothing.

Richard spent most of his time in town and at the waterfront and was seldom home during the day. His absence didn't bother Mary. She was grateful not to have to withstand his scrutiny of her days, how she still sat in the gloomy parlor with the portrait and how she picked at her food. Above all, she didn't want him to know too much about how she spent her mornings. Almost every day after Richard left the house, Mary gave detailed instructions to Maude and walked the two blocks down William Street to Caroline's. There she sat for a while in the kitchen with Phoebe.

Their conversations were more informal than ever now that Phoebe was no longer Mary's employee and the servant didn't hesitate to offer her opinions about everything from when to transplant the basil to what tonic Mary should take to improve her appetite.

When Caroline finished her accounts and her instructions to the servants, she and Mary set out for the Point. Mary knew Richard wouldn't approve, but she also knew that the excursions were good for her. The exercise helped increase her stamina and thinking about things other than her dead baby gradually raised her spirits. She could feel a tiny flower of optimism growing in her heart just as the new baby was growing in her belly.

Conditions at the Point had improved during the weeks Mary had been absent. Julia and her family had retrieved some of the original boards from their shack and collected others that had blown in during the storm. They rebuilt their shelter inland, not far from where it stood before. Maggie helped carry the wood and Ephraim drove the nails Caroline provided. The old weathered white boards contrasted with the newly found green ones and, with its contrasting stripes and tilted roof, the shanty had an air of gaiety that belied the severity of the lives spent in it.

Julia was worried about Ephraim. She told Mary and Caroline how, as his cough increased, his energy diminished. He often had to rest as he worked on the new shed. Sometimes shortness of breath overcame him and he bent double until he stopped wheezing.

"He's been complaining about pains in his knees and hips, too," Julia reported one day. "And I hear him awake at night, although he won't talk about it."

Caroline asked Phoebe to go with them to the camp. Ephraim wouldn't consent to being examined, certainly not by a woman, so Phoebe had to form her opinion from discrete observations.

"It's almost certainly consumption," she said as the three women walked home. "I don't know much that can be done for it except to make the person comfortable. I've heard of folks who survive it, but they've been young and healthy when they were infected and had a strong will to live. I'll make up packets of horehound for Julia to prepare for him. It should help the cough and maybe it will give him some appetite, too. Camomile will help him sleep. Mary, are there still nasturtiums growing by the cistern? Pick some of those for a salad the next time you come. They're tasty and pretty and some say they're restorative."

Mary agreed, silently grateful that she'd stopped Maude just before she ripped out the nasturtiums, having mistaken them for penny weed.

Two days later Mary again presented herself at Caroline's red door.

"Phoebe's made up the packets of remedies, but I can't go with you and neither can she," Caroline said. "The captain of that big schooner refused the pilot's help. Most say he was too cheap to pay him. Anyway, he said he knew this channel like the back of his hand. Evidently he exaggerated. He ran into those rocks on the south side of the island. The ones that stick right up out of the water at low tide. Stove in the hull. Now he'll be here until they finish the repairs. From what I hear, that may be quite a while because the shipyard is taking its time, probably out of spite. In the meantime, I have my hands full running a guest house for the passengers and crew."

Mary smiled. "That's a change from your usual patronage, isn't it?"

"It's more similar than you might think," said Caroline. "And there will be some of the other, too. This came at a good time for me because two of my girls just left for the mainland. I've lost the revenue from their services so I'm glad to use their rooms for paying guests, even if I wind up changing beds myself and helping with the extra laundry. Who knows, I might have a new business if this works out."

Mary walked to the Point alone. As she approached the cheerful green and white shack, she saw Julia scurry back and forth several times from the shanty to the nearby brush. Mary walked as quickly as she dared over the irregular stones.

"I'm so glad to see you!" Julia reemerged at the edge of the scrub. Her hands were full of rags and she carried a short board under one arm. "Ephraim's having a coughing fit inside and Maggie fell and turned her ankle looking for firewood. I'm trying to take care of them both and keep an eye on Jonny, but I can't stay long enough in one place to make a difference anywhere. Maggie's too heavy to carry and I have to splint her ankle so she can hobble back on her own." She wiped the sweat from her forehead on her sleeve.

"Go on. Take care of Maggie," reassured Mary. "I have Phoebe's medicines for Ephraim. I'll take care of him and Jonathan until you come back."

Inside, Ephraim sat in the shadow on a packing crate, his face buried in a white rag. Fortunately, Jonny was happily occupied in the corner pushing sea shells from one place to another and putting them into a wooden bowl, then emptying it and starting again. Mary gave the child an affectionate pat on the head and rumpled his hair before she turned her attention to Ephraim.

The old man's coughing frightened her. He hacked so deeply and with such force that it seemed he must be tearing up the lining of his lungs. She placed her bag on the floor and touched his shoulder. "It's Mary," she reassured him. "I've come with medicines that will help you." She could feel the heat of his fever through his shirt.

Ephraim raised his head in recognition. His pale skin and sunken eyes said more than words.

"Let me help you lie down while I make up these teas."

"If I lie down it gets worse," he rasped. Mary shivered when she saw the spots of green sputum and streaks of blood on the rag he had used to cover his face.

She kindled the last of the firewood to boil water. Outside at the little stone fireplace she could still hear Ephraim's hacking. Relying on the power of the infusions, she willed the water to boil quickly and then for the teas to steep to the necessary strength. At last, she was ready with two bowls, one of horehound and the other of camomile. She offered the horehound first.

"Let me hold the bowl," she said. "If it spills, we'll have to start all over. Lean your head back a little so you can drink." He complied, but the angle made him choke when he tried to swallow and he coughed violently, spraying tea and sputum all over himself and Mary.

"I'm sorry," he mumbled deeply.

"Never mind," said Mary, wiping her face and bodice with the hem of her skirt. "Don't be discouraged. Take another drink. I want you to empty the bowl. Take small sips so you won't choke again." With enormous effort, Ephraim kept drinking. He pressed his lips together tightly when a cough threatened to overcome him. Finally he drained the bowl. After a while, his coughing became shallower and minutes instead of seconds passed between outbursts.

"Now, eat this fresh salad I brought," Mary coaxed. "Isn't the nasturtium in it pretty? You can even eat the flowers. Eat the little salad and drink this other bowl of tea and see if you don't feel better." Ephraim acquiesced and within an hour he agreed to lie down on some of Julia's rag rugs. When Julia and Maggie appeared at the door, flushed from exertion, he dozed quietly, although a deep rumble in his chest served as a reminder that this was only a respite.

"I thought we'd never get back!" exclaimed Julia. "But my girl's a fighter." She hugged Maggie as she helped her turn around to sit on the crate. Maggie's left ankle was supported by a crude splint of boards and rags. "She leaned on me the whole way and we were like one big animal with three legs. Believe me. It's no way to be."

Mary recounted her time alone with Ephraim. "You'd better wash up," advised Julia. "I have some soap left still. I don't know what kind of ailment he's got, but you sure don't want it." Julia was right. Mary had been too busy to think about herself. She didn't have the heart to tell her Phoebe's diagnosis of consumption.

They shared bread Mary had brought and some fish leftover from the previous night's dinner. Mary gave Julia instructions for brewing and administering the infusions and set out for home. She smiled and hummed and barely noticed the piercing rays of the sun directly overhead or the dust she kicked up as she walked up the path.

"I'd started to worry about you Mrs. Randall." Maude greeted her as she climbed the front steps. "I wanted to ask you about cleaning the parlor. Is it all right if I move the chair with that picture on it so I can sweep the floor? I'll do my best to put it right back where it belongs."

"Yes, of course," Mary replied, irritated by the tactless reminder of her sorrow. A dark cloud slid over the late summer sun, portending an afternoon shower. Mary's optimism and satisfaction faded with the sunshine.

CHAPTER 26

"Maude isn't nearly as good a cook as Phoebe was," Richard commented one September evening at supper as he sawed at his pigeon breast. "I've never had a bird so tough."

"I'd say Maude doesn't compare well to Phoebe in any way," replied Mary, looking him straight in the eyes.

Richard looked at his dinner plate. He paused to chew and raised his gaze. "I haven't wanted to discuss this until I was sure of the possibilities, but now I feel certain and I've made my decision. I'll sail again in two weeks or so depending on the weather. It will be my last wrecking trip and only partially wrecking, at that. I also plan to sail north to St. Augustine and make provision for my new business."

Mary's eyes widened and she started to speak, but her husband continued before she could form the question.

"I told you the difficulties surrounding wrecking these days. The situation hasn't improved and my profits keep dwindling. I'm going to open a chandlery here in Key West. It's difficult to buy high quality fittings locally and it's almost impossible for a captain to anticipate his needs and stock up. Look at that passenger ship that missed the channel. Granted they're not breaking their backs to get it repaired, but things would go faster if it weren't for the lack of screws, bolts, and ropes. Caroline is making a lot of money renting rooms, but the captain's losses increase every day. He'd pay a nice premium for readily available parts."

"I thought the sea was your first love. When we first married, I was even jealous of her. Won't you miss the long voyages?"

"As I see it, this is a practical decision. I can follow the romance of the sea as a wrecker, but I'm not going to keep making money at it. I'm not suited to carrying cargo or passengers, nor is the Osprey. We have a fine, deep harbor here. Even if wrecking ends completely, this will always be a busy seaport and every sort of ship needs a chandlery. I'll do my sailing when I travel to the mainland three or four times a year to restock."

"Have you rented space for the business?"

"I'll just handle fittings and equipment - ropes and screws and cleats and winches and the like. Maybe I'll carry a few charts and compasses. Cottrill and Fitch already handle clothing and food staples. I don't want to compete with them. Since I won't have any perishables, I can store my goods in a corner of Tift's warehouse. I see no need to increase my overhead by paying rent to somebody else for a storefront so I'll run the business from here. We're only two blocks from the waterfront. They'll come that little distance if I have a good inventory. I must have foreseen something like this when I built the house. My office has an exterior door. I can work from there and you won't have strangers walking through your house."

Mary didn't know what to think. It seemed like a workable plan, but what a change it would make in her daily life! If Richard worked from the house, he'd know her every coming and going. And while his clients might not parade through the parlor to do business, they'd still be around. Bit by bit he was nibbling away at her independence. First it was Phoebe, now he was going to install a business in her home.

"It seems to me enough to have sailors walking through my yard and into my house," she said.

"They'll go no farther than the front office," he said. "I'm convinced that this is the best plan for our future prosperity. You'll hardly notice the difference."

Ah, but you'll notice some things you didn't know about, thought Mary. *I think I'll start telling you about my days gradually so the information doesn't come as too much of a shock. You may be in charge of decisions about business and the house, but I won't let you dictate how I spend my free time, even if you don't approve. I intend to continue to visit Phoebe and to help Julia and her family.*

* * *

Richard sailed in early October. Mary remembered how his departures had once been occasions for sadness and how she'd felt his absences as loss. Now she was glad to see him go and she treasured these days of independence, knowing they were her last, at least for a while. Not only was he going to be in the house to oversee her, her waistband was getting tight. She was using yarn to expand it as she had during her first pregnancy, but the trick was reaching its limits and soon she'd have to relinquish her normal clothes for maternity shifts and accept confinement to the house until after the baby's birth. Yes, she'd better make the most of her time now!

"I don't know if the Captain will allow it, but I'll be glad to come for your lying in," said Phoebe one morning as they sat in Caroline's kitchen.

"I haven't thought about it. Maybe I don't want to face it," admitted Mary. "I want nothing more than for you to be with me, but I doubt very much if he'll agree. I don't trust Maude for a minute unless she has explicit instructions for her every move and I can hardly go through labor and tell her what to do all at once, can I? I'd better see if I can find a midwife with good references. If you hear of anyone, please tell me."

Mary walked to the Point at least three times a week, sometimes more. The sunshine warmed her shoulders and the sea breeze stirred the leaves and ruffled her hair. Caroline accompanied her as often as she was able, but the guest house business increasingly demanded her presence. Her support for the folks at the Point became more moral and financial as her business improved. Mary missed her company, but she also enjoyed the solitude of the walk. She breathed most deeply and thought most clearly walking outdoors. Here she gained the strength and composure to deal with the rest of her life. Happily, things were improving. She accepted Maude for what she was and no longer resented her for being so different from Phoebe. Best of all, the pain of baby Richard's death was starting to dissipate. She had Maude drive a nail in the parlor wall and she hung that sad, sad, painting, now framed, beside the door. She still looked at it often, but she cried less and thought more about the future than the past.

Mary also drew satisfaction from the equilibrium of life at the Point. Julia had resumed hooking rugs. Maggie helped by tearing rags into strips and together they made several dozen a week. The durable, inexpensive rugs had become popular in Key West homes, especially for children's rooms, and the dry goods store sent a man once a month to buy whatever Julia had available. Often she bartered for staples and clothing, so the family ate and dressed better than before. Jonathan was healthy and about ready to walk and Ephraim, although he still coughed, seemed stronger as long as he drank the horehound and camomile infusions.

I have good reason to be proud of them, thought Mary. *These people have worked for what they've accomplished, but I've helped. I don't think they could have done it without me.*

By the end of October, Mary bulged beyond the ability of yarn to expand her waistband. She had Maude unpack the maternity shifts from the trunk and wash and iron them. She resigned herself to the months of idleness and confinement she knew lay ahead. It was probably just as well. She seemed to have caught a cold. Runny eyes and a cough were making her miserable. She'd get over it sooner if she rested and drank the echinacea infusions Phoebe sent.

"Please make an effort to visit the Point and report to me," begged Mary. "I'll feel completely isolated if I don't have news from there."

"I'll go as often as I can," said Caroline. "I know how much it means to you. After all, I was the one to take you there in the first place. Now you worry about those folks more than I do. How does Richard like your charitable work?"

"Richard should be content when he comes home." Mary avoided Caroline's question. She didn't want to detail the efforts she took to conceal her frequent visits to the Point. "The household is running smoothly and he can look forward to the birth of another son, at least he's sure it's another boy. Those are the things that matter to him."

* * *

"I found everything I wanted and was able to buy it at a good price," Richard flushed with excitement as he recounted his successful journey. They sat on the veranda between his office and the front steps. From here they could observe the evening comings and goings of the neighbors. "I never thought I'd enjoy spending so much money at once, but I can envision the profit it's going to mean for me. During the next months I'll organize my stock and maybe I'll do a little business from Tift's. After the child is born, I'll move the operation here."

"I'm glad you decided to wait. The thought of lying in labor upstairs while captains provision their ships below is hardly appealing." Mary tried to make a joke of it, but really, it wasn't funny!

"I wouldn't do that!" he exclaimed righteously. He reached over and patted her bulging belly. "I want only the best for you and my son."

Mary had long since given up trying to point out that the baby might be a girl. She just smiled. "I think I may have found a good midwife. Susan Baxter used her and they say . . . " A cough interrupted her and she held her handkerchief to her lips. "Excuse me. They say Susan is very finicky. I'd have Phoebe if you'd allow it. Will you reconsider?"

"I recognize your fondness for the woman, but Phoebe is out of the question in view of what happened before. I know Martin Baxter. He's a sensible man. That midwife might be good. Why don't you talk to her?"

Mary stifled another cough and rose to go inside for some horehound. Richard took her hand and asked, "Are you ill? You seem tired and sometimes your coughing goes on and on."

"It's nothing," she said. "It's the pregnancy that makes me tired. As for the cough, it's just a lingering cold. I'll be fine." She didn't like to admit it, but her cough was becoming chronic and she didn't like it one bit. She had to make the horehound infusions stronger and stronger to control it. Maude had noticed and suggested a little laudanum might help. Mary dismissed the idea out of hand. Nevertheless, she must find a way to unobtrusively visit Caroline's and talk to Phoebe about a more effective remedy.

* * *

"November 14. This would have been our first son's first birthday," observed Richard one morning as he dipped bread into his breakfast tea.

"I'd rather not dwell on that," Mary said. Thinking about the anniversary only made her sad again. She didn't want to remember that awful despair. Today she planned to slip out and see Phoebe. If Richard would just leave! She went to the kitchen house to give Maude instructions about supper. Maybe cooking the pigeons longer in a cooler part of the oven would tenderize them. Maude always tended to rush things and the crispness of the fowls' outer skin suggested that they had been cooked quickly at high heat.

"The captain is looking forward to roast pigeon tonight," she began tactfully. "I'd like to suggest that you try . . . Oh!" Mary exclaimed as she sat on the nearby bench.

"What is it, Mrs. Randall?"

"I had a cramp, almost like labor." She gripped the table. "Oh, there's another one. But it's too soon. I'm sure it's not time for this baby to be born. I haven't even retained the midwife." Whether it was time or not, the contractions were familiar.

"Let me help you to bed," offered Maude as she took her arm and helped her to stand. Mary didn't protest. The stairway was too narrow for the women to climb side by side, so Mary went first and Maude pushed her buttocks from behind. Mary sat limply on the bed.

"Lie down now, Mrs. Randall." Maude unlaced Mary's boots and lifted her feet to help her recline.

"What's going on?" Richard hurried into the room and knelt by the bed. Another pain overwhelmed Mary and she doubled up, almost hitting him in the face with her knee.

"I think the baby's coming," she gasped. "This shouldn't happen for at least another month, I'm sure, but it's coming anyway. I don't know what to do."

Richard planted a kiss on her cheek and stood. "I'll go get help," he said as he left the room. "I'll be back as soon as I can."

Mary knew she should try to relax, but the pains swept over her when she least expected it and she was frightened. Maude brought her cool water to sip and moist cloths for her forehead.

The contractions became longer and more frequent. Early or not, there was no question the baby was coming. Where was Richard? Surely he'd be back with the midwife soon! A flood of warm fluid drenched the bed. Her water had broken. At the same time, she heard Richard's voice below and an unfamiliar heavy step on the stairs.

"Labor started a little soon, did it? Well, there's nothing to worry about. I'll take care of everything." Doctor Hawthorne let himself into the room. Mary stiffened. She'd hoped never to see him again. Her mind spun with the terrible images of the last time he'd been called on. She saw him bleed her screaming son and little Richard dead on the bed where she was lying now. She screamed as the doctor lifted the sheet and pulled her legs apart to examine her. She didn't want him to touch her! Now, the pains came more and more quickly and became unbearably intense. She couldn't think beyond pushing the baby out and ending the torture.

"Push, now! Push. You're almost there." Doctor Hawthorne's voice seemed miles away She gathered what little strength she had left and pushed again, grunting with the effort.

She felt the head push free and the rest of the body slid between her legs.

"It's a boy," announced the physician.

Mary relaxed. It was over! "Let me see," she said.

Doctor Hawthorne seemed not to hear her. He leaned over the newborn and slapped its back. Then he turned it on its right side and began to rub his hand along its spine downward from the base of its head over and over again.

Mary turned partially on her side and craned to look. The baby hadn't cried. It was hardly breathing and there were long pauses between its gasps for air. She could see the little fingers extended as if they were reaching out for her. They were blue.

"Get a bucket of warm water, clean rags, and the kitchen bellows. Now!" Maude ran from the room and soon returned with them.

The doctor wiped out the infant's mouth and nose and, holding him under the arms, plunged him into the water up to his chin. The baby gave a little squeal, almost like a chick peeping, then he was quiet again.

"All right. Hold him here. Don't let him sink. I'm going to massage his back again. We must make him take some strong breaths to start his lungs and his heart in a regular pattern." Wide-eyed with terror, Maude did as she was told. All Mary could see of her son was his head sticking out of the bucket. His lips and eyelids were blue. Doctor Hawthorne sighed and took the bellows. "Tip him back," he ordered. He pushed the corner of a rag into the child's left nostril and held the bellows to the right. He puffed the bellows gently by holding them under his left arm and covered the little mouth with his right. He removed the bellows and pressed firmly against the baby's stomach. Then he repeated the procedure. Mary screamed in horror at the unearthly scene. Then the tiny mouth opened wide and she realized her own scream was drowning out the baby's cries. She clamped her mouth shut. Yes, he was crying vigorously and gulping big breaths of air between howls!

Doctor Hawthorne put the bellows aside and resumed rubbing his back. It seemed like an eternity before he instructed Maude, "Lift him out gently and dry him."

Mary fell back on the pillow, overcome by fatigue and relief. The doctor lay her son across her stomach. "He gave me quite a scare, but he'll be fine now. We call that a 'mute birth.' It seems to be caused by a valve between the two sides of the heart that doesn't close the way it should. When he took the first vigorous breath, he shocked the heart into beating strongly and that closed the open valve. Look. His fingers are starting to turn pink." He held up the baby's right hand for her to see and she enclosed it in her own.

"Thank you, Doctor," Mary had to speak loudly to be heard over her son's howling. "I was afraid he would die."

"You needn't worry now. The crisis is over. But you're right. The danger was very real for a while. It was a good thing I was here. Midwives often don't know what to do in these cases. They're not common and only seem to occur when the birth occurs early. He's rather small. How long had the pregnancy progressed?"

"I expected him to be born in January."

"And it's November. I suppose he's about seven months along. Well, one good thing about having him born now is that it made your work easier. You had a very short labor." He patted her shoulder. "I'll be going. I'll tell your husband he can see you now."

CHAPTER 27

Richard paused at the door and stared at the wailing infant and blood-soaked sheets. When Mary smiled her encouragement, he stepped tentatively into the bedroom. The baby kept yelling. "He's certainly making a racket!" Richard shouted to be heard.

"It's a wonderful sound!" Mary exclaimed. "He was completely silent when he was born. He started to turn blue because he couldn't breathe and his heart wasn't pumping. Doctor Hawthorne puffed air into his lungs with the bellows and finally he started to breathe and cry."

Richard's eyes widened and he knelt beside the bed. "I didn't know the child was in such danger. Are you all right? This birth didn't take very long compared to the first time."

"I'm tired, but I'll be all right. The worst of it was the fear. At first I was afraid of Doctor Hawthorne. Then I was afraid the baby was going to die. It was a good thing you brought the doctor. I never heard of a 'mute birth' and I had no idea what to do and certainly Maude didn't either. But everything's fine now. Listen to him! What shall we name him?"

"We'll name him Richard after me."

Mary's smile faded. "Our first son was Richard and he died. I think this little one should have a different name."

"Every man should have a namesake, a son to share his father's honor and reputation along with his name," Richard said solemnly. "I want our son to be Richard. If you like, we can name him Richard T. You know, use the T for Tuggy that's my nickname since I tugged the house over here. Of course he'll have a nickname of his own. He's roaring like a bull. How about Bull Randall?"

"Richard T., then, but Bull doesn't suit him at all; he's so small. Let's wait. Something will come along."

"As you like. His name is the important thing. The nickname can wait." Richard kissed her on her lips and then her forehead. "Now, do you suppose you can think of a way to get him to quiet down a little?"

"Where's Maude?" Mary brushed tangled hair away from her face. "Everything's a mess! The baby hasn't been washed yet and these bloody sheets are sticky and disgusting. I want her to change the bed and tidy the room and I need a clean chemise. And I want to nurse this little fellow. That should quiet him down for a while. I'd like a glass of water and a bowl of soup. And have her bring some horehound tea. My throat is rough and sore."

Maude needed two trips to bring the tray for Mary and the warm water to bathe the baby. She was panting when she took him to wash him.

"Hold him on a towel on your lap and don't let go of him as you wipe him," Mary cautioned. "After all he's been through, he doesn't need to fall on the floor and break his bones."

"Yes, Ma'am, I'll be careful."

She was careful, but terribly slow. Mary didn't know whether to laugh or exclaim in exasperation. It seemed like Maude took twice as long to wash the child as even Richard would have done. Then she fumbled with the bed sheets and tore one as she tried to tuck it in. When she pulled out another from the wardrobe, she dropped the whole stack of clean bed linen willy nilly on the floor and had to resort it.

Finally Mary stiffly pulled herself between clean sheets

reclined against the pillows. She savored the smell of the sun-dried pillowcases as she put her son to her breast. He sucked greedily even though her milk wouldn't start to flow for a day or so. His appetite was a good sign. Best of all, while he nursed, he was quiet. It was the first peace in the room since he'd started to breathe.

"I've heard it said that a baby cries to strengthen its lungs," said Maude.

"If that's so, I guess we should be thankful," replied Mary. "Those lungs almost didn't survive birth."

"I'll try to be thankful, Ma'am, but all that wailing gets on my nerves."

"I'm sure he'll be more placid as he gets used to being out in the world. He'll develop a schedule, won't you, honey?" she affectionately stroked his cheek as he sucked. He closed his eyes and rested. Mary was reassured by the regular rise and fall of his chest. At least when he was howling there was no question of his being alive. She had little sympathy with Maude's nerves; she was sure he'd soon quiet down. She already looked forward to the day when both of them would be strong enough to visit Caroline and Phoebe.

The baby seemed to have other ideas. Mary didn't have a chance of regaining her strength if she couldn't get some sleep and that didn't seem likely. Baby Richard developed a pattern of nursing, resting briefly, then crying inconsolably. Rocking him didn't help. Neither did rubbing his back or his stomach. Sometimes carrying him around with his head cradled against her shoulder and patting his back calmed him for a while. But the minute she put him back in the cradle, he'd start in again.

"When is this going to stop, Mary?" asked Richard when the baby was a week old. "Even in the room across the hall with my head under my pillow I can't sleep. I don't want to spend my nights on the boat, but I've got to get some rest."

"Think how it is for me," Mary replied. Dark circles surrounded her eyes. "I've tried everything I can think of. I'm sure he's not ill. There's no fever and his bowels are normal. I don't detect any pain in his crying. This just seems to be how he wants to spend his time right now and I can't do anything about it. I'm tempted to take him into the bed with me and try to get some sleep while he's at my breast, but I'm afraid I'll roll over on him. I don't know what to do!"

"I know you want to suckle him yourself, but I'm going to tell Maude to find a wet nurse. You can put him to bed in the servants' quarters and close the doors. The nurse can feed him at night and maybe we can get some sleep."

Mary reluctantly agreed. Although she felt guilty the next day when Maude reported that she'd found a willing wet nurse, that night, she slept ten hours straight. She woke only twice, once because she heard the distant sound of her baby crying and again with a cold sweat that soaked her night dress. She dismissed it as a reaction to the stress of the last weeks and put on a fresh chemise. She climbed back between the sheets and immediately fell asleep.

In the morning, when Mary went to retrieve her son, he was crying. "How did he do last night?" she asked Maude as she lifted him to her shoulder. She could tell from his protruding stomach that he'd been well fed and he was clean and dry.

"Well, he ate all right, but he didn't sleep down here, either. That girl spent most of the night with her breast in his mouth," said Maude. "I'm not sure how long she's going to last. She has her own baby to tend during the day. She thought she was hired just to give a feeding in the middle of the night, not put up with this constant wailing. She left early and he's cried ever since, although I can't believe he can be hungry. Me, I'm going to have to nap this afternoon if I'm to do my work and be able to prepare supper."

"This can't go on forever," said Mary. She paced slowly and gently patted the baby's back. His crying abated, although it didn't stop. "I benefitted from the night's rest and it's important that I continue to sleep well because I'm still coughing from that cold and I need to recover my strength from childbirth. Visit the wet nurse when you do your shopping and tell her I will double her pay. That should sustain her interest in continuing, in spite of the unpleasantness."

The additional money was persuasive. The nurse arrived immediately after supper and Mary deposited her son in the kitchen with her. Mary woke only a few times and she felt stronger. She coped better with the fussy baby now that she could rest. Richard reported growing sales from his newly acquired stock of ships' goods. Maude napped in the afternoons. Things seemed to have settled down into a tolerable routine.

Mary reconstructed the sling she once used to carry the first baby and one day while her husband was occupied with customers, she took her son down the street to visit Caroline and Phoebe.

"He does love to howl, doesn't he?" Phoebe raised her voice to be heard, but she laughed as she spoke. "My little brother was like this. He hollered until he was three months old. Then he stopped. Just like that. Nobody knew why. We were sure glad, though. I guess you can appreciate that."

"I certainly can!" exclaimed Mary. Phoebe's story reassured her. The specter of illness and abnormality always lurked in the background of her thoughts about the child. "Did he grow up to be healthy?"

"The only thing about him was that he was lazy. You could hardly get him out of bed for breakfast. My mother always said he was trying to catch up on the sleep he missed as an infant. He was five when I was taken to the Bahamas. I never saw him after that."

* * *

The new setup seemed to work. Maude reported that baby Richard, now five weeks old, was finally sleeping for hours at a time every night (although she herself still required her afternoon nap). Encouraged, Mary once tried to take him back into her bedroom, but as soon as she lay him in the crib, he started to wail. She turned him from his back to his stomach, changed his diaper, and tried to rock him to quiet him. When nothing worked, she took him back to the servants' quarters.

As she became used to her newly-regained nocturnal peace, she postponed moving her son upstairs. Her maternal guilt faded and some mornings she lingered long beyond sunrise, snuggled in the warmth of the soft sheets. After all, she needed strength and patience to deal with her squalling son the rest of the day.

"I'm going to begin selling supplies from my office here," Richard announced one evening. "I want you to help me in two ways. First, take that squalling child out of the house for a few hours in the morning when I expect customers."

Mary beamed. Just when she felt well enough to consider going to the Point, he was asking her to leave the house. "Of course," she said.

"Let me finish," he continued. "The second thing is that I want your help keeping the accounts for the business. I need to record transactions - who bought what and when and for how much. I'm selling at a good pace, but I'm losing track of my inventory. I want you to consolidate my papers into a single ledger. You can leave the baby with Maude as you do at night. If it's necessary to keep him quiet, we'll bring in the wet nurse for a few more hours. It's worth it to me."

Again he was giving with one hand and taking with the other! She knew she could do what he asked, yet she already regretted the time she'd spend away from her son. But, how could she say no?

"I'll be glad to help."

"We'll start tomorrow," said Richard. "This business is already growing beyond my most ambitious hopes. With your help I can expand without worrying about the details."

Now Mary was out the door every morning before nine, carrying her child in his sling. The motion of walking calmed him some. He was quiet for the short trip down the street to Caroline's and for at least half the journey to the Point. After that, he resumed his noisy outbursts, and was only quiet when Mary nursed him. He sucked feverishly, as if to compensate for the two months he'd missed in the womb, but he didn't seem to grow in proportion to the amount of milk he drank. At the same time, Mary's breasts were becoming raw and sore from so much pulling at them. She considered starting him on cereals and soaked bread. She'd never heard of a child starting solid foods at just two months, but this might be the exception.

Mary had expected to feel liberated with her new schedule. So recently, a few hours away from the house had seemed unattainable. Now her absence was required, and it had lost its aura of privilege. She began to feel like an exile. At first Caroline welcomed her, but after an hour or so, it became clear that she had her own business to attend to. Even Phoebe had to excuse herself to finish her chores. It was the same thing at the Point. Daily habits and responsibilities weren't easily interrupted.

To Mary's surprise, the afternoons were more rewarding. When Maude carried away the lunch dishes, Mary spread out the papers on the dining room table. Richard was right. If the accounts weren't organized soon, important information would be lost permanently. Receipts, memos, and IOUs were tied in random bundles. Some were dated and some not. A few were signed. Others gave no hint of who the buyer or debtor might be. It was frustrating how her husband had glossed over important details. Gradually Mary established a system, filing papers in dated envelopes and making corresponding entries in a lined ledger.

"You absolutely must remember who it was who bought a dozen brass cleats and five replacement winches in January," she insisted one day as Richard walked though the dining room on his way to the privy. "It's already February and I'd like very much to concentrate on current activities. If I don't track down that sale, I'm afraid it will be permanently lost. From what I can see, whoever bought those things didn't pay for them in full."

Richard shoved his hands into his pockets and concentrated on the toes of his boots like an errant schoolboy. "I'm as bewildered as you are by that one," he said. "But I don't have an inkling who it might have been or how much he owes me. I'm making a fine profit this month. I guess I'll just have to forget about that debt, if it is one, and hope the buyer's honest and comes to make it right.

"Since you've started taking care of the details, this business is much easier for me. I have a talent for seeing who needs what and convincing them to buy it, but then I'm on to the next one. I need you to organize the records and make sense out of it all."

Mary welcomed his praise. She worked hard to organize the piles of paper and she was glad to know he recognized her efforts. Contrary to her expectations, baby Richard seemed to benefit from the new schedule, too. Most evenings he returned from the servants' rooms drowsy and placid and usually didn't fuss until after his parents finished supper.

"I think Maude has discovered how to manage him," observed Mary. "I'm glad to be able to say she does something well. There for a while I wasn't sure."

"She can still learn a thing or two about cooking," said Richard with a wry smile. "Do you think the baby's growing? He doesn't seem as big as I remember the first one to have been at three months."

"I sometimes wonder the same thing," said Mary. "But we must remember this one was born early. It's not fair to compare him to his brother."

CHAPTER 28

"I knew my chandlery would succeed!" Richard burst in on Mary's afternoon bookkeeping. "Key West is becoming a port of destination because captains can count on my having what they need and they know they can get it without delay. I thought it was a beautiful day when William Curry brought me his local trade. That was nothing compared to this! I'm becoming a celebrity around town because it's my chandlery's reputation that clinched the retail fleets' calling here. They're coming! For the next two weeks ships from England, Spain, Portugal and Italy are going to stop in Key West. Mary, this is my great opportunity. You'll have to work more than usual. It's more important than ever for me to know my inventory and keep track of credit and receipts. Otherwise, it will all become a tangle of confusion. You, my dear, will keep me on track. You'll have to stay home and work at least part of every morning."

"Have you forgotten the reason I leave the house in the morning is to give you peace and quiet to conduct your affairs? What will I do with the baby?" Mary asked. She saw the imperatives of business gnawing into her independence as surely as the slugs had chewed half the leaves off the pepper plants last week.

"Let Maude watch him. If he starts to cry, you can nurse him. It's about time his fussing came to an end, isn't it? I've never heard of such a demanding child."

Evidently Maude was lingering outside the door, because at the mention of her name she came right in. "Begging your pardon, Captain, but if I'm to watch the young master in the mornings, I'll need help with the scouring and cleaning. The child will occupy a good part of my time, you know."

"Find a girl to do menial work for two hours, then," Richard replied. "But no longer than that, and get someone for a reasonable wage. Sometimes I think that baby sucks my money like he sucks his mother's milk."

"Do I need to remind you the extra help is the price of our peace at night and my work for you during the day?" asked Mary. "If anyone is taking advantage of you, I don't know about it." Richard's jaw tightened. Mary knew her words had hit home. She didn't pursue the subject because Maude was there and he let it drop, too.

* * *

Richard worked for days in the warehouse sorting and labeling his products so he could find them when he needed them. He came home covered with cobwebs and moldy-smelling dust. By the first Monday of March, he was ready for what Richard predicted would be an onslaught of European captains and mates desperate for fittings to complete their voyages to South America and the Gulf Coast. On the sixth of the month, a few schooners and a passenger ship anchored in the channel and dories transferred the crews to Key West. Richard had on hand almost everything they wanted to buy. As the week went on, the traffic increased to the point that he only came home after dark. Mary worked all morning, ate her lunch in the kitchen and nursed the baby; then she rushed back to the dining room to try to reach the bottom of the current stack of papers before Richard brought another one.

She leaned over her ledgers until her shoulders ached and her fingers were permanently stained by dark blue ink. Condensation ran down the sides of the bottle and stained the oak table with intertwined rings forming a blue chain that randomly wove down its middle. Mary rubbed the wood with fine sand and lemon oil, but the ink had absorbed so deeply that the marks were indelible reminders of her labors. Sometimes her eyes strained to decipher the smudged penciled records of a transaction and when she stepped out into the sun, the unaccustomed light forced her to squint or close her eyes altogether. Even the brightness on the other side of her eyelids was more than she could stand.

Friday night Mary and Richard sat on the upstairs veranda. As the full moon brightened the sky, the railing cast thin bars of shadow along the pine floor. They hoped the second floor was far enough removed from the street to discourage entreaties for after-hours purchases. One evening a first mate had burst in on their dinner, mistaking the open door for an invitation to procure a dozen mast hoops after the chandlery closed.

"When I was wrecking, we worked hard when a ship foundered and when there were storms. But there was rest in between. This is unrelenting. I feel I have to be available for every potential client, because if he loses interest or leaves port without buying, he'll be gone forever," said Richard.

"I'd dearly like some rest," said Mary. "How lovely it would be to take a stroll with young Richard or to sit in the shade and listen to the spring birds."

"I'll close on Sunday. No business, whatsoever. They'll expect that, anyway. I'll go down to the Osprey early. I haven't seen my own ship all week. You can garden and relax. Then we'll spend the afternoon together."

She was up at first light. Richard had already gone. She woke Maude to make tea and was glad to see young Richard asleep in his kitchen cradle. The wet nurse was nowhere to be seen. She must have left early to care for her own family.

Mary didn't linger over her breakfast and the baby was still full from his last feeding, so they were ready to go in no time. As she walked away from town, her son snuggled against her chest in the sling as if he were compensating for time missed listening to her heartbeat in the womb. She relished his closeness and the slightly milky smell that surrounded him. The sun and exertion warmed her and she strolled leisurely, savoring the time for reflection.

Mary didn't think she loved this baby less than the first one, but between his unsupportable bawling and the demands of Richard's business, she certainly spent less time with him. She treasured the few moments, usually when he'd just been fed, when he smiled and relaxed and she could enjoy cuddling him. Maybe she imagined it, but his crying seemed to be abating. When she retrieved him from Maude he often was drowsy and his wild sucking had eased. Mary was grateful on both counts. *He's entered a new stage of his development,* she thought. *It's about time!* Thanks to the enduring peace, Richard and Mary were reunited in their bedroom and their son continued to spend his nights with the servants.

She stopped for a minute to watch a little brown warbler in the grass, twitching its tail to expose a bright patch of yellow on its underside that matched its lemon-colored throat. She turned her son so he could see the bird. "See how he walks around in the grass." Richard gurgled appreciatively. She laid him between her knees facing her. "You're tiny like the bird, aren't you? Maybe I should call you Richard Bird. At least you're quiet today. You're so much more pleasant when you're not screaming." She stroked his forehead with her finger and noticed that it was warm and moist and his pupils looked dilated. The bright sun must be a shock to him after being indoors so much. She'd make this a quick trip. She knew what could happen if she overdid it.

Julia and Maggie had new red skirts and shawls and Jonny played on a crimson cloth. "Mr. Fitch received a big shipment of red yard goods," explained Julia. "He gave us some in exchange for our batch of rugs. It's good quality and should last for a long time."

"It's certainly cheerful," said Mary as she shared the jar of cool tea that she'd brought. "We won't have to worry about losing you in the woods when you're wearing that skirt! Where's Ephraim?

He's all right, isn't he?"

"Ephraim's off fishing. He seems to feel stronger as the days get longer. He still coughs and gets short of breath, but I don't worry about him the way I once did. He refuses to let me make him a new shirt, though. Says he can't stand the color red." Julia smiled affectionately.

Mary enjoyed the companionable chat. When Richard started to fuss, Mary gave him her breast and recounted all the trouble she'd suffered with her newborn.

"I don't know what I would have done if one of mine had been that way. You're lucky to have the means to hire help," said Julia. "He's a lovely child, despite his crying. I think he looks more like you than your first child."

"I worry about him because he's so small," confessed Mary.

"He's little, but I'm sure when he starts to grow, he won't stop." Julia's confidence was reassuring. After all, she was raising two healthy children under very difficult circumstances.

Mary visited for a little more than an hour, then set out for town. She'd planned to stop at Caroline's before going home, but she thought better of it. As much as she wanted to see her friends, she didn't think it was prudent. She was breathing hard as she climbed the slight incline toward home. The baby wasn't the only one who needed to get used to being outside! She was surprised to find herself looking forward to a quiet afternoon.

The afternoon passed quickly and pleasantly. Richard read the local Register and a three-week-old Boston Globe that a sailor had given him. Mary worked on a needlepoint cushion she'd started months ago and young Richard rested quietly in his crib staring at the porch ceiling and sucking on his own hand. Mary was tempted to try putting him in his own crib next to her bed, but she thought better of it. She was glad to again have her husband beside her at night and she didn't want to imperil that. There would be time enough to reestablish the child's presence upstairs.

* * *

It was still dark when she awoke. Richard was shaking her by the shoulders and calling her name as if from a distance.

She had dreamed she was climbing a tall, sandy hill. For some reason, she urgently had to get to the top, but her feet kept slipping out from under her and there was no handhold to help her stand.

"What?" she coughed and panted from the exertion of the climb. Couldn't he wait until she got to the crest of the hill?

"What's the matter with you?" he asked. "Your coughing woke me and you're sweating like it's August."

"It was a terrible nightmare," she replied. "I don't know why I was coughing. I must have breathed too much spring pollen when I was out. Maybe that's what caused the dream. I hope so. It was awful." She coughed again. "I'm sorry I woke you. I'll go down and get some horehound from the kitchen."

She sat, retrieved her nightgown from the floor where she'd dropped it earlier, and pulled it over her head. The bright moon lit her way as she padded barefoot down the stairs. She walked gingerly across the dirt between the house and the kitchen. She didn't want to step on a scorpion out on its own nocturnal errand. The night was perfectly still except for an insomniac tree frog and the sound of her own muted footsteps. Good! The baby must be asleep.

She eased open the kitchen door and stepped in. The cradle stood by the trestle table. All she could see of her baby was the back of his head sticking out from under the red cotton blanket Julia had given her. Maude snored gently from her cot in the corner. It was all so peaceful, Mary thought. But where was the wet nurse? She was supposed to be there all night, but there was no sign of her. The table was bare except for two amber bottles, different only in their size. The larger one was empty; the smaller one held only two inches of liquid. When she shook it, tiny brown particles rose from the bottom. A chill shot through the nape of Mary's neck and crept down her spine.

Laudanum.

She tiptoed over and lightly lay her hand on her baby's back. He barely moved. She held her little finger next to his nostril. She could scarcely feel his breath.

"Richard!" she screamed. "Rich-ard!" She didn't know if she was shouting for her husband or her son.

Startled from sleep, Maude jerked from her cot and looked around for the source of the noise. "What? Is there a fire? What's happening?"

"You!" hissed Mary. "You explain right now what those bottles are doing on the table."

"Oh, that," said Maude with apparent relief. "That's just a little Godfrey's Cordial. I used up the little bottle the captain gave me and bought some more at the apothecary. I was going to ask you to reimburse me for it the next time I get paid."

"Do you know what's in Mr. Godfrey's little cordial?" Mary shrieked. "Poison, is what! You didn't give that to my baby, did you?"

"I take it myself. It helps me sleep. I only gave him a little." Maude's defensiveness spoke volumes about her guilt.

"And where is the wet nurse?"

"She just stepped out for a minute." Maude's eyes shifted from Mary to the door as if she might bolt. Richard appeared in the doorway wearing nothing but his trousers.

"What on earth is going on here?" he asked.

"I don't know the whole story yet." Mary spat out the words and she shook all over. "This woman has been drugging our baby to make him sleep. The wet nurse we've been paying is nowhere to be found. My guess is that the two have been splitting the nurse's wages and plying Richard with laudanum. No wonder he stopped crying and eating. He's been drugged most of the time." She crossed the room in three quick strides and slapped Maude with all her strength. Blood ran from the servant's nose down her lips and onto her chin. She sat heavily on the cot.

"Help me, Richard," Mary said. "We have to get him to Doctor Hawthorne. His breathing is weak and I'm afraid. It can't wait until tomorrow."

CHAPTER 29

"I'll get your shoes and a shift. Wrap the baby and I'll meet you at the street." Richard took the steps two at a time. Mary turned to Maude. "You!" she shouted. "Get out of here! Take everything you own and nothing more. If there's a grain of salt missing, you'll wish you never took even a breath. Give me your keys. The house is better left unlocked than in your care." She wrapped the red sheet snugly around her baby and went to meet her husband.

She pulled a wrinkled house dress over her head and stuffed her bare feet into her shoes. Richard carried the child and Mary kept up by grasping his elbow and letting him pull her along as they rushed up the street.

"The doctor has his surgery downtown on Duval Street, but he lives in a big house somewhere on this side of Eaton," said Richard. "I went there once. I'm sure I'll know it when I see it." They'd only gone a block and a half when he exclaimed, "Look there! I'm sure that's it."

They climbed the three broad steps and Richard crashed the brass knocker against the solid wood door as if to break it down. It seemed like no one would answer, but finally a middle-aged woman appeared. Her hair was tangled and a sweater was thrown over her long nightgown.

"What is it?" she asked through clenched teeth.

"It's an emergency, a matter of life and death. This is Doctor Hawthorne's house, isn't it?" Richard asked.

"It's our baby. He's been poisoned." Mary pulled back the sheet so the woman could see the child. "Doctor Hawthorne saved him from a mute birth just months ago. He must save him again now."

The woman's features relaxed and she spoke gently. "I'm Mrs. Hawthorne. The doctor told me about the birth. Come in. I'll wake him." She showed them into a spacious parlor and lighted a table lamp. "Please sit down and make yourselves as comfortable as possible," she said, indicating an overstuffed sofa under the window. "I'll get the doctor."

Richard and Mary stood near the door. They could hear Doctor Hawthorne shouting at his wife, but they couldn't make out the words. He banged down the stairs and burst into the parlor.

"Captain Randall, I wouldn't expect you to unnecessarily raise a man from his bed in the middle of the night, so I'm sure you have good reason for presenting yourself in my home at this hour."

Richard opened his mouth, but Mary interrupted before he could speak. "You saved our son's life when he was born. If you don't save him now, your trouble will have been wasted. The maid has been pacifying him with laudanum. I'm afraid she's poisoned him!" She took the baby from Richard and held him out like a doll. "Please help him," she pled.

"Come into the dining room where the light is brighter," Doctor Hawthorne growled as he led the way down the hall. "I can examine him on the table there." Mrs. Hawthorne lighted all the lamps and the chandelier and Mary squinted in the sudden glare. The doctor lay baby Richard on the polished mahogany table and pulled back the red blanket. The boy didn't budge, unaffected by the cool air on his naked skin or the bright lights overhead. The doctor put his index fingers against the palms of the baby's hands. Then he raised a knee with one hand and thumped it smartly with the index finger of the other. Nothing brought a response. He pushed up one eyelid with his thumb and peered into the unseeing eye. Then he repeated the examination on the other side. Lastly he sniffed the infant's breath.

"Laudanum, you said? I think you're right. Some kind of opium, anyway. I can smell it on his breath and he's heavily sedated. How long has this been going on?" he asked.

"We aren't sure," said Mary. "Apparently the maid and the wet nurse deceived us. They pretended to feed and care for him when really they were drugging him so they wouldn't be bothered. We just discovered it and came straight to you."

"You were right to come. He's not sleeping; he's insensible and hardly breathing. What I'm about to do may be very unpleasant for you, but believe me, it's necessary. I'll try to explain as we go along so you can understand the importance of my methods. I'm going to make him swallow mustard water so he'll vomit and empty his stomach of whatever poison is still there. If he won't swallow it, I'll use a tube to get it into him. At the same time, I want him to move as much as possible. Mrs. Randall, take his arms and wave them up and down like a bird's wings. Be gentle. He's tiny and frail, but we need to make his blood pulse quickly to clean his system."

As Mary followed the doctor's instructions, she thought sadly of the little bird they'd seen the previous morning. The warbler had been so tiny, yet so full of life. Young Richard wretched uncontrollably.

"Good," said Doctor Hawthorne. "That's a first step. Now, keep fanning his arms while I splash cold water on him and rub him with a rough towel. My goal is to stimulate his nervous system so he won't succumb to the drug. He mustn't sleep or he'll sink into oblivion again. I can't do this by myself. I need your help."

Mary conscientiously flapped her son's arms while the doctor splashed water on him and rubbed him. Then he pinched the baby's skin starting at his legs and working his way up to his cheeks. Mary's arms tired and Richard relieved her.

The moon faded and the sky grew gray as they worked silently. Finally Doctor Hawthorne spoke. "I've exhausted my medical knowledge. We've had some success. He could have slipped away there during the night and he's still with us. Go home now. Someone should sit with him at all times and be sure there is always some physical stimulation – rubbing, tapping, coolness, heat – whatever you can think of."

"There are some herbal tonics that I think might help. Do you object to my trying them?" asked Mary.

"As you know, I don't hold much stock with that kind of thing. Just be careful not to make matters worse. Who knows what might happen? Consult that servant of yours."

"Phoebe is no longer with us, but I know where to find her." Mary watched Richard's face to read his reaction.

"The point is to try everything that might be beneficial. We must leave no stone unturned," said the doctor.

Richard nodded solemnly.

"You'll know he's improving when he cries and takes the breast again," Dr. Hawthorne continued. "Go home now. Take turns working with him and see if you can get some help so you can rest. I'll stop by in the afternoon to see if there's been any progress."

* * *

Mary knew Caroline's household rose early so while Richard went home with the baby, she trotted down the street in the other direction. She went around the house to the kitchen door and rushed in without knocking.

"Please come help me," she pled. "My baby's sick, maybe dying. I'll explain as we go." Phoebe dropped her apron on the trestle table and turned briefly to her employer who sat at the table in her dressing gown drinking her tea.

"Go, go!" exclaimed Caroline. "I can finish making breakfast. Hurry, now."

Phoebe made a tea of thyme, basil, sage, and rosemary. "These herbs taste and smell good," she said. "Most folks don't know part of the reason they like them is that they're invigorating. We mustn't make the infusion too strong, though. In excess, the herbs will have the opposite effect and make things worse. Miss Mary, I want you to drink some, too. It will help maintain your energy and spirits and it will pass into your milk so when he starts to nurse again, you can medicate him naturally without forcing more liquids down his throat." Mary smiled at the sound of the familiar "Miss Mary" and felt as much braced by the words as by the tonic. She followed both Phoebe's instructions and the doctor's since they weren't contradictory.

Monday, Richard painted "NO BUSINESS TODAY" on a board and nailed it to a post near the street. Mary, Phoebe, and Richard took turns dosing the boy on a regular schedule, massaging him, and flexing his arms and legs. Caroline came at odd hours to relieve whomever most needed rest. Day and night blended into one as they continued their ministrations, ate little, and rested sitting erect, always alert for a new sound or symptom. Tuesday, when Caroline offered to have Phoebe move back to William Street, Mary was overjoyed.

Doctor Hawthorne came every afternoon. He nodded and pronounced his not particularly heartening opinion that at least the situation wasn't any worse.

"If only he'd cry again," said Mary. "Finding relief from that endless crying was what led us to this awful state. Now I'd give anything to hear it again."

"It would be a very good sign," agreed the doctor. "So would some interest in feeding. Have you put him to your breast?"

"I tried just before you came," said Mary. "He didn't react. He turned his head toward me and my milk rushed down in anticipation, but he didn't even open his mouth."

Wednesday and Thursday passed in a blur of sameness. By Friday, Mary began to despair.

"We've followed all the good advice we've been given, and nothing is working," she said to Richard. "I want to take him out in the sunshine. Maybe he'll respond to natural warmth." She lay him on his red blanket in a sunny spot next to the kitchen garden and sat by him to wave away the flies and mosquitoes and massage his legs. After about an hour, the spring sun started to redden his skin, so she carried him to the kitchen and dabbed him in cool water before spooning the mid-day dose of infusion down his throat and drinking her own. She rubbed his bare stomach and tickled the bottoms of his feet. If he felt any sensation, he didn't show it.

On Saturday, she had another idea. "Let's take him to the ocean. Maybe the salt water will remind him of his life in the womb and when we take him out, he'll become conscious of the world as if he'd just been born."

"Do you really think it will help?" Richard asked. "Do you think anything will?"

"I don't know," said Mary. "Please help me try."

They walked to the end of William Street and then single file along the path that wound to the Atlantic shore. Mary walked ahead along the familiar path and Richard followed, carrying his son. When they reached the rocky shore, Mary unwrapped him. She cradled his head in one hand and his shoulders in the other and held him feet first into the surf.

"Richard, support his feet and fanny so he won't be scratched by the rocks and sand," she ordered.

The waves that lapped onto the shore had been tamed by their long trip over the coral reef and they gently rocked the infant as they rolled over his chest and slid back to their source. The March sea was cool. "My hands are getting cold. I'm sure he is, too. I think we should go home," said Richard after ten minutes.

Just then a stronger wave surprised them by surging over the baby's face. Mary pulled him back anxiously. He choked and coughed.

"Did you see that? Quick, let me see if he'll suck." She tore open her blouse and pushed her breast against his lips. A little seawater dribbled from the corner of his mouth, but he didn't respond to the milk that trickled from Mary's swollen nipple.

"Let's go home. I don't know what else to do." Mary wrapped the blanket and handed the child to his father. They walked back without speaking.

"No change. Nothing at all," pronounced Mary when Phoebe

met them on the veranda. They resumed their previous routine. Sometime after midnight Mary's head threatened to burst, it ached so.

"Lie on the sofa and rest," said Richard. "I'll call you if he improves."

She half-reclined, half-sat and closed her eyes. She must have fallen asleep because when she opened them again, early morning light filtered through the shutters. She'd turned her neck in her sleep and it hurt to straighten it.

She found Richard sitting on the top step of the veranda. He cradled his son and hummed tunelessly as he rocked back and forth. Mary stood unnoticed behind him. Intuition told her not to go further and she stood watching for minutes that seemed like an hour. Finally she found the resolve to face the truth.

"He's dead, isn't he?" she asked.

"He died just before the sun rose," said Richard. Still rocking, he looked up at her with eyes red from crying and sunken from lack of sleep. "He just went completely limp. I felt for his pulse and there wasn't any and he didn't move or breathe. He started to get cold almost right away. I've been with men when they died and the warmth of life stayed with them for hours, even days. But life left this little fellow all at once. Poor thing. I suppose he never stood a chance." His voice tapered to a sigh and he lowered his chin to his chest, hugging his dead son. Mary sat down, put her arm around him, and leaned against his shoulder. She had no more tears, no more words, no more hope.

Richard built the little casket himself from a pine packing crate that had held brass cleats. Mary and Phoebe washed the body. Mary wrapped her baby in a flannel blanket she had hemmed before he was born. They buried this child late in the afternoon with his casket touching his brother's.

"He wasn't even five months old," marveled Mary as she plodded along the too-familiar path to the cemetery. "He barely lived at all." Richard took her arm to steady her. "I think you loved the two of them enough to last for eternity," he said.

"I hope so," she replied. "That's where they are now."

CHAPTER 30

Mary sat on the love seat on the veranda and stared at the kitchen garden dappled by the afternoon sun. It was a blur of green and gray-brown. She didn't even try to focus on the remains of the late-winter vegetables. The clusters of little lavender flowers at the tips of the blue-green rosemary sprigs were lost in the haze. It was as if her eyes were covered with a permanent sheet of tears that didn't overflow.

Richard sat beside her with his eyes closed and his head bowed. He held his hands in his lap and vigorously rubbed the scar on his left hand with his right thumb. Finally, Mary noticed. "You'll hurt yourself if you rub so hard, she said."

"My pain is so great. Nothing can add to it," he replied.

"I know." Mary gently took his hands in hers and kissed them. She rose and went to the parlor. At first she thought to divert her mind by working at a half-finished embroidered hand towel. It was no use. She couldn't focus on that either.

Phoebe tiptoed into the room. "I've made some strong tea to fortify you, Miss Mary."

Mary smiled and a single tear ran down her cheek. Phoebe's kindness was so reliable. "I can't drink it right now," Mary said. "I don't think I can eat, either. I believe I'll go lie down."

She removed her outer clothes and slipped into bed in her chemise. She stared vacantly at the ceiling trying to keep her mind still and empty. If she wasn't careful, the terrible picture of Richard rocking their dead baby would reappear and she'd go through it all again. Pretty soon Richard came and lay on his back beside her. She knew he must have his own tragic visions, but she couldn't help him any more than he could help her. She found his open right hand between them and nestled her left hand over it. They lay all night without moving.

Before sunrise, Mary wiggled out from under the covers, trying not to wake Richard, who had fallen into a raspy, snoring sleep. Yesterday's lethargy was gone and Mary was filled with frantic energy. She bolted her breakfast and tore into the project she had set for the day.

She found the laudanum bottles still on the kitchen table. She took them to the side yard and poured the remaining poison into the privy. Then she threw the bottles into the darkness as hard as she could. She smiled grimly when she heard the glass shatter on the rocks that lined the hole.

When she came back in the house, Richard was eating. "After you finish, I want you to help me break up the cradle so it'll fit in the stove," she said. "I'm going to burn everything that had to do with them."

"Don't you think you're getting carried away?" asked Richard. "Let's just put the things back in the attic for a while. We'll have more children. Cradles are expensive to replace, you know."

"I can't bear to see their things!" she replied.

"I'll do whatever you want if it will console you." He broke the cradle into pieces and shoved it into the firebox of the kitchen stove.

Mary stuffed all the baby clothes and blankets, even the pretty eyelet sheets Sara had sent, into the raging fire. She shut the door and walked away without looking back. She lifted the painting of the dead Bubb off the wall and had Phoebe carry it to the attic.

Richard stayed home most of the time, but he kept to himself. The remainder of the spring fleets had come and gone while they were consumed with their son's illness, so there were no more sales or deliveries to keep him busy. He sat in his office or on the porch and polished the brass fittings until they glowed. Polishing metals seemed to become an obsession for him. When he finished all the fittings, he started on the household silver.

Business associates from town heard about their loss and called during the afternoons. Richard smiled and nodded gravely when they offered their condolences. Mary smiled weakly and excused herself as soon as she could. Their words of sympathy rang hollow. How could they appreciate her suffering? She was secretly glad that she hadn't made many friends in Key West. She wanted to be alone.

She withdrew from everything, even Richard. When the first boy died, she'd yearned for Richard's sympathy. Now she felt trapped inside an impenetrable bubble that kept her pain from dissipating and that repelled even her husband's efforts to comfort her. In her craving for solitude, she'd sometimes wander away from the house. Where once her purposeful strides carried her to the Point, now her tentative steps meandered aimlessly. Sometimes she'd stop to rest at the stone Methodist church on Eaton Street. She'd sit for a few minutes, sometimes as long as an hour, while she caught her breath. She liked to ruffle through the pages of the hymnal. There she found songs about grief and suffering that matched her own melancholy.

"I'm worried about you," said Caroline one day toward the end of April. "It's been over a month since your baby died. Don't you think it's time for you to renew your interest in life? You haven't been to the Point at all. You just wander around or sit staring into space. It's not healthy!"

"I have difficulty believing my health is of much consequence," replied Mary. She lowered her eyes.

"I wish you'd let me help, but there's nothing I can do for you if you won't accept it," said Caroline. "I'll come again the day after tomorrow," she said as she left.

Phoebe stayed on at William Street, although there wasn't much physical work to do. Meals were simple and cleaning was undemanding.

"Come out in the garden," she'd coax. "The weeds know it's spring. They'll take over if we don't get to work." Sometimes Mary made the effort to go with her, but usually she ended by sifting the sandy dirt through her fingers, mindless of the weeds. That's what she was doing one day when Julia and Maggie walked into the yard. "Happy May Day!" they exclaimed. "Look, we've brought you four orchids we found in bloom and a bright new rug for your bedroom."

Mary jumped with surprise and squinted up into the sunshine. "Is everything all right?" she asked anxiously. "Where's little Jonathan? Nothing's happened to him, has it?"

"Of course not. Jonny's fine," said Maggie. "We wanted to see you and Caroline offered to babysit for a few hours. Not that she's had any experience, but we won't be gone long."

"How silly of me to worry when I didn't see him," said Mary more calmly. "Come inside where we can all sit down."

Phoebe brought tea and they chatted about familiar details of life at the Point. Mary remarked that Maggie had grown taller. Julia didn't mention Ephraim until Mary asked her directly. "I suppose he's as well as can be expected," she said vaguely.

Mary recognized her friends were trying to cheer her, but she wished they'd go away and leave her alone. When they did leave after only an hour, she was exhausted from the effort of being pleasant so as not to offend them.

As the days dragged on in their sameness and sadness, Mary ignored every effort to raise her spirits and, finally, no one tried anymore, not even Richard.

"The spring fleets managed to deplete my inventory. Do you mind if I sail up to St. Augustine and buy more before the summer storms get underway?" he asked one evening as they sat outside.

"It doesn't matter to me," said Mary. She was preoccupied and tired. That annoying cough had returned and she wasn't sleeping well. As she lay awake in the dark, she was haunted by memories of Ephraim's hacking, so much like her own. She couldn't forget the day when he'd spat all over her when she'd tried to help him take his medicine. He had consumption. She barely dared ask herself if now she had it, too. None of Phoebe's remedies seemed to help and Mary became resigned to the coughing and fatigue. In a perverse way they seemed to enhance her despondency.

"Maybe there's something I can bring back that will cheer you, a new lamp, for example. Remember the one I described after my last trip? You seemed to like it then."

"There is something I want, but I don't know if you can find it in St. Augustine," Mary said. "I want my sons to have a beautiful grave marker made of marble and engraved with their names and their ages. I want it to cover the whole grave so they will always be protected from the elements. Yes, look for the marble while you're away. I'll have the engraving done here so I can oversee it. Buy a white piece that will symbolize their innocence and be sure it's of fine quality to show how much we valued their short lives."

Richard agreed to look. Since he planned to be away only a short time, it took him less than two weeks to supply the Osprey and check her fittings. Having some parts on hand turned out to be a bonus, because some cleats and hooks had suffered from disuse during the months the schooner sat in port and had to be replaced. He sailed before the end of May.

His absence neither cheered nor depressed Mary. Her health deteriorated slowly as if her dejection gnawed away at her vitality. Normally, her strong will might have shored her up, but it was as if she lost a little more interest in living with every cough.

"Miss Mary, I've tried every infusion and balm and compress I can think of and nothing's making you better. You just get sicker no matter what I try to do for you. I never thought I'd see this day, but I want you to visit Doctor Hawthorne." Phoebe pushed the heels of her hands deep into the bread dough with such vigor that it shot out fragrant little puffs of yeasty flour.

"You think it's consumption, don't you?" Mary asked. It was the first time she'd said the word aloud.

Phoebe glared. Then she gave her undivided attention to the dough, thrusting her hands even harder than before. "I don't know, Miss. But I think it's high time you find out."

SAND DOLLAR

* * *

The next morning Mary washed and dressed carefully. Somehow it seemed to her that extreme cleanliness and good grooming might improve the doctor's diagnosis. She had no difficulty finding the Duval Street surgery and seated herself on a bent wood chair in the waiting room just a few minutes after ten. The place smelled of alcohol and bleach. *At least,* she thought nervously, *the place is clean.* Soon Doctor Hawthorne presented himself at the inner door.

"Mrs. Randall! To what do I owe this visit?"

"Doctor, I must know the source of these complaints I suffer. I cough more and more frequently. I'm tired. And I wake almost every night in a cold sweat. I thought at first these were reactions to my grief, but three months have passed and my symptoms only seem to worsen. Phoebe has tried every conceivable remedy and nothing has succeeded. It was she who persuaded me to consult you. I'm afraid it may be consumption."

"I see," said Doctor Hawthorne rubbing his right temple as if it would help him think. He called in his nurse to help the observations since it would be improper for him to examine a female patient's body anywhere she was normally covered by her street clothing. She coughed into a handkerchief, looked into the light, coughed again with the nurse's ear against her chest, recounted a history of the night sweats she experienced and the fatigue that only seemed to worsen, even on the few nights when she slept well.

"I think there is reason for concern," the doctor said at last as he seated himself behind his desk. "I'd like your husband to come with you this afternoon and we can discuss the situation together."

"Captain Randall has sailed for St. Augustine. I don't expect him back for at least another week. I don't want to wait that long for your conclusions. I am capable of understanding your diagnosis and following directions for treatment." Mary pursed her lips in annoyance. Why should her husband's presence be necessary, or desirable, for that matter?

"I can understand your anxiety, Mrs. Randall. I'm afraid my conclusions are unpleasant and, judging from experience, I suspect you will resist the treatments I will propose. This might be easier for us both if Captain Randall were here, but since that's impossible, I will respect your sense of urgency." He stood and turned to look out the window. When he turned and sat back down his jaw was set and his eyes were stern.

"You are definitely suffering from consumption."

Mary inhaled sharply.

"I recommend the usual treatment as described by Doctor Rush. That includes regular bloodletting and purging, a meat diet, and confinement indoors. I strongly advise a mild opium preparation such as the one that bears Mr. Godfrey's name to calm your tussis."

"Doctor. Your so-called cures were involved in the deaths of both my sons. How can you possibly think I can accept them as cures for me?"

"Now you understand my interest in having your husband present, Mrs. Randall. In spite of your sad associations with the treatment, it is the one you should pursue. Less respectable sources recommend alternative cures such as eating boiled mice and smoking cow dung, but I assure you, they are unproven and, frankly, ridiculous. I urge you to begin my regimen now. You can choose from a number of laudanum products at the apothecary without my script. Start taking that immediately to promote sleep and increase your strength."

"How can I possibly do as you say?" Mary sighed.

Doctor Hawthorne frowned as he stood and formally opened the examining room door. "As you wish," he said. "Your husband is welcome to consult with me upon his return." Mary strode past him and slammed the front door as she stepped into the bright heat outside. She trembled with anger and fear. She was seriously ill and needed medical care, yet she was convinced she would die of the treatment.

She panted and her head spun by the time she reached William Street and she braced herself against the veranda to catch her breath before trying to climb the steps. Phoebe was in the garden picking beetles from the squash vine and either didn't see her or chose to let her speak first.

"I'm not hungry. I'm going upstairs to rest," Mary said. Once there, she refused to leave the bedroom. Phoebe brought trays of soup and fruit and fresh bread, but nothing tempted her appetite or awakened her interest. She ate a little and sipped at the tea and water to keep Phoebe from complaining too much, but that was all. Sitting at the shuttered window and reclining on the bed, her days were as still as her nights. She inhabited a mindless sort of meditation that led her to ever-increasing emptiness instead of harmony and understanding.

She didn't know how much time passed before Richard came home. His quiet, gentle words slid delicately into the void she'd contrived. "Mary, Mary, my dear. I'm home." He sat on the edge of the bed and stroked her hair and rubbed her hands while she told him about her visit to the doctor and his conclusions.

"I'll see him tomorrow. Surely there's more hope in the situation than you understand. Now, you come downstairs with me and eat a decent supper. Phoebe's gone out to buy a pigeon. Think of it! A tender, moist pigeon in a pool of its own juices next to fresh green boiled peas."

Mary couldn't help smiling. He'd found a fleck happiness in this dark, miserable life. She'd come downstairs and try to eat.

The next morning Richard left the house early. Mary drank tea and waited. It felt better to have him home. Maybe she had made too much out of her sickness. As he suggested, hope was sure to be disguised in the words that had frightened her. She'd listened for the worst news and she'd heard it. She wasn't that ill, after all. She'd soon be well. Maybe she'd become pregnant again and finally have the family she wanted.

It was mid-afternoon when he returned. "Come down to the waterfront to see the beautiful marble I found for you in St. Augustine," he said. "Then we'll go watch the sunset from the pier."

"Don't you want to talk about my treatment?" Mary asked.

"Didn't you visit Doctor Hawthorne?"

"That can wait. It's a beautiful afternoon and I want to share it with you. Get dressed and as soon as you come downstairs, we'll go."

What on earth is he thinking? She wondered as she brushed her hair. The mystery invigorated her. She dressed and went down, looking forward for the first time in months to unexpected pleasure.

"It's beautiful!" she exclaimed when he uncovered two marble slabs which leaned against a post. "The creamy white doesn't look like stone at all and the faint pink lines look like threads woven into a luxurious fabric. I'll be so glad to have such a lovely covering there. But there's so much of it. I'm sure those two slabs are much more than we need for our one grave."

"It was a bargain. I paid only a little more for two pieces than I would have paid for one. The man was going out of business and I think he just wanted to get rid of it. I'm sure I can sell it without any trouble."

Arm in arm they strolled out on the dock to watch the sun go down. It had been over a year since they'd done this. Transported back to happier times, Mary allowed optimism to raise her spirits. There were just enough clouds in the sky to catch the sun's rays and disperse them into shades of blue and pink and orange. Then, in an instant, the sun dropped below the horizon leaving behind multicolored streaks. They sat looking to the west until the last color had faded from the sky.

"Still no green flash," mused Mary. "I doubt that I'll ever see one. But I'll keep looking." She leaned against Richard's shoulder. "So tell me what the doctor had to say. You know, he wanted to talk to you in the first place, but I wouldn't stand for it. He was probably right. I heard only what I chose to hear and at the time I was lonely and sad. Let me guess. I'll soon be well and soon our family will grow. I think I feel better already."

Richard's attention didn't seem to move from the horizon. Finally he cleared his throat and pressed his arm around her waist. "You understood Doctor Hawthorne's diagnosis and the care he thinks is indicated. He spent a very long time explaining the details of the situation to me. You are very sick. It's not something we can ignore. You already have the cough and the night sweats. We probably won't have more children because consumption usually sterilizes women. You may experience pain in your joints and your back. There are some other, less common symptoms, but if you are conscientious in the treatment, they can probably be avoided."

Mary slumped forward and hung her head. So that was it! Cheerfulness was an illusion and her only confidence could be in increasing pain and disability. No more children, ever. She stood and dug her clenched hands into her pockets.

"I told him you'll start treatment tomorrow morning," Richard said.

"I'd rather die!" exclaimed Mary. Richard reached out to hug her, but she recoiled. "Leave me alone!" she shouted and she turned and walked alone toward home.

CHAPTER 31

On the walk home Mary wished more than once that she hadn't rebuffed Richard so vigorously. She would have welcomed his strong arm to help her along. She got up the stairs dragging herself hand over hand on the railing. When she finally reached her goal, she leaned heavily against the inside of the bedroom door. She locked it, not bothering to light a lamp and slid to the floor with her back against the bottom drawer of her grandmother's dresser. Bending her knees, she pressed her spine and the back of her head against the antique cherry. Years of lemon oil rubbed into the wood gave it a lingering smell that reminded her of her mother and growing up on Green Turtle Cay. *Is this what it was like for her mother?* Mary wondered. *Was she really ill and just waiting for the end?* She remembered Ann to be weak and whining, consumed by the trivia of daily existence. Maybe Mary misjudged her. Were those irritating habits her mother's way of coping with a downward spiral of health and vitality that led to certain invalidism and undignified death? From where Mary sat, that looked like her own future and she wasn't at all sure how to deal with it.

Should she write home? She hadn't written since March after the second baby died. Her mother's letter of condolence had seemed strained. Sara's wasn't much better. After all, what could they possibly say to comfort her? No, she wouldn't write. They could never understand the bleak hopelessness that enveloped her. She'd keep to herself as she always had.

She heard Richard's step on the stairs and ignored his soft tap on the door. He went into the front bedroom and shut the door. Good. She wanted to be alone. There was nothing he or anyone else could do to help her now! She slipped away from the dresser to lie on the floor and pulled the little rag rug under her head for a pillow. She spent the night on the floor drifting in and out of consciousness and mulling over what alternatives remained to her. She knew it didn't matter if she followed Dr. Hawthorne's instructions or not. Consumption was always fatal. She wouldn't submit herself to those treatments. If she died a little sooner, what difference would it make? Richard was already a widower, whether he knew it or not.

However, there were a few things she must do. Richard would certainly take another wife soon after she died. She'd overheard Sara's stories of how the new wife always worked to erase the memory of the former household. Mary knew if she didn't see to her sons' grave marker, it would never be done and they would lie forgotten and nameless, surrounded only by bricks and cement. She wouldn't allow that to happen.

When she heard the roosters start to crow, she rolled to one side and stiffly sat up. Pulling herself up to stand, she dropped her wrinkled clothes on the floor, dressed in fresh ones, and eased herself down the stairs. She recognized the aroma of the herbal infusion Phoebe had set out for her.

"Is there anything I can do for you?" Richard asked solicitously when he came to the table. Mary saw the worry lines around his eyes and how he rubbed his scar incessantly.

"No, nothing," she replied. She shook her head. Her situation was far beyond anyone's ability to intervene.

She spent the morning quietly, reading and staring into space. After lunch when Richard walked down to the waterfront, she went in the opposite direction to the sexton's little house to inquire about stone carvers. As it happened, there were two, a local man who mostly inscribed cornerstones for municipal buildings and an Italian who had stopped for a while in Key West five years ago and never left. She went behind the house and found Renaldo DaVana working on a headstone for Euphemia Curry's stillborn son.

"Just a minute, please," he said when Mary spoke. "I want to finish the outline of the little lamb. I'll lose the feeling of it if I stop. The marble talks to me through my hands as I work. I only help it become more beautiful. But if I interrupt it, the feeling may be lost."

Mary watched silently as he slowly carved out the relief and gradually coaxed the rounded soft form of the lamb from the angular hardness of the stone. By the time he finished, she knew he would create the memorial she wanted. She contracted for his services, paying half of his fee on the spot so he would give her work priority. He recommended two idle grave diggers to haul the marble slabs to the cemetery.

"Can I give you the money to pay them?" Mary asked. "I don't want to be bothered by another trip over here tomorrow." And I don't know if I'm strong enough to make an extra trip, she thought.

"Of course, Signorina. They are reliable men and you will have no worries. But you can trust me. I won't pay them until the job is done."

* * *

"He's going to cut the boys' stone to exactly cover their grave," she told Richard later. "That means a piece about thirty inches by sixty so the smaller one you bought will be perfect. He'll make a thinner, smaller headstone, too and there will be almost no waste. He'll engrave the children's names - first Richard's, then Richard T. below. I wanted to include their dates of birth and death and their exact ages when they died, but there's not enough space, so I told him to leave off the ages."

"You've given this a lot of thought," said Richard. "It's not a very cheerful undertaking. Are you sure it's not reawakening painful memories you'd rather forget?"

"Quite sure." Mary replied in a businesslike tone. "It's very educational. I'm enjoying learning about stone and stone cutting and lettering styles." And I'm taking care of some very important business that may not be done otherwise, she thought. "It's very interesting. Mr. DaVana will use capital Roman letters for the whole stone, larger ones for the beginnings of names and smaller ones for the rest. That combination is classic, but not too ponderous for young children. I was tempted to have him carve a lamb or an angel, but I decided against further ornamentation because when he sketched it, I preferred the simpler design. The bottom third of the stone is bare, at least for now. I'd like to put a pretty verse there, but that can be done later."

"Do you want me to look at the plans?"

"Not really. I'll see to it. That way you'll more appreciate it when it's finished in a few weeks."

* * *

"Your Mr. DaVana has done a good job," Richard said when Mary took him to see the finished work. He rubbed a tear from his cheek with the back of his hand and hugged her against him. "They lived for such a short time. Sometimes I forget what a painful time it was."

I never forget, said Mary to herself. The pain is part of me. She patted his shoulder affectionately. "I have an idea for the other piece of marble," she said. "I want it for my own grave."

"How can you say such a thing? You're becoming morose." He held her at arms length and stared at her incredulously.

"I'm not morose, I'm realistic," she replied. "I cough more every day and I'm getting hoarser and weaker. There are days when the pain in my joints makes it almost impossible to get out of bed and walk down the stairs. I don't complain because it won't do any good, but it's true. I don't need anyone to tell me my consumption is acute and I'm going to die. When that time comes,

I want to lie right here next to my sons. And I want a pretty headstone as tall as I am and a table stone that tells about my life. Look, " she said, pointing to the two marble slabs, "I'm going to have Mr. DaVana make these just the way I want them and they'll be ready when you need them. You gave me a fine house to live in. Now let me have a suitable grave."

When Richard looked at her, his eyes were veiled. *He doesn't want to tell me that he knows I'm dying,* Mary thought. *All right. We'll pretend for now, because if we don't, the torment of reality will tear us to shreds.*

Richard looked away and took her hand. "Let's go home now. We can spend the afternoon in the shade of the veranda."

* * *

Mr. DaVana installed the small stones on the Richards' grave and Mary told him her plan for the larger ones.

"I don't know," he said. "I've never seen anybody plan their stone before dying. People do that for you after you die. I'll do as you say, of course, but think about it, Mrs. Randall. It's very unusual."

Unusual or not, it was what she wanted and the prospect of seeing her own grave before she died gave her a sense of completion about her life she hadn't had before. She worried, though, about what the inscription should be. She'd seen plenty of them in the cemetery on Green Turtle Cay, but nothing lingered in her memory. "Beloved Mother and Wife" was a perfectly nice sentiment, but it didn't say anything about the person who lay there.

The summer heat and humidity seemed unusually oppressive this year. Maybe she just didn't have the stamina to resist them anymore. By September, Mary was weary from the weather as well as her ailment. One morning the top drawer of the dresser jammed as she tried to take out fresh linen. She wiggled it from side to side and jerked on both drawer pulls. The drawer came loose and Mary fell back on the bed. The drawer landed on its side and the contents spilled all over the floor.

"Damn," whispered Mary out loud. "Damn, damn, damn. Will nothing work out right?"

She leaned on a chair to ease the pain of kneeling as she put things right, but it hurt too much. She'd get dressed and ask Phoebe to do it for her. Then she saw a paper wedged in the side groove of the drawer bottom. It was brown with age and the edges had begun to flake away. She carefully pulled it free. "Hymn 48 = L.M. by John Wesley" it read. How odd. She didn't remember anyone in the family going to church much. Maybe it had been there since her grandmother's time.

"1 PASS a few swiftly-fleeting years,
And all that now in bodies live
Shall quit, like me, the vale of tears,
Their righteous sentence to receive.
2   But all, before they hence remove,
May mansions for themselves prepare
In that eternal house above;
And, O my God, shall I be there?"

She read the first stanza again. It seemed to have been written expressly for her. So! Here was the verse for her stone. In her excitement, she temporarily forgot her aches. She dressed and set out for the cemetery, leaving the dresser drawer and its contents on the bedroom floor.

"This is it. This is what I want engraved on both the headstone and the table stone," she told Mr. DaVana. "It will fit won't it?'

He assured her that he could make it fit and, at her urging, began the design, drawing on the blank side of a brown paper bag from Cottrell and Fitch. She watched until even her excitement couldn't mask her aching back and fatigue. She resigned herself to seeing the finished plan when he brought it to William Street the next day.

"I've drawn it to match the children's stone," explained Mr. DaVana as he smoothed the paper on the dining room table.

"It's lovely," said Mary, not wanting to hurt his pride. "But I wonder if you might make it more feminine. For example, can you vary the letters? They don't have to be all capitals, do they? And maybe you can use a slanting design. Isn't that what you call italic?

"Go ahead and sketch in the specifics. I was born on October 17, 1822. You can put September as the death month and fill in the details afterward."

"Mrs. Randall, you don't know when you might die!"

"Please do as I ask." Once again she paid half of the fee in advance and that seemed to put an end to his arguments and apprehension.

She couldn't wait to see the completed work. Two weeks dragged by before Mr. DaVana sent word that he had finished. It was all she could do to walk the three blocks to the cemetery, but it was worth the effort. When she saw the carved marble, she knew it was perfect. The stones stood propped against the Richards' grave. She couldn't take her eyes off the delicate engraving and the marble's milky softness. She caressed the polished stone with her fingertips, then pressed her flushed cheek against its coolness. "At least this will turn out the way I hope," she whispered as she rubbed her sore back. "And it won't die or be washed away. It will last forever."

The laborious three-block trek home was a grim reminder of Mary's waning strength. She didn't know how many more times she could make that trip. But now that all the grave stones were finished to her satisfaction, she'd only have to walk back there once more.

"Miss Mary, do you have a fever again?" Phoebe asked when she served Mary's soup. "I understand you don't want to do all the things the doctor wanted, but you're not taking care of yourself. You're just not being sensible."

Mary docilely drank her soup and lay down for a nap. She was glad to rest and organize her thoughts.

"You seem to feel much better," Richard observed on Sunday.

"I do!" Mary exclaimed. "Let's go watch the sunset again tonight."

They sat on an empty wooden packing crate and Mary began to

reminisce. She gripped Richard's hand tightly when she recalled the early days of their courting, how she'd first spurned his attention and then found comfort with him when she discovered her father's misconduct. They laughed together at her silliness at their wedding when she'd learned the power of rum. Mary recounted the days when Richard built their house, then took it apart again to bring it to Key West. They sat and relived happy times and looked at the horizon long after the sun dipped beneath it.

Finally, Richard said, "We should go home. Phoebe will be crabby if we're too late for supper."

After the long walk to the dock and sitting so long in one spot, Mary needed help to stand. "Do you want me to find a cart?" asked Richard. "You don't look like you're going to make it home on your own."

"I'm afraid you're right," Mary said. "I'll wait here until you find one."

The ride home was bumpy, but far better than the long walk would have been. Phoebe's scowl softened when she saw Richard help Mary up the steps. "You two are smiling like newlyweds." she said. "I remember when you looked just like that the first time."

After supper, Richard helped Mary climb the stairs and undress. He lay beside her, cradling her body against his own like a child. In the morning, he dressed and slipped out of the room without waking her.

Mary was even stiffer than usual when she woke, but she had her plan to keep her moving. Phoebe knocked at the door with tea and bread on a tray. "I thought after last night, you might be tired," she said.

"Thank you," Mary replied. She patted the bed next to her. "Come. Sit with me while I eat."

We don't need to talk anymore, thought Mary. *We've been through so much together. I wonder if she knows. I wonder if she'll miss me or if she'll feel I'm still with her.*

When Phoebe took the tray, Mary dressed in her fine ruffled blouse, fastened the enamel forget-me-not necklace around her throat, and put on the matching earrings. She left the house while Phoebe was still washing up.

Just as Doctor Hawthorne had said, Godfrey's Cordial was as easy to acquire as a spool of white thread. "Enjoy your day," said the cheerful pharmacy clerk as he wrapped the bottle in brown paper. "Indeed I will," Mary replied with a cheerful smile.

She took her parcel and turned up Angela Street. She followed the familiar cemetery paths to the spot where her sons' grave broke the evenness of the ground and sat on the Richards' grave. A mockingbird sang from the top of a frangipani. Did she always see the same bird, or was there a whole flock of them? Maybe generations of mockingbirds came there to witness her grief.

For a moment, she lost her resolve. She stood and gazed at the pretty stones that she'd wanted so much. Maybe she didn't want them after all! Not now, anyway. Even as she considered that, a hoarse cough shook her chest and she admitted once and for all that her future was out of her hands. She couldn't choose what was going to happen, only when. She unwrapped her parcel and shook the bottle. Tiny undissolved particles of opium floated in the alcohol. She removed the cork, shrinking from the bitter odor of the laudanum. She inhaled deeply, turned her head, and held her breath. Then she tipped her head back and drank until every drop drained from the bottle.

"I won't have to wait long now," she said to the mockingbird.

At first she felt giddy. It was like the time she drank too much rum. Then her heart began to pound and perspiration broke out on her temples and throat. She started to cry out, but the crisis passed. She slid to the ground and supported herself on one arm so she could look at her pretty marble grave stones. They looked like sentinel angels, their wings unfurled to embrace her in welcome. She felt light and calm. Nothing hurt.

"Shall quit, like me, the vale of tears," she read aloud. She stopped abruptly. She heard babies crying. She couldn't tell where the sound came from. It was everywhere, near and far away, but she was certain of the sound.

"Don't cry," she whispered. "I'm coming."

LaVergne, TN USA
07 October 2009
160148LV00003B/144/A